RIVER GOD
Volume II

Ancient Egypt. Land of the Pharaohs. A kingdom built on gold. A legend shattered by greed, the Valley of the Kings now lying ravaged by war, as the weak inherit the cherished crown. In this the second volume of Wilbur Smith's magnificent chronicle of a corrupted civilisation and of the lives of those who fight to change it, Taita, the formidable eunuch slave, continues his narration of the story that describes a dream—to restore the glory and the grandeur of the Pharaoh of Pharaohs on the glittering banks of the River Nile.

MEDITERRANEAN

MEMPHIS (CAIRO)

LOWER
KINGDOM

EGYPT ABNUB

SAFAGA

THEBES
(KARNAK
& LUXOR)

UPPER
KINGDOM

ASSOUN
First cataract

Second
cataract

R
E
D

S
E
A

Third
cataract

Fourth
cataract

Fifth
cataract

ATBARA

Atbara River

Sixth
cataract

QEBUI (KHARTOUM)

CUSH

Pharaoh's
Tomb

ADBAR
SEGED

RIVER GOD

Volume II

Wilbur Smith

LP
F

EAGLE LARGE PRINT

HAMPTON, NEW HAMPSHIRE

Library of Congress Cataloging-in-Publication Data

Smith, Wilbur A.
    River god / Wilbur Smith.
        p. cm.
    ISBN 0–7927–2017–2 (hardcover)
    ISBN 0–7927–2016–4 (softcover)
    1. Eunuchs—Egypt—Thebes (Extinct city)—Fiction.
    2. Slaves—Egypt—Thebes (Extinct city)—Fiction.
    3. Thebes (Egypt: Extinct city)—Fiction.
    4. Egypt—History—to 332 B.C.—Fiction.
    5. Large type books.   I. Title.
[PR9405.9.S5R58   1994b]
823—dc20   93–49515
                                                                  CIP

Published in Large Print by arrangement with St Martin's Press.

The right of Wilbur Smith to be identified as author of this work has been asserted by him in accordance with the Copyright, Designs and Patents Act 1988.

The hieroglyphs write the name of the god of the Nile inundation, Hapi, from the papyrus of Ani (P BM 10470).

Printed in Great Britain

This book, like so many others before it, is for my wife, Danielle Antoinette.

The Nile that flows through this story has both of us in her thrall. We have spent days of delight voyaging together upon her waters and idling upon her banks. As we are, so is she a creature of this very Africa of ours.

Yet this great river runs neither so strongly nor so deeply as my love for you, my darling.

RIVER GOD

Pharaoh's joy and pride in his heir were unbounded. He declared a nativity feast in his honour. For one entire night the citizens of Upper Egypt sang and danced in the streets, and gorged on the meat and wine that Pharaoh provided, and they blessed the Prince Memnon with every bowlful that went down their gullets. The fact that he was the son of my Lady Lostris, whom they loved, made the occasion of his birth all the more joyous.

So young and resilient was my mistress that within days, she was well enough to appear before the full court of Egypt, bearing her infant at her breast. Seated on the lesser throne below that of the king, she made a picture of lovely young motherhood. When she opened her robe and lifted out one of her milk-swollen breasts and before the assembled court gave the infant suck, they cheered her so loudly as to startle the infant. He spat out the nipple and roared at them in scarlet-faced outrage, and the nation took him to its heart.

'He is a lion,' they declared. 'His heart is pumped up with the blood of kings and warriors.'

Once the prince had been quieted again, and his mouth stopped up with the nipple, Pharaoh rose to address us, his subjects.

'I acknowledge this child to be my issue and the direct line of my blood and succession. He is my first-born son, and shall be Pharaoh after me. To you noble lords and ladies, to all my subjects, I commend the Prince Memnon.'

The cheers went on and on, for no one amongst them wanted to be the first to fall silent and bring

1

his loyalty into question.

During all of this I stood with other servants and slaves of the royal household in one of the upper galleries which overlooked the hall. By craning my head, I was able to pick out the tall figure of Lord Tanus. He was standing in the third rank below the throne with Nembet and the other military commanders. Although he cheered with the rest of them, I could read the expression on his broad, open face that he strove to disguise. His son was claimed by another and it was beyond his power to prevent it. Even I, who knew and understood him so well, could only guess at what agony he was suffering.

When at last the king ordered silence and he had their attention once more, he continued, 'I commend to you also the mother of the prince, the Lady Lostris. Know all men that she sits now closest to my throne. From this day forward she is elevated to the rank of chief consort and the senior wife of Pharaoh. From henceforth, in name she will become Queen Lostris, while in precedence and preferment she ranks after the king and his prince alone. Furthermore, until the prince has reached the age of his majority, Queen Lostris shall act as my regent and, when I am unable to do so, she will stand at the head of the nation in my stead.'

I do not think there was a soul in all the Upper Kingdom who did not love my mistress, except perhaps some of the royal wives who had been unable to provide the king with a male heir, and who now found themselves outranked by her and superseded in the order of precedence. All the rest showed their love in the acclaim with which they greeted this pronouncement.

To end the ceremony of the naming of Pharaoh's heir, the royal family left the hall. In the main courtyard of the palace, Pharaoh mounted the sledge of state, and with Queen Lostris seated at his side and the prince in her arms, they were drawn by the span of white bullocks down the Avenue of Rams to the temple of Osiris to make sacrifice to the god. Both sides of the sacred avenue were lined a hundred deep by the citizens of Thebes. With a mighty voice they demonstrated their devotion to the king and their love for the queen and her new-born prince.

That night, as I waited on her and the child, she whispered to me, 'Oh, Taita, did you see Tanus in the crowd? What a day of mixed joy and sorrow this has been. I could have wept for my love. He was so tall and brave, and he had to watch and listen when his son was taken from him. I wanted to jump to my feet in all that throng and cry out, "This is the son of Tanus, Lord Harrab, and I love them both."'

'I am pleased for the sake of all of us, Your Majesty, that for once you were able to restrain that wayward tongue of yours.'

She giggled. 'It is so strange to have you call me that—Your Majesty—it makes me feel like an impostor.' She transferred the prince from one breast to the other, and at the movement he released from both ends of his tiny body a double blast of air which in volume and resonance was truly imperial.

'It is apparent that he was conceived in a wind-storm,' I remarked drily, and she giggled again and then immediately afterwards sighed

3

dolefully.

'My darling Tanus will never share these intimate moments with us. Do you realize that he has not yet held Memnon in his arms, and it is possible he never will? I think I am about to cry again.'

'Restrain yourself, mistress. If you weep, it might sour your milk.' A warning which was untrue but effective in bending her to my will. She sniffed back her tears.

'Is there no way that we can let Tanus enjoy our baby as we do?'

I thought about it for a while and then made a suggestion which caused her to cry out with pleasure. As if to endorse what I had said, the prince broke resounding wind once more.

The very next day when Pharaoh came to visit his son, the queen put my suggestion into effect. 'Dear and divine husband, have you given thought to selecting official tutors for Prince Memnon?'

Pharaoh laughed indulgently. 'He is still only an infant. Should he not first learn to walk and talk, before he is instructed in other skills?'

'I think his tutors should be appointed now, so they can grow to know him, and he them.'

'Very well.' The king smiled, and took the child on to his knee. 'Who do you suggest?'

'For his schooling we need one of our great scholars. Some person who understands all the sciences and mysteries.'

The king's eyes twinkled. 'I cannot think of one who answers that description,' and he grinned at me. The child had altered Pharaoh's disposition; since Memnon's birth, he had become almost jovial, and for a moment I expected him to wink at me. However, his new, congenial attitude to life did not extend quite that far.

The queen continued, unruffled by this exchange, 'Then we need a soldier well versed in the warlike arts, and the exercise of arms to train him as a warrior. He should, I think, be young and of good breeding. Trustworthy, of course, and loyal to the crown.'

'Who do you suggest for that position, my dear? Very few of my soldiers answer to all those virtues.' I do not think there was any guile or malice in Pharaoh's question, but nevertheless my mistress was no fool. She inclined her head gracefully and said, 'The king is wise, and knows who, from all his generals, best suits that role.'

At the very next assize the king announced the prince's tutors. The slave and physician, Taita, was to be responsible for Memnon's schooling and deportment. This surprised very few, but there was a buzz of comment when the king went on, 'For his training in arms and in military tactics and strategy, the Great Lion of Egypt, Lord Harrab, shall henceforth be responsible.' Accordingly it became the duty of Lord Harrab, when he was not on campaign, to wait upon the prince at the beginning of each week.

While my mistress waited for her quarters in the new palace that I was building across the river to be completed, she had moved from the harem into a wing of the grand vizier's palace that overlooked the water-garden I had built for her father. This was in accordance with her new status as the senior wife and consort. The weekly audience that Prince Memnon held for his official tutors took place under the barrazza, with Queen Lostris in

5

attendance. Very often there was a score of other officials or courtiers present, and occasionally Pharaoh himself arrived with all his train, so we were under considerable constraint.

However, once in a while there were just the four of us present. On the very first occasion that we had such privacy, Queen Lostris placed the prince in his father's arms for the first time and I was witness to the incoherent joy with which Tanus looked down into the face of his son. Memnon rose to the occasion by puking down the front of his father's uniform, but even then Tanus would not relinquish him.

From then onwards we reserved any special event in the child's life for when Tanus was with us. Tanus fed him his first spoonful of gruel, and the prince was so startled by this unaccustomed fare that he screwed up his face and spat the offending mess down his chin. Then he howled loudly for his mother's milk to wash the taste from his mouth. Queen Lostris took him on her lap and while Tanus watched fascinated, she gave him the breast. Suddenly Tanus reached across and tweaked the nipple from the tiny mouth. This amused everybody but the prince and me. Memnon was outraged at this cavalier treatment and made that fact known, while I was shocked. I imagined the king arriving unexpectedly to find the Great Lion of Egypt with a right royal handful which he seemed in no hurry to relinquish.

When I quite rightly protested, my mistress told me, 'Don't be such a prim old woman, Taita. We are only having a little innocent fun.'

'Fun, yes. However, there is some doubt as to the innocence of it,' I muttered, for I had seen

6

both their faces light up at the intimate touch, and sensed their mutual passion like thunder in the air. I knew that they could not restrain themselves for much longer, and that even Tanus' sense of duty and honour must in the end succumb to so great a love as theirs.

That very evening I visited the temple of Horus and made a generous sacrifice. Then I prayed and asked the god, 'May the prophecy of the Mazes be not too long delayed, for they cannot help themselves. It will mean death and disgrace to all of us.'

Sometimes it is best for men not to attempt to interfere with destiny. Our prayers can be answered in ways which we do not expect and do not welcome.

 I was physician to the prince, but in truth he had little need of my medical skills. He was blessed with his father's rude and abundant health, and precocious strength. His appetite and digestion were exemplary. Anything placed in his mouth was devoured with leonine voracity, and promptly re-emerged from his nether end in the desired shape and consistency.

He slept without interruption and woke bellowing for food. If I showed him a finger, he would watch it move from side to side with those huge dark eyes, and the moment it came within range, he would seize it and attempt to haul himself into a sitting position. In this he succeeded sooner than any other child that I had attended.

He raised himself and crawled at the age when others had only begun to sit up. He took his first tottering step when others would only begin to crawl.

Tanus was present on that remarkable day. He had been on campaign for the past two months, for the forces of the red usurper had captured Asyut. That city was the pivot on which our northern defences turned, and Pharaoh had ordered Tanus down-river with all his fleet to retake the city.

Much later I heard from Kratas just how terrible had been the fighting, but in the end Tanus breached the walls and was at the head of his beloved Blues when they broke in. They drove the pretender from the city and back beyond his own borders with bloody losses.

Tanus sailed back to Thebes and the gratitude of the kingdom. Pharaoh laid another chain upon his shoulders, the Gold of Valour, and made up the back-pay of all the troops who had helped him achieve this victory.

Tanus came almost directly from the king to the barrazza in the water-garden where we were waiting for him. While I stood guard at the gateway, Tanus and my mistress embraced with all the fire that had burned up so brightly while they had been apart. At last I had to separate them, for that embrace could lead in only one direction.

'Lord Tanus,' I called sharply, 'Prince Memnon grows impatient.' Reluctantly they drew apart, and Tanus went to where the infant sprawled naked on a robe of jackal skins that I had spread for him in the shade. Tanus went down on one knee before him.

'Greetings, Your Royal Highness. I bring you

8

tidings of the triumph of our arms—' Tanus mocked him lovingly, and Memnon gave a happy shout as he recognized his father, and then the sparkling gold chain caught his eye. With a mighty heave he hoisted himself to his feet. He took four lurching steps, seized the chain and clung to it with both hands.

All of us applauded this feat, and, supporting himself by the chain, Memnon beamed about him, accepting this praise as his due.

'By the wings of Horus, he has as sharp an eye as you do for the yellow metal, Taita,' Tanus laughed.

'It is not the gold that draws him, but the winning of it,' my mistress declared. 'One day he too will wear the Gold of Valour upon his chest.'

'Never doubt it!' Tanus swung the boy high, and Memnon shrieked with pleasure and kicked his legs to urge Tanus to further rough play.

Thus, for Tanus and me, the child's advances seemed to mark the change of seasons, just as surely as did the rise and fall of the river. On the other hand my mistress's life revolved around those hours spent alone with the child and the man. Each interval between Tanus' visits seemed too long for my mistress to support, each visit too short for her to bear.

The inundation of that summer was as benevolent as any that we had forecast at the ceremony of the waters in Elephantine. When the flood receded, the fields glistened under their new coat of black mud. In their turn, they were soon obliterated by the dense green stands of corn and fruit. By the time the prince took his first upright step the granaries of Egypt were brimming, and the larders of even the poorest of her subjects were filled. On the west bank the Palace of Memnon was taking shape, and the war in the north was running in our favour. The gods smiled on Pharaoh and all his realm.

The only discontent in all this was that the two lovers, though close enough to touch, were cleaved apart by a gulf wider than the valley in which we lived. Each of them on separate but numerous occasions taxed me with the prophecy of the Mazes of Ammon-Ra, as though I were personally responsible for the fulfilment of the dream visions. It was in vain to protest that I was merely the mirror in which the future was reflected, and not the one who moved the stones on the bao board of destiny.

The old year died, and the river began to rise once more, completing the endless cycle. This was the fourth flood that the Mazes had foretold. I, as much as any of them, expected my vision of the Mazes to be fulfilled before the end of the season. When this did not happen, both my mistress and Tanus taxed me severely.

'When will I be free to go to Tanus?' Queen Lostris sighed. 'You must do something, Taita.'

'It is not me, but the gods, whom you must question. I can pray to them, but that is all I can do.'

Then another year passed without any change in our circumstances, and even Tanus was bitter. 'So much faith I have placed in you that I have based my future happiness on your word. I swear to you, Taita, that if you do not do something soon—' He broke off and stared at me. The threat was all the more forceful for not being spoken.

Yet another year drifted past, and even I began to lose faith in my own prophecy. I came to believe that the gods had changed their minds, or that what I had seen was my own wishful fantasy.

In the end Prince Memnon was almost five years old and his mother twenty-one, when the messenger came flying wild-eyed from the north, in one of our scouting galleys.

'The Delta has fallen. The red pretender is dead. The Lower Kingdom is in flames. The cities of Memphis and Avaris are destroyed. The temples are burned to the ground and the images of the gods thrown down,' he shouted to the king, and Pharaoh replied, 'It is not possible. I long to believe this despatch, but I cannot. How could this thing come to pass without our knowledge? The usurper was possessed of great force, for more than fifteen years we have been unable to overthrow him. How has this been accomplished in a day, and by whom?'

The messenger was shaking with fear and exhaustion, for his journey had been onerous, and he knew how the bearers of disastrous tidings were treated in Thebes.

'The red pretender was destroyed with his sword

still in the scabbard. His forces were scattered before the war trumpets could sound the alarm.'

'How was this accomplished?'

'Divine Egypt, I know not. They say that a new and terrible enemy has come out of the East, swift as the wind, and no nation can stand before his wrath. Though they have never seen him, our army is in full retreat from the northern borders. Even the bravest will not stay to face him.'

'Who is this enemy?' Pharaoh demanded, and for the first time we heard the fear in his voice.

'They call him the Shepherd King. The Hyksos.'

Tanus and I had jested with that name. We would never do so again.

 Pharaoh called his war council into secret conclave. It was only long afterwards that I learned from Kratas all that transpired in those deliberations. Tanus, of course, would never break his oath of secrecy, not even to me or my mistress. But I was able to worm it out of Kratas, for that lovable, brawling oaf was not proof against my wiles.

Tanus had promoted Kratas to the rank of Best of Ten Thousand, and had given him the command of the Blue Crocodile Guards. The bond between them was still as solid as a granite stele. Thus, as a regimental commander, Kratas was entitled to a seat on the war council, and although at his lowly rank he was not called upon to speak, he faithfully relayed all that was said, to me and my mistress.

The council was divided between the ancients,

12

headed by Nembet, and the new blood of which Tanus was the leader. Unfortunately the final authority lay with the old men, and they forced their archaic views upon the others.

Tanus wanted to draw our main forces back from the frontier and to set up a series of deep defences along the river. At the same time, he intended sending forward scouting and reconnaissance parties to assess and study the nature of the mysterious enemy. We had spies in all of the northern cities, but for some unknown reason no reports from them had as yet been received. Tanus wanted to gather these in and study them, before he deployed his main force to battle.

'Until we know what we are facing, we cannot devise the correct strategy to meet it,' he told the council.

Nembet and his faction countered any of Tanus' suggestions. The old admiral had never forgiven Tanus for his humiliation on the day he saved the royal barge from destruction. His opposition to Tanus was based on principle rather than on reason or logic.

'We will not yield a cubit of our sacred soil. To suggest it is cowardice. We will meet the enemy and destroy him wherever we find him. We will not dance and flirt with him like a gaggle of village maidens.'

'My lord!' roared Tanus, incensed by the suggestion of cowardice. 'Only a fool, and an old fool at that, will make a decision before he knows the facts. We have no scrap of intelligence to act upon—'

It was in vain. The seniority of the three generals

13

above Tanus on the army lists prevailed in the end.

Tanus was ordered north immediately, to steady and rally the retreating army. He was to hold the frontier, and make his stand on the boundary stones. He was forbidden to make a strategic withdrawal to the line of hills before Asyut, which was the natural defensive line, and from which the city walls provided a second line of defence. He would have the fleet and the northern army corps under his direct command, with three hundred warships to provide the transport, and to command the river.

In the meantime, Nembet would bring in the rest of the army, even those regiments on the southern border with Cush. The black threat from the African interior must be ignored now in the face of this more pressing danger. As soon as they were assembled, Nembet would rush these reinforcements northwards to join up with Tanus. Within a month, there would be an invincible army of sixty thousand men and four hundred galleys lying before Asyut. In the meantime, Tanus must hold the frontier at all costs.

Nembet ended with a strict injunction. 'Lord Harrab is further ordered to hold all his forces on the border. He is not to indulge in raids or scouting forays to the north.'

'My Lord Nembet, these orders blindfold me, and bind my sword-arm. You are denying me the means of conducting this campaign in a prudent and efficient manner,' Tanus protested in vain. Nembet sneered with the satisfaction of having forced his authority upon his young rival, and in having gained a measure of retribution. On such petty human emotions pivots the destiny of

14

nations.

Pharaoh himself announced his intention of taking his rightful place at the head of his army. For a thousand years the pharaoh had been present on the field whenever the decisive battles of history had been fought out. Although I had to admire the king's courage, I wished he had not chosen this moment to demonstrate it. Pharaoh Mamose was no warrior, and his presence would do little to enhance our chances of victory. There might be some bolstering of morale when the troops saw him in the van, but on balance he and his train would be a greater hindrance than assistance to Lord Tanus.

The king would not travel northwards to the battle-front alone. His entire court would attend him, including his senior wife and his son. The queen must have her retinue and Prince Memnon his tutors, and so I would be going north to Asyut and the battle-front.

Nobody knew nor understood this enemy. I felt that my mistress and the prince were being placed in unnecessary danger. On the other hand, the safety of a slave was of no account, except to the slave himself. I slept little the night before we sailed northwards on the flood of the river for Asyut and the battle-front.

The farther north we sailed, the more numerous and troublesome were the rumours and reports coming down from the front to feed upon our contentment and confidence, like locusts upon the standing crops. Often during the voyage, Tanus came aboard our vessel, ostensibly to discuss these with me. However, on each visit he spent some time with the prince and his mother.

I have never held with the custom of women following the army into battle. In times of peace or war, they are a marvellous distraction—even a warrior of Tanus' calibre could be diverted from his main purpose. All his mind should have been on the task ahead, but when I told him so, he laughed and clapped my shoulder.

'They give me a reason to fight. Don't worry, old friend, I shall be a lion defending his cub.'

Soon we encountered the first elements of the retreating army, straggling groups of deserters who were looting the villages as they fled southwards along the banks of the river. With very little ceremony and no hesitation at all, Tanus beheaded several hundred of them and had their heads spiked on spears and planted along the bank as an example and a warning. Then he gathered up the others and regrouped them under reliable officers. There were no further desertions and the troops stood to the colours with a new spirit.

Our flotilla came to the walled city of Asyut, overlooking the river. In defiance of his orders from Nembet, Tanus left a small strategic reserve of five thousand men here under the command of

Remrem. Then we sailed on northwards to take up our positions on the border, there to await the approach of the mysterious Shepherd King.

The fleet lay at anchor across the river in its battle formations, but the vessels were under skeleton crews. The fighting men were disembarked with the main body of infantry and deployed upon the east bank of the river.

I prevailed upon Pharaoh to allow my mistress and the prince to remain on board the large and comfortable barge that had brought them here. It was cooler and healthier out on the water, and their escape would be swifter if our army met with any reverse of arms.

The king went ashore with the army, and set up his camp on the higher ground above the inundated fields. There was a deserted village here; years ago the peasants had fled from this disputed border with the false pharaoh. There were always foraging troops and bloody little skirmishes hereabouts, and the farmers had given up any attempts to work these fertile but dangerous fields. The name of the derelict village was Abnub.

The flood of the Nile had begun to subside some weeks prior to our arrival at Abnub, and although the irrigation canals were still running strongly, and the fields were morasses of black mud, the main waters had retreated back between the permanent banks of the Nile.

Within the restrictions placed upon him by Nembet, Tanus set about preparing to meet the threat. The regiments encamped in their order of battle. Astes commanded the fleet on the river, Tanus himself had the centre with his left flank anchored on the Nile, while Kratas had the right

17

wing.

The desert stretched to the eastern horizon, dun and forbidding. No army could survive out in that burning, waterless waste. It was our right flank, secure and impregnable.

All that we knew of the Hyksos was that he had come overland, and that he possessed no fleet of his own. Tanus expected to meet him on land, and to fight an infantry engagement. Tanus knew that he could prevent the Hyksos from crossing the river, and so he should be able to bring him to battle on the field of his own choice. Ideally, this would not have been at Abnub, but Nembet had made that decision for him.

The village of Abnub stood on a low ridge with open untended fields around it. At least it commanded a good view, and the enemy would be under our observation long before it could engage and drive in our pickets.

Tanus had thirty thousand of the finest troops in Egypt under his command. I had never seen such a large force. Indeed, I doubt that an army of this size had ever before been assembled in the valley of the Nile. Soon Nembet would arrive with another thirty thousand. Then it would be the greatest army in history.

I went with Tanus to inspect them, and the troops' morale had soared since he had taken command in person. Perhaps the presence of Pharaoh in the camp had also helped to steady them. They cheered Tanus as he strode along their massed ranks, and I felt much encouraged and relieved at the multitudes of their host, and the spirit in them.

I could not imagine an enemy powerful enough

to overwhelm us. There were twelve thousand archers with polished leather helmets and padded leather breastplates that would stop an arrow, except if it were fired at very short range. There were eight thousand heavy spearmen, with long shields of hippo-skin as tough and hard as bronze. The ten thousand swordsmen in leopard-skin caps were also armed with slingshots, the stones from which could split a skull at fifty paces.

I felt more confident with each day that passed, as I watched Tanus exercising these huge masses of armed men. Yet it worried me that we still knew so little about the Hyksos and the forces that he commanded. I pointed out to Tanus that the war council had forbidden him to send land forces forward to reconnoitre, but had said nothing of vessels being used for this purpose.

'You should have been a law scribe,' Tanus laughed, 'you can make words dance to any tune you play.' But he ordered Hui to take a single squadron of fast galleys northwards as far as Minieh, or until he encountered the enemy. This was the same Hui whom we had captured at Gallala, and who had been one of Basti's Shrikes. Under Tanus' favour, that young rogue had advanced swiftly, and now commanded a squadron of galleys.

Hui had strict orders to avoid action and to report back within four days. Dutifully, he returned on the fourth day. He had reached Minieh without seeing another ship or encountering any resistance. The villages along the river were all deserted, and the town of Minieh itself had been sacked and was in flames.

Hui had, however, captured a handful of

19

deserters from the false pharaoh's shattered army. These were the first persons we had questioned who were actual eye-witnesses of the Hyksos invasion. However, none of them had ever stood to engage and actually fight the Shepherd King. They had all fled at his first approach. Their reports were therefore so far-fetched and garbled as to be completely incredible.

How could we believe in the existence of an army that sailed across the open desert on ships that were as swift as the wind? According to our informants, the dust-clouds that hung over this strange fleet were so tall as to obscure their numbers and to strike terror into any army that watched their advance.

'These are not men,' the prisoners reported, 'they are fiends from the underworld, and they ride on the devil winds out of the desert.'

Having questioned the prisoners carefully, and finding that even hot coals on their heads could not make them alter their stories, Tanus ordered their summary execution. He did not want these wild tales circulating and spreading despondency amongst our forces who had only recently regained their courage.

 On the tenth day of waiting at Abnub, we received word that Nembet was at last on his way with reinforcements, and that he expected to reach Asyut within the next two weeks. The effect on the men was marvellous to behold. They were transformed at a stroke from sparrows to eagles.

Tanus issued an extra ration of beer and meat to celebrate the news, and the cooking-fires were a field of stars upon the plain before Abnub. The luscious odour of burning mutton fat filled the night, and the sound of laughter and singing only died away in the final watches.

I had left my mistress on board the barge with her son, and had come ashore in response to a summons from Tanus. He wanted me to attend the final war council with his regimental commanders. 'You are always a well of ideas and wisdom, you old rascal. Perhaps you can tell us how to sink a fleet of ships that comes sailing over dry land?'

Our deliberations went on until after midnight, and for once I was able to contribute very little of value. It was too late to return to the ship that night, so Tanus gave me a straw mattress in the corner of his tent. I awoke before dawn, as was my habit, but Tanus was gone from his bed, and beyond the coarse linen wall of the tent, the camp was already astir. I felt guilty of indolence, and hastened out to watch the dawn breaking over the desert.

I climbed the hill behind the camp. From there I looked first towards the river. The blue smoke from the cooking-fires was smeared out across the surface, mingling with the streamers of river mist. The riding lamps on board the ships were reflected in the dark waters. It was still too dark and far to pick out the vessel upon which my mistress lay.

I turned then towards the east and saw the light bloom over the desert with the nacreous glow of pearly oyster-shells. The light hardened and the desert was soft and lovely, the hillocks and dunes shaded with mauve and soft purple. In the limpid air the horizons seemed close enough to touch with an outstretched hand.

Then I saw the cloud suspended on the horizon beneath the unblemished aquamarine sheen of the sky. It was no larger than the end of my thumb, and my gaze wandered past it and then drifted back to it. I felt no initial alarm, for I had to stare at it for a while before I realized that it was moving.

'How strange,' I murmured aloud. 'The beginning of the *khamsin*, perhaps.' But it was out of season, and there had been no charging of the air with those malevolent forces which herald the desert storms. The morning was cool and balmy.

Even as I pondered it, the distant cloud spread and grew taller. The base of the cloud was upon the earth, not suspended above it, and yet it was too swift and wide to be of any earthly origin. A flock of birds might move that fast, locusts may rise that thickly to the skies, but this was neither of these things.

The cloud was ochre-yellow, but at first I could not believe it was dust. I have watched herds of scimitar-horned oryx galloping through the dunes in their hundreds upon their annual migrations, but they had never raised a dust-cloud such as this. It might have been the smoke from a fire, but there was nothing out there in the desert to burn. It had to be dust, and yet I still could not wholly believe it. Swiftly it grew, and drew ever closer, while I stared in wonder and in awe.

Suddenly I saw reflected light twinkle at the base of the towering cloud. Instantly I was transported back to the vision of the Mazes of Ammon-Ra. This was the same scene. The first had been

22

fantasy, but this was reality. I knew that those beams of light were shot from war armour and from blades of polished bronze. I started to my feet, and alone upon the hilltop I shouted to the wind a warning that nobody heard.

Then I heard the war trumpets sounding in the camp below me. The pickets on the heights had at last seen the approaching dust-cloud and sounded the alarm. The sound of the trumpets was a part of my vision. Their urgent warning shrilled in my ears and threatened to split my skull, it thrilled my blood and chilled my heart. I knew from my vision that on this fateful day a dynasty would fall and the locusts from the East would devour the substance of this very Egypt. I was filled with dread, and with terror for my mistress and the child that was part of the dynasty.

The camp below me was a tumult of men running to arms. Their armour glinted and their spear-heads sparkled as they brandished them on high. They were bees from the overturned hive, massing and swarming in disarray. The shouts of the sergeants and the rallying cries of the captains were almost drowned by the braying horns.

I saw Pharaoh carried from his tent in the centre of a knot of armed men. They hustled him up the slope of the hill to where his throne was set amongst the rocks, overlooking the plain and the wide sweep of the river. They lifted him to the throne and placed the crook and the flail in his hands and the tall double crown upon his head. Pharaoh sat like a marble statue with an ash-white face, while below him his regiments fell into their battle formations. Tanus had trained and exercised them well, and out of the confusion of the first

23

alarm, order swiftly emerged.

I ran down the hill to be near the king, and so rapid was the response of Lord Tanus' divisions that by the time I reached the foot of his throne, his army lay upon the plain like a coiled serpent to meet the menace of that boiling yellow dust-cloud that swept down upon it.

Kratas stood with his division on the right flank. I could recognize his tall figure on the first slope of the hill. His regimental officers were grouped around him, their plumes nodding and waving in the light morning breeze from the river. Tanus and his staff were directly below me, close enough for me to overhear their conversation. They discussed the advance of the enemy in cool, academic tones, as though this were a sandbox problem at an officers' training course.

Tanus had disposed his force in the classical formations. His heavy spearmen formed the front ranks. Their shields were interlocked and the spears' butts grounded. The bronze spear-heads sparkled in the early sunlight, and the men's demeanour was calm and grave. Drawn up behind them were the archers. Their bows were strung and ready. Behind each man stood his quiver boy with bundles of spare arrows. During the battle they would gather up the expended arrows of the enemy to replenish their own bundles. The swordsmen were in reserve, light and quick troops that could rush in to stop a breach or to exploit a weak point in the enemy formations.

The moves of any battle were like those of the bao board. There were classic openings with set defences that had been developed over the centuries. I had studied these and written three of the definitive scrolls on military tactics that were the prescribed reading of officers training in Thebes.

Now, reviewing Tanus' dispositions, I could find no fault in them, and my confidence soared. How could an enemy prevail against this mighty host of trained and battle-hardened veterans, and their brilliant young general, who had never lost a battle?

Then I looked once more beyond our ranks at that ominous, rolling yellow cloud, and my confidence wavered. This was something beyond military tradition, beyond the experience of any general in all our long, proud history. Were these mortal men that we were facing, or, as rumour suggested, were they fiends?

When I stared into the swirling clouds, they were now so close that I could make out dark shapes in the dun and gloomy veils of dust. My skin crawled with a kind of religious horror as I recognized the shiplike shapes that our prisoners had warned us of. But these were smaller and swifter than any vessel that had ever been launched on water, swifter even than any creature that had ever moved upon the surface of the earth.

It was difficult to follow one of these shapes with the eye, for they were ethereal and quick as moths in the light of a lantern. They wheeled and wove and disappeared in the moving clouds, so that when they reappeared, it was impossible to tell whether it was the same or another like it. There was no way to count their numbers, or even to guess at what followed the first ranks of their advance. Behind them, the dust-cloud extended back to the horizon from which they had come.

25

Although our own ranks stood firm and steady in the sunlight, I could sense the wonder and trepidation that gripped them all. The studied conversation of Tanus' officers had dried up, and they stood in silent awe and watched the enemy deploy before us.

Then I realized that the dust-cloud was no longer advancing upon us. It hung in the sky, and gradually began to settle and clear, so that I was able dimly to make out the stationary vehicles in the vanguard. But I was now so confused and alarmed that I could not tell whether there were a thousand of them or more.

We would learn later that this hiatus was always part of the Shepherd King's attack plan. I did not know it then, but during this lull they were regrouping and watering and gathering themselves for the final advance.

A terrible stillness had fallen on our ranks. It was so profound that the whisper of the breeze was loud through the rocks and the wadis of the hill on which we stood. The only movement was the flutter and swirl of our battle standards at the head of each division. I saw the Blue Crocodile banner waving in the centre of our line, and I took comfort from it.

Slowly, the dust-clouds subsided and row after row of the Hyksos' craft were revealed to us. They were still too distant to make out details, but I saw that those in the rear were much larger than those leading their army. It seemed to me that they were roofed over with sails of cloth or leather. From these I saw that men were unloading what looked like large water jars and carrying them forward. I wondered what men could consume such large

26

quantities of water. Everything these foreigners did was a puzzle and made no sense to me.

The silence and the waiting drew out until every muscle and nerve in my body screamed out with the strain. Then suddenly there was movement again.

From the front ranks of the Hyksos' formations some of these strange vehicles started towards us. A murmur went up from our ranks as we saw how fast they were moving. After that short period of rest, they seemed to have doubled their speed. The range closed and another cry went up from our host as we realized that these vehicles were each being drawn by a pair of extraordinary beasts.

They stood as tall as the wild oryx, with the same stiff, upstanding mane along the crest of their arched necks. They were not horned like the oryx, but their heads were more gracefully formed. Their eyes were large and their nostrils flared. Their legs were long and hoofed. Striding out with a peculiar daintiness, they seemed merely to brush the surface of the desert.

Even now, after all these years, I can recapture the thrill of gazing at a horse for the first time. In my mind the beauty of the hunting cheetah paled beside these marvellous beasts. At the same time we were all filled with fear of them, and I heard one of the officers near me cry out, 'Surely these monsters are killers, and eaters of human flesh! What abomination is this that is visited upon us?'

A stirring of horror ran through our formations, as we expected these beasts to fall upon us and devour us, like ravening lions. But the leading vehicle swung away and sped parallel to our front rank. It moved on spinning discs, and I stared at it in wonder. For the first few moments I was so stunned by what I was looking at that my mind refused to absorb it all. If anything, my first sight of a chariot was almost as moving as the horses that drew it. There was a long yoke-pole between the galloping pair, connected to what I later came to know as the axle. The high dashboard was gilded with gold leaf and the side-panels were cut low to allow the archer to shoot his arrows to either side.

All this I took in at a glance, and then my whole attention focused on the spinning discs on which the chariot sailed so smoothly and swiftly over the rough ground. For a thousand years we Egyptians had been the most cultured and civilized men on earth; in the sciences and the religions we had far outstripped all other nations. However, in all our learning and wisdom we had conceived nothing like this. Our sledges churned the earth on wooden runners that dissipated the strength of the oxen that dragged them, or we hauled great blocks of stone over wooden rollers without taking the next logical step.

I stared at the first wheel I had ever seen, and the simplicity and the beauty of it burst in upon me like lightning flaring in my head. I understood it instantly, and scorned myself for not having discovered it of my own accord. It was genius of the highest order, and now I realized that we stood to be destroyed by this wonderful invention in the same way as it must have annihilated the red usurper in the Lower Kingdom.

The golden chariot sped across our front, just out of bowshot. As it drew opposite us, I dragged my gaze from those miraculously spinning wheels and the fierce and terrifying creatures that drew

28

them, and I looked at the two men in the cockpit of the chariot. One was clearly the driver. He leaned out over the dashboard and he seemed to control the galloping team by means of long plaited cords of leather attached to their heads. The taller man who stood behind him was a king. There was no doubting his imperial bearing.

I saw instantly that he was an Asian, with amber skin and a hooked, aquiline nose. His beard was black and thick, cut square across his breastplates, curled and intricately plaited with coloured ribbons. His body armour was a glittering skin of bronze fish-scales, while his crown was tall and square; the gold was embossed with images of some strange god and set with precious stones. His weapons hung on the side-panel of the chariot, close to his hands. His broad-bladed sword in its leather and gold scabbard had a handle of ivory and silver. Beside it, two leather quivers bulged with arrows, and each shaft was fletched with bright feathers. Later I would come to know how the Hyksos loved gaudy colours. The king's bow on its rack beside him was of an unusual shape that I had never seen before. It was not the simple, clean arc of our Egyptian bows; on the Hyksos bow, the upper and lower limbs recurved at the tips.

As the chariot flew down our line, the king leaned out and planted a lance in the earth. It was tipped with a crimson pennant, and the men around me growled in perturbation. 'What is he doing? What purpose does the lance serve? Is it a religious symbol, or is it a challenge?'

I gaped at the fluttering pennant, but my wits were dulled by all that I had seen, it meant nothing to me. The chariot sped on, still just out of bowshot, and the crowned Asian planted another lance, then wheeled and came back. He had seen Pharaoh on his throne and he halted below him. The horses were lathered with sweat, it foamed on their flanks like lace. Their eyes rolled ferociously and their nostrils flared so that the pink mucous lining was exposed. They nodded their heads on long, arched necks and their manes flew like the tresses of a beautiful woman in the sunlight.

The Hyksos greeted Pharaoh Mamose, Son of Ra, Divine Ruler of the Two Kingdoms, May He Live For Ever, with contempt. It was a laconic and ironic wave of a mailed hand, and he laughed. The challenge was as clear as if it had been spoken in perfect Egyptian. His mocking laughter floated across to us, and the ranks of our army growled with anger, a sound like far-off thunder in the summer air.

A small movement below me caught my attention, and I looked down just as Tanus took one step forward and flung up the great bow Lanata. He loosed an arrow and it rose in a high arcing trajectory against the milky-blue sky. The Hyksos was out of range to any other bow, but not to Lanata. The arrow reached its zenith and then dropped like a stooping falcon, full at the centre of the Asian king's chest. The watching multitude gasped with the length and power and aim of that shot. Three hundred paces it flew, and at the very last moment the Hyksos threw up his bronze shield and the arrow buried its head in the centre of the target. It was done with such contemptuous ease that we were all amazed and confounded.

Then the Hyksos seized his own strangely

shaped bow from the rack beside him. With one movement he nocked an arrow, and drew and let it fly. It rose higher than Tanus had reached, and it sailed over his head. Fluting like the wing of a goose, it dropped towards me. I could not move and it might have impaled me without my attempting to avoid it, but it passed my head by an arm's-length and struck the base of Pharaoh's throne behind me. It quivered in the cedar strut like an insult, and the Hyksos king laughed again and wheeled his chariot and sped away, back across the plain, to rejoin his own host.

I knew then that we were doomed. How could we stand against these speeding chariots, and the recurved bows that so easily outranged the finest archer in our ranks? I was not alone in my dreadful expectations. As the squadrons of chariots began their final fateful evolutions out on the plain and sped towards us in waves, a moan of despair went up from the army of Egypt. I understood then how the forces of the red pretender had been scattered without a struggle, and the usurper had died with his sword still in its scabbard.

On the run, the flying chariots merged into columns four abreast and came directly at us. Only then did my mind clear, and I started down the slope at full pelt. Panting, I reached Tanus' side and shouted at him, 'The pennant lances mark the weak points in our line! Their main strike will come through us there and there!'

Somehow the Hyksos had known our battle order, and had recognized the lapse in our formation. Their king had planted his pennants exactly between our divisions. The idea of a spy or a traitor occurred to me even then, but in the

31

urgency of the moment I thrust it aside, and it was for the moment forgotten.

Tanus responded to my warning instantly, and shouted an order for our pickets to race forward and seize the pennants. I wanted him to move them, so that we could receive the enemy thrust on our strongest front, but there was no time for that. Before our pickets could reach and throw down the markers, the spear-head of flying chariots bore down upon them. Some of our men were shot down with arrows from the bouncing, swerving chariots. The aim of the enemy charioteers was uncanny.

The survivors turned and raced back, trying to regain the illusory safety of our lines. The chariots overhauled them effortlessly. The drivers controlled the galloping, plunging teams of horses with a lover's touch. They did not run their victims down directly, but swerved to pass them at the length of less than a cubit. It was only then that I noticed the knives. They were curved outwards from the spinning hub of the wheels like the fangs of some monstrous crocodile.

I saw one of our men struck squarely by the whirling blades. He seemed to dissolve in a bright cloud of blood. One of his severed arms was thrown high in the air and the bleeding chunks of his mutilated torso were dashed into the rocky earth as the chariot flew on without the least check. The phalanx of chariots was still aimed directly at the lap in our front line, and though I heard Kratas yelling orders to reinforce it, it was far too late.

The column of chariots crashed into our defensive wall of shields and spears, and tore through it as though it were as insubstantial as a

32

drift of river mist. In one instant our formation, that had stood the assault of the finest Syrian and Hurrian warriors, was cleaved and shattered.

The horses spurned our strongest and heaviest men under their hooves. The whirling wheel-knives hacked through their armour and lopped off heads and limbs, as though they were the tenderest shoots of the vine. From the high carriages the charioteers showered arrows and javelins into our tightly packed ranks, then they tore on through the breach they had forced, passing entirely through our formations, fanning out behind us and driving at full tilt along our rear files, still hurling their missiles into our unprotected rear.

When our troops turned to face this assault on their rear, another phalanx of racing chariots crashed into them from the open plain. The first assault split our army in twain, dividing Tanus from Kratas on the right wing. Then those that followed so swiftly cut up the two halves into smaller, isolated groups. We were no longer a cohesive whole. Little bands of fifty and a hundred men stood back-to-back and fought with the courage of the doomed.

Across the plain on wings of swirling dust, the Hyksos came on endlessly. Behind the light two-wheeled chariots followed the heavy four-wheeled war carts, each carrying ten men. The sides of the carts were screened with sheep fleeces. Our arrows slapped ineffectually into the thick, soft wool, our swords could not reach the men in the high body of the carts. They shot their points down into us and broke up the confused masses of our fighting men into scattered knots of terrified survivors. When one of our captains rallied a few men to counter-attack them, the war carts wheeled away and stopped out of range. With their awful recurved bows, they broke up our gallant charges, and the moment we wavered, they came rolling back upon us.

I was intensely aware of the moment when the conflict ceased to be a battle and became nothing more than a massacre. The remains of Kratas' division out on our right flank had fired the last of their arrows. The Hyksos had picked out their captains by their plumed helmets and shot nearly every one of them down. The men were disarmed and leaderless. They broke into rout. They threw down their weapons and ran for the river. But it was not possible to outrun a Hyksos chariot.

The broken troops ran into Tanus' divison below the hillock, and tangled with it. With their panicking, struggling masses they clogged and smothered what little resistance Tanus was still capable of offering. The terror was infectious and the centre of our line broke and tried to fly, but the deadly chariots circled them, like wolves around the flock.

In all that chaos, in the bloody shambles and the tumult of defeat, only the Blues stood firm around Tanus and the Crocodile standard. They were a little island in the torrent of defeated men, even the chariots could not break them up, for, with the instinct of a great general, Tanus had gathered them and pulled them back into the one patch of rocks and gulleys where the Hyksos could not come at them. The Blues were a wall, a bulwark around the throne of Pharaoh.

Because I had been at the king's side, I was in

34

the centre of this ring of heroes. It was difficult to keep my feet, for all around me men struggled and surged, washed back and forth by the waves of battle, like seaweed clinging to a rock in the full stream of tide and surf.

I saw Kratas fight his way through from the shattered right wing to join us. His plumed helmet attracted the Hyksos arrows and they flew around his head thickly as locusts, but he came through unscathed, and our ring opened for him. He saw me, and he laughed with huge delight. 'By Seth's steaming turds, Taita, this is more fun than building palaces for little princes, is it not?' He was never famous for his repartee, was Kratas, and I was too busy staying on my feet to bother with a reply.

He and Tanus met close to the throne. Kratas grinned at him like an idiot. 'I'd not have missed this for all Pharaoh's treasure. I want one of those Hyksos sledges for myself.' Neither was Kratas one of Egypt's greatest engineers. Even now he still believed that the chariots were some type of sledge. That was as far as his imagination reached.

Tanus tapped the side of his helmet with the flat of his sword in greeting, and although his tone was light, his expression was grim. He was a general who had just lost a battle and an army, and an empire.

'Our work here is finished for today,' he told Kratas. 'Let us see if these Hyksos monsters can swim as well as they run. Back to the river!' Then, shoulder-to-shoulder, the two of them shoved their way through the ranks towards the throne where I still stood.

I could see over their heads, over the periphery

of our little defensive ring, out over the plain where our broken army was streaming away towards the river, still harried by the squadrons of chariots.

I saw the golden chariot of the Hyksos king wheel out of formation and cleave its way towards us, trampling our men under the flying hooves and chopping them up with the glittering wheel-knives. The driver brought the horses to a rearing, plunging halt before he reached the barrier of rocks which protected us. Balancing easily on the footplates, the Hyksos drew his recurved bow and aimed at me, or so it seemed. Even as I ducked, I realized that the arrow was not meant for me. It shrieked over my head and I turned to watch its flight. It struck Pharaoh high in the chest, and buried half its length in his flesh.

Pharaoh gave a hoarse cry and tottered on his high throne. There was no blood, for the shaft had plugged the wound, but the feathers were a pretty scarlet and green. Pharaoh slid sideways and collapsed forward towards me, and I opened my arms to receive him. His weight bore me to my knees, so I did not see the Hyksos king's chariot wheel away, but I heard his mocking laughter receding as he dashed back across the plain to lead the slaughter.

Tanus stooped over me as I held the king. 'How badly is he struck?' he demanded.

'He is killed,' the reply rose to my lips unthinkingly. The angle of entry and the depth of the wound could mean that only one outcome was possible, but I choked off the words before they were spoken. I knew that our men would lose heart if Great Egypt was slain. Instead I said, 'He is hard hit. But if we carry him back aboard the state

36

barge, he may recover.'

'Bring me a shield here!' Tanus roared, and when it came we gently lifted Pharaoh on to it. There was still no blood, but I knew his chest was filling like a wine jar. Quickly, I felt for the head of the arrow, but it had not emerged from his back. The point was still buried deep within the cage of his ribs. I snapped off the protruding shaft, and covered him with his linen shawl.

'Taita,' he whispered. 'Will I see my son again?'

'Yes, Mighty Egypt, I swear it to you.'

'And my dynasty will survive?'

'Even as the Mazes of Ammon-Ra have foretold.'

'Ten strong men here!' Tanus bellowed. They crowded around the makeshift litter, and lifted the king between them.

'Form the tortoise! Close up on me, the Blues!' With interlocking shields, the Blues formed a wall around the king.

Tanus raced to the Blue Crocodile which still waved in our midst and tore it from its pole. He wound it around his waist and knotted the ends across his belly.

'If the Hyksos want this rag, they had better come and take it from me,' he shouted, and his men cheered this piece of foolish bravado.

'All together now! Back to the ships! At the double!'

The moment we left the shelter of our little rocky redoubt, the chariots came at us.

'Leave the men!' Tanus had found the key. 'Kill their beasts!' As the first chariot bore down upon us, Tanus flexed Lanata. His bowmen drew with him, and they all fired on his example.

37

Half our arrows flew wide, for we were running over uneven ground and the archers were winded. Others struck the bodywork of the leading chariot, and the shafts snapped or pegged into the wood. Still other arrows rattled off the bronzed plates that covered the chests of the horses.

Only one arrow flew hard and true. From the great bow Lanata it sang with the wind in its feathers, and struck the offside horse in the forehead. The creature went down like a rockslide, tangling the traces and dragging its team-mate down in a cloud of dust and kicking hooves. The charioteers were hurled from the cockpit as the carriage somersaulted, and the other chariots veered away to avoid the wreckage. A jubilant shout went up from our ranks, and our pace picked up. This was our first success in all that dreadful day, and it manned and encouraged our little band of Blues.

'On me, the Blues!' Tanus roared, and then, incredibly, he began to sing. Immediately the men around him shouted the opening chorus of the regimental battle hymn. Their voices were strained and rough with thirst and effort, and there was little tune or beauty to it, but it was a sound to lift the heart and thrill the blood. I threw back my head and sang with them, and my voice soared clear and sweet.

'Horus bless you, my little canary,' Tanus laughed at me, and we raced for the river. The chariots circled us with the first wariness to their manoeuvres that they had demonstrated all that day. They had seen the fate of their comrade. Then three of them swung across the front of our tortoise, and in vee-formation charged at us

38

head-on.

'Shoot at the heads of the beasts!' Tanus shouted, and led them with an arrow that brought another horse crashing to its knees. The chariot overturned and was smashed to pieces on the stony ground, and the other vehicles in the formation veered away.

As our formation passed the shattered chariot, some of our men ran out to stab the squealing horses that were trapped in the wreckage. Already they hated and feared these animals with an almost superstitious dread, which was reflected in this vindictive piece of cruelty. They killed the fallen charioteers also, but without the same rancour.

With two of their chariots destroyed, the Hyksos seemed reluctant to attack our little formation again, and we were rapidly approaching the morass of muddy fields and flooded irrigation ditches that marked the river-bank. I think that at that stage I was the only one of us who realized that the wheeled enemy could not follow us into the swamp.

Although I ran beside the king's litter, I could see, through the gaps in our ranks, the dying acts of the battle that were being played out around us.

Ours was the only surviving detachment that still showed any cohesion. The rest of the Egyptian army was a formless and terrified rabble streaming across the plain. Most of them had thrown aside their weapons. When one of the chariots drove at them, they dropped to their knees and held up their hands in supplication. The Hyksos showed them no quarter. They did not even waste arrows upon them but swung in close to chop them to tatters with the spinning wheel-knives, or to lean out of the cockpit with the lance and cut them down, or to smash in their skulls with the stone-headed maces. They dragged the victim behind them, still spiked on the lance, until the barbed spear-head disengaged, and only then did they leave the crumpled corpse lying in their dust.

I had never seen such butchery. I had never read of anything like it in all the accounts of ancient battles. The Hyksos slaughtered our people in their thousands and their tens of thousands. The plain of Abnub was like a field of dhurra corn after the reapers had been through it with their scythes. Our dead were piled in drifts and windrows.

For one thousand years our armies had been invincible and our swords had triumphed across the world. Here on the field of Abnub an age had come to an end. In the midst of this carnage the Blues sang, and I with them though my eyes burned with tears of shame.

The first irrigation ditch was just ahead when another chariot formation swung out on our flank and came driving hard at us, three abreast. Our arrows fell all about them, but they came on with the horses blowing hard through gaping red mouths and with the drivers screaming encouragement at them. I saw Tanus shoot twice, but each time his arrows were deflected or were cheated by the erratic swerve and bounce of the chariots. The formation thundered into us and broke the tortoise of interlocking shields.

Two of the men carrying Pharaoh's litter were cut to shreds by the wheel-knives, and the wounded king was tumbled to the earth. I dropped to my knees beside him and covered him with my own body to protect him from the Hyksos lances, but the chariots did not linger. It was their concern never to allow themselves to become entangled or surrounded. They raced on and clear before our men could reach them with the sword. Only then did they wheel and regroup, and come back.

Tanus reached down and hauled me to my feet. 'If you get yourself killed, who will be left to compose a hero's ode to us?' he scolded me, then he shouted for men. Between them they picked up the king's litter and ran with it for the nearest ditch.

I could hear the squeal of the chariot wheels bearing down on us, but I never looked back. In ordinary circumstances I am a strong runner, but now I outdistanced the litter-bearers as though their feet were chained to the earth. I attempted to hurdle the ditch, but it was too wide for me to cross in a single leap, and I landed knee-deep in the black mud. The chariot that was following me struck the bank of the ditch and one of its wheels shattered. The body of the vehicle toppled into the ditch and almost crushed me, but I managed to throw myself aside.

Swiftly the Blues stabbed and hacked the horses and men as they lay helplessly in the mud, but I took the moment to wade back to the chariot.

The up-ended wheel was still spinning in the air. I placed my hand upon it as I studied it, and let it rotate beneath my fingers. I stood there only as long as it took me to draw three deep breaths, but at the end of that time I had learned as much about wheel construction as any Hyksos, and had the first inkling of the improvements I could make to it.

'By Seth's melodious farts, Taita, you'll have us

41

all killed, if you start daydreaming now!' Kratas yelled at me.

I shook myself and seized one of the recurved bows from the rack on the side of the chariot body and an arrow from the quiver. I wanted to examine these at my leisure. Then I waded across the ditch with them in my hand, just as the squadron of chariots came thundering back, running parallel to the ditch and firing their arrows down amongst us.

The men carrying the king were a hundred paces ahead of me, and I was the last of our little band. Behind me the charioteers roared with frustration that they were unable to follow us, and they shot their arrows around me as I ran. One of them struck my shoulder, but the point failed to penetrate and the shaft glanced away. It left a purple bruise which I only discovered much later.

Although I had started from so far behind them, I caught up with the litter-bearers by the time we reached the main bank of the Nile. The river-bank was crowded with the survivors of the battle. Nearly all of these were weaponless and very few were unwounded. They were all driven by a single desire, to return as swiftly as possible to the ships that had brought them down-river from Thebes.

Tanus singled me out and called me to him as the litter-bearers came up. 'I place Pharaoh in your hands now, Taita. Take him on board the royal barge and do all you can to save his life.'

'When will you come aboard?' I asked him.

'My duty is here, with my men. I must save all of them that I can, and get them embarked.' He turned from me and strode away, picking out the captains and commanders from amongst his beaten rabble, and shouting his orders.

I went to the king and knelt beside the litter. He was still alive. I examined him briefly and found that he hovered on the edge of consciousness. His skin was as clammy-cold as that of a reptile, and his breathing was shallow. There was only a thin rime of blood around that arrow-shaft which had seeped up from the wound, but when I laid my ear to his chest I heard the blood bubbling in his lungs with each breath he drew, and a thin red snake of it crawled from his mouth down his chin. I knew that whatever I could do to save him, I must do quickly. I shouted for a boat to take him out to the barge.

The litter-bearers lifted him into the skiff, and I sat in the bilges beside him as we sculled out to where the great state barge lay anchored in the main flow of the current.

 The king's suite crowded the ship's side to watch us approach. There was a gaggle of the royal women and all those courtiers and priests who had taken no part in the fighting. I recognized my mistress standing amongst them as we drew closer. Her face was very anxious and pale, and she held her young son by his hand.

As soon as those on board the barge looked down into our skiff and saw the king on his litter, with the blood on his face that I had been unable to wipe away, a terrible cry of alarm and mourning went up from them. The women keened and wailed, and the men howled with despair, like dogs.

Of all the women, my mistress stood closest at hand as the king was lifted up the ship's side and his litter laid on the deck. As the senior wife, hers was the duty to attend him first. The others gave her space as she stooped over him and wiped the mud and the blood from his haggard face. He recognized her, for I heard him breathe her name and ask for his son. My mistress called the prince to him, and he smiled softly and tried to raise his hand to touch the boy, but he did not have the strength, and the hand dropped back to his side.

I ordered the crew to carry Pharaoh to his quarters, and my mistress came to me quickly and asked low and urgently, 'What of Tanus? Is he safe? Oh, Taita, tell me that he is not slain by this dreadful enemy!'

'He is safe. Nothing can harm him. I have given you the vision of the Mazes. All this was foreseen. But now I must go to the king, and I will need your help. Leave Memnon with his nursemaids, and come with me.'

I was still black and crusted with river mud, and so was Pharaoh, for he had fallen in the same ditch as I had. I asked Queen Lostris and two of the other royal women to strip and bathe him and lay him on fresh white linen sheets, while I returned to the deck to bathe in buckets of river water that the sailors hauled up over the side. I never operate in filth, for I have found by experience that for some reason it affects the patient adversely and favours the accumulation of the morbid humours.

While I was thus occupied, I was watching the east bank where our broken army was huddled behind the protection of ditch and swamp. This sorry rabble had once been a proud and mighty

44

force, and I was filled with shame and fear. Then I saw the tall figure of Tanus striding amongst them, and wherever he moved, the men stood up out of the mud, and reassembled into the semblance of military discipline. Once I even caught the sound of ragged and unconvincing cheers on the wind.

If the enemy should send their infantry through the swamps now, the slaughter and the rout would be complete. Not a man of all our mighty army would survive, for even Tanus would be able to offer little resistance. However, although I peered anxiously into the east, I could make out no sign of infantry shields in phalanx or the sparkle of advancing spear-heads at the shoulder-slope.

There was still that terrible dust-cloud hanging over the plain of Abnub, so the chariots were at work out there, but without enemy infantry falling upon him, Tanus could still salvage some little comfort out of this dreadful day. It was a lesson I was to remember, and which stood us in good stead in the years ahead. Chariots might win the battle, but only the foot-soldiers could consolidate it.

The battle out there on the river-bank was now entirely Tanus' affair, while I had another battle to fight with death in the cabin of the state barge.

 'We are not entirely without hope,' I whispered to my mistress, when I returned to the king's side. 'Tanus is rallying his troops, and if any man alive is capable of saving this very Egypt from the Hyksos, he is the one.' Then I turned to the king, and

45

for the moment all else was forgotten but my patient.

As is often my way, I murmured my thoughts aloud as I examined the wound. It was less than an hour, measured by a water-clock, since the fateful arrow had struck, and yet the flesh around the broken-off stub of the shaft was swollen and empurpled.

'The arrow must come out. If I leave the barb in there, he will be dead by tomorrow's dawn.' I had thought the king could no longer hear me, but as I spoke, he opened his eyes and looked directly into mine.

'Is there a chance that I will live?' he asked.

'There is always a chance.' I was glib and insincere. I heard it in my own voice, and the king heard it also.

'Thank you, Taita. I know you will strive for me, and I absolve you now from all blame, if you should fail.' This was generous of him, for many physicians before me have felt the strangling-rope as punishment for letting the life of a king slip through their fingers.

'The head of the arrow is deeply lodged. There will be a great deal of pain, but I will give you the powder of the Red Shepenn, the sleeping-flower, to still it.'

'Where is my senior wife, Queen Lostris?' he asked, and my mistress replied immediately, 'I am here, my lord.'

'There is aught that I would say. Summon all my ministers and my scribes, that my proclamation may be witnessed and recorded.' They crowded into the hot little cabin and stood in silence.

Then Pharaoh reached out to my mistress.

'Take my hand, and listen to my words,' he ordered, and she sank down beside him and did as she was ordered, while the king went on speaking in a soft and breathless whisper.

'If I should die, Queen Lostris will stand as regent for my son. I have learned in the time that I have known her that she is a person of strength and good sense. If she were not, I would not have laid this charge upon her.'

'Thank you, Great Egypt, for your trust,' Queen Lostris murmured low, and now Pharaoh spoke directly to her, although every person in the cabin could hear him.

'Surround yourself with wise and honest men. Instruct my son in all the virtues of kingship that you and I have discussed. You know my mind on all these matters.'

'I will, Majesty.'

'When he is old enough to take up the flail and the crook, do not attempt to withhold it from him. He is my lineage and my dynasty.'

'Willingly I shall do what you order, for he is not only the son of his father, but my son also.'

'While you rule, rule wisely and care for my people. There will be many who seek to wrest the emblems of kingship from your grasp—not only this new and cruel enemy, this Hyksos, but others who stand even closer to your throne. But you must oppose them all. Keep the double crown intact for my son.'

'Even as you say, divine Pharaoh.'

The king fell silent for a while and I thought that he had slipped over the edge into unconsciousness, but suddenly he groped for the hand of my mistress again.

'There is one last charge I have for you. My tomb and my temple are incomplete. Now they are threatened, as is all my realm, by this terrible defeat that we have suffered. Unless my generals can stop them, these Hyksos will sweep on to Thebes.'

'Let us petition the gods that it does not come to pass,' my mistress murmured.

'I charge you most strictly that you will see me embalmed and interred with all my treasure in accordance with the strictest protocols of the *Book of the Dead.*'

My mistress was silent. I think that she realized even then just what an onerous charge this was that Pharaoh had laid upon her.

His grip upon her hand tightened until his knuckles turned white, and she winced. 'Swear this to me on your own life and hope for immortality. Swear it before my ministers of state and all my royal suite. Swear it to me in the name of Hapi, your patron god, and on the names of the blessed trinity, Osiris and Isis and Horus.'

Queen Lostris looked across at me with a piteous appeal in her eyes. I knew that once she had given it, she would honour her word at all and any cost to herself. In this, she was like her lover. She and Tanus were bound by the same code of chivalry. I knew also that those close to her must expect to pay the same price. An oath to the king now might one day return to burden us all, Prince Memnon and the slave Taita included. And yet there was no manner in which she could gainsay the king as he lay upon his death-bed. I nodded to her almost imperceptibly. Later I would examine the finer points of this oath, and like a law scribe I would mould it a little closer to reasonable interpretation.

'I swear on Hapi, and on all the gods,' Queen Lostris said, softly but clearly, and there would be a hundred times in the years ahead when I would wish she had not done so.

The king sighed with satisfaction and let her hand slip from his. 'Then I am ready for you, Taita. And for whatever fate the gods have decreed. Only let me kiss my son once more.'

While they brought our fine young prince to him, I drove the crowd of nobles from the cabin with little ceremony. Then I prepared a draught of the Red Shepenn for him and made it as strong as I dared, for I knew that pain could undo all my best efforts and destroy my patient as swiftly as a slip of my scalpel.

When he had drunk it all, I waited for the pupils of his eyes to contract to pinpoints, and for the lids to droop over them. Then I sent the prince away with his nursemaids.

 On leaving Thebes I had expected to have to deal with arrow wounds, so I had brought my spoons with me. I had designed this instrument myself, although there was a quack in Gaza and another in Memphis who both claimed it was their invention. I blessed the spoons and my scalpels in the lamp flame, and then washed my hands in hot wine.

'I do not think it is wise to use one of your spoons when the head of the arrow is so deep and so near the heart,' my mistress told me as she

49

watched my preparations. There are occasions when she speaks as though the student had outpaced the master.

'If I leave the arrow, it will certainly mortify. I will have killed him just as surely as if I had chopped his head off his shoulders. This is the only way that I will have a chance of saving him.'

For a moment we looked into each other's eyes, and we spoke without words. This was the vision of the Mazes of Ammon-Ra. Did we wish to avoid the benevolent consequences to ourselves?

'He is my husband. He is Pharaoh.' My mistress took my hand to emphasize her words. 'Save him, Taita. Save him, if you can.'

'You know that I will,' I answered.

'Do you need me to help you?' She had assisted me so very often before. I nodded my assent, and stooped over the king.

There were three ways that I might have attempted to withdraw the arrow. The first would be to pluck it out. I have heard of a surgeon in Damascus who bends down the supple branch of a tree and attaches this to the shaft. When he releases the branch, the arrow is whipped out of the living flesh by the strength of the sapling. I have never tried such brutal treatment for I am convinced that very few men would survive it.

The second method would be to push the arrow through the limb or the torso until the barbed head emerges on the far side. To achieve this, it can be driven along its original path with a mallet, like a nail through a plank. Then the barb is sawn off and the shaft drawn free. This treatment is almost as brutal as the first.

My method is the Taita spoon. I have named the

spoon after myself in all modesty, for the claims of those others are spurious, and posterity needs to be informed of my genius.

Firstly, I examined the Hyksos arrow that I had salvaged along with the bow from the overturned chariot. I was surprised to find that the arrow-head was of worked flint rather than of bronze. Of course, flint is cheaper and easier to procure in quantity, but I have seldom known a general who tries to economize when setting out to seize a kingdom. This flint arrow-head spoke eloquently of the Hyksos' limited resources, and suggested a reason for his savage attack upon this very Egypt. Wars are fought for land or wealth, and it seemed that the Hyksos was short of both these commodities.

I had to hope that the arrow-head buried in Pharaoh's breast was of the same shape and design. I matched a pair of my spoons to the razor-edged piece of stone. My spoons are of various sizes, and I selected a pair that enclosed the head snugly, masking the wicked barbs with smoothly polished metal.

By this time, the drug had worked its full magic, and Pharaoh lay unconscious upon his cloud-white linen sheets, with the snapped-off arrow standing out as far as my forefinger from the skin, which was wrinkled with age and covered with the frosted curls of his body hair. I laid my ear on his chest once more and heard his breath sigh and gurgle in his lungs. Satisfied that he still lived, I greased the spoons that I had selected with mutton fat, to lubricate their entry into the wound. I laid the spoons close at hand and took up one of my keenest scalpels.

51

I nodded to the four strong guards that Queen Lostris had selected for me while I was busy with my preparations, and they took hold of Pharaoh's wrists and ankles and held him down firmly. Queen Lostris sat at the king's head and placed the wooden tube from my medical chest between his lips and deep back into his throat. This would keep his windpipe clear and open. It would also prevent him from biting or swallowing his own tongue, or grinding his teeth together and snapping them off, when the pain assaulted him too fiercely.

'First I have to enlarge the wound around the shaft to enable me to reach the head of the arrow,' I muttered to myself, and I pressed the point of the scalpel down along the line of the shaft. Pharaoh's whole body stiffened, but the men held him down remorselessly.

I worked swiftly, for I have learned that speed is crucial in an operation of this nature, if the patient is to survive. I opened a slit on each side of the shaft. The human skin is tough and elastic and would inhibit the entry of the spoons, so I had to get through it.

I dropped the knife and took up the pair of lubricated spoons. Using the arrow-shaft as a guide, I eased them deeper and deeper into the wound, until only the long handles still protruded.

By this time Pharaoh was writhing and twisting in the grip of his restrainers. Sweat was pouring from every pore of his skin, and running back over his shaven skull with its stubble of thin grey hair. His screams rang through the tube in his mouth, and reverberated through the hull of the barge.

I had taught myself to ignore the agonized distress of my patients, and I slid the spoons

52

deeper into the widely distended mouth of the wound until I felt them touch the flint of the arrow-head. This was the delicate part of the operation. Using the handles like a pair of tweezers, I levered the spoons apart and worked them over the arrow-head. When I felt them close of their own accord, I hoped that I had entirely enclosed the coarse flint and masked the barbs.

I took a careful grasp of the handles of the spoons and of the reed shaft of the arrow, and pulled back on them all together. If the barbs were still free, they would have immediately snagged in Pharaoh's flesh and resisted my pull. I could have shouted aloud with relief as I felt it all begin to yield. Still, the suction of the wet and clinging flesh was considerable, and I had to use all my strength to draw the shaft.

Pharaoh's agony was dreadful to hear and behold, as the mass of reed and stone and metal was dragged through his chest. The Red Shepenn drug had long ago ceased to be of any effect, and the pain was raw and savage. I knew I was doing fearful damage, and I could feel tissue and sinew tearing.

My own sweat ran down into my eyes and burned and half-blinded me, but I never released my pull until suddenly the blood-smeared arrow came free in my hands and I staggered backwards across the cabin and crashed into the bulkhead. I leaned against it for a moment, exhausted with the effort. I watched the dark, half-congealed blood trickle and spurt from the wound for a long moment, before I could rally myself and stagger back to stem it.

I smeared the wound with precious myrrh and

crystallized honey, and then bound it up tightly with clean linen bandages. As I worked, I recited the incantation for the binding up of wounds:

I bind thee up, oh creature of Seth.
I stop up thy mouth.
Retreat before me, red tide.
Retire before me, red flower of death.
I banish you, oh red dog of Seth.

This was the recitation for a bleeding wound caused by blade or arrow. There are specific verses for all types of wound, from burns to those inflicted by the fangs or claws of a lion. Learning these is a large part of the training of a physician. I am never certain in my own mind as to just how efficacious these incantations are; however, I believe that I owe it to my patients to employ any possible means at my disposal for their cure.

In the event, Pharaoh seemed much easier after the binding-up, and I could leave him sleeping in the care of his women and go back on deck. I needed the cool river airs to revive me, for the operation had drained me almost as much as it had Pharaoh.

By this time it was evening, and the sun was settling wearily upon the stark western hills and throwing its last ruddy glow over the battlefield. There had been no assault by the Hyksos infantry, and Tanus was still bringing off the remains of his vanquished army from the river-bank to the galleys anchored in the stream.

I watched the boatloads of wounded and exhausted men passing our anchored barge, and I felt a deep compassion for them, as I did for all our people. This would be for ever the most dire day in our history. Then I saw that the dust-cloud of the Hyksos chariots was already beginning to move southwards towards Thebes. The clouds were incarnadined by the sunset to the colour of blood. It was for me a sign, and my compassion turned to dread.

 It was dark by the time that Tanus himself came aboard the state barge. In the light of the torches he looked like one of the corpses from the battlefield. He was pale with fatigue and dust. His cloak was stiff with dried blood and mud, and there were dark, bruised shadows under his eyes. When he saw me, his first concern was to ask after Pharaoh.

'I have removed the arrow,' I told him. 'But the wound is deep and near the heart. He is very weak, but if he survives three days, then I will be able to save him.'

'What of your mistress and her son?' He always asked this, whenever we met.

'Queen Lostris is tired, for she helped me with the operation. But she is with the king now. The prince is as bonny as ever and sleeps now with his nurses.'

I saw Tanus reel on his feet, and knew that he was close to the end of even his great strength. 'You must rest now—' I began, but he shook off my hand.

'Bring lamps here,' he ordered. 'Taita, fetch your writing-brushes and ink-pots and scrolls. I must send a warning to Nembet, lest he walk into

55

the Hyksos trap even as I did.'

So Tanus and I sat half that night on the open deck, and this was the despatch for Nembet that he dictated to me:

I greet you Lord Nembet, Great Lion of Egypt, Commander of the Ra division of the army of Pharaoh. May you live for ever!

Know you that we have encountered the enemy Hyksos at the plain of Abnub. The Hyksos in his strength and ferocity is a terrible foe, and possessed of strange, swift craft that we cannot resist.

Know you further that we have suffered a defeat and that our army is destroyed. We can no longer oppose the Hyksos.

Know you further that Pharaoh is gravely wounded and in danger of his life.

We urge you not to meet the Hyksos in an open field, for his craft are like the wind. Therefore take refuge behind walls of stone, or wait aboard your ships, to turn the enemy aside.

The Hyksos has no ships of his own, and it is by means of our ships alone that we may prevail against him.

We urge you to await our coming before committing your forces to battle.

I call the protection of Horus and all the gods down upon you.

It is Tanus, Lord Harrab, Commander of the Ptah division of the army of Pharaoh, who speaks thus.

I wrote out four copies of this message, and as I completed each, Tanus called for messengers to

56

carry them to the Lord Nembet, Great Lion of Egypt, who was advancing from the south to reinforce us. Tanus sent two fast galleys speeding up-river, each with a fair copy of the despatches. Then he put his best runners ashore on the west bank, the opposite side of the river from the Hyksos army, and sent them off to find Nembet.

'Surely one of your scrolls will win through to Nembet. You can do no more until morning,' I reassured him. 'You must sleep now, for if you destroy yourself, then all of Egypt is destroyed with you.'

Even then he would not go to a cabin, but curled on the deck like a dog, so that he could be instantly ready for any new emergency. But I went to the cabin to be near my king and to give comfort to my mistress.

I was on deck again before the first glimmer of dawn. I arrived to hear Tanus giving orders to burn our fleet. It was not for me to question this decision, but he saw me gape incredulously at him, and when the messengers had been sent away he told me brusquely, 'I have just received the roll-call from my regimental commanders. Of the thirty thousand of my men who stood yesterday on the plain of Abnub to meet the chariots of the Hyksos, only seven thousand remain. Five thousand of those are wounded, and many will still die. Of those who are unwounded, very few are sailors. I am left with only sufficient men to work half our fleet. I must abandon the rest of our ships, but I cannot let them fall into the hands of the Hyksos.'

They used bundles of reeds to start the fires, and once they were set, they burned fiercely. It was a sad and terrible sight to watch, even for me and my mistress, who were not sailors. For Tanus it was far worse. He stood alone in the bows of the state barge, with despair and grief in every line of his face and in the set of those wide shoulders, as he watched his ships burn. For him they were living things, and beautiful.

Before all the court my mistress could not go to his side where she belonged, but she took my hand surreptitiously, and the two of us mourned for Tanus and for all Egypt as we watched those gallant craft burn like torches. The roaring pillars of flame from each vessel were sullied with black smoke, but still their ruddy light rivalled the approach of the sunrise.

At last Tanus gave the order to his hundred remaining galleys to weigh anchor, and our little fleet, laden with wounded and dying men, turned back into the south.

Behind us, the smoke from the funeral pyre of our fleet stood high into the early morning sky, while ahead of us the yellow dust-cloud stretched taller and wider along the east bank of the Nile as the chariot squadrons of the Hyksos drove deeper into the Upper Kingdom, towards helpless Thebes and all her treasures.

It seemed that the gods had turned their backs on Egypt and deserted us completely, for the wind, which usually blew so strongly from the north at this season of the year, died away completely, and then sprang up again with renewed vigour from the south. Thus we were forced to contend with both current and wind, and our ships were deeply laden with their cargoes of wounded. We were slow and heavy in the water, with the depleted crews slaving at the oars. We could not keep pace with the Hyksos army, and it drew away from us inexorably.

I was absorbed with my duties as physician to the king. However, on every other vessel in the fleet, men whom I could have saved were dying in their scores. Every time that I went on deck for a little fresh air and a short break from my vigil at the bedside of Pharaoh, I saw corpses being thrown over the side of the other galleys near us. At each splash there was a swirl of crocodiles beneath the surface. Those awful reptiles followed the fleet like vultures.

Pharaoh rallied strongly, and on the second day I was able to feed him a small bowl of broth. That evening he asked to see the prince again, and Memnon was brought to him.

Memnon was already at the age when he was as restless as a grasshopper and as noisy as a flock of starlings. Pharaoh had always been good with the boy, if inclined to over-indulgence, and Memnon delighted in his company. Already he was a beautiful boy, with clean, strong limbs and his mother's skin and great dark green eyes. His hair was curled like the pelt of a new-born black lamb, but in the sunlight, it was sparked with the flames of Tanus' ruddy mop.

Pharaoh's delight in Memnon was even more poignant than usual. The child and the promise that he had wrung from my mistress were his hope of immortality. Against my wishes he kept the child with him until after sunset. I knew that Memnon's boundless energy and his demands for attention were tiring the king, but I could not intervene until it was time for the prince's supper

59

and he was led away by his nurses.

My mistress and I stayed on at the king's bedside, but he fell almost instantly into a death-like sleep. Even without his white make-up, he was as pale as the linen sheets on which he lay.

The next day was the third since the wounding, and therefore the most dangerous. If he could survive this day, then I knew I could save him. But when I woke in the dawn the cabin was thick with the musky stench of corruption. When I touched Pharaoh's skin, it burned my fingers like a kettle from the hearth. I called for my mistress, and she came stumbling through from her alcove behind the curtain where she slept.

'What is it, Taita?' She got no further, for the answer was plain upon my face. She stood beside me as I unbound the wound. The binding-up is a high art of the surgeon's skills, and I had sewn the linen bandages in place. Now I snipped the threads that held them and peeled them away.

'Merciful Hapi, pray for him!' Queen Lostris gagged at the stench. The crusted black scab that corked the mouth of the wound burst open, and thick green pus poured out in a slow and viscous stream.

'Mortification!' I whispered. This was the surgeon's nightmare, this evil humour that struck upon the third day and spread through the body like winter fire in the dry papyrus beds.

'What can we do?' she asked, and I shook my head.

'He will be dead before nightfall,' I told her, but we waited beside his bed for the inevitable. As the word spread through the ship that Pharaoh was dying, so the cabin filled with priests and women

60

and courtiers. We waited in silence.

Tanus was the last to arrive, and he stood at the back of the throng with his helmet under his arm, in the position of respect and mourning. His gaze rested not on the death-bed, but upon Queen Lostris. She kept her face averted from his, but I knew that she was aware of him in every fibre of her body.

She covered her head with an embroidered linen shawl, but above the waistband of her skirt, she was naked. Since the prince had been weaned, her breasts had lost their heavy burden of milk. She was as slim as a virgin, and childbirth had not scarred her bosom or her supple belly with silver lines of striae. Her skin was as smooth and unblemished as though it had been freshly anointed with perfumed oil.

I laid wet cloths upon Pharaoh's burning body in an attempt to cool the fever, but the heat evaporated the moisture and I was forced to change them at short intervals. Pharaoh tossed about restlessly and cried out in delirium, haunted by all the terrors and monsters of the other world, who waited to receive him.

At times he recited snatches from the *Book of the Dead*. From childhood the priests had taught him to memorize the book that was the key and the map through the shades to the far fields of paradise:

The crystal path has twenty-one turnings.
The narrow way is thin as the blade of
    bronze.
The goddess who guards the second pylon
is treacherous and her ways are devious.

61

Lady of flame, whore of the universe,
with the mouth of a lioness,
your vagina swallows men up,
they are lost in your milky dugs.

Gradually his voice and his movements became
weaker, and a little after the sun had made its
noon, he gave one last shuddering sigh and was
still. I stooped over him and felt for the life-throb
in his throat, but there was none, and the skin was
cooling under my touch.

'Pharaoh is dead,' I said softly, and closed the
lids over his staring eyes. 'May he live for ever!'

The mourning cry went up from all who were
assembled there, and my mistress led the royal
women in the wild ululation of grief. It was a
sound that chilled me and made invisible insects
crawl upon my skin, so I left the cabin as soon as I
was able. Tanus followed me out on to the deck
and seized my arm.

'You did all in your power to save him?' he
demanded roughly. 'This was not another of your
devices?'

I knew that this unkind treatment of me was an
expression of his own guilt and fear, so I was gentle
in my reply. 'He was slain by the Hyksos arrow. I
did all that was in my power to save him. It was the
destiny of the Mazes of Ammon-Ra, and there is
no guilt or fault in any of us.'

He sighed and placed one strong arm around my
shoulders. 'I had not foreseen any of this. I thought
only of my love for the queen and for our son. I
should rejoice that she is free, but I cannot. Too
much is lost and destroyed. All of us are merely
grains of dhurra corn in the grinding-mill of the

Mazes.'

'There will be a time of happiness for all of us hereafter,' I reassured him, although I had no basis for this claim. 'But there is still a sacred duty on my mistress, and through her, on you and me also.' And I reminded him of the oath that Queen Lostris had sworn to the king, that she would preserve his earthly body and give it proper burial to allow his *Ka* to move on to the fields of paradise.

'Tell me how I can help in this,' Tanus replied simply, 'but remember that the Hyksos is sweeping through the Upper Kingdom ahead of us, and I cannot guarantee that Pharaoh's tomb will not be violated.'

'Then, if needs be, we must find another tomb for him. Our first concern must be to preserve his body. In this heat it will be decaying and crawling with maggots before the sun sets. I am not skilled in the embalmer's art, but I know of only one way in which we can keep our trust.'

Tanus sent his sailors down into the barge's hold, and they swung up one of the huge clay jars of pickled olives from our stores. Then, under my instructions, he emptied the jar and refilled it with boiling water. While the water was still hot, he mixed into it three sacks of the finest-quality sea salt. Then he filled four smaller wine jars with the same brine and set them all out on the deck to cool.

In the meantime I was working alone in the cabin. My mistress had wanted to help me. She felt that it was part of her duty to her dead husband, but I sent her away to care for the prince.

I slit open Pharaoh's corpse down his left flank from ribs to hip-bone. Through this opening I

63

removed the contents of chest and belly, freeing them along the diaphragm with the knife. Naturally, I left his heart in place, for this is the organ of life and intelligence. I left the kidneys also, for these are the vessels of water and represent the sacred Nile. I packed the cavity with salt and then sutured it closed with cat-gut. I did not have an embalming-spoon to push up through the nostrils and remove that soft yellow mush from the gourd of the skull, so I left it in place. In any event, it was of no importance. The viscera I divided into its separate parts: liver, lungs, stomach and entrails. I washed out the stomach and intestines with brine, which was a loathsome task.

When this was done, I took the opportunity to examine the king's lungs minutely. The right lung was healthy and pink, but the left lung had been pierced by the arrow, and had collapsed like a punctured bladder. It was filled with rotten black blood and pus. I was amazed that the old man had lived so long with such an injury. I felt that I was absolved. No physician could have saved him, and there was no fault or failure in my treatment.

At last I ordered the sailors to bring in the cooled jars of brine. Tanus helped me to fold Pharaoh's body into the foetal position and we placed him in the olive vat. I made certain that he was completely immersed in the strong brine. We packed his viscera into the smaller Canopic wine jars. We sealed all the jars with pitch and wax, and lashed them securely into the reinforced compartment below decks in which the king stored his treasure. I think Pharaoh must have been content to rest thus, surrounded by gold and bars of silver.

I had done my best to help my mistress make good her vow. In Thebes I would hand the king's body over to the embalmers, if the Hyksos had not arrived there first, and if the city and its inhabitants still existed by the time we reached it.

 When we reached the walled city of Asyut, it was apparent that the Hyksos had left only a small force to invest it, and had continued southwards with their main army. Even though it was merely a detachment with less than a hundred chariots, the Hyksos besiegers were far too strong for us to attack them with our decimated army.

Tanus' main aim was to rescue Remrem and his five thousand, who were within the city walls, and then to push on up-river to join forces with Lord Nembet and his thirty thousand reinforcements. Anchored out in the main stream of the river, secure from attack by those deadly chariots, Tanus was able to signal his intentions to Remrem on the city walls.

Years before, I had helped Tanus draw up a system of signals, using two coloured flags by means of which he could spell out a message to any other within sight, across a valley, from peak to peak, or from city wall to plain and river. With the flags Tanus was able to warn Remrem to be ready for us that night. Then, under cover of darkness, twenty of our galleys raced into the beach below the city walls. At the same moment, Remrem threw open the side-gates, and, at the head of his regiment, fought his way through the Hyksos pickets. Before the enemy were able to harness their horses, Remrem and all his men were safely embarked.

Immediately, Tanus signalled the rest of the flotilla to weigh anchor. He abandoned the city of Asyut to sack and plunder, and we bore on upstream under oars. For the rest of that night, whenever we looked back over the stern, we saw the flames of the burning city lighting the northern horizon.

'Let those poor bastards forgive me,' Tanus muttered to me. 'I had no choice but to sacrifice them. My duty lies south of here in Thebes.'

He was soldier enough to make the hard choice without flinching, but man enough to grieve bitterly over it. I admired him then as much as I loved him.

Remrem told us that our signal frigates had sailed past Asyut the previous day, and that by now the despatches that I had drawn up on Tanus' behalf must be in Lord Nembet's hands.

Remrem was also able to give us some intelligence and news of the Hyksos, and his sweep to the south. Remrem had captured two Egyptian deserters and traitors who had gone over to the enemy and who had entered Asyut to spy on the defenders. Under torture they had howled like the jackals they were, and before they died, had told Remrem much about the Hyksos that was of value and interest to us.

66

The Hyksos king, whom we had so disastrously encountered on the plain of Abnub, was named Salitis. His tribe was of Semitic blood and originally a nomadic and pastoral people who had lived in the Zagros mountains near Lake Van. In this my first impression of these terrible Asians was confirmed. I had guessed at their Semitic origins from their features, but I wondered how a pastoral people had evolved such an extraordinary vehicle as a wheeled chariot, and where they had found that marvellous animal that we Egyptians now spoke of as a horse, and feared as though it were a creature from the underworld.

In other areas it seemed that the Hyksos were a backward people. They were unable to read or write, and their government was a harsh tyranny by their single king and ruler, this bearded Salitis. We Egyptians hated him and feared him even more than we did those wild creatures that drew his chariot.

The chief god of the Hyksos was named Sutekh, the god of storms. It needed no deep religious instruction to recognize in him our own dreaded Seth. Their choice of god was fitting, and their behaviour did the god honour. No civilized people would burn and plunder and murder as they did. The fact that we torture traitors cannot be weighed in the same scale as the atrocities committed by these barbarians.

It is a truth that I have often observed, that a nation chooses its gods to suit its own nature. The Philistines worship Baal, and cast live infants into the fiery furnace that is his mouth. The black Cushite tribes worship monsters and creatures from the underworld with the most bizarre rituals.

67

We Egyptians worship just and decent gods who are benevolent towards mankind and make no demands for human sacrifice. Then the Hyksos have Sutekh.

It seemed that Remrem's captives were not the only Egyptian traitors travelling with the enemy host. With a hot coal in his anus, one of Remrem's captives had told of some great Egyptian lord from the Upper Kingdom who sat upon King Salitis' war council. When I heard this, I remembered how I had wondered at the knowledge that the Hyksos had displayed of our order of battle upon the plain of Abnub. I had guessed then at the presence of a spy among them who knew our secrets.

If any of this was true, then we must expect that the enemy knew all our strengths and weaknesses. They must know the plans and defences of all our cities. Especially they would know of that rich treasure that Pharaoh had accumulated in his funerary temple.

'Perhaps this explains the haste with which King Salitis is driving on towards Thebes,' I suggested to Tanus. 'We can expect them to attempt a crossing of the Nile at the first opportunity that presents itself to them.' And Tanus cursed bitterly.

'If Horus is kind, he will deliver this traitorous Egyptian lord into my hands.' He punched his fist into the palm of his other hand. 'We must prevent Salitis from crossing the river, our ships are the only advantage that we hold over him. I must exploit them to full advantage.'

He stamped about the deck, and looked up at the sky. 'When will this foul wind swing back into the north? Every hour the enemy's chariots draw farther ahead of us. Where is Nembet's fleet? We must join our forces and hold the river-line.'

 That afternoon on the poop-deck of the royal barge the state council of Upper Egypt convened before the throne. The high priest of Osiris represented the spiritual body, Lord Merkeset the chancellor stood for the temporal body of the state, and Tanus, Lord Harrab stood for the military authority.

Between them the three lords lifted Queen Lostris to the throne of this very Egypt, and placed her son upon her lap. While every man and woman on board the barge raised their voices in a loyal salute, the other ships of the fleet sailed past, and even the wounded soldiers dragged themselves to the rail to cheer the new regent and the young heir to the great throne of Egypt.

The high priest of Osiris strapped the false beard of the kingship upon my mistress's chin, and it did nothing to detract from her beauty and manifest womanhood. Lord Merkeset bound the lion's tail around her waist and settled the tall red and white crown upon her brow. Finally, Tanus mounted the throne to place the crook and golden flail in her hands. Now Memnon saw the shining toys that Tanus carried towards him, and reached out to snatch them from him.

'A king indeed! He knows the crook is his by right,' Tanus applauded proudly, and the court roared their approval of this precocious behaviour.

I think this was the first time that any of us had laughed since that dreadful day on the field of

Abnub. It seemed to me that the laughter was a catharsis, and that it marked a new beginning for all of us. Up until that moment we had been overwhelmed by the shock of defeat and the loss of Pharaoh. But now, as the great lords of Egypt went forward one at a time to kneel before the throne on which sat this lovely young woman and her royal child, a fresh spirit sprang up in all of us. We were rescued from the apathy of despair, and our will to fight and to endure was resuscitated.

Tanus was last of all of them to kneel before the throne and swear his allegiance. As she looked down upon him, Queen Lostris' adoration for him was so evident that it suffused her lovely face and shone like the sunrise from those dark green eyes. I was amazed that no other in all that throng seemed aware of it.

That evening after the sun had set, my mistress sent me to the bridge of the state barge with a message for the commander of her armies. She summoned him to a council of war in the main cabin. This time Tanus dared not refuse her, for he had very recently sworn an oath of obedience.

This extraordinary war council of which I was the only witness had barely begun, before the new regent of Egypt imperiously banished me from the cabin, and sent me to guard the door and turn away all other visitors. The last glimpse that I had of them as I drew the heavy curtain was as they fell into each other's arms. So great was their need, and so long had they been denied, that they rushed at each other like deadly enemies joining in mortal combat, rather than lovers.

The happy sounds of this engagement persisted for most of the night, and I was relieved that we were not at anchor but driving on up-river in haste to join with Lord Nembet. The clunk and swish of the oars, the boom of the drum setting the stroke and the chants of the rowers on their benches almost drowned out the tumult in the royal cabin.

When he came to the poop-deck at the change of the night-watch, Tanus had the smile and the satisfied air of a general who had just won a famous victory. My mistress followed him on deck shortly afterwards, and she glowed with a new and ethereal beauty that startled even me, who was accustomed to her loveliness. For the rest of that day she was loving and kind to all around her, and found numerous occasions to consult the commander of her army. Thus Prince Memnon and I were able to spend most of the day together, a circumstance that suited both of us very well.

With the prince's dubious assistance I had already started carving a series of wooden models. One of these was a chariot and wooden horses. Another was a wheel on an axle that I was experimenting with.

Memnon stood on tiptoe to watch the wheel spin smoothly on its miniature hub.

'A solid disc is too heavy, don't you agree, Mem? See how swiftly it loses momentum and slows down.'

'Give it to me!' he demanded, and snatched at the spinning disc. It flew from his chubby fingers, dashed to the deck and shattered into four almost equal segments.

'You are a Hyksos ruffian,' I told him sternly, which he seemed to take as a great compliment, and I went down on my knees to gather up my poor model.

71

The broken segments still lay in a circular pattern, and, before my hand touched them, I had a strange aberration of vision. In the eye of my mind, the solid segments of wood became spaces, while the cracks between them appeared solid.

'Sweet breath of Horus! You've done it, Mem.' I hugged him. 'A rim supported by struts from the hub! When you are Pharaoh, what other miracles will you perform for us?'

Thus did the Prince Royal, Memnon the first of that name, Ruler of the Dawn—with just a little help from his friend—conceive of the spoked wheel. Little did I dream then that one day the two of us together would ride to glory upon it.

 We came upon the first of the Egyptian dead before noon. He came floating down the river with his bloated belly buoying him up, and his face gazing blankly at the sky. There was a black crow perched upon his chest. It picked out his eyes and threw back its head to swallow them one at a time.

In silence we stood at the ship's rail and watched the dead man float serenely by.

'He wears the kilt of the Lion Guards,' Tanus said quietly. 'The Lions are the spear-head of Nembet's army. I pray to Horus that there will be no others following this one down the river.'

But there were. Ten more, then a hundred. More and still more, until the surface of the river from bank to bank was carpeted by floating corpses. They were thick as the leaves of the water-hyacinth which clog the irrigation canals in summer.

At last we found one who still lived. He was a captain of the Lion Guards who had been seconded to Nembet's staff. He clung to a mat of floating papyrus stems in the current. We fished him from the water and I attended to his wounds. The head of a stone mace had shattered the bones of his shoulder and he would never use that arm again.

When he had recovered sufficiently to speak, Tanus squatted beside his mattress.

'What of Lord Nembet?'

'Lord Nembet is slain, and all his staff with him,' the captain told him hoarsely.

'Did Nembet not receive my despatch warning him of the Hyksos?'

'He received it on the eve of the battle, and he laughed as he read it.'

'Laughed?' demanded Tanus. 'How could he laugh?'

'He said that the puppy was destroyed—forgive me, Lord Tanus, but that was what he called you—and now sought to cover his stupidity and cowardice with spurious messages. He said that he would fight the battle in the classic manner.'

'The arrogant old fool,' Tanus lamented. 'But tell me the rest of it.'

'Lord Nembet deployed upon the east bank, with the river at his back. The enemy fell upon us like the wind, and drove us into the water.'

'How many of our men escaped?' Tanus asked softly.

'I believe that I am the only one of those who went ashore with Lord Nembet who survived. I saw no other left alive. The slaughter upon the

73

river-bank was beyond my power to describe to you.'

'All our most famous regiments decimated,' Tanus mourned. 'We are left defenceless, except for our ships. What happened to Nembet's fleet? Was it anchored in midstream?'

'Lord Nembet anchored the greater part of the fleet, but he beached fifty galleys in our rear.'

'Why would he do that?' Tanus stormed. 'The safety of the ships is the first principle of our standard battle plan.'

'I do not know Lord Nembet's mind, except he may have kept them at hand to re-embark our troops expeditiously, should your warning have proved justified.'

'What then is the fate of our fleet? Nembet lost our army, but did he save the ships?' Tanus' tone was rough with anger and distress.

'Of the ships that were anchored in midstream, most are scuttled and burned by the skeleton crews. I saw the flames and the smoke even from where I lay on my papyrus float. A few of the others cut the anchor-lines and fled south towards Thebes. I shouted to the crews as they sailed past me, but so great was their terror that they would not heave-to and pick me from the water.'

'The fifty ships that lay upon the beach—' Tanus broke off and drew a deep breath before he finished the question. 'What has become of the squadron that was beached?'

'It has fallen into the hands of the Hyksos.' The captain trembled as he answered, for he dreaded Tanus' anger. 'I looked back as I drifted with the current, and I saw the enemy swarming aboard the galleys on the beach.'

Tanus stood up and strode to the bows. He stared upstream from where the corpses and the scorched and blackened planks of Nembet's fleet still drifted down upon the steady green flow of the river. I went to stand at his side, to be ready to halter his rage when it came.

'So the proud old fool has sacrificed his life, and the lives of all his men, simply to spite me. They should build a pyramid to his folly, for Egypt has never seen the like of it.'

'That is not all his folly,' I murmured, and Tanus nodded grimly.

'No, not all his folly. He has given the Hyksos the means to cross the river. Sweet milk of Isis' breast, but once they are across the Nile we are truly finished.'

Perhaps the goddess heard him call her name, for at that moment I felt the wind that had blown so long into our faces veer. Tanus felt it also. He spun on his heel and roared an order to his officers on the poop-deck.

'The wind turns fair. Make a general signal to the fleet. Set all sail. Relieve the men at the oars every hour by the water-clock. Drummers, increase the beat to flank speed. Make all haste southwards.'

The wind settled strongly into the north. Our sails filled and stiffened like the bellies of pregnant women. The drums gave the rowers the stroke, and we breasted the flow of the river as the whole battle-fleet raced southwards.

'All thanks to the goddess for this wind,' Tanus shouted. 'Divine Isis, let us be in time to catch them on the water.'

The state barge was slow and ungainly. She began falling astern of the fleet. It seemed that the fates had intervened once more, for Tanus' old galley that he had loved so well, the *Breath of Horus*, was sailing close to us in the formation.

She was under a new captain now, but she was still a formidable little vessel, built for speed and attack. The sharp bronze ramming-horn protruded from her bows, just above the water line. Tanus hailed her alongside the barge and transferred his Blue Crocodile standard into her, taking over the command from her new captain.

My place was with my mistress and the prince. I am not certain how I found myself on board the *Breath of Horus*, standing on the poop beside Tanus, as we tore along upstream. Sometimes I am guilty of folly almost as monumental as that recently demonstrated by Lord Nembet. I remember only that as soon as the state barge began to fall away astern, I began bitterly to regret my impetuosity. I thought of telling Tanus that I had changed my mind, and asking him to put about and drop me once more on the deck of the barge. But after one glance at his face, I decided that I would rather face the Hyksos again.

From the deck of the *Breath of Horus*, Tanus issued his orders. By flag and voice-hail, they were passed from vessel to vessel. Without slackening the pace of our advance, Tanus redeployed the fleet. He gathered up the galleys around him, as he forged his way to the head of the flotilla.

The wounded and those no longer fit to fight

were transferred to the slower vessels which fell back to keep pace with the state barge. The faster galleys in the van were cleared for action. They were manned mostly by Remrem's fresh troops whom we had relieved from the siege of Asyut. They were spoiling for a chance to avenge the disgrace of Abnub. Tanus hoisted the Blue Crocodile standard at his masthead of the *Breath of Horus*, and they roared with the lust of battle. How swiftly he had been able to stiffen their spirit since that bloody defeat!

The signs of Nembet's recent catastrophe became ever more obvious with each league that we covered. The corpses and wreckage and all the flotsam of war were stranded in the papyrus beds on each side of the river. Then, at last, in the sky ahead of us we saw once again the dust of the chariots mingling with the smoke from the cooking-fires of the Hyksos camp.

'It is as I had hoped,' Tanus exulted. 'They have halted their headlong advance on Thebes, now that Nembet has presented them with the means of crossing the river. But they are not sailors, and they will have difficulty embarking their men and chariots. If Horus is kind, we will arrive in time to help them on their way.'

In extended battle order we swept around the last wide bend of the river, and we found the Hyksos before us. By one of those happy freaks of war, we had arrived precisely at the moment that they were fully committed to the crossing of the Nile.

There were the fifty captured galleys straggling across the river in the most lubberly fashion. The sails and sheets were in a tangle and every oarsman

77

was keeping his own stroke. The paddles were splashing and crab-catching. The steering of each vessel was shaky and erratic, completely out of phase with the ships around it.

We could see that most of the Hyksos manning the decks were in full bronze armour. Clearly they had not realized just how difficult it is to swim in that state of dress. They stared at us in consternation as we bore down upon them. Now at last the roles were reversed. We were in our element, and they were flying in the wind like a torn sail.

I had a few moments to study the enemy, as we closed. The vast bulk of the Hyksos army was still upon the east bank. They had gone into bivouac, and they were so numerous that their encampment stretched away to the foothills of the desert, as far as I could see from the deck of the *Breath of Horus*.

King Salitis was sending only a small force across the river. Almost certainly they were under orders to race down the west bank and to capture the funerary temple of Pharaoh Mamose, before we were able to remove the treasure.

We bore down rapidly on the convoy of Hyksos ships, and I shouted to Tanus above the beat of the drums and the bloodthirsty cheers of our rascals, 'They have taken their horses across already. Look over there!'

Almost unprotected, except for a few armed guards, there was a huge herd of these terrible animals gathered on the west bank. I guessed there were several hundred of them; even at this distance, we could make out their long, flowing manes and tails streaming in the strong north wind. They were a disturbing sight to us. Some of the men around me shuddered and swore with loathing of them. I heard one of them mutter darkly, 'The Hyksos feed those monsters of theirs on human flesh, like tame lions or jackals. That is the reason for this slaughter. They must have food for them. We can only guess how many of our comrades are already in their bellies.'

I could not contradict him, and I even had a queasy feeling in my guts that he might be speaking the truth. I turned my attention from those beautiful but gory monsters to the galleys in the stream ahead of us.

'We have caught them taking the chariots and the men over,' I pointed out to Tanus. The decks of Nembet's captured vessels were piled high with chariots and equipment, and crowded with the Hyksos charioteers who were being ferried across. As they realized their predicament, some of the Hyksos tried to turn and run back for the east bank. They collided with the ships that followed them, and locked together, they drifted helplessly on the current.

Tanus laughed savagely to see their confusion, and shouted into the wind, 'General signal. Increase the beat to attack speed. Light the fire-arrows.'

The Hyksos had never experienced an attack with fire-arrows, and at the thought of what was coming, I laughed with Tanus, but nervously. Then suddenly I stiffened and my laughter choked off.

'Tanus!' I seized his arm. 'Look! Look at the galley dead ahead! On the poop. There is our traitor.'

For a moment Tanus did not recognize the tall,

stately figure at the rail of the galley, for he wore fish-scale armour and a tall Hyksos war helmet. Then abruptly he roared with anger and outrage, 'Intef! Why did we not guess it was him?'

'I see it so clearly now. He has guided Salitis to this very Egypt. He went east and deliberately tempted the Hyksos with accounts of the treasures of Egypt.' My outrage and hatred matched those of Tanus.

Tanus threw up the bow Lanata and loosed an arrow, but the range was long and the point glanced off Lord Intef's armour. I saw his head jerk round at the shock, and he looked across the water directly at us. He singled us out, Tanus and myself, and for a moment I thought I saw fear in his eyes. Then he ducked out of sight below the gunwale of the galley.

Our leading squadron flew into the pack of confused and milling shipping. With a tearing crunch, our bronze ramming-horn struck Intef's galley amidships, and I was thrown off my feet by the impact. When I struggled up again, the oarsmen had already backed water, and with another rending screech of timbers we disengaged from the stricken ship.

At the same time, our archers were pouring a heavy rain of fire-arrows into her. The heads were bound with pitch-soaked papyrus stems that burned like comets, each leaving a trail of sparks and smoke as they flew into the sails and top hamper. The north wind fanned the flames and they leaped up the rigging with a fiendish exuberance.

The waters flooded in through the gaping hole we had ripped in her belly, and she listed over sharply. The sails caught fire and burned with startling rapidity. The heat singed my eyelashes even at that distance. The heavy mainsail, burning fiercely, fluttered down over the deck, trapping the crew and crowded charioteers beneath it. Their screams shrilled in our ears as their hair and clothing burst into flames. I remembered the plain at Abnub and felt no pity as they leaped in flames from the ship's side and were drawn under by the weight of their armour. Only a swirl of ripples and a lingering puff of steam marked where each of them had disappeared.

All down the line, the Hyksos galleys were burning and sinking. They had neither the experience nor the skill to counter our attack, and they were as helpless as we had been before the assault of their chariots. Our ships backed off and charged again, crushing in their hulls and sending torrents of flaming arrows into them.

I was watching the first galley that we had attacked, seeking another glimpse of Lord Intef. She was almost gone when suddenly he reappeared. He had thrown off his helmet and his armour, and wore only a linen breech clout. He balanced easily on the gunwale of the sinking ship, and then, as the flames reached out to embrace him, he joined his hands above his head and dived overboard.

He was a son of the Nile, at home in her waters. He knifed through the surface, and came up a minute later and fifty paces from where he had struck, with his long wet hair sleeked back, so that he looked like a swimming otter.

'There he goes!' I screamed at Tanus. 'Run the swine under.'

Instantly Tanus gave the order to turn the *Breath of Horus*, but quick as the helmsman was on the steering-oar, she was slow to come around. Meanwhile, Lord Intef slipped through the water like a fish, reaching out overarm for the east bank and the protection of his Hyksos allies.

'Swing hard!' Tanus signalled his starboard bank of oars, and they thrust the bows around. As soon as we were on line with the swimmer, Tanus gave the order to pull together, and we shot in pursuit. By now Lord Intef was far ahead and close in to the bank, where five thousand Hyksos archers waited with their long recurved bows strung and ready to give him covering fire.

'Seth piss on them!' Tanus yelled in defiance. 'We will take Intef out from under their noses.' And he drove the *Breath of Horus* directly at them, bearing down upon the lone swimming figure.

As we came within range of the shore, the Hyksos loosed a volley at us that darkened the sky, and their arrows fell in a whistling cloud around us. They dropped so thickly that the deck soon bristled with them like the quills in a goose's wing, and some of our sailors were struck and fell writhing and bleeding from their benches.

But we were already close on Intef, and he looked back over his shoulder and I saw the terror in his face as he realized he could not escape our sharp prow. I ignored the arrows and ran to the bows to scream down at him, 'I hated you from the first day we met. I hated every loathsome touch. I want to watch you die. You are evil! Evil!'

He heard me. I saw it in his eyes, and then his dark gods intervened yet again. One of the sinking Hyksos galleys drifted down upon us, spouting fire and smoke. If she had touched us we would have gone up with her in a tower of flame. Tanus was forced to put the steering-oar over, and to signal urgently for his oarsmen to back-water. The burning galley drifted between the shore and where we lay heaved-to. Lord Intef was hidden from my view, but when the burning galley was past, I saw him again. Three brawny Hyksos charioteers were dragging him from the water and up the steep bank.

He paused at the top of the bank and looked back at us, and then disappeared from sight, leaving me trembling with rage and frustration. Our men were still being struck down by the falling arrows, so Tanus gave the order, and we wheeled away and sped back to join in the destruction of those few vessels of the convoy that were still afloat.

As the last of these listed over and then rolled on to her back, the green Nile waters poured into her and quenched the flames in a hissing cloud of steam. Our archers leaned over the side and shot the few surviving Hyksos who splashed weakly on the surface.

Immediately they were all drowned, Tanus turned his attention to the west bank and to the small party of the enemy and the herd of horses that were stranded there. As our galley sped in to the shore, the Hyksos herders scattered and ran, but our men leaped ashore, sword in hand, and raced after them. The Hyksos were charioteers, and accustomed to riding into battle. Our lads were foot-soldiers and trained to run. Like a pack of hounds after a jackal, our men isolated and surrounded them. They hacked them down and left a hundred bleeding corpses scattered across the green fields of standing dhurra corn.

I had jumped ashore behind the first wave of our troops. I had serious business in mind. There was no point in making models and designing chariots without a means of driving the spoked wheels that I had seen in my imagination.

It required an enormous act of courage on my part to start towards that herd of terrible creatures that the Hyksos herders had abandoned close to the water's edge. Each step was an effort of will, for there were many hundreds of them, and they were obviously restless and alarmed by the shouting and the running of men and the clash of arms. I was certain that at any moment they would rush at me like wounded lions. I imagined them gobbling my still warm and twitching flesh, and my courage evaporated and I could go no closer. From a distance of a hundred paces, I stood staring in dreadful fascination at these savage predators, but I was poised to turn and rush back to the safety of the galley at the first sign of an attack.

This was the first opportunity that I had been given to study these animals. They were mostly of a dun colour, but with subtle shadings of bay and chestnut and roan. One or two of them were as black as Seth. They stood as tall as a man, with a full barrel-chest, and long necks that arched gracefully. Their manes were like the tresses of a beautiful woman, and their hides glowed in the sunlight, as though they had been burnished.

One of those nearest to me threw back its head and rolled its upper lip, and I recoiled as I saw the great square white teeth that lined its jaw. It kicked its hind-legs and emitted such a terrifying neighing sound that I turned and started back towards the ship with some alacrity.

Then a hoarse yell from one of our soldiers near me arrested my cowardly retreat. 'Kill the Hyksos monsters!'

'Kill the monsters!' The cry was taken up by the others.

'No!' I screamed, and my concern for my own safety was forgotten. 'No! Save the horses. We need them.'

My voice was lost in the angry war-cry of our troops, as they rushed at the herd of horses, with their shields raised and their swords still dripping with the blood of the herders. Some of the men paused to nock arrows to the bow and fire them into the herd.

'No!' I cried, as a glossy black stallion reared and screamed, with an arrow standing out of his withers.

'No! Please, no!' I cried again, as one of the sailors ran in with a light war-axe and hacked through the fetlock joint of a young mare. She was crippled by the blow and could not escape the next stroke of the axe that caught her between the ears and dropped her kicking in the dust.

'Leave them! Leave them!' I pleaded, but the arrows brought down a dozen of the animals, and the swords and axes maimed and killed a dozen more before the herd broke under the assault, and three hundred horses bolted and went galloping out in a mass across the dusty western plain towards the desert.

I shaded my eyes to watch them go, and it seemed to me that part of my heart went with them. When they had disappeared, I ran to protect and tend to those animals that were left maimed and arrowed amongst the papyrus beds. But the soldiers were ahead of me. So great was their fury that they gathered around the fallen carcasses. In a frenzy of hatred, they plunged their blades into the unresisting flesh and hacked at the broken heads.

A little to one side stood an isolated clump of papyrus reeds. Behind this, and screened from the rampaging soldiers, stood the black stallion that I had first seen hit by an arrow. He was sorely struck and staggering as he limped forward, the arrow deep in his chest. Without thought for my own safety, I ran towards him, and then stopped as he turned to face me.

Only then did I realize my danger. Here was a wounded beast that, like a lion in the same straits, must surely charge at me. The stallion and I stared at each other, and I felt fear fall away like a discarded cloak from my shoulders.

His eyes were huge and swimming with pain. Gentle eyes, beautiful eyes that made my heart swell with pity. He made a soft, fluttering sound, and limped towards me. I held out my hand and touched his muzzle and it felt like warm Arabian silk. He came directly to me, and pressed his forehead to my chest in a gesture of trust and appeal that was almost human. I knew that he was asking for my help.

Instinctively I flung my arms around his neck and embraced him. I wanted more than anything in my life at that moment to save him, but from his nostrils warm blood trickled down my chest. I knew he was hit through the lungs and that he was dying. He was far beyond any help that I could give him.

86

'My poor darling. What have those stupid, ignorant bastards done to you?' I whispered. Dimly in my distress and spiritual agony, I realized that my life had changed again, and that this dying creature had made that change. Somehow I seemed to sense that, in the years ahead, wherever I left my footsteps in the African earth, the hoof-prints of a horse would lie beside them. I had found another great love to fill my days.

The stallion made that fluttering sound once more and his breath was warm on my skin. Then his legs collapsed under him and he fell heavily on his side and lay gasping air into his punctured lungs. Bright red bubbles frothed from the wound in his chest. I went down beside him, and lifted that noble head into my lap and waited with him until he died. Then I stood up and went back to where the *Breath of Horus* was beached.

It was difficult to see my way, for my own hot tears blinded me. Once again I cursed myself for a soft and sentimental fool, but that never did much to help me brace myself. I was always so vulnerable to suffering in another creature, human or otherwise, especially in one that was noble and beautiful.

'Damn you, Taita! Where have you been?' Tanus railed at me as I scrambled aboard. 'There is a battle raging. The whole army cannot wait around while you have another of your famous daydreams.' Yet for all his bluster, he had not deserted me.

Tanus would not even hear me out, but cut brusquely across my request for leave to follow the herd of runaway horses out into the desert, and for men to go with me.

'I want no truck with those foul and unholy creatures!' he shouted at me. 'I only regret that my men let them escape and that they did not slaughter the lot of them. Let us hope that the lions and the jackals make good that default.' I realized then that he hated them as much as did the most ignorant lout in his regiments.

'Were you there on the plain of Abnub?' I do not usually indulge in loud argument, but his intransigence infuriated me. 'Or was that some other dull-witted oaf standing beside me? Did you not see the future charge at you on hooves and wheels and chop your men to jackal-food? Do you not understand that without chariot and horse, you and this Egypt we know are finished?'

This amicable discussion was taking place on the poop-deck of the *Breath of Horus*. Tanus' officers were silent and stiff with shock to hear a slave address a Great Lion of Egypt and the commander of all her armies as a dull-witted oaf. However, I was past all restraint and I rushed on.

'The gods have given you this wonderful gift. Three hundred horses placed in your hands! I will build you the chariots to go with them. Are you so blind that you cannot see it?'

'I have my ships!' Tanus roared back at me. 'I don't need these foul man-eating beasts. They are an abomination in the face of decent men and all benevolent gods. They are creatures of Seth and

88

Sutekh, and I want no part of them.'

Too late I realized that I had pushed Tanus into a position from which he could not retreat. He was a clever and intelligent man, until his pride hamstrung his reason. I moderated my tone and made my voice mellifluous.

'Tanus, please listen to me. I have held the head of one of these animals in my hands. They are strong, but strangely gentle. Their eyes shine with the intelligence of a faithful dog. They do not eat meat—'

'How could you tell that from one brief touch?' he sneered at me, still proud and affronted.

'The teeth,' I answered. 'They do not possess the fangs or claws of a carnivore. Pigs are the only hoofed creatures that eat flesh, and these are no pigs.'

I saw him waver at last, and I pressed my advantage. 'If that is not enough, look then at the stores that the Hyksos have brought across the river. Do they need that mountain of fodder to feed a pride of meat-eating lions?'

'Meat or fodder, I will not argue further. You have heard my decision. We will let those cursed horses perish in the wilderness. That is my decision, and it is final.' He stamped away, but I muttered under my breath, 'Final, is it? We will see about that.'

There have been very few occasions when I have not been able to have my own way with my mistress, and hers was now the highest authority in this very Egypt. I went to her that very evening, as soon as the royal barge came once more under the protection of the war galleys.

Without the knowledge of her commander and

lover, I showed her the tiny working model of a chariot with the miniature carved horses in the traces, which I had crafted for her. Queen Lostris was enchanted by it. Naturally she had never seen the squadrons of war chariots in full flight, and had not conceived for them the same hatred as had the bulk of her army. Having captured her full attention with the model chariot, I then described the death of the stallion in such harrowing detail that both of us were reduced to tears. She can resist my tears as little as I am able to resist hers.

'You must go immediately and rescue these marvellous animals from the desert. When you have them, I order you to build a squadron of chariots for my armies,' she cried.

If Tanus had spoken to her before I had the chance to persuade her, I doubt that she would have given that order, and the history of our world would have been very different. As it was, Tanus was furious with my deception, and we came as close to a permanent rift in our relationship as we ever had in all the years.

It was fortunate that I had been summarily ordered ashore by Queen Lostris, and was able to escape the full force of his wrath. I had only a few hours in which to gather around me a few helpers, and the chief of these was the most unlikely of them all.

I had never taken to Hui, the Shrike whom we had captured at Gallala and who had commanded one of the galleys which Tanus had scuttled at Abnub. He was now a captain without a ship, and a man looking for a reason to go on. He sought me out as soon as rumour of my mission spread through the fleet.

'What do you know about horses?' he challenged me, which was a question I was not prepared to answer at that moment.

'Obviously not as much as you do?' I made it a cautious question.

'I was once a syce,' he boasted, in his usual endearing fashion.

'And what creature is that?'

'A groom, one who cares for horses,' he replied, and I stared at him in amazement.

'Where did you ever see a horse before that bloody day at Abnub?' I demanded.

'As an infant my parents were killed, and I was captured by a tribe of barbarians who roamed the plains far to the east, a year's travel beyond the Euphrates river. My captors were people of the horse and, as a child, I lived each day with those animals. Mare's milk was my food and I slept beneath the horses' bellies for shelter in the night, for a slave was not allowed into the tents of the tribe. When I escaped from slavery, it was upon the back of my favourite stallion. He carried me fast and far. But he died long before we reached the Euphrates.'

Thus Hui was with me when a galley set down my small party of reluctant horse-catchers upon the west bank. Sixteen men were all that I could recruit, and most of them were the dregs and riff-raff of the army. Tanus had seen to it that none of his best men would join me. He could not countermand the word of the regent of all Egypt, but he made it as difficult as he could for me to carry out her orders.

At Hui's suggestion, I had equipped my men with light linen ropes and bags of crushed dhurra

91

corn. All of them, except Hui and myself, were terrified to the point of incontinence by the mere thought of the creatures that we had set out to follow. When I woke in the morning after our first night's camp, I found that every single one of these stalwarts had disappeared, and I never saw them again.

'We will have to turn back,' I despaired. 'There is nothing we can do alone. Lord Tanus will be pleased. This was exactly what he knew would happen.'

'You are not alone,' Hui pointed out cheerfully. 'You have me.' This was the first time that my feelings began to warm towards the young swaggerer. We divided the load of ropes and the leather bags of crushed corn, and we went on.

By this time the tracks of the horses were three days old, but they had stayed together in a single herd and so had beaten a road that was easy to follow. Hui assured me that the herd instinct was strong amongst them, and that with such lush grazing along the river-bank, they would not have wandered far. He was certain they would not have gone out into the desert, as I had feared that they might.

'Why would they do that? There is no food or water for them out there.' And in the end Hui proved right.

With the coming of the Hyksos, the peasants had deserted their farms and gone into the shelter of the walled towns. The fields were untended and the corn half-grown. We found the herd before noon the second day. It was spread out and grazing peacefully in one of the fields. Even after my experience with the wounded stallion, I was still rather nervous of these mysterious creatures.

'It will surely be a difficult and dangerous matter to capture a few of them,' I confided in Hui, seeking his reassurance and advice. At this stage, the notion of capturing all three hundred horses had not even occurred to me. I would have been satisfied with twenty, and delighted with fifty of them. I imagined that we would be forced to run each of them down and bind it with the ropes we had brought with us for that purpose.

'I have heard that you have the reputation of being a very clever slave,' Hui grinned at me, cocky and delighted by his superior understanding of the subject. 'Clearly, it is a reputation that is ill-founded.'

He showed me how to twist and braid a halter from the ropes. We made a dozen of these before he was satisfied. Then each of us armed himself with one of these and a leather sack of crushed corn, and we started towards the grazing herd. Following Hui's example, we never walked directly towards them, but strolled obliquely at a leisurely pace past the animals in the fringe of the herd.

'Slowly now,' Hui cautioned me, when they flung up their heads and studied us with that peculiarly frank and almost childlike gaze that I would come to know so well.

'Sit down.' We sank into the standing corn and remained motionless, until the horses started feeding again. Then we moved forward until they became restless once more.

'Down,' Hui ordered, and when we were crouched in the corn, he went on, 'They love the sound of a gentle voice. When I was a child, I sang to my horses to quieten them. Watch this!' He started to sing a refrain in a strange language, which I presumed was the barbaric tongue of his childhood captors.

Hui's voice was as melodious as the squawking of crows squabbling over the rotting carcass of a dead dog. The nearest horses stared at us curiously. I laid my hand on Hui's arm to quieten him. I was certain that the herd must find his efforts at song as distressing as I did.

'Let me try,' I whispered. I sang the lullaby that I had composed for my prince.

Sleep, little Mem, who rules the dawn,
sleep, little prince, who will rule the world,
rest that curly head, filled with wondrous
      dreams,
rest those arms, make them strong for sword
      and bow.

One of the mares closest to us took a few steps towards me, and when she stopped, she made that same soft fluttery sound with her lips. She was inquisitive, and I sang on softly and seductively. She had a foal at her heels, a lovely little bay-coloured creature with an appealing head and pricked-up ears.

With my special feeling for and understanding of birds and animals, I was already beginning to recognize the desirable points of breed in these new animals. I was learning swiftly and instinctively how to deal with them. I was no longer completely reliant on Hui to instruct me.

Still singing gently, I scooped up a handful of the crushed cornmeal and held it out to the mare. I could see at once that she had been hand-fed before, and that she understood my offer. She blew noisily through wide nostrils, and took another few paces towards me. Even now I can remember the thrill that almost stopped the beating of my heart when she took the last pace up to me, and delicately lowered her muzzle into my hand to taste the white meal. It powdered her whiskers as she ate, and I laughed with the joy and excitement of it. She made no effort to pull away from me as I slipped my other arm around her neck and laid my cheek softly against hers to inhale the strange, warm smell of her hide.

'The halter,' Hui reminded me softly, and I slipped it over her head, as he had shown me.

'She is yours,' Hui said.

'And I am hers,' I replied without thinking, but it was true. We had captured each other.

The rest of the herd had watched all this. As soon as the halter was on the mare, they settled down and trustingly allowed Hui and me to walk freely amongst them. They came to eat from the hand and allowed us to lift their hooves and stroke their necks and massive shoulders.

All this seemed to me at the time to be miraculous, but after only a little consideration I realized that it was quite natural. They were accustomed from birth to being handled and petted, to being fed and harnessed. They had lived always with the close and constant presence of man. The true miracle came later, when I realized that they recognized affection, and that they were able to return it in full measure.

Hui had selected and haltered one of the other mares, all the time lecturing me and displaying his learning and experience in matters equine. I was in such a euphoric mood that for once his bumptiousness did not annoy me.

'Very well,' he said at last, 'we will mount up now.' And to my utter astonishment he placed both hands on his mare's back, drew himself up and flung one leg over her, to sit astride her back. I gawked at him in disbelief, expecting the mare to react violently, to rear up and dash Hui to earth, or, at the very least, to seize his naked leg in those powerful white teeth and drag him from his perch. She did none of these things, but stood quietly and subserviently.

'Hi up, my darling!' he called to her, and dug his heels into her ribs. The mare started forward obediently, and when he urged her on again she broke into a trot and then a gallop. Hui guided her effortlessly in a manner that was not then apparent to me. Horse and rider traced out elegant patterns of movement across the field, and then circled back to where I stood.

'Come up, Taita. Try a gallop!' I could see that he was expecting me to refuse, and it was that which made me overcome my reluctance. I would not allow the little whippersnapper to have the better of me.

My first attempt at mounting up was unsuccessful, but the mare stood stoically, and Hui laughed. 'She has a great deal to teach you. You should call the poor animal Patience.' I did not see the humour of it then, but the name stuck and the mare was Patience from then onwards.

'Pull yourself higher before you swing your leg over, and be careful not to trap your balls under you when you come down,' Hui counselled, and then howled with laughter. 'And that's a piece of advice that you need not worry about. My guess is that you would love still to have a pair of those to sit on!'

All the warm feelings I was beginning to have towards Hui cooled again at that sally, and I threw myself on to the mare's back and clung with both hands around her neck, in fear of broken limbs and cracked skull.

'Sit up straight!' Hui began my instruction, and Patience assisted me with her sweet and forgiving nature.

I surprised myself by thinking of these creatures in human terms, but over the following days as we rode south towards Thebes, I discovered that they could be stupid or clever, suspicious or trusting, dour or mischievous, friendly or aloof, brave or timid, nervous or phlegmatic, long-suffering or impatient, surprising or predictable—in short, as close to man in temperament as any creature that walks on four legs. The more I learned about them, the more I wanted to learn. The longer I spent working with them, the more I grew to love them.

I rode ahead on Patience, her foal at heel. The herd trailed after us compliantly, all three hundred and sixteen of them. Hui brought up the rear to sweep up any stragglers. With each league we covered, I became more confident and proficient upon Patience's back, and the rapport between us became firmer. The mare became an extension of my own body, but so much swifter and stronger than my own feeble limbs. It felt so natural and right to be astride that broad and sturdy back that I was amazed that so few others were willing to share the experience with me.

Perhaps it was not only the terror that had struck them so devastatingly on the plain of Abnub, but also the words and attitude of Tanus, Lord Harrab that affected the regiments of our army. Whatever the reason, I could find no Egyptian who would mount upon the back of a horse, except Hui and, very much later, Prince Memnon. Of course, they learned to husband and breed the horse and care for him. Under my tutelage they became dexterous and dashing charioteers, but I never saw a man of them mounted on horseback, save only myself and Hui and the prince. When the chariots that I would design with their light, spoked wheels swept all before them, and made Egypt the master of this creation, Tanus never followed our example, and I never heard him express a kind sentiment towards those willing and brave animals who dragged him into battle.

Even in later years, when the horse was commonplace through all our realm, it was considered somehow indecent and obscene to mount them. When the three of us rode past astride, many of the common people spat on the ground three times and made the sign against the evil eye.

 All that was in the future as I led my herd up the west bank of the river towards Thebes, and we arrived to the gratitude of my mistress, and to a gruff and unenthusiastic welcome from the commander-in-chief of the Egyptian armies.

'Just keep those evil brutes out of my sight,' Tanus told me. He still had not forgiven me for going above him to my mistress.

In fairness to him, he had more than enough excuse for his evil temper. The safety of the state and our nation were in the direst jeopardy. There had never been a time in our history when our civilization was so threatened by the barbarian.

Already Asyut was lost, and the whole east bank of the river as far as Dendera. Completely undaunted and undeterred by the naval reverse that Tanus had inflicted upon him, King Salitis with his chariots had swept on and surrounded the walled city of Thebes.

Those walls should have withstood siege for a decade, but that reckoned without the baleful presence of Lord Intef in the camp of the enemy. It transpired that while still grand vizier of the Upper Kingdom, he had secretly ordered the construction of a concealed passage beneath the city walls. Even I who knew most of his other secrets had never suspected this, and Lord Intef had murdered the workmen who had carried out this construction, so that he alone was aware of its existence. I have no idea why he should have constructed the tunnel in the first place, except that his devious mind was much given towards such devices. The palace was riddled with trap-doors and concealed corridors, like the warren of a rabbit or the lair of a desert fox.

When Lord Intef disclosed its existence to him, King Salitis sent a small party of his best men through the secret passage, and once within the walls, they stormed the unsuspecting Egyptian guards on the main gate, slaughtered them and threw the gates wide. The main Hyksos horde poured into the city, and within days of the siege commencing, the city was lost and half her inhabitants massacred.

From the west bank where Tanus now had his headquarters in the half-built Palace of Memnon, we could see the burnt and blackened roofs of those buildings in the city across the river that the Hyksos had put to the torch. Each day we watched the dust-clouds of their chariots, as they raced up and down the far bank, and the glint of their spear-heads at the shoulder-slope, as they prepared for the battle that all of us knew was coming.

With his sadly depleted fleet, Tanus had thus far managed to hold the river-line, and during my absence had beaten back another attempt by the Hyksos to get across the Nile in strength. However, our defences were thinly spread, for we had to guard a great sweep of the river, while the Hyksos could make a crossing at any point they chose. We learned from our spies on the east bank that they had commandeered every single craft they could lay hands on, from barge to skiff. They had captured many of our boatmakers, and had them at work in the boatyards of Thebes. Of course, we could be sure that Lord Intef would give them pertinent advice in all these matters, for he must have been every bit as eager as the barbarian Salitis to seize Pharaoh's treasure.

The crews of our galleys stood to arms every watch of the day and night, and Tanus only slept when he could, which was not often. Neither my mistress nor I saw much of him, and when we did, he was haggard and short-tempered.

Every night saw the arrival on the west bank of many hundreds of refugees. Of both sexes and all ages, they crossed the Nile in an odd assortment of rafts and small craft. Many of the stronger ones even swam the wide stretch of water. All of them were desperate to escape the Hyksos terror. They brought us horror-stories of rapine and plunder, but also detailed and up-to-date news of Hyksos movements.

Of course we welcomed these people, they were countrymen and relatives, but their numbers strained our resources. Our main granaries had all been in Thebes, and most of the herds of cattle and sheep had fallen into the hands of the enemy. Queen Lostris gave me the responsibility of gathering up all the supplies of grain and the herds on the west bank. I drew up lists and rosters for rationing our supplies of meat and grain. Fortunately, the date palms were in full bearing, and the supply of fish from the river was inexhaustible. The Hyksos could never starve us out.

My mistress had also appointed me Master of the Royal Horse. There was no intense competition for this appointment, particularly as no pay or privileges were attached to it. I made Hui my deputy, and he managed, by means of bribes, threats and blackmail, to recruit a hundred grooms to help him care for our little herd. Later we would train them as our first chariot-drivers.

It was no hardship for me to make time every day to visit our makeshift stables in the necropolis. The mare Patience always came running to greet me, and I carried corn-cakes for her and her foal. Often I was able to sneak Prince Memnon away from his mother and his nurses and carry him into the stables on my shoulders. He squealed with excitement as soon as he saw the horses.

I held the prince on my lap as Patience and I galloped along the river-bank, and he made clucking noises and rocked his little backside, imitating the way in which I urged Patience to a harder gallop. I made certain that the route we followed on these rides would never cross Tanus' path. He had still not forgiven me, and if he had seen his son on the back of a cursed horse, I knew that I would have been in physical danger.

I also spent a great deal of my time in the armoury workshop of Pharaoh's funerary temple, where I had the assistance of some of the finest craftsmen in the world to help me build my first chariot. It was here, while working on the design of these vehicles, that I conceived devices that were to become our first line of defence against the Hyksos chariots. These were simply long wooden staves sharpened at both ends, and with the points fire-hardened. Each of our infantrymen would carry ten of these in a bundle upon his back. At the approach of a squadron of cavalry, the staves were planted in the earth at an angle, with the points at the level of the horses' chests. Our men took up their positions behind this barrier of wicked spears, and fired their arrows over them.

When I demonstrated these to Tanus, he threw his arm around my shoulders for the first time since our quarrel over the horses, and said, 'Well, at least you have not turned senile on me yet,' and I knew that I had been at least partially forgiven.

The ground that I had gained with him here was almost completely lost over the affair of the Taita chariot.

My workmen and I at last completed the first

chariot. The dashboard and sides were of split bamboo, woven into basketwork. The axle was of acacia wood. The hubs were of hand-forged bronze, greased with mutton fat, and the spoked wheels were bound with bronze rims. It was so light that two charioteers could lift it between them, and carry it over broken ground where the horses could not pull it. Even I realized that it was a masterpiece, and the workmen called it the Taita chariot. I did not object to the name.

Hui and I harnessed up two of our best horses, Patience and Blade, and took the Taita chariot for its first gallop. It took us some time to learn how to control the rig, but we learned swiftly, and the horses were bred to this and showed us the way. In the end, we were flying across the ground, and hurtling through tight turns at full gallop.

When we drove back into the stables, flushed with excitement and jubilant with our achievement, both of us were convinced that our chariot was swifter and handier than any that the Hyksos could send against us. We tested and modified this creation of mine for ten full days, working by lamplight in the armoury until the late watches of every night, before I was satisfied that I could show it to Tanus.

Tanus came to the stables with surly reluctance, and balked at climbing up into the cockpit of the chariot behind me.

'I trust this contraption of yours as much as I trust those cursed brutes who tow it,' he grumbled, but I was persuasive, and at last he stepped up gingerly on to the footplate and we were off.

At first I kept the horses to an easy trot, until I felt him relaxing and, despite himself, beginning to enjoy the exhilarating ride. Then I pushed them into a canter. 'See the speed of it. You can be upon the enemy before he knows you are there,' I exulted.

Tanus laughed for the first time, and I was encouraged. 'With your ships you rule the river. With this chariot you rule the land. Between the two, you rule the world. Nothing can stand against you.' I was careful not to disparage his beloved ships, or to make unfavourable comparisons.

'Is this your best speed?' he shouted in the wind and the pounding of hooves. 'With a fair wind, *Breath of Horus* is faster than this.' Which was a lie and a challenge.

'Hold on to the sides and take a deep breath,' I warned him. 'I am going to take you up where the eagles fly,' and I let Patience and Blade go.

No man has ever travelled faster. The wind seared our eyes, and the tears pouring from them were blown back into our hair.

'Sweet breath of Isis!' Tanus shouted with excitement. 'This is—' I never knew what he thought this was. Tanus never finished his sentence, for at that instant our off-wheel hit a rock and the rim exploded.

The chariot capsized and somersaulted, and both Tanus and I were thrown high and clear. I struck the hard earth with a force that should have crippled me, but I was so concerned with how Tanus would be affected by this little mishap, and how my dreams and plans would be dashed, that I felt no pain.

I bounded to my feet and saw Tanus crawl to his bleeding knees twenty paces beyond me. He was coated heavily with dust and seemed to have lost the skin from one half of his face. He tried to maintain his dignity as he pushed himself upright and staggered back to the wrecked chariot, but he was limping heavily.

He stood for a long minute gazing down at the shattered ruins of my creation, and then abruptly he let out a roar like a wounded bull, and launched such a mighty kick at it that it flipped over again, as though it were a child's toy. He turned on his heel without even a glance in my direction and limped away. I did not see him again for a week, and when we did meet, neither of us mentioned the chariot.

I think that might have been the end of the matter, and we would never have assembled our first chariot squadron, if it had not been for the fact that the stubbornness of my mistress's pride surpassed even that of her lover. She had given me the original order, and would not now retract it. When Tanus tried to inveigle her into doing so, he merely made my position stronger. Hui and I rebuilt the chariot within three days, and another identical to it.

By the time the embalmers in the funerary chapel had completed the ritual seventy days of royal mummification, we had our first squadron of fifty chariots, and had trained drivers for them.

 Since we had returned to the Palace of Memnon from our defeat at the battle of Abnub, my mistress had been occupied with the business of state thrust upon her by the regency. Long hours were spent with her ministers and advisers.

It was now that the initial training which I had given her in the Palace of Elephantine was to bear fruit. I had taught her to pick her way unerringly through the labyrinth of power and influence. She was just twenty-one years of age, but she was a queen, and ruled like one.

Very occasionally she encountered a problem which particularly vexed or perplexed her. Then she sent for me. I would drop my work in the armoury or the stables or in the small scribery that she had set aside for me just down the corridor from her audience chamber, and I would rush to her side.

On occasion I spent days sitting below her throne and steering her through some troublesome decisions. Once again, my ability to read the lips of men without hearing their words stood us in good stead. Some nobleman at the back of the audience never realized, as he plotted or schemed with his neighbour, that I was relaying his exact words to my mistress. She swiftly acquired a reputation of sagacity and prescience. Neither of us enjoyed much rest during these dark and worrisome days.

Even though our days were full, our nights were long. Those interminable councils of war and of state lasted well past midnight. No sooner was one crisis averted, than another loomed before us. Each day the Hyksos threatened us more directly, and Tanus' hold on the river-line weakened.

Slowly, a sense of doom and despair permeated all of us. Men smiled little and never laughed out loud. Even the play of the children was muted and subdued. We had only to look across the river, and the enemy was there, gathering himself, growing stronger each day.

After seventy days, the mummification of Pharaoh was completed. My early efforts in preserving the king's body had been highly successful, and the grand master of the guild of embalmers had commended me in the presence of my mistress. He had found no evidence of decay when he removed the king's corpse from the olive jar, and even his liver, which is the part most subject to mortification, was well preserved.

Once the king had been laid out on the diorite slab in his mortuary chapel, the grand master had inserted the spoon up his nostril and scooped out the curdled contents of his skull which the pickle had hardened to the consistency of cheese. Then, still in the foetal position, the king was placed in the bath of natron salt with only his head left uncovered by the harsh fluid. When he was removed from the bath thirty days later, all the fatty tissue had dissolved, and the outer layers of the skin had peeled off, except for that of the head.

They laid him upon the mottled stone slab once again and straightened him into an extended position. He was wiped and dried, and his empty stomach was filled with linen pads soaked in resins and wax and then sutured closed. Meanwhile, his internal organs were desiccated and placed in their milk-coloured alabaster Canopic jars, which were then sealed.

For the remaining forty days, the body of the king was allowed to dry out thoroughly. The doors of the chapel had been aligned with the direction of the warm, dry prevailing winds, so that they blew over the funeral slab. By the end of the ritual period of seventy days, Pharaoh's body was as dry as a stick of firewood.

His nails, which had been removed before he was soaked in the natron bath, were replaced and fixed in position on his fingers and toes with fine threads of gold wire. The first layer of pure white linen bandages was wound into place around his body, leaving his head and neck exposed. The binding was meticulous and intricate, with the bandages crossing and criss-crossing each other in elaborate patterns. Under the bindings were laid charms and amulets of gold and precious stones. The bandages were then soaked with lacquer and resins that dried to a stony hardness.

Now it was time for the ceremony of Opening-the-Mouth, which traditionally was performed by the dead pharaoh's next of kin. Memnon was too young to take this part, so his regent was called in his stead.

My mistress and I went to the chapel together in the gloom of dawn, and we were witnesses as the linen sheet that covered the king was drawn aside. Pharaoh's head was miraculously preserved. His eyes were closed and his expression was serene. The embalmers had rouged and painted his face, and he looked better in death than he had in life.

While the high priest of Ammon-Ra and the grand master of the guild of embalmers prepared the instruments for the ceremony, we sang the Incantation against Dying for the Second Time.

He is the reflection and not the mirror.
He is the music and not the lyre.
He is the stone and not the chisel that forms
    it.
He will live for ever.
He will not die a second time.

Then the high priest handed my mistress the golden spoon and led her by the hand to the funeral slab.

Queen Lostris stooped over the body of Pharaoh and laid the spoon of life upon his painted lips.

I open thy lips that thou mayest speak once
    more,
I open thy nostrils that thou mayest breathe.

She intoned the words and then touched his eyelids with the spoon.

I open thy eyes that thou mayest behold
    once more the glory
of this world, and the nether-world of the
    gods where you
shall dwell from this day forward.

She touched the spoon to his bandaged chest.

I quicken your heart, so that you may live
    for ever.
You shall not die a second time.
You shall live for ever!

Then we waited while the embalmers bound up Pharaoh's head in the neat swathes of bandages and painted them with resin. They moulded the resin-wet bandages to the shape of his face beneath them. Finally, they placed over his blind bandaged face the first of the four funeral masks.

This was the same funeral mask that we had watched being fashioned from pure gold. While he was still alive, Pharaoh had posed for the sculptor, so the mask was amazingly lifelike. The eyes of shining rock-crystal and obsidian seemed to gaze upon me with all the humanity that the man beneath the mask had once possessed. The cobra head of the *uraeus* rose from the noble brow, regal and mystical.

Then the wrapped mummy was placed in the golden inner coffin, which was sealed, and this went into the second golden coffin with another death-mask embossed upon the lid. Half the treasure recovered from Lord Intef's hoard had gone to make up that enormous weight of precious metal and jewels.

There were seven coffins in all, including the massive stone sarcophagus standing upon the golden sledge, which waited ready to carry Pharaoh along the causeway to his tomb in the gaunt hills. But my mistress refused to give her sanction for this to happen.

'I have given my sacred vow. I cannot place my husband in a tomb that may be plundered by the Hyksos barbarians. Pharaoh will lie here until I am able to make good my promise to him. I will find a secure tomb in which he may lie through eternity. I have given my word that no one will disturb his rest.'

 The wisdom of Queen Lostris' decision to delay the entombment was proved three nights later. The Hyksos made a determined effort to cross the river, and Tanus barely succeeded in turning them back. They made the attempt on an unguarded stretch of the river two miles north of Esna. They swam their horses across in a mass, and then followed with an armada of small boats which they had carried overland from Thebes in order to conceal their intentions from us.

They actually succeeded in making a beachhead on the west bank before Tanus could rush his galleys to the spot, but he arrived before they could unload their chariots and harness the horses to them. Tanus destroyed their boats with the chariots still on board, and he then had almost three thousand Hyksos stranded on our side of the river. Their horses scattered and bolted away into the night when Tanus' troops made their first charge.

Without their chariots the Hyksos were on even terms with our troops, but they had no means of escape and they fought with grim determination. In numbers they were almost evenly matched, for Tanus had managed to bring up only one full regiment. The rest of his army was thinly spread along the west bank. The fighting was bloody and ferocious, confused by the darkness which was lit only by the burning vessels that Tanus had fired on the beach.

It was only by the wildest coincidence, or by another nudge from the gods, that Hui and I had brought our little squadron of fifty chariots and fledgling charioteers to Esna on training manoeuvres. In truth, we had driven these twenty miles from Thebes principally to escape from Tanus' disapproval and interference.

We were encamped in the sacred grove of tamarind trees beside the temple of Horus at Esna. I was exhausted after a long day of galloping and

111

manoeuvring at high speed. On return to our encampment, Hui had produced a jar of remarkably palatable wine, and I had been somewhat intemperate in my sampling of it. I was dead asleep when Hui staggered into my tent and shook me awake.

'There are fires burning on the bank of the river downstream,' he told me, 'and when the wind shifts, you can hear the sound of cheering, and a little while ago I thought I heard many voices singing the battle hymn of the Blues. I think there is a fight going on down there.'

I was as unsteady on my feet as he was, and reckless with wine, as I shouted for him to rouse the camp and harness the horses. We were all still novices, and it was almost dawn by the time we had caught the horses and put them in the traces. In the chilly drift of the river mist and the gloomy shiver of dawn, we trotted along the north road in column of route, two chariots abreast. I was driving the lead chariot, while Hui had command of the rear-guard. Our fifty chariots had been reduced to thirty by the previous day's exercises, for I had not yet succeeded in perfecting my spoked wheels. They had an alarming tendency to fly to pieces when driven at speed, and almost half my force was out of action.

The passage of the wind over my bare chest made me shiver again, and counteracted the bravado of the wine. I was beginning to hope that Hui had been mistaken, when suddenly from far ahead there came that unmistakable chorus of shouting and cheering, and the clank and clash of bronze on bronze that could mean only one thing. Once you have heard them, the sounds of battle

112

are not readily forgotten or mistaken. The rough farmer's track we were following along the river-bank took a turn to the left. As we came through it, the field lay open before us.

The sun was just above the horizon, and it had turned the surface of the river into a shimmering sheet of beaten copper that was painful to the eye. The ships of Tanus' squadron lay just off-shore, crowding in close to, in an attempt to bring the archers on the decks in range of the Hyksos, and to cut off any retreat across the river.

The stranded Hyksos regiment was making a stand in the centre of a field of knee-high green corn. They had formed a circle, facing outwards, shoulder to shoulder, with their shields locked together and their spears thrust forward. As we came into view, they had just repulsed another attempt by Tanus' troops to break their circle. The Egyptian regiment was pulling back to regroup, leaving their dead and wounded scattered around the periphery of the enemy circle.

I am no soldier, although I have written scrolls on the conduct of war. I had accepted the rank of Commander of the Royal Horse, thrust upon me by my mistress, with the deepest reluctance. I had intended simply to perfect my chariot, train the first squadron, and then hand it over to Hui or some other person more suited to the warlike professions.

I was cold and still half-drunk as I heard my voice giving the order to deploy in arrow-head formation. It was the evolution that we had practised the previous day, and the chariots that followed mine flared out on either side with reasonable proficiency. I was acutely aware of the sound of hooves in the soft earth and the creak of the chariot harness, the squeal of the wheels turning on their metal-lined hubs, and the rattle of javelins as my charioteers drew their darts from the quivers. I looked left and right, reviewing our little squadron drawn up in the shape of an arrow-head with my chariot at the apex. It was a formation I had copied from the Hyksos. I drew a deep breath.

'Squadron will advance!' I screamed, and my voice shrilled with fear. 'At the gallop, forward!'

I had only to lift my left hand that held the traces, and Patience and Blade bounded forward. I was almost thrown over backwards, but I grabbed at the dashboard with my free hand, and we went straight at the Hyksos circle.

Beneath me the chariot leaped and jolted over the lumpy ploughed earth, and I looked over the plunging hindquarters of my horses and saw the wall of Hyksos shields, glittering and impenetrable in the early sunlight, drawing closer with every stride we took.

On either side of me, men were howling and cheering to hide their terror, and I howled with them, like a pariah dog at full moon. The horses were snorting and neighing, and suddenly Patience lifted the long plume of her tail and began to fart in rhythm and in time to her own stride. This struck me as immoderately funny. My howls of terror turned to screams of laughter. The helmet that I had borrowed from Hui was too large for me. It bounced off my head and the wind flung my hair out behind me.

Patience and Blade were the fastest pair in the squadron, and our chariot pulled ahead of the rest of the formation. I tried to slow our charge by

114

hauling back on the traces, but Patience would have none of it. Her glee was evident, she was as excited as any of us, and she straightened her neck and ran away with me.

We tore through the retiring lines of Egyptian infantry coming back from the failed assault on the Hyksos circle, and they scattered out of our path and gawked at us in astonishment.

'Come on!' I howled with laughter. 'We will show you the way!' They turned and followed us back towards the enemy at the run. Behind me, I heard the trumpeters sounding the charge, and the braying horns seemed to spur our horses. Out on my right I saw Tanus' battle standard waving, and recognized his crested helmet standing taller than the other men around him.

'What do you think of my cursed brutes now?' I yelled at him, as we tore past, and Patience farted again, bringing on fresh gales of my nervous laughter.

The chariot on my left was running almost level with me, and then its near-side wheel burst under the strain and it went flying end over end, throwing the charioteers, and bringing the horses down screaming. The rest of us tore on without a check.

The first rank of the enemy was now so close that I could see their eyes staring at me over the top edge of their shields. Their arrows hissed around my ears. I could make out clearly the figures of beasts and demons embossed on their tall metal helmets, see the beads of sweat glittering in their plaited and beribboned beards, hear their chanted war-cry—and then we were into them.

My horses leaped together into the barrier of shields and it shattered before the weight and fury of our charge. I saw a man tossed head-high, and heard his bones crackle like kindling in the fire. On the footplate behind me, my javelineer was making deadly practice. I had chosen him as the best from amongst all my recruits, and he proved my choice now, as he stood firm and hurled his darts down into the enemy.

In succession the following chariots tore into the gap we had opened, and we hardly checked as we raced through, breaking out through the far side of the Hyksos circle, then wheeling in pods of three and coming back at them.

Tanus seized the moment and threw his infantry into the breach that we had torn open. The Hyksos formation broke up into knots of struggling men. These in turn disintegrated, and the Hyksos panicked and ran for the river. The moment they came within range, the archers on the decks of our galleys sent clouds of arrows over them.

Ahead of me there was an isolated pocket of Hyksos warriors still fighting back-to-back, and holding off our men. I swerved the chariot and drove at them in full gallop. Before I reached them, my right wheel burst asunder, the light carapace of the chariot flipped over, and I soared free and then, with a gut-tearing lurch, fell back to earth. My head struck first, and my eyes filled with stars and meteors of bright light. Then there was only darkness.

I woke again under the awning on the deck of Tanus' flagship. I found myself lying on a sheepskin mattress, with Tanus leaning over me. As soon as he saw that I was conscious, he masked the expression of concern and worry that had twisted his features.

116

'You crazy old fool.' He forced a grin at me. 'What, in the name of Horus, were you laughing about?'

I tried to sit up, but my head ached abominably and I groaned, then clutched his arm as it all came back to me.

'Tanus, the enemy horses that swam across last night—I must have them.'

'Don't worry that battered head of yours. I have already sent Hui to gather them up,' he assured me. 'If I am to have five hundred of those contraptions of yours for my new chariot division, I will need a thousand of those cursed brutes to pull them. However, those new-fangled wheels of yours are more dangerous than a regiment of Hyksos. I will not ride with you again until you do something about them.'

For a moment it did not penetrate my aching skull, then I realized that it had happened. Tanus had quashed his pride, and given in to me. My orphan chariot squadron was at last to be part of the standing army, and he would give me the men and gold to build five hundred more. He would even ride with me again, if only I could fix my wheels.

But what truly filled me with joy was that he had forgiven me at last, and we were friends once more.

The success of my chariots at Esna, and the feeling of confidence that it instilled in us all, were short-lived. Secretly, I had expected and dreaded what would happen next. It was the enemy's logical move, and both Salitis and Lord Intef should have made it much earlier.

We knew that when he swept through the Lower Kingdom, Salitis had captured most of the fleet of the red pretender intact. Those ships were lying abandoned in the docks of Memphis and Tanis in the Delta. However, there must be droves of renegade Egyptians from the usurper's navy available to Salitis, and even if that were not the case, it would certainly be possible to recruit enough mercenary Syrian sailors in Gaza and Joppa, and the other ports along the eastern coast of the great sea, to man several hundred of these galleys and transports.

I had realized that this must happen, but I had refrained from warning either Tanus or my mistress of the likelihood, for I did not wish to add to the feeling of gloom, and heighten the despondency of our people. I had searched my heart for a counter to this move when Salitis and Intef made it, but there was none that I could think of. Therefore, since I could do nothing to allay these fears, I thought it best to keep them to myself.

When it finally happened, and our spies on the east side of the river opposite Asyut warned us of the approach of this fleet from the Delta, Tanus rushed his own ships northwards to meet them.

His fleet was superior in every way to the one which Salitis and Intef had assembled, but the battle they fought lasted for almost a week before Tanus destroyed or drove them back into the Delta.

However, Salitis had brought his transports up behind the screen of fighting galleys, and while the river battle still raged, he was able to embark almost two full regiments of horse and chariot, and ferry them intact to our side of the river, without our galleys being able to reach them.

These regiments comprised nearly three hundred of Salitis' fast war chariots, his elite divisions which he led himself. At last he had turned our flank. There was nothing to stop him now, as his chariots came bowling southwards along our side of the river. All our galleys could do was to try to keep pace with the dust-cloud he threw up, as he raced for the funerary temple of Mamose and all its treasures.

 Queen Lostris called her war council when the news of the Hyksos crossing reached us in the Palace of Memnon. She addressed her first question to Tanus.

'Now that he is across the river, can you check the barbarian?'

'I can slow him down, perhaps,' he replied frankly. 'We have learned a great deal about him. We can wait for him behind walls of stone, or behind barriers of the sharp staves that Taita has equipped us with. But Salitis need not give battle. His chariots are so fast that he can swing around our positions as he did at Asyut. No, I cannot stop him.'

Queen Lostris looked at me. 'Taita, what about your chariots? Can they not give battle to the Hyksos?'

'Your Majesty, I have forty chariots that I can send in to meet him. He has three hundred. My chariots are swifter than those of Salitis, but my men cannot match his in skill and training. There is also the matter of the wheels. I have not perfected them. Salitis will overwhelm and destroy us very easily. If I am given the time and the material, I can build new and better chariots with wheels that do not burst, but I cannot replace the horses. We dare not risk the horses. They are our only hope for eventual victory.'

While we thus debated, another messenger arrived, this time from the south. He had fled to us on the current and the wind, so his news was only a day old. Tanus ordered him into the council chamber, and the messenger fell to his knees before Queen Lostris.

'Speak, fellow,' Tanus invited him. 'What do you have to tell us?'

The messenger stuttered in fear of his life, 'Divine Majesty, while our fleet was busy at Asyut, the barbarian made another crossing at Esna. They swam the horses over as they did before, but this time there were none of our galleys ready to turn back their boats. Two Hyksos regiments are across. Their horses are in the traces and they are coming on a cloud of dust, swiftly as the flight of the swallow. They will be here in three days.'

None of us spoke until Tanus had sent the man away with orders that he be fed and cared for. The messenger, who had expected to be killed, kissed Queen Lostris' sandals.

When we were alone, Tanus said softly, 'Salitis has four regiments across the river. Six hundred chariots. It is over.'

'No!' my mistress's voice shook with the force of her denial. 'The gods cannot desert this very Egypt now. Our civilization cannot perish. We have too much to give to the world.'

'I can fight on, of course,' Tanus agreed. 'But in the end it will all be the same. We cannot prevail against their chariots.'

My mistress turned back to me. 'Taita, I have not asked you before, because I know how dearly it costs you. But I must ask you now before I make the final decision. I ask you to work the Mazes of Ammon-Ra for me. I must know what the gods require of us.'

I bowed my head in acquiescence, and whispered, 'I will fetch my chest.'

 The site that I chose for the divination was the inner sanctuary of the shrine to Horus in the half-completed Palace of Memnon. The shrine had not yet been dedicated to the god, and his image had not yet been set up, but I was certain that Horus had already cast his benevolent influence over the building.

My mistress sat before me with Tanus at her side, and watched in fascination as I drank the witches' potion to open the eyes of my soul, my *Ka*, the little bird-like creature that lives in the heart of every one of us, and which is our alter ego.

I laid the ivory Mazes before them and asked both Queen Lostris and Tanus to stroke and handle them, to endow them with their spirit and the spirit of the nation that they represented, this very Egypt. As I watched them divide the stacks of ivory counters, I felt the drug in my blood grow stronger, and the beat of my heart slowed as the little death crept over me.

I took up the two remaining Mazes from the last stack, and I held them to my breast. They began to grow hot against my skin, and my instinct was to draw back from the darkness that I felt coming over me. Instead, I surrendered to it and let it carry me away.

I heard my mistress's voice, as though from a great distance. 'What will become of the double crown? How can we resist the barbarian?'

The visions began to form before my eyes, and I was carried up into the days that were still to come, and I saw events that had not yet come to pass.

The morning sunlight was streaming through the aperture in the roof and striking the altar of Horus, when at last I returned from the far journey of the Mazes. I was shaken and nauseated with the effect of the hallucinatory drug, giddy and trembling with the memories of the strange sights that I had seen.

My mistress and Tanus had stayed with me during the long night. Their anxious faces were the first things that I saw on my return, but they were still so distorted and wavering that I thought they were part of the vision.

'Taita, are you all right? Speak to us. Tell us what you saw.' My mistress was concerned. She

122

could not hide the guilt she felt at having forced me to enter the Mazes of Ammon-Ra once more.

'There was a serpent.' My voice still echoed strangely in my own ears, as though I stood apart. 'A great green serpent that crawled through the desert.'

I saw the puzzled expression on their faces, but I had not yet considered the meaning of it all myself, so I could give them no guidance.

'I am thirsty,' I whispered. 'My throat is dry and my tongue like a stone covered with moss.'

Tanus fetched a jar of wine and poured it into the bowl for me, and I drank greedily.

'Tell us of the serpent,' my mistress demanded, as soon as I lowered the bowl.

'There was no end to its sinuous body, and it shimmered green in the sunlight. It crawled through a strange land, in which lived tall naked men and strange and wonderful beasts.'

'Could you see the head or the tail of the serpent?' my mistress asked, and I shook my head.

'Where were you? Where did you stand?' she insisted. I had forgotten how keenly she enjoyed my visions, and what pleasure she took in interpreting them.

'I was riding upon the back of the serpent,' I answered. 'But I was not alone.'

'Who was with you?'

'You were at my side, mistress, and Memnon with you. Tanus was on my other hand, and the serpent carried us all.'

'The Nile! The serpent was the river,' she cried triumphantly. 'You foresaw a voyage that we were making upon the river.'

'Which way?' Tanus demanded. He was as rapt

123

as she was. 'Which way did the river run?'

I made an effort to recall every detail. 'I saw the sun rise on my left hand.'

'South!' he cried.

'Into Africa,' said my mistress.

'At last I saw the heads of the serpent ahead of us. The body of the serpent was bifurcated, and on each branch was a head.'

'Does the Nile have two branches?' my mistress wondered aloud. 'Or is there some deeper meaning to the vision?'

'Let us hear the rest of what Taita has to tell us,' Tanus stopped her speculation. 'Continue, old friend.'

'Then I saw the goddess,' I went on. 'She sat upon a high mountain. Both the heads of the serpent worshipped her.'

My mistress could not restrain herself. 'Which of the goddesses did you see? Oh, tell me quickly who it was.'

'She had the bearded head of a man but the breasts and the pudenda of a woman. From her vagina she spurted out two great streams of water into the open mouths of the double-headed serpent.'

'It is the goddess Hapi, the river god,' Queen Lostris whispered. 'She generates the river within herself, and pours it out to flow through the world.'

'What else did the vision show you?' Tanus demanded.

'The goddess smiled at us, and her face shone with love and benevolence. She spoke in a voice that was the sound of the wind and the sea. The sound of thunder on the peaks of far-away

124

mountains.'

'What did she say to us?' Queen Lostris asked in awe.

'She said, "Let my child come to me. I will make her strong so that she will prevail and my people will not perish in the face of the barbarian."' I repeated the words that still beat like a drum in my head.

'I am the child of the river goddess,' said my mistress simply. 'At birth I was dedicated to her. Now she summons me, and I must go to the place where she dwells at the end of the Nile.'

'This is the same voyage that Taita and I contemplated once before,' Tanus mused. 'And now the goddess commands it. We cannot refuse her.'

'Yes, we must go, but we will come back,' my mistress vowed. 'This is my land, this very Egypt. This is my city, this beautiful Thebes of the hundred gates. I cannot leave them for ever. I will return to Thebes. This I swear and I call upon the goddess Hapi to witness my oath. We shall return!'

 The decision to fly to the south, up above the cataracts into the wild and unexplored land beyond, was one that Tanus and I had made once before. The first time had been to escape the wrath and vengeance of Pharaoh. Now we were flying from an even more merciless foe. It was almost as though the gods were determined that we should undertake this voyage, and that they would not be denied.

There was little time for us to make our

preparations for such a fateful departure. The Hyksos were coming down on us from two directions, and our pickets reported that their cohorts would be in view from the roof of the Palace of Memnon within three days at the very latest.

Tanus placed Kratas in charge of half his available force and sent him to meet King Salitis who was driving hard from Asyut in the north and was likely to be the first column to reach the necropolis and the palace. Kratas had orders to fight a running battle. Using the staves and defending every fortified position, he was to delay Salitis as long as was possible, without risking being cut off or overwhelmed. When he could hold them no longer, he was to evacuate his men on to the galleys.

Tanus himself took the other half of our army and moved south to fight another delaying battle against the Hyksos division coming at us from Esna.

While they were thus engaged, my mistress was to embark our people and all their possessions aboard the remaining ships of our fleet. My mistress delegated this duty to Lord Merkeset, but of course she made me his assistant. Lord Merkeset was not only well into his dotage, but had recently taken to himself a sixteen-year-old wife. He was not, therefore, of much use either to himself or to me. The entire planning and execution of the evacuation fell squarely on my shoulders.

However, before I could turn my mind to this, I had to take care of my horses. Even at this early stage I realized with stark clarity that they were the

126

key to our survival as a nation and a civilized people. With those animals that we had captured at Esna, we now had several thousand in our herd. I split this herd into four parts so that they could more readily find grazing on the march. Further, the smaller herds would throw up less dust, and it would be easier for them to avoid the Hyksos scouts.

I sent Hui and my charioteers and grooms south with these herds towards Elephantine, with orders to avoid the river-bank down which the Hyksos chariots were advancing and to keep inland, closer to the edge of the desert.

Once the horses were despatched, I could turn my attention to the humans. I realized that we were limited by the number of ships available as to how many of our people were able to accompany us on the long voyage. I was certain that almost every Egyptian wanted to be part of the exodus. The cruelty and ferocity of the Hyksos were evident in every city they burned and in every atrocity that they inflicted on our people. All the unknown dangers of the African wilderness were preferable to these bloodthirsty monsters who were racing down upon us in their chariots.

In the end I calculated that we could accommodate only twelve thousand souls aboard the escaping fleet, and I reported this to my mistress.

'We will have to be ruthless in those we select and those we leave behind,' I told her, but she would not listen to my advice.

'These are my people. I would give up my own place rather than leave one of them to the Hyksos.'

'But, Majesty, what about the old and the

decrepit? The sick and the very young?'

'Every citizen will be given the choice of coming with us. I will not leave a greybeard or a beggar, a day-old infant or a leper. They are my people, and if they cannot go, then Prince Memnon and I will stay with them.' Of course, she mentioned the prince to make doubly certain of her victory over me.

The ships would be gunwale-deep under this great weight of humanity, but I had no choice. Still, I had some satisfaction in first embarking all the most useful and creative citizens. I chose men from every trade and profession, masons and weavers, coppersmiths and potters, tanners and sailmakers, scribes and artists, shipbuilders and carpenters, all of them leaders in their particular discipline. These I saw safely on board the waiting transports. It gave me a particular pleasure to allocate the most uncomfortable berths in the most squalid vessels to the priesthood and the law scribes, those blood-sucking fleas on the healthy body of the state.

When all of these were boarded, I allowed the rabble to come swarming on to the wharf below the temple.

As a result of my mistress's intransigence, I had to be careful in choosing what cargo we would load. There would be no room for idle fripperies. I gathered up the weapons and tools and the raw materials that we would need to build up another civilization in the unknown lands. For the rest of the cargo I tried in every way to reduce weight and bulk. For instance, rather than grain and fruits, I loaded the seeds of every desirable plant in clay jars sealed with pitch and wax.

Every deben-weight of cargo that we loaded in our holds meant that something else must be left behind. Our voyage might last ten years or a lifetime. The road would be hard. We knew that the great cataracts lay ahead of us. We dared not burden ourselves with anything but the most essential, but then there remained my mistress's promise to Pharaoh. There was barely room for the living—how much space could we afford to give over to the dead?

'I gave my vow to the king as he lay dying,' my mistress insisted. 'I cannot leave him here.'

'Your Majesty, I will find a secure hiding-place for the king's body, an unmarked grave in the hills where no man will find him. When we return to Thebes, we will exhume him, and give him the royal burial that you promised him.'

'If I break my vow, the gods will desert us and our voyage will be doomed. The body of the king must go with us.'

One glance at her expression warned me that there would be no profit in further argument. We opened the massive granite sarcophagus and lifted out the six inner coffins. Even these were so bulky that it would have needed a galley to carry them alone.

I made a decision without consulting Queen Lostris. I had the workmen remove only the two innermost golden coffins. These we covered with a thick linen canvas shroud which we stitched over them as protection. The size and weight were thus reduced to acceptable proportions, and we stowed these two canvas-covered coffins in the hold of the *Breath of Horus*.

The bulk of Pharaoh's treasure, all the gold and

silver and the precious stones, was packed into cedar-wood boxes. I ordered the goldsmiths to strip the bullion from the discarded coffins and from the wooden frame of the great funeral sledge, and melt it down into bars. I was secretly delighted to be the instrument of destruction of that tasteless monstrosity. The treasure chests and the bars of bullion were carried down to the wharf and loaded on board the waiting ships. I distributed these so that every ship carried at least one chest or a stack of bullion bars. In this way, the risk that the entire treasure could be lost at a single stroke of misfortune was greatly reduced.

There was much of the funerary treasure that we could not take with us, all the furniture and the statuary, the ceremonial armour and the boxes of *ushabti* statues, and of course the ungainly framework of the hearse from which I had stripped the gold. Rather than have it fall into the hands of the Hyksos, we piled all of this in the temple courtyard, and I personally hurled a burning torch on top of the mountain of treasure, and watched it burn to ashes.

All this was done in dreadful haste, and before the last ship was loaded the lookouts on the roof of the palace shouted the warning that the dust-clouds of the Hyksos chariots were in sight. Within the hour, our exhausted and battle-weary troops who, under command of Tanus and Kratas, had been fighting the long grim rear-guard action, began to pull back into the necropolis, and to embark on the waiting galleys.

I met Tanus as he came up on to the causeway at the head of a squad of the guards. So far, by dint of courage and sacrifice, he and his men had managed to win a few extra days for us to complete the evacuation. They could do no more, and the enemy was driving them in.

When I waved and called his name, Tanus saw me and shouted over the heads of the crowd, 'Queen Lostris and the prince? Have they gone aboard the *Breath of Horus?*'

I forced my way through the throng to his side. 'My mistress will not leave until all her people are on board the ships. She ordered me to take you to her as soon as you arrived. She is waiting for you in her quarters in the palace.'

He looked at me aghast. 'The enemy are pressing us hard. Queen Lostris and the prince are more precious than all this rabble. Why did you not force her?'

I laughed. 'She is not an easy lady to force. You should know that as well as I do. She will leave none of her people to the Hyksos.'

'Seth blast that woman's pride! She will get all of us killed.' But his harsh words were belied by the expression of pride and admiration on his dusty, sweat-streaked face, and he grinned at me. 'Well, if she will not come on her own, we shall have to go and fetch her.'

We pushed our way through the long lines of passengers, laden with bundles of their possessions and carrying their infants, that were streaming down to the dock to go aboard the ships. As we hurried along the causeway, Tanus pointed over the battlements at the ominous clouds of dust bearing down upon us from both directions.

'They are moving faster than I had believed possible. They have not even halted to water their horses. Unless we speed up the embarkation, they will catch us with half our people still ashore,' he said grimly, and pointed down on to the wharf below us.

The wharf was wide enough to allow only two vessels to come alongside at one time. The masses of refugees clogged the causeway and congested the entrance gates to the dock. Their weeping and lamentation added to the confusion, and at that moment someone at the rear of the column screamed, 'The Hyksos are here! Run! Save yourselves! The Hyksos are here!'

The panic spread through the crowd and it surged forward mindlessly. Women were crushed against the stone gates, and children were trampled under foot. All order and control were breaking down, decent and dignified citizens and disciplined soldiers were being reduced to a desperate mob struggling for survival.

I had to use the sharpened stave I carried to force a way through them, as Tanus and I fought our way back towards the palace. At last we broke out of the crowd and ran to the palace gates.

The halls and corridors were empty and deserted except for a few looters who were picking through the empty rooms. They ran when they saw Tanus. He was a dreadful sight, gaunt and dusty and battle-worn, with a ruddy stubble of beard covering his jaw. Ahead of me, he burst into the private quarters of the queen, and we found her chamber unguarded and the door standing wide. We rushed through it.

My mistress sat alone on the terrace under the spreading vine, with Prince Memnon on her lap. She was pointing out to him the fleet of ships on the Nile below the terrace, and the two of them were enthusing over the spectacle.

'Look at the pretty ships.'

Queen Lostris stood up smiling when she saw us, and Memnon slid off her lap and ran to Tanus.

Tanus swung him up on to his shoulder, and then embraced my mistress with his free hand.

'Where are your slaves? Where are Aton and Lord Merkeset?' Tanus demanded.

'I sent them to the ships.'

'Taita says that you refused to go yourself. He is very angry with you, and rightly so.'

'Forgive me, dear Taita.' Her smile could light my life, or break my heart.

'Rather beg the forgiveness of King Salitis,' I suggested stiffly. 'He will be here soon enough.' I seized her arm. 'Now that this rude soldier of yours has at last arrived, can we please go to the ships?'

We hurried from the terrace and back through the palace corridors. We were entirely alone, even the looters and the thieves had disappeared like rats into their holes. The only one of us who was completely unconcerned was Prince Memnon. For him it was another jolly game. Sitting astride Tanus' shoulders, he dug in his heels and shouted, 'Hi up!' as he had learned from me when we were riding Patience.

We raced across the palace gardens to the stone staircase that led up on to the causeway. That was the shortest way to the temple dock. As we hurried along the causeway, I realized that circumstances had changed drastically in the time that had passed since we had left to fetch my mistress and the prince from the palace. Ahead of us the causeway was deserted, the last of the refugees had gone on board the ships in the dock. Beyond the stone battlements I could see their masts moving slowly down the canal towards the open river.

With a hollow feeling in the pit of my stomach, I realized that we were the last persons left ashore, and that we still had half a mile to cover before we reached the empty dock. All of us stopped together, and watched the last galleys sail away.

'I told the captain to wait,' I groaned, 'but with the Hyksos so close, their only concern is with their own safety.'

'What can we do now?' my mistress breathed, and even Memnon's happy cries dried up.

'If we can reach the river-bank, surely Remrem or Kratas will see us and send in a skiff to pick us up?' I suggested, and Tanus agreed immediately.

'This way! Follow me!' he cried. 'Taita, see to your mistress.'

I took her arm to help her along, but she was as strong and agile as a shepherd boy and ran easily at my side. Then suddenly I heard the horses, and the squeal of chariot wheels. The sounds were unmistakable and terrifyingly near at hand.

Our own horses had left three days ago, and must be well on their way to Elephantine by this time. Our own chariots were dismantled and loaded in the holds of the departing fleet. The chariots I heard now were still out of sight below the wall of the causeway, but we knew to whom they belonged.

'The Hyksos!' I said softly, and we stopped in a tight little group. 'It must be one of their advance scouting parties.'

'It sounds like only two or three of their chariots,' Tanus agreed, 'but that is enough. We are cut off.'

134

'It seems that we have left it a little late,' said my mistress with a calmness that I knew was feigned, and she looked at Tanus and myself with complete trust. 'What do you suggest now?'

Her effrontery flabbergasted me. Her obstinacy was entirely responsible for our predicament. If she had followed my urging we would all of us have been on the *Breath of Horus* and making our way up-river to Elephantine by this time.

Tanus held up his hand for silence, and we stood and listened to the sounds of the enemy chariots driving along the pathway at the foot of the wall. The closer they came, the more certain it became that this was only a small advance party.

Suddenly the sounds of turning wheels stopped, and we heard the horses blowing and stamping, then men's voices speaking a harsh and guttural tongue. They were just below us, and Tanus made another urgent signal for silence. Prince Memnon was not accustomed to restraint, nor to keeping the peace against his inclinations. He also had heard and recognized the sounds.

'Horses!' he shouted in his usual high and ringing tones. 'I want to see the horses.'

There was an instant outcry. Hyksos voices shouted orders, and weapons rattled in their scabbards. Then heavy footfalls pounded upon the stone staircase as a party of the enemy came dashing up on to the causeway.

Their tall helmets appeared above the stone balustrade just ahead of us, and then the rest of them came into view. There were five of them in a body and they rushed up at us with drawn swords, big men with fish-scale shirts of mail and brightly coloured ribbons in their beards. But one of them was taller than the rest. I did not recognize him at first, for he had grown a beard and decorated it with ribbons in the Hyksos fashion, and the visor of his helmet hid half his face. Then he shouted in that voice that I would never forget, 'So it's you, young Harrab! I killed the old dog, and now I will kill his puppy!'

I should have known that Lord Intef would be the very first of them to come sniffing like a hungry hyena after Pharaoh's treasure. He must have raced ahead of the main Hyksos division to be the first into the funerary temple. Despite his boast, he did not rush to meet Tanus, but waved the band of Hyksos charioteers forward to do the job for him.

Tanus swept Prince Memnon from his shoulders and tossed him to me as though he were a doll.

'Run!' he ordered. 'I will buy you a little time here.' He rushed the Hyksos while they were still bunched on the staircase and had no room to wield their swords. He killed the first one cleanly, with that thrust through the throat which he always performed so skilfully.

'Don't stand there gawking,' he shouted over his shoulder. 'Run!'

I was not gawking, but with the child clutched to my chest, I knew how futile was his command. Burdened as I was, I would never reach the river-bank.

I stepped to the parapet of the causeway and glanced over. There were two Hyksos chariots parked directly below me, with the horses blowing and stamping in the traces. Only one man had been left to hold them, while his companions rushed up the staircase. He stood at the heads of

136

the two teams and his whole attention was fixed on his charges. He had not seen me on the causeway above his head.

Still clutching Memnon, I threw my legs over the parapet and pushed myself outwards. The prince shrieked with alarm as we dropped. From the top of the causeway to where the Hyksos charioteer stood was four times the height of a tall man. I might easily have broken a leg in the fall, except that I landed neatly on the unsuspecting Hyksos' head. The impact broke his neck; clearly I heard the vertebrae snap, and he crumpled under us, breaking our fall.

I scrambled to my feet, with Memnon howling in outrage at this rough treatment, but there was more of it to follow. I dropped him into the cockpit of the nearest chariot and looked up at my mistress. She was peeping over the parapet high above me.

'Jump!' I shouted. 'I will catch you!' She never even hesitated, but flung herself over the edge so promptly that I was not yet braced to receive her. She came hurtling down on top of me, with her short skirts blowing up and exposing those long sleek thighs. She hit me squarely and knocked the wind out of my lungs. We went down together in a heap.

I scrambled up wheezing for breath, and dragged her to her feet. I shoved her roughly over the footplate of the chariot and shouted at her, 'See to Memnon!' She grabbed him just as he tried to escape from the cockpit of the chariot. He was still howling with anger and fright. I had to scramble over the top of them to reach the reins and take control of the horses.

'Hang on tight!' The pair of horses responded instantly to my hands, and I wheeled the whole rig smartly under the wall. One wheel bounced over the body of the man that I had killed with my fall.

'Tanus!' I screamed. 'This way!'

High above us he jumped up on to the parapet, and balanced there easily, exchanging parry and thrust with the group of charioteers who bayed around him, like hounds around a treed leopard.

'Jump, Tanus, jump!' I yelled, and he stepped out over the edge of the stone wall and let himself drop. With his cloak billowing around his head and shoulders, he landed astride the back of the off-side horse. His sword jerked out of his hand and clattered on the hard earth, and Tanus threw both arms around the animal's neck.

'Hi up!' I called to the pair, and whipped the end of the reins around their hindquarters. They surged forward into a full gallop. I steered them across the pathway and into the open fields that led down to the river-bank. I could see the sails of our fleet out there in midstream, and I could even recognize the pennant of the *Breath of Horus* flying amongst the forest of masts. We had half a mile to go to reach the bank, and I glanced over my shoulder.

Lord Intef and his men had rushed down the staircase. Even as I watched, they were climbing up into the other chariot. I cursed myself that I had not disabled it. It would have taken only a moment to cut the traces and chase away the horses, but I had been in a panic to get my mistress and the prince away.

Now Lord Intef was coming after us. His chariot had not covered a hundred paces before I realized

138

that it was faster than the one I was driving. Tanus'
weight on the back of the off-side horse was
hampering its gallop; he was a heavy man and he
still clung to its neck with both arms. He seemed
frozen with terror. I think that this was the first
time that I had ever seen him truly afraid. I have
seen him stand firm and shoot down a charging
lion with his bow, but the horse terrified him.

I tried to ignore the following chariot, and I
looked ahead and concentrated all my newly
acquired skill on piloting us over the open
cultivated fields and through the maze of irrigation
canals and ditches to the bank of the Nile. The
Hyksos chariot was heavy and unwieldy, compared
to my Taita vehicle. The solid wooden wheels with
their glinting and turning knives around the rims
bit deeply into the clay loam of the ploughed lands,
and all that bronze armour and ornamentation on
the dashboard and side-frames weighed us down.
The horses must have been driven hard before I
took control of them. They were lathered with
sweat and white froth dripped from their muzzles.

We had not covered half the distance to the
river-bank when I heard the shouts of the Hyksos
charioteer closing with us, and the pounding of
hooves. I glanced back to see them not three
lengths behind. The driver was lashing the horses
with a whip of knotted leather tails and yelling at
them in that coarse and ugly language. Beside him,
Lord Intef was leaning out eagerly over the
dashboard. His ribboned beard was streaming
back on either side of his jaw, and his handsome
features were lit by the rapture of the hunter.

He shouted at me, and his voice carried over the
sounds of the two labouring teams of horses.

'Taita, my old darling, do you still love me? I want you to prove it once more before you die.' And he laughed. 'You are going to kneel in front of me and die with your mouth full.' My skin prickled with insects' feet of horror at the image his words conjured up.

There was an irrigation ditch ahead of us, and I swerved to run alongside it, for the sides were deep and sheer. The Hyksos chariot followed us round, gaining on us with every stride.

'And you, my lovely daughter, I will give you to the Hyksos soldiers to play with. They will teach you a few tricks that Harrab forgot to show you. I don't need you, now that I have your brat.' Queen Lostris clutched the prince closer to her chest and her face was pale and set.

I understood Lord Intef's design immediately. A child of the royal blood of Egypt, even as a satrap of the Hyksos, would command the loyalty of all our people. Prince Memnon was the puppet through which King Salitis and Lord Intef intended to rule the two kingdoms. It was an ancient and effective device of the conqueror. I pushed my horses to their utmost, but they were tiring and slowing, and Lord Intef closed with us so swiftly that he no longer needed to shout to make himself heard.

'Lord Harrab, this is a pleasure long delayed. What shall we do with you, I wonder? First, you and I will watch the soldiers entertain my daughter—' I tried to stop my ears to his filth, but his voice was insidious.

I was still gazing ahead, concentrating on the rough and dangerous ground, but from the corner of my eye I saw the heads of the Hyksos pair draw level with our vehicle. Their manes flowed back, and their eyes were wild as they tore up beside us at full gallop.

I looked back at them. The burly Hyksos archer on the footplate behind Intef nocked an arrow to his short recurved bow. The range was so short that even from the bouncing and leaping platform, he could not miss hitting one of us.

Tanus was out of the fight. He had dropped his sword. He was still clinging to the neck of the horse on the side furthest from the overtaking chariot. I had only my little dagger, and Queen Lostris was down on her knees trying to shield the prince with her own body.

It was only then that I realized the mistake that the Hyksos driver had made. He had pushed his team of horses into the gap between us and the deep irrigation ditch. He had left himself no room to manoeuvre.

The archer lifted his bow and drew the fletchings of the arrow to his lips. He aimed at me. I was looking into his eyes over the barbed flint of the arrow-head. His brows were black and dense and bushy, his eyes as dark and implacable as those of a lizard. The Hyksos horses were running level with the hub of my near-side wheel, and I gathered my reins and swerved towards them. The flashing bronze knives that stood out of my wheel-rims buzzed softly as they spun towards the legs of the horses.

The Hyksos driver shouted with consternation as he realized his error. His horses were trapped between the ditch and those cruel knives. The blades were less than a hand-span from the knees of the big bay stallion running nearest to me.

At that same instant, the Hyksos archer loosed his arrow, but my sudden swerve had beaten him also. The arrow seemed to fly quite slowly towards my head, but this was an illusion produced by my terror. In reality it flashed like a beam of sunlight over my shoulder, the flint edge touched my ear, and a drop of blood dripped from the grazed skin on to my chest.

The other driver had tried to counter my swerve by turning away from me, but now his far wheel was running along the lip of the irrigation ditch. It was crumbling away beneath the bronze-bound rim, and the chariot lurched and teetered on the edge.

I gathered my horses and swung them again, turning into the other chariot. My wheel-blades hacked into the legs of the nearest horse, and the poor beast squealed with agony. I saw pieces of skin and hair fly into the air above the sideboard of my chariot, and I steeled myself to the whinnying cry of the horse, and turned hard into him again. This time blood and bone chips flew in a mush from the broken legs, and the horse went down, kicking and squealing, pulling his team-mate down with him. The Hyksos chariot went over the edge of the ditch. I saw the two passengers in the cockpit thrown clear, but the driver was carried over and crushed beneath the capsized truck and the heavy, spinning wheels.

Our own chariot was now tearing along dangerously close to the edge of the ditch, but I managed to gather the horses and bring them back in hand.

'Whoa!' I slowed them, and turned to look back. A cloud of dust hung over the ditch where the

Hyksos chariot had disappeared. I brought my team down to a trot. The river-bank was two hundred paces ahead, and nothing stood in our way to safety.

I turned for one last look behind me. The Hyksos archer, who had fired his arrow at me, lay in a crumpled and broken heap where he had been thrown. Lord Intef lay a little further from the edge of the ditch. I truly believe I might have left him there if he had not stirred, but at that moment he sat up and then pushed himself unsteadily to his feet.

Suddenly all my hatred of him came back to me with such force and clarity that my mind seethed with it. It was as though a vein had burst behind my eyes, for my vision darkened, and was glazed over with the reddish sheen of blood. A savage, incoherent cry burst from my throat, and I wheeled the horses in a tight circle until we were headed back towards the causeway.

Lord Intef stood directly in my path. He had lost his helmet and his weapons in the fall, and he seemed half-dazed, for he swayed upon his feet. I whipped the horses up into a gallop once more, and the heavy wheels rumbled forward. I aimed the chariot directly at him. His beard was dishevelled and the ribbons in it sullied with dust. His eyes also were dull and bemused, but as I drove the horses down on him, suddenly they cleared and his head came up.

'No!' he shouted, and began to back away, throwing out his hands towards me as if to fend off the massive carriage and the running horses. I aimed directly for him, but at the last moment, his dark gods defended him one last time. As I was

143

right upon him, he threw himself to one side. I had seen him staggering and I had supposed that he was weak and helpless. Instead, he was as quick and nimble as a jackal pursued by the hounds. The chariot was heavy and unwieldy, and I could not turn it swiftly enough to follow his side-step and dodge.

I missed him and went on by. I wrestled with the reins, but the horses carried me on a hundred paces before I could get them under control and swing the heavy vehicle round again. By the time we came around, Intef was running for the shelter of the ditch. If he reached it, he would be safe—I realized that. I swore bitterly as I drove the team after him.

It was then that his gods finally abandoned him. He had almost reached the ditch, but he was looking back over his shoulder at me, and he was not watching his footing. He ran into a patch of clay clods, hard as rocks, and his ankle turned under him. He fell heavily but rolled back on to his feet like an acrobat. He tried to run again, but the pain in his broken ankle brought him up. He hobbled a pace or two and then tried to hop forward towards the ditch on one leg.

'You are mine at last!' I screamed at him, and he spun around to face me, balanced on one leg as I drove the chariot down on him. His face was pale, but those leopard eyes blazed up at me with all the bitterness and hatred of his cruel and twisted soul.

'He is my father!' my mistress cried at my side, holding the prince's face to her bosom so that he would not see it. 'Leave him, Taita. He is of my blood.'

I had never disobeyed her in my life, this was the

first time. I made no move to check the horses, but gazed into Lord Intef's eyes, for once without fear.

At the very end, he almost cheated me again. He flung himself sideways, and such were his agility and his strength that he twisted himself clear of the truck and the wheels of the chariot, but he could not quite avoid the wheel-knives. One of the spinning blades hooked in the fish-scale links of his coat of mail. The point of the knife tore through the armour and hooked in the flesh of his belly. The knife was spinning and his entrails snagged and wrapped around it, so that his guts were drawn out of him, as though he was one of those big blue perch from the river being disembowelled by a fishwife on the market block.

He was towed along behind us by the slippery ropes of his own entrails, but he fell slowly behind as more coils and tangles of his gut were torn from his open stomach cavity. He clutched at them with both hands, as they were stripped out of him, but they slid through his fingers like some grotesque umbilical cord that bound him to the turning wheel of the chariot.

His screams were a sound that I wish never to hear again as long as I live. The echoes of them still sometimes haunt my nightmares, so that in the end he inflicted his last cruelty upon me. I have never been able to forget him, as I would so dearly have wished.

When at last the gruesome rope by which he was being dragged across the black earth snapped, he was left lying in the centre of the field. At last those cries of his were stilled, and he lay without movement.

I pulled up the horses and Tanus slid down off

145

the back of his mount and came back to the chariot. He lifted my mistress and the prince down and held them close to his chest. My mistress was weeping.

'Oh, it was so terrible! Whatever he did to us, he was still my father.'

'It's all right now,' Tanus hugged her. 'It's all over now.'

Prince Memnon was peering back over his mother's shoulder at the sprawling figure of his grandfather with all the fascination that children have with the macabre. Suddenly he piped up in that ringing treble, 'He was a nasty man.'

'Yes,' I agreed softly, 'he was a very nasty man.'

'Is the nasty man dead now?'

'Yes, Mem, he is dead. Now we can all sleep better at nights.'

I had to drive the horses hard along the river-bank to catch up with our departing flotilla, but at last I drew level with Kratas' galley, and he recognized us in the unfamiliar vehicle. Even across that wide stretch of water, his astonishment was apparent. Later he told me that he had believed we were safely aboard one of the leading ships of the flotilla.

I turned the horses loose before I left the chariot. Then we waded out into the water to reach the small boat which Kratas sent in to pick us up.

The Hyksos would not let us go that easily. Day after day, their chariots pursued our flotilla down both banks of the Nile as we fled southwards.

Whenever we looked back over the stern of the *Breath of Horus*, we saw the dust of the enemy columns following us. Very often the dust was mingled with the darker clouds of smoke that rose from the towns and villages on the river-banks which the Hyksos burned as they sacked them. As we passed each of the Egyptian towns, a flock of small craft sailed out to join our fleet, so that our armada increased in numbers with each day that passed.

There were times, when the wind was unfavourable, that the columns of chariots overhauled us. Then we saw their cohorts gleaming on the banks on either side of us, and heard their harsh but futile jeers and challenges ring out across the water. However, eternal Mother Nile gave us her protection, as she had over the centuries, and they could not reach us out on the stream. Then the wind would veer back into the north and we drew ahead of them once more, and the dust-clouds fell back on to the northern horizon.

'Their horses cannot keep up this chase much longer,' I told Tanus on the morning of the twelfth day.

'Don't be too smug about it. Salitis has the lure of the treasure of Pharaoh Mamose and the legitimate heir to the double crown,' Tanus replied simply. 'Gold and power have a marvellous way of

147

stiffening a man's resolve. We have not seen the last of the barbarian yet.'

The next morning the wind had changed again, and the chariots slowly gained upon us once more, and overtook the leading ships of our flotilla just as we approached the Gates of Hapi, the first of the granite walls that constricted the river below Elephantine. Between them the Nile narrowed to less than four hundred paces across from bank to bank, and the black granite cliffs rose almost sheer on each side. The flow of the current was full against us as it swirled through the Gates of Hapi, so that our speed bled off and Tanus ordered fresh men to the rowing-benches.

'I think you are right, Taita. This is where they will be waiting,' he told me grimly, and then almost immediately afterwards he pointed ahead. 'There they are.'

Leading the fleet, the *Breath of Horus* was just entering the gates, so we had to throw our heads back to look up the cliff-faces. The figures of the Hyksos archers high up on the rocky ledges were foreshortened by the angle, so that they appeared as grotesque dwarfs.

'From that height they could shoot their arrows clear across from bank to bank,' Tanus muttered. 'We will be in easy range for most of this day. It will be hard on all of us, but more especially on the women and the children.'

It was even worse than Tanus expected. The first arrow, fired at our galley from the cliffs above us, left a trail of smoke against the blue vault of the sky as it arced down and struck the water only a cubit ahead of our bows.

'Fire-arrows,' Tanus nodded. 'You were right

148

once again, Taita. The barbarian does learn quickly.'

'It's easy enough to teach an ape new tricks.' I hated the Hyksos as much as any man in the fleet.

'Now let us see if your bellows can pump water into a ship as well as they pump it out,' Tanus said.

I had anticipated this attack with fire and so, for the last four days, I had been working on those galleys that Tanus had fitted with the water-pumps which I had designed for him. Now, as each of our vessels came up, Tanus ordered the captain to lower his sails, and we pumped water over the decks and soaked the rigging. Leather buckets were filled and placed ready upon the decks, and then one of the galleys escorted the ship into the granite-lined gut of the river and the rain of Hyksos fire-arrows.

It took two full days to get the flotilla through, for the cliffs blanketed the wind. It was hot and still in the gap, and each ship had to be rowed all the way against the current. The arrows fell upon us in pretty, sparking parabolas, rapping into the masts and the decks. Each of them started its own blaze that had to be quenched by the bucket chains or by the leather hoses of the pumps on the escort galley. There was no way for us to retaliate against this attack, for the archers were high up on the cliff-faces. They were well out of range of our own less powerful bows. When Remrem led a shore party to dislodge them from their perches, they were able to fire down on his men and drive them back into the boats with heavy losses.

Those vessels that won through were all scarred with black scorched patches. Many others were less fortunate. The flames aboard them had beaten
149

the buckets and the pumps and engulfed them. They had to be cut free and left to drift down on the current, causing pandemonium amongst the rest of the fleet coming up into the gap. In most cases we managed to take the crew and passengers off before the flames were out of hand, but with some we were too late. The screams of the women and the children in the heart of the flames were enough to stop the blood in my heart. I am left for ever with an image from that dreadful day of a young woman leaping from the deck of a burning barge with her long hair wreathed in flames, like a wedding garland.

We lost over fifty ships in the Gates of Hapi. There were mourning banners flying on every ship as we sailed on towards Elephantine, but at least the Hyksos seemed to have exhausted themselves and their horses in this long chase southwards. The dust-clouds no longer besmirched our northern horizon, and we had a respite in which to mourn our dead and repair our vessels.

However, none of us believed that they had given up entirely. In the end, the lure of Pharaoh's treasure must prove too much to resist.

 Confined as we were to the deck of the galley, Prince Memnon and I spent much time together sitting under the awning on the poop-deck. There he listened avidly to my stories, or watched me design and whittle the first model of a new bow for our army, based on the Hyksos recurved type. He had by now learned the old trick of asking questions to keep my attention focused upon him.

'What are you doing now, Tata?'

'I am making a new bow.'

'Yes, but why?'

'All right, I will tell you. Our own single-curve bows, apart from lacking the same power and carry, are too long to be used from the chariot.' He listened gravely. Even when he was an infant I had tried never to indulge in baby-talk with him, and I always addressed him as an equal. If sometimes he did not understand, at least he was happy with the sound of my voice.

'I am now totally convinced that our future lies with the horse and chariot, I am sure that Your Royal Highness agrees with me.' I looked up at him. 'You love horses too, don't you, Mem?'

He understood that well enough. 'I love horses, especially Patience and Blade,' he nodded vehemently.

I had already filled three scrolls with my musings and diagrams of how I conceived these military assets could be used to best advantage. I wished that I was able to discuss these in detail with Tanus, but the Great Lion of Egypt's interest in matters equine was grudging and superficial.

'Build the cursed things if you must, but don't keep chattering about them,' Tanus told me.

The prince was a much more receptive audience, and while I worked, we conducted these long discussions, which were only much later to bear their full harvest. As a companion, Memnon's first choice was always Tanus, but I was not far behind in his affections, and we spent long, happy hours in each other's company.

From the very first he was an exceptionally

151

precocious and intelligent child, and under my influence he developed his gifts more swiftly than any other I had ever instructed. Even my mistress at the same age had not been as quick to learn.

I had made Memnon a toy bow of the design I was studying, and he mastered it almost immediately and could soon shoot one of his tiny arrows the full length of the galley's deck, much to the agitation of the slave girls and nursemaids who were usually his targets. None of them dared bend over when the prince was armed with his bow, he seldom missed an inviting pair of feminine buttocks at under twenty paces.

After his bow, his favourite toy was the miniature chariot and horse that I had carved for him. I had even made the tiny figure of a charioteer to stand in the cockpit, and reins for him to drive the pair. The prince promptly named the mannikin Mem, and the horses were christened Patience and Blade. He crawled tirelessly up and down the deck, pushing the chariot in front of him, making appropriate horsy noises and uttering cries of 'Hi up!' and 'Whoa!'

For such a small boy he was always aware of his surroundings. Those sparkling dark eyes missed very little of what was happening around him. It was no surprise to me when he was the first of any of the crew of the *Breath of Horus* to spot the strange figure far ahead of us on the right bank of the river.

'Horses!' he shrieked, and then moments later, 'Look, look! It is Hui!'

I rushed up to where he stood in the bows, and my heart soared as I realized that he was right. It was Hui astride Blade coming down the river-bank to meet us at a full gallop.

'Hui has got the horses through to Elephantine. I forgive him all his other sins and stupidities. Hui has saved my horses.'

'I am very proud of Hui,' said the prince gravely, imitating my words and intonation so exactly that my mistress and all those around us burst out laughing.

 We were given a respite once we reached Elephantine. There had been no sign of the pursuing chariots for so many days that a new optimism spread through the fleet and the city. Men started speaking of abandoning the flight to the south, and of remaining here below the cataracts to build up a new army with which to oppose the invader.

I never allowed my mistress to be seduced by this spirit of confidence which was rooted in such shallow soil. I convinced her that my vision of the Mazes had shown us the true path and that our destiny still lay to the south. In the meantime, I continued my preparations for the voyage unabated. I think that by this time, it was the adventure itself that had cast its spell over me, even more than the necessity of running from the Hyksos.

I wanted to see what lay beyond the cataracts, and in the nights after a full day's work in the docks, I sat up into the late watches in the palace library, reading the accounts of men who had taken that first step into the unknown before us.

They wrote that the river had no end, that it ran

on to the very ends of the earth. They wrote that after the first cataract, there was another more formidable, one that no man or ship could ever surmount. They said that to voyage from the first cataract to the next was a full year of travel, and still the river ran on.

I wanted to see it. More than anything in my life I wanted to see where this great river, that was our life, began.

When at last I fell asleep in the lamplight over the scrolls, I saw again in my dream the vision of the welcoming goddess seated on a mountain-top, with the twin spouts of water gushing from her great vagina. Although I had slept but little, I awoke with the dawn, refreshed and excited, and I rushed back to the docks to continue the preparations for the journey.

I was fortunate in that most of the ropes for our shipping were woven and braided in the sail-yards here in Elephantine. Thus I had the pick of the finest linen cables at my disposal. Some of these were as thick as my finger, and others as thick as my thigh. With them I filled every available space in the holds of the ships not already crammed with stores. I knew just how desperately we would need these, when we came to the cataracts.

It was not surprising that here in Elephantine those of our company with faint hearts and weak resolve made themselves known. The rigours of the flight from Thebes had convinced many of these that the compassion and mercy of the Hyksos were preferable to a continuation of the voyage into the burning southern deserts where even more savage men and beasts awaited them.

When Tanus heard that there were so many

154

thousands of these citizens anxious to desert from the fleet, he roared, 'Damned traitors and renegades! I know what to do with them.' And he expressed his intention of turning his legions upon them, and driving them back on board the ships.

At first he had my mistress's support in this. Her motives were very different from his. She was concerned only with the welfare of her subjects, and her vow that she would leave none of them to the Hyksos terror.

I had to spend half the night arguing with both of them before I could convince them that we were better off without reluctant passengers. In the end, Queen Lostris issued a decree that any person who wished to remain in Elephantine might do so, but she added a neat little touch of her own to the proclamation. This was read aloud in every street of the city, and upon the docks where our ships lay.

I, Queen Lostris, regent of this very Egypt, mother of Prince Memnon, the heir to the double crown of the two kingdoms, now deliver to the people of this land my solemn promise.

I make oath before the gods and call upon them to witness it. I swear to you that on the majority of the prince, I shall return with him to this city of Elephantine, here to elevate him to the throne of Egypt and place the double crown upon his brow that he may cast out the oppressor and rule over you with justice and in mercy all the days of his life.

It is I, Queen Lostris, regent of this very Egypt, who speaks thus.

This act and declaration increased one hundredfold the love and the loyalty that the common people felt towards my mistress and the prince. I doubt that in all our history there had ever been a ruler so cherished as was she.

When the lists were drawn up of those who would come with us beyond the cataracts, I was not surprised to see that it comprised most of those whose loyalty and skills we most valued. Those who wished to stay in Elephantine were the ones we were happiest to lose, including most of the priesthood.

However, time would prove that those who remained behind us in Elephantine were of great value to us also. During the long years of the exodus they kept alive the flame in the hearts of the people, the memory of Prince Memnon and the promise of Queen Lostris to return to them.

Gradually, through all the long, bitter years of the Hyksos tyranny, the legend of the return of the prince spread through the two kingdoms. In the end, all the people of Egypt, from the first cataract to the seven mouths of the Nile in the great Delta, believed that he would come back, and they prayed for that day.

 Hui had my horses waiting for me on the fields of the west bank, below the orange dunes hard by the river. The prince and I visited them every day, and although he was growing heavier, Memnon rode upon my shoulder to have a better view over the herd.

By now Memnon knew all his favourites by name, and Patience and Blade came to eat corn-cakes from his hand when he called them. The first time he rode upon her back without my hand to steady him, Patience was as gentle with him as she was with her own foal, and the prince shouted out loud with the thrill of cantering alone around the field.

Hui had learned a great deal about the management of the herds on the march, and using this knowledge, we planned in detail for their welfare on the next stage of the journey. I also explained to Hui the role that I wished the horses to play in the passage of the cataracts, and set him and the charioteers and grooms to work plaiting and splicing harness.

At the very first opportunity, Tanus and I went up-river to scout the cataract. The water was so low that all the islands were exposed. The channels between them were so shallow that in places it was possible for a man to wade through without the water covering his head.

The cataracts extended for many miles, a vast confusion of shining, water-worn granite boulders and serpentine streams that wriggled and twisted their way between them. Even I was daunted and discouraged by the task that lay ahead of us, while Tanus was his usual brutally straightforward self.

'You won't be able to push a skiff through here without ripping the belly out of it. What will you do with a heavily laden galley? Carry it through on the back of one of your cursed horses?' he laughed, but without the least trace of humour.

We started back to Elephantine, but before I reached the city, I had made up my mind that the

157

only way forward was to abandon the ships and go on overland. The hardships that this course would bring down upon us were difficult to imagine. However, I reckoned that we might be able to rebuild the flotilla on the river-banks above the cataracts.

When we returned to the palace on Elephantine Island, Tanus and I went directly to the audience chamber to report to Queen Lostris. She listened to everything that we told her, and then shook her head.

'I do not believe that the goddess has deserted us so soon,' and she led us and all her court to the temple of Hapi on the south tip of the island.

She made a generous sacrifice to the goddess, and we prayed all that night and asked for the guidance of Hapi. I do not believe that the favour of the gods can be bought by cutting the throats of a few goats and placing bunches of grapes upon the stone altar, nevertheless, I prayed with all the fervour of the high priest, although by dawn my buttocks ached hideously from the long vigil on the stone benches.

As soon as the rays of the rising sun struck through the doors of the sanctuary and illuminated the altar, my mistress sent me down the shaft of the Nilometer. I had not reached the bottom step before I found myself ankle-deep in water.

Hapi had listened to our prayers. Although it was weeks early, the Nile had begun to rise.

The very day after the waters began to rise, one of our fast scouting galleys that Tanus had left to watch the movements of the Hyksos cohorts came speeding up-river on the wings of the north wind. The Hyksos were on the march again. They would be in Elephantine within the week.

Lord Tanus left immediately with his main force to prepare for the defence of the cataracts, leaving Lord Merkeset and myself to see to the embarkation of our people. I was able to prise Lord Merkeset off the belly of his young wife just long enough for him to sign the orders which I had prepared for him so meticulously. This time we were able to avoid the chaos and panic that had overtaken us at Thebes, and the fleet prepared to sail for the tail of the cataracts in good order.

Fifty thousand Egyptians lined both banks of the river, weeping and singing psalms to Hapi and waving palm-fronds in farewell as we sailed away. Queen Lostris stood in the bows of the *Breath of Horus* with the little prince at her side, and both of them waved to the crowds on the bank as they passed slowly up-river. At twenty-one years of age, my mistress was at the zenith of her beauty. Those who gazed upon her were struck with an almost religious awe. That beauty was echoed in the face of the child at her side, who held the crook and the flail of Egypt in his small, determined hands.

'We will return,' my mistress called to them, and the prince echoed her, 'We will return. Wait for us. We will return.'

The legend that would sustain our blighted and

159

oppressed land through its darkest times was born that day on the banks of the mother river.

 When we reached the tail of the cataract the following noon, the rock-studded gorge had been transformed into a smooth green chute of rushing waters. In places it tumbled and growled in white water and froth, but it had not yet unleashed its full and terrible power.

This was the moment in the life-cycle of the river most favourable to our enterprise. The waters were high enough to allow our ships through without grounding in the shallows, but the flood was not yet so wild and headstrong as to hurl them back and dash them to driftwood on the granite steps of the cataract.

Tanus himself managed the ships, while Hui and I, under the nominal command of Lord Merkeset, managed the shore party. I placed the jovial old man, with a large jar of the very best wine on his one hand and his pretty little sixteen-year-old wife on the other, under a thatched shelter on the high ground above the gorge. I ignored the garbled and contradictory orders that the noble lord sent down to me from time to time over the ensuing days, and we got on with the business of the transit of the first cataract.

The heaviest linen lines were laid out upon the bank, and our horses were harnessed in teams of ten. We found out quickly enough that we were able to bring forward ten teams at a time—one hundred horses—and couple them to the main ropes. Any greater numbers were unmanageable.

In addition to the horses, we had almost two thousand men upon the secondary ropes and the guide-lines. Horses and men were changed every hour so that the teams were always fresh. At every dangerous turn and twist of the river, we stationed other parties upon the bank, and on the exposed granite islands. These were all armed with long poles to fend the hulls off the rocks as they were dragged through.

Our men had been born on the river-banks and understood their boats and the moods of the Nile better than they did their own wives'. Tanus and I arranged a system of horn signals between the ships and the shore party that functioned more smoothly even than I had hoped.

On board the vessels, the sailors were also armed with poles to punt themselves forward and to fend off the bows. They sang the ancient river shanties as they worked, and the *Breath of Horus* was the first to make the attempt. The sound of song and the cries of the horse-handlers mingled with the muted thunder of the Nile waters as we hauled her forward and she thrust her bows into the first chute of smoothly racing waters.

The green waters piled up against her bows, but their thrust was unable to overcome our determination and the strength of two thousand men and one hundred straining horses. We dragged the *Breath of Horus* up the first rapid, and we cheered when she glided into the deep green pool at the head.

But there were six miles still to go. We changed the men and horses and dragged her bows into the next tumbling, swirling stretch of broken water in

161

which the rocks stood like the heads of gigantic hippopotami ready to rip out her frail timbers with fangs of granite. There were six miles of these hellish rapids to negotiate, with death and disaster swirling around every rock. But the ropes held, and the men and the horses plodded on and upwards in relays.

My mistress walked along the bank beside the teams of sweating men. She looked as fresh and cool as a flower, even in the baking sunlight, and her laughter and banter gave them fresh purpose. She sang the working songs with them, and I joined with her in the chorus. We made up fresh words as we went along. The men laughed at the saucy couplets and hauled on the ropes with renewed strength.

Prince Memnon rode on the back of Blade, in the leading team of horses. Hui had tied a rope around the horse's chest behind the front legs to give him a hand-hold, because Memnon's legs were still too short to afford him a firm grip, and stuck out at an undignified angle on each side of Blade's broad back. The prince waved back proudly at his father on the poop-deck of the galley.

When at last we broke out into the deep, unruffled flow of the main river above the rapids, the working chant of the boatmen turned to a hymn of praise to Hapi, who had seen us through.

Once my mistress had gone back on board the galley, she called for the master mason. She ordered him to cut an obelisk from the granite massif that hemmed in the gorge. While we laboured to bring the rest of the fleet through the gorge, the masons worked with fire and chisel to

162

lift a long, slender column of mottled stone from the mother lode. When they had freed it from the matrix, they chiselled the words that my mistress dictated to them, using the pharaonic hieroglyphics in which her name and that of the prince were enclosed in the royal cartouche.

As we proceeded with the transit of the cataract, we became more expert with each pace we gained against the river.

It had taken us a full day to bring the *Breath of Horus* up the rapids. Within the following week we were making the transit in half that time, and we had five or six vessels in the gorge simultaneously. It was almost a royal procession with one galley coming up behind the other, stem to stern. Ten thousand men and nearly a thousand horses were in the traces at any one time.

There were over a hundred vessels moored along the bank in the quiet, deep green reach of the Nile above the rapids, when the Hyksos fell upon us once more.

King Salitis had been delayed by his sack and plunder of the city of Elephantine, and he had not realized immediately that we had continued on up-river with the great bulk of Pharaoh's treasure in the holds of our galleys. Everything that he knew about the river, all that his spies and Lord Intef had been able to tell him, had convinced him that the cataracts were a barrier that could not be navigated. He had wasted all that time in the city of Elephantine before setting after us again.

He had ransacked the city and the palace on the island; he had paid informers and tortured captives in an attempt to learn what had become of the treasure and the prince. The citizens of Elephantine had served their prince well. They had held out against the Hyksos in order to give our flotilla a chance to complete the transit.

Of course, it could not last indefinitely, and at last some poor soul broke under the torture of the tyrant. King Salitis harnessed up his horses yet again and came storming after us into the gorge of the cataract.

However, Tanus was well prepared to meet him. Under his command, Kratas and Remrem and Astes had made their dispositions with care. Every single man who could be spared from the work of hauling the ships through the gorge was sent back to help defend it.

The terrain was our greatest ally. The gorge was steep and rocky. The path along the bank was narrow and twisted with the broken ground crowding down upon it. At every turn of the river there rose high bluffs and cave-riddled cliffs, each of them a natural fortress for us to exploit.

In the confines of the gorge the chariots were unable to manoeuvre. They were unable to leave the river and make a detour around the gorge through the open desert. There was neither water nor fodder for their horses out there in the sandy wastes, and the going was soft and treacherous. Their heavy chariots would have bogged down and been lost in the trackless desert, before they could reach the river again. There was no alternative for them, they were forced to come at us in single file along the narrow river-bank.

164

On the other hand, Kratas had been given ample grace in which to improve the natural defences of the ground by building stone walls in the most readily defensible places. He positioned his archers in the cliffs above these obstacles, and set up man-made rock-slides on the high ground overlooking the pathway.

As the Hyksos vanguard came up the gorge, they were met with a downpour of arrows from stone-walled redoubts on the high ground above them. Then, when they dismounted from their chariots and went forward to clear the stone barriers that had been placed across the track, Kratas yelled the order and the wedges were knocked from under the rock-slides balanced on the lip of the precipice.

The landslides came tumbling and rolling down upon the Hyksos, sweeping men and horses and chariots off the bank into the surging green waters of the Nile. Standing on the top of the cliff with Kratas, I watched their heads go bobbing and spinning through the cascades, and heard their faint and desperate cries echoing from the cliffs, before the weight of their armour pulled them below the surface and the river overwhelmed them.

King Salitis was tenacious. He sent still more of his legions forward to clear the pathway, and others to climb up the cliffs and dislodge our troops from the heights. The Hyksos' losses in men and horses were frightful, while we were almost unscathed. When they laboured up the cliffs in their heavy bronze armour, we rained our arrows down upon them. Then, before they could reach our positions, Kratas ordered our men to fall back to the next prepared strongpoint.

There could be only one outcome to this one-sided encounter. Before he had fought his way halfway up the gorge, King Salitis was forced to abandon the pursuit.

Tanus and my mistress were with us on the cliff-tops when the Hyksos began their retreat back down the gorge. They left the path strewn with the wreckage of their chariots and cluttered with abandoned equipment and the detritus of their defeat.

'Sound the trumpets!' Tanus gave the order, and the gorge echoed to the mocking fanfare that he sent after the retreating Hyksos legions. The last chariot in that sorry cavalcade was the gilded and embossed vehicle of the king himself. Even from our perch on top of the precipice, we could recognize the tall and savage figure of Salitis, with his high bronze helmet and his black beard flowing back over his shoulders. He raised his bow, that he held in his right hand, and shook it at us. His face was contorted with frustration and rage.

We watched him out of sight. Then Tanus sent our scouts after them to follow them back to Elephantine, in case this was a ruse, a false withdrawal. In my heart I knew that Salitis would not come after us again. Hapi had fulfilled her promise, and offered us her protection once more.

Then we turned, and followed the pathway made by the wild goats along the precipice, back to where the flotilla was moored.

The masons had finished work on the obelisk. It was a shaft of solid granite three times the height of a man. I had marked out the proportions and the shape of it upon the mother rock before the masons had made their first cut. Because of this, the lines of the monument were so elegant and pleasing that it appeared to be much taller, once it was set on the summit of the bluff above the last wild stretch of the cataract, overlooking the scene of our triumph.

All our people gathered below it, as Queen Lostris dedicated the stone to the goddess of the river. She read aloud the inscription that the masons had engraved upon the polished stone.

I, Queen Lostris, Regent of Egypt and widow of Pharaoh Mamose, the eighth of that name, mother of the Crown Prince Memnon, who shall rule the two kingdoms after me, have ordained the raising of this monument.

This is the mark and covenant of my vow to the people of this very Egypt, that I shall return to them from the wilderness whence I have been driven by the barbarian.

This stone was placed here in the first year of my rule, the nine-hundredth year after the building of the great pyramid of Pharaoh Cheops.

Let this stone stand immovable as the pyramid until I make good my promise to return.

Then, in sight of all the people, she placed the

Gold of Valour upon the shoulders of Tanus and Kratas and Remrem and Astes, all those heroes who had made possible the transit of the cataract.

Then, last of all, she called me to her, and as I knelt at her feet, she whispered so I alone might hear, 'How could I forget you, my dear and faithful Taita? We could never have come this far without your help,' she touched my cheek lightly, 'and I know how dearly you love these pretty baubles.' And she placed around my neck the heavy Gold of Praise. I weighed it later at thirty deben, five deben heavier than the chain that Pharaoh had bestowed upon me.

On the way back down the side of the gorge, I walked beside my mistress to hold the sun-shade of ostrich feathers over her head, and she smiled at me more than once. Each smile was more precious to me than the heavy chain upon my shoulders.

The following morning we went back on board the *Breath of Horus* and turned our bows once more towards the south. The long voyage had begun.

 We found that the river had changed its mien and character. It was no longer the broad and serene presence that had comforted and sustained us all our lives. This was a sterner, wilder being. There was little gentleness and compassion in its spirit. It was narrower and deeper. The land on each side of it was steeper and more rugged, and the gorges and nullahs were crudely gouged from the harsh earth. The brooding and darkling cliffs frowned down upon us with furrowed brows.

In some places the bottom lands along the banks narrowed down so that the horses and cattle and sheep had to pass in single file along the crude track that the wild goats had trodden between the cliffs and the water. In other places the track disappeared completely, as the bluffs and the cliffs pushed boldly into the flood of the Nile. Then there was no way forward for our herds. Hui was forced to drive them into the river and swim them across the green expanse of water to the far bank, where the cliffs had retreated and left the way open for them to pass.

As the weeks wore on, we saw little sign of any human presence. Once, our scouts found the worm-eaten hull of a crude dugout canoe washed up on a sand-bank, and upon the bottom land an abandoned cluster of huts. The sagging roofs were thatched with reeds and the sides were open. There were the remains of fish-smoking racks and the ashes of the fires, but that was all. Not a shard of pottery or a bead to hint at who these people might be.

We were anxious to make our first contact with the tribes of Cush, for we needed slaves. Our entire civilization was based on the keeping of slaves, and we had been able to bring very few of them with us from Egypt. Tanus sent his scouts far ahead of the fleet, so that we might have good warning of the first human habitations in ample time to organize our slave-catchers. I found no irony in the fact that I, a slave myself, spent so much of my time and thought in planning the taking of other slaves.

All wealth can be counted in four commodities, land and gold and slaves and ivory. We believed that the land that lay ahead of us was rich in all of these. If we were to grow strong enough to return and drive the Hyksos from our very Egypt, then we must discover this wealth in the unexplored land to which we were sailing.

Queen Lostris sent out her gold-finders into the hills along the river as we passed. They climbed up through the gorges and the dry nullahs, scratching and digging in every likely spot, chipping fragments off the exposed reefs of quartz and schist, crushing these to powder, and washing away the dross in a shallow clay dish, hoping always to see the gleaming precious tail remaining in the bottom of the dish.

The royal huntsmen went out with them to search for game with which to feed our multitudes. They searched also for the first sign of those great grey beasts who carry the precious teeth of ivory in their monstrous heads. I made vigorous enquiry through the fleet for any man who had ever seen one of these elephant alive, or even dead. Though their teeth were a commonplace throughout the civilized world, there was not a single man who could help me in my enquiries. I felt a strange and unaccountable excitement at the thought of our first encounter with these fabulous beasts.

There was a host of other creatures inhabiting this wild land, some of them familiar to us and many that were strange and new.

Wherever reeds grew upon the river-bank, we found herds of hippopotami lying like rounded granite boulders in the shallows. After long and erudite theological debate, it was still uncertain whether these beasts above the cataract belonged to the goddess, as did those below, or whether they were royal game belonging to the crown. The priests of Hapi were strongly of one persuasion, and the rest of us, with an appetite for the rich fat and tender flesh of these animals, were of the opposite opinion.

It was entirely by coincidence that at this point the goddess Hapi chose to appear to me in one of my celebrated dreams. I saw her rise from the green waters, smiling beneficently, and place in my mistress's hand a tiny hippopotamus no bigger than a wild partridge. As soon as I awoke, I lost no time in relaying the substance of this weird and thrilling dream to the regent. By now my dreams and divination were accepted by my mistress, and therefore by the rest of our company, as the manifest will and law of the gods.

That evening we all feasted on luscious river-cow steaks grilled on the open coals on the sand-bank against which the ships had moored. My reputation and popularity, which were already high throughout the fleet, were much enhanced by this dream. The priests of Hapi alone were not carried along by the general warmth of feeling towards me.

The river teemed with fish. Below the cataract, our people had fished the river for a thousand years and longer. These waters were untouched by man or his nets. We drew from the river shining blue perch heavier than the fattest man in our company, and there were huge catfish, with barbellate whiskers as long as my arm, that were too strong and weighty to be captured in the nets. With a flick of their great tails they ripped the linen threads as though they were the fragile webs of spiders. Our men hunted them in the shallows with spears, as

171

though they were river-cows. One of these giants could feed fifty men with rich yellow flesh that dripped fat into the cooking-fires.

In the cliffs above the river hung the nests of eagles and vultures. From below they appeared like masses of driftwood, and the droppings of the huge birds painted the rocks beneath them with streaks of shining white. The birds floated above us on wide pinions, circling and swaying on the heated air that rose from the black rocks of the gorge.

From the heights, flocks of wild goats watched us pass with regal and disdainful mien. Tanus went out to hunt them on their airy crags, but it was many weeks before he succeeded in bringing back one of these trophies. They had the eyesight of vultures and the agility of the blue-headed rock lizards that could run effortlessly up a vertical wall of granite.

One of these old rams stood as tall as a man's shoulder. His beard flowed from his chin and throat to sweep the rock on which he posed. His horns curled upon themselves from mighty crenellated bases. When Tanus finally brought him down, it was with an arrow shot across a gorge a hundred paces deep, from peak to pinnacle of these rugged hills. The goat dropped into the gulf and twisted over and over in the air before it hit the rocks below.

Because of my passionate interest in all wild things, after he had skinned out and butchered the carcass, Tanus carried the head and the horns home for me. It took all his vast strength to bring down such a burden from those murderous crags. I cleaned and bleached the skull and set it up on the bows of our galley as a figurehead, as we sailed on into the unknown.

 The months passed, and below our keels the river began to dwindle away as the inundation abated. As we passed the sheer headlands, we could see the height of the river measured upon the cliff where all the previous inundations had left their watermarks.

At night Memnon and I sat up on deck as late as his mother would allow us, and together we studied the stars that illuminated the firmament of the sky with a milky radiance. I taught him the name and the nature of each of these fiery points of light and how they affected the destiny of every man born under them. By watching the heavenly bodies, I was able to determine that the river was no longer taking us directly into the south, but that we were veering towards the west. These observations stirred up another heated controversy amongst the scholars and the wise men of our company.

'The river is taking us directly to the western fields of paradise,' suggested the priests of Osiris and Ammon-Ra. 'It is a ruse of Seth. He wishes to confuse and confound us,' argued the priests of Hapi, who up until now had exerted undue influence over our councils. Queen Lostris was a child of their goddess, and it had been generally accepted by most of us that Hapi was the patron of our expedition. The priests were angry to see their position weakened by this wayward perambulation of the river. 'Soon the river will turn south once more,' they promised. It always appalls me to watch how unscrupulous men manipulate the wishes of the gods to coincide with their own.

Before the matter could be resolved, we came to the second cataract.

This was as far as any civilized man had ever ventured, and not one of them had reached further. When we scouted and surveyed the cataract, the reason for this was abundantly evident. These rapids were more extensive and formidable than those we had already negotiated.

Over a vast area, the stream of the Nile was split by several massive islands and hundreds of smaller ones. It was low-water now, and at most places the bed of the river was exposed. A maze of rock-strewn canals and branches extended for miles ahead of us. We were awed by the grandeur and menace of it.

'How do we know that there is not another cataract, and then another, guarding the river?' those who were easily discouraged asked each other. 'We will expend our strength and in the end find ourselves trapped between the rapids without the strength to advance or retreat. We should turn back now, before it is too late,' they agreed amongst themselves.

'We will go on,' decreed my mistress. 'Those who wish to turn back now, are free to do so. However, there will be no vessels to carry them nor horses to draw them. They will return on their own, and I am certain the Hyksos will bid them a hearty welcome.'

There were none who accepted her magnanimous offer. Instead, they went ashore on the fertile islands that choked the course of the river.

The spray from the rapids during the flood, and the water filtering up through the soil during low ebb, had transformed these islands into verdant forests, in stark contrast to the dry and terrible deserts on either bank. Springing from seeds brought down by the waters from the ends of the earth, tall trees, of a kind that none of us had ever seen before, grew on the silt that Mother Nile had piled up on the granite foundation of the islands.

We could not attempt a transit of these rapids until the Nile brought down her next inundation and gave us sufficient depth of water for our galleys. That was still many months away.

Our farmers went ashore and cleared land to plant the seeds that we had brought with us. Within days the seed had sprouted, and in the hot sunlight the plants seemed to grow taller under our eyes. Within a few short months the dhurra corn was ready to be harvested, and we were gorging on the sweet fruits and vegetables that we had missed so much since leaving Egypt. The muttering amongst our people died away.

In fact these islands were so attractive, and the soil so fertile, that some of our people began to talk about settling here permanently. A delegation from the priests of Ammon-Ra went to the queen and asked for her permission to erect a temple to the god on one of the islands. My mistress replied, 'We are travellers here. In the end we will return to Egypt. That is my vow and promise to all my people. We will build no temples or other permanent habitation. Until we return to Egypt we will live as the Bedouin, in tents and huts.'

I now had at my disposal the timber from those trees we had felled upon the islands. I was able to experiment with these and to explore their various properties.

There was an acacia whose wood was resilient and strong. It made the finest spokes for my chariot wheels of any material which I had so far tested. I put my carpenters and weavers to work on reassembling the chariots that we had brought with us, and building new ones from the woods and bamboos that grew on the islands.

The flat bottom lands were several miles wide on the left bank below the cataract. Soon our squadrons of chariots were training and exercising upon these smooth and open plains once more. The spokes of the wheels still broke under hard driving, but not as frequently as they once had. I was able to entice Tanus back on to the footplate; however, he would not ride with any driver but myself.

At the same time, I was able to complete the first successful recurved bow upon which I had been working since we had left Elephantine. It was made from the same composite materials as was Lanata, wood and ivory and horn. However, the shape was different. When it was unstrung, the upper and lower limbs were curved out and away from the archer. It was only when the weapon was strung that they were forced back into the familiar bow shape, but the tension in the stock and the string was multiplied out of all proportion to the much shorter length of the bow.

176

At my gentle insistence, Tanus finally agreed to shoot the bow at a series of targets that I had erected upon the east bank. After he had shot twenty arrows he said little, but I could see that he was astonished by the range and accuracy of it. I knew my Tanus so well. He was a conservative and a reactionary to the marrow of his bones. Lanata was his first love, both the woman and the bow. I knew it would be a wrench for him to acknowledge a new love, so I did not pester him for an opinion, but let him come to it in his own time.

It was then that our scouts came in to report a migration of oryx from out of the desert. We had seen several small herds of these magnificent animals since we had passed the first cataract. Usually they were grazing upon the river-bank, but they fled back into the desert as our ships sailed towards them. What our scouts reported now was a massive movement of these animals such as took place only very occasionally. I had witnessed it just once before. With the freak occurrence of a thunderstorm in the desert fastnesses once in twenty years or so, the flush of green grass that sprang from the wet earth would attract the scattered herds of oryx from hundreds of miles around.

As they moved towards the fresh grazing grounds, the herds amalgamated into one massive movement of animals across the desert. This was happening now, and it offered us the chance of a change of diet and the opportunity to run our chariots in earnest.

For the first time, Tanus showed a real interest in my chariots, now that there was game to pursue with them. As he took his place on the footplate of my vehicle, I noticed that it was the new recurved bow that he hung on the rack, and not his faithful old Lanata. I said not a word, but shook up the horses and headed them towards the gap in the hills that offered us a route out of the narrow valley of the Nile and gave access to the open desert.

We were fifty chariots in the squadron, followed by a dozen heavy carts with solid wheels that carried sufficient fodder and water for five days. We trotted in column of route, two vehicles abreast, and with three lengths between the files. This had already become our standard travelling formation.

To keep down the weight, we were stripped to loin-cloths, and all our men were in superb physical condition from long months of work on the rowing-benches of the galleys. Their muscled torsos were all freshly oiled and gleamed in the sunlight, like the bodies of young gods. Each chariot carried its brightly coloured recognition pennant on a long, whippy bamboo rod. We made a brave show as we came up the goat track through the hills. When I looked back down the column, even I, who never was a soldier, was affected by the spectacle.

I did not clearly recognize the truth then, but the Hyksos and the exodus had forced a new military spirit upon the nation. We had been a race of scholars and traders and priests, but now, with the determination of Queen Lostris to expel the tyrant, and led by Lord Tanus, we were fast becoming a warlike people.

As we led the column over the crest of the hills, and the open desert lay ahead of us, a small figure stepped out from behind the last pile of rocks where it had been lying in ambush.

'Whoa!' I reined down the horses. 'What are you doing out here so far from the ships?'

I had not seen the prince since the previous evening, and had believed that he was safe with his nursemaids. To come across him here on the edge of the desert was a shock, and my tone was outraged. At that time he was not quite six years of age, but he had his toy bow over his shoulder and a determined expression on his face that mirrored that of his father, when Tanus was in one of his most intractable moods.

'I am coming on the hunt with you,' said Memnon.

'No, you are not,' I contradicted him. 'I am sending you back to your mother this very instant. She will know how to deal with small boys who sneak out of the camp without telling their tutors where they are going.'

'I am the crown prince of Egypt,' declared Memnon, but his lip trembled despite this weighty declaration. 'No man durst forbid me. It is my right and my sacred duty to lead my people in time of need.'

We had now moved on to dangerous ground. The prince knew his rights and his responsibilities. It was I who had taught them to him. However, in all truth, I had not expected him to exercise them so soon. He had made it an affair of royal protocol, and it was difficult, even impossible, to argue with him. Desperately I sought for an escape.

'Why did you not ask me before?' I was merely bidding for time.

'Because you would have gone to my mother,' he said with simple honesty, 'and she would have supported you, as she always does.'

'I can still go to the queen,' I threatened, but he looked back into the valley where the ships were small as toys, and he grinned at me. We both knew that I could not order the entire squadron to drive all that way back.

'Please let me come with you, Tata,' he changed his tune. The little devil was attacking me on all fronts. I found it impossible to resist him when he exerted all his charm. Then I was struck with inspiration. 'Lord Harrab is the commander of this expedition. You must ask him.'

The relationship between these two was a strange one. Only three of us—the two parents and myself—were aware of Memnon's true paternity. The prince himself thought of Tanus as his tutor and the commander of his armies. Although he had come to love Tanus, he still held him in considerable awe. Tanus was not the type of man that a small boy, even a prince, would trifle with.

The two of them looked at each other now. I could see Memnon was pondering his best plan of attack, while I could feel Tanus trembling with the effort of holding back his laughter.

'Lord Harrab,' Memnon had decided on the formal approach, 'I wish to come with you. I think it will be a very useful lesson for me. After all, one day I will have to lead the army.' I had taught him logic and dialectic. He was a student to be proud of.

'Prince Memnon, are you giving me an order?' Tanus managed to cover his amusement with a horrific scowl, and I saw tears begin to well up in the prince's eyes.

He shook his head miserably. 'No, my lord.' He

was a small boy once more. 'But I would very much like to come hunting with you, please.'

'The queen will have me strangled,' said Tanus, 'but hop up here in front of me, you little ruffian.'

The prince loved Tanus to call him a ruffian. It was a term that he usually reserved for the men of his old Blues regiment, and it made Memnon feel that he was one of them. He let out a yelp of glee and almost tripped over his own feet in his haste to obey. Tanus reached down and caught his arm. He swung him up and placed him securely between us on the footplate.

'Hi up!' Memnon shouted to Patience and Blade, and we drove out into the open desert, but not before I had sent a messenger back to the fleet with a message for the queen to tell her that the prince was safe. No lioness could be as fierce as my mistress in the care of its cub.

When we struck the migration road, it was a broad swathe of churned sand many hundreds of yards wide. The hooves of the oryx are broad and splayed to cover the soft desert sands. They leave a distinctive track, the shape of a Hyksos spear-head. Many thousands of the huge antelope had passed this way.

'When?' Tanus asked, and I dismounted to examine the trail. I took Memnon down with me, for I never missed an opportunity to instruct him. I showed him how the night breeze had eroded the spoor, and how small insects and lizards had superimposed their own tracks over those of the herd.

'They passed here yesterday evening at sunset,' I gave my opinion, and had it endorsed by the prince. 'But they are travelling slowly. With luck we can catch them before noon.'

We waited for the wagons to come up. We watered the horses, and then went on, following the broad trodden road through the dunes.

Soon we found the carcasses of the weaker animals that had succumbed. They were the very young and the oldest, and now the crows and the vultures squawked and squabbled over their remains, while the little red jackals slunk around the fringes, hoping for a mouthful.

We followed the broad road until at last we saw the thin filtering of dust upon the southern horizon, and we quickened our pace. When we topped a line of rugged hills whose crests danced in the heat-mirage, we saw the herds spread out below us. We had reached the area where the thunderstorm had broken weeks before. As far ahead as we could see, the desert had been transformed into a garden of flowers.

The last rains might have fallen here a hundred years ago. It seemed impossible, but the seeds of that harvest had lain sleeping all that time. They had been burned and desiccated by sun and desert wind, while they waited for the rains to come once again. For any who doubted the existence of the gods, this miracle was proof. For any man who doubted that life was eternal, this held out the promise of immortality. If the flowers could survive thus, then surely the soul of man, which is infinitely more wonderful and valuable, must also live for ever.

The landscape below us was painted with shades of soft greens, the contours and the outlines of the hills were picked out with sweeps of darker green. This formed a background to the wonderful rainbow of colour that lit the earth. The flowers grew in banks and drifts. The blooms of each variety seemed to seek the company of their own kind, as do the herds of antelope and the flocks of birds. The orange-coloured daisies grew in pools and lakes together, those with white petals frosted entire hillsides. There were fields of blue gladiolus, scarlet lilies and yellow ericas.

Even the wiry brush plants in the gorges and nullahs, that had seemed seared and dried as mummies of men dead a thousand years, were now decked in fresh robes of green, with wreaths of yellow blooms crowning their ancient blasted heads. Lovely as it now was, I knew that it was ephemeral. Another month and the desert would triumph again. The flowers would wither on the stem, and the grass would turn to dust and blow away on the furnace blasts of the winds. Nothing would remain of this splendour except the seeds, tiny as grains of sand, waiting out the years with a monumental patience.

'Such beauty should be shared with the one you love,' Tanus breathed in awe. 'Would that the queen were with me now!'

That Tanus had been so moved by it proved the glory of the spectacle. He was a soldier and a hunter, but for once he gave no thought to the quarry, but gazed upon the spectacle with a religious awe.

It was a shout from Kratas in one of the following chariots that roused us from this reverie of beauty. 'By Seth's stinking breath, there must be ten thousand of them down there.'

The oryx were spread out to the green silhouette of the farther hills. Some of the old bulls were

183

solitary, keeping all others away, but the rest of them were in herds of ten or a hundred, and some of the herds were beyond count. They were merely huge tawny stains, like cloud shadow upon the plains. It seemed to me that every oryx in all of Africa was gathered here.

We watered the horses again before the hunt began. This gave me a chance to go forward and to gaze down upon this great concourse of living things. Of course, I took Memnon with me, but when I tried to lead him by the hand he disentangled his fingers from my grip. 'Don't hold my hand in front of the men, Tata,' he told me solemnly. 'They will think I am still a baby.'

As we stood on the sky-line, the nearest animals raised their heads and regarded us with mild curiosity. It occurred to me that they had probably never before seen a human being, and that they detected no danger in our presence.

The oryx is a magnificent creature, standing as tall as a horse, with the same full, flowing, dark tail that sweeps the ground. Its face is painted with intricate whorls and slashes of black upon a pale, sand-coloured mask. A stiff, dark mane runs down the neck, enhancing the horse-like appearance, but its horns are like those of no other animal created by the gods. They are slim and straight and tipped like the dagger on my belt. Almost as long as the animal that bears them is tall, they are formidable weapons. Whereas all other antelope are meek and inoffensive, preferring flight to aggression, the oryx will defend itself even against the attack of the lion.

I told Memnon of their courage and their powers of endurance, and explained how they could live their entire lives without drinking water from pool or river. 'They take their water from the dew, and from the desert roots and tubers which they dig out of the earth with their hooves.'

He listened avidly, for he had inherited the love of the chase in his father's blood, and I had taught him to revere all wild things.

'The true huntsman understands and respects the birds and the animals that he hunts,' I told him, and he nodded seriously.

'I want to be a true huntsman and a soldier, just like Lord Tanus.'

'A man is not born with such gifts. He must learn them, in the same way that you must learn to be a great and just ruler.'

I felt a pang of regret when Tanus called to me that the horses were watered, and I looked back to see the charioteers mounting up. I would have preferred to spend the rest of that day with my prince watching the royal show upon the plains below me. I went back reluctantly to take up the reins and to drive our chariot back to the head of the column.

On the footplates of the other chariots, the archers had their bows strung, and the fever of the hunt gripped every man. They were like hounds on a short leash with the scent in their nostrils.

'Ho, Lord Tanus!' Kratas shouted across to us. 'A wager on the outcome?'

Before Tanus could reply, I murmured, 'Take one for me. The old braggart has never shot from the back of a flying chariot.'

'Clean kills only,' Tanus called back to him. 'Any animal with another man's arrow in it, not to count.' Every archer marked the shaft of his arrow with his own motif, so that he might claim it later.

Tanus' mark was the Wadjet, the wounded Eye of Horus. 'One gold deben for each oryx with your arrow in it.'

'Make it two,' I suggested. 'One for me.' I am not a gambling man, but this was not a gamble. Tanus had his new recurved bow, and I was the best charioteer in the whole of our army.

We were still novices, but I had studied the Hyksos' use of the chariot. Every evolution that their squadrons had performed on that terrible day on the plain of Abnub was graven on my memory. To me this was not merely a hunt for meat and sport, but practice and training for the much greater game of war. We had to learn to run our formations to the very best advantage and to control them in the full flight and confusion of battle, while circumstances changed with every movement of the enemy, and every chance and hazard of war.

As we trotted down on to the plain, I gave the first signal, and the column split into three files. Smoothly we opened up like the petals of a lily. The flankers curled out like the horns of a bull to surround the quarry, while my column in the centre deployed into line abreast, with three chariot lengths between our wheel-hubs. We were the chest of the bull. The horns would hold the enemy while we came up and crushed him in our savage embrace.

Ahead of us, the scattered herds of gazelle threw up their heads and gazed at us with the first stirring of alarm. They began to drift away, gathering up their fellows as they passed, small herds combining into larger, the way that a single boulder rolling down the slope will bring down the landslide. Soon

186

the entire plain was alive with moving oryx. They cantered with a peculiar rocking motion, and dust rose in a pale mist and hung over their swaying backs. Their long, dark tails swished from side to side.

I held my own squadron down to a walk. I did not want to tire the horses too soon with a long, stern chase. I was watching the denser, taller dust-clouds thrown up by the two flanking columns circling swiftly out on each side of the herd.

At last they came together far ahead, and the ring was closed. The herds of oryx slowed down as they found their escape-route blocked. They began to mill in confusion as those in the lead turned back and ran into the ranks that followed.

Obedient to my orders, once the flanking columns had completed the encircling movement, they also slowed to an easy walk, and turned in towards the centre of the circle. We had the huge herd of oryx in our fist, and slowly we closed our grip upon them. Most of the bewildered animals came to a halt, uncertain in which direction to run. Every way they gazed, they saw the lines of chariots bearing down upon them.

Closer we came, at a steady walk, and our horses were still fresh and eager to run. They had sensed the excitement, and threw their heads, fighting with the traces, snorting and rolling their eyes until the whites showed. The oryx herd began to move again, but in no definite direction. They milled upon themselves, making uncertain dashes in one direction before coming up short and then swinging around and rushing back again.

I was pleased with the control and discipline of

187

our squadrons. They held their formations rigidly, without bunching up and leaving gaps in the ranks. The signals that I gave were repeated down the line and acted upon instantly. We were at last becoming an army. Soon we would be able to meet any foe on favourable terms, even the Hyksos veterans who had spent their entire lives on the footplate of a chariot.

I reached behind me and took Prince Memnon by the arm. I drew him forward and placed him against the dashboard. I wedged him there with my own body, and he gripped the front panel. Now Tanus had both hands free to shoot his bow, and the prince was safe.

'Let me take the reins, Tata. I will drive,' Memnon pleaded. I had let him drive before, so he meant it seriously, though he was barely tall enough to see over the dashboard. I dared not laugh at him, for he took himself very seriously.

'Next time, Mem. This time just watch and learn.'

At last we were less than a hundred paces from the nearest oryx, the pressure was too great for them to tolerate. Led by one scarred old cow, a hundred of them charged straight at our line in a mass. At my signal we shortened our line until we were running hub to hub, a solid wall of horses and men, and the trumpeters sounded the charge. I lashed my team into a full gallop and we raced headlong to meet them.

Tanus was firing past my right shoulder. I could watch each of his arrows fly out across the closing gap. This was the first time he had shot from a running chariot, and his first three arrows flew wide of the mark, as the chariot careered into the herd of racing oryx. But he was a master archer, and he adjusted his aim swiftly. His next arrow took the old cow, who was still leading the charge, full in the chest. It must have split her heart, for she went down, nose into the sand, and rolled over her own head. The animals following her swerved out on either side of her, offering Tanus broadside targets. It was fascinating to watch his next two arrows curl away and fall behind the racing oryx.

The temptation is always to shoot directly at a running target, and not at the place in the empty air ahead of it, where it will be when the arrow reaches it. This calculation of forward aim is further complicated by the movement of the chariot in relation to the target. I was trying to give him the easiest shot by turning the chariot with the run of the game. All the same, I was not surprised when two more of Tanus' arrows missed behind the target.

Then, like the master of the bow that he is, he adjusted his aim, and the following arrow plunged feathers-deep into the chest of the next oryx. He killed three more with three arrows, while all around us the hunt disintegrated into the wild confusion of battle, and dust obscured all but the closest glimpses of running chariots and racing animals.

I was driving close behind a pair of oryx, overhauling them slowly, when the flying hooves of one of them threw up a chip of sharp flint the size of the last joint of my thumb. Before he could duck, it struck Memnon on the forehead, and when he looked up at me I saw the blood trickling from the shallow cut above his eye.

'You are hurt, Mem,' I cried, and started to rein

189

down the horses.

'It is nothing,' he told me, and used the corner of his shawl to mop the blood. 'Don't stop, Tata! Keep after them. Kratas will beat us, if you don't.'

So I drove on into the dust, and beside me Tanus' bow sang its awful song, and the prince yipped and yelped with excitement like a puppy the first time that it chases a rabbit.

Some of the oryx broke free of our lines and escaped into the open desert, while others were turned back into the trap. Men shouted with excitement and triumph, horses whinnied, and the oryx snorted and bellowed as the arrows slapped into them and brought them crashing down in a tangle of flying hooves and scimitar horns. All around us was the thunder of hooves and wheels, and we were immersed in the yellow fog of dust.

There is a limit to how long even the finest and most willing team of horses can be driven at full gallop. When finally I reined Patience and Blade down to a walk, the dust had caked like mud in the sweat that lathered their flanks, and they hung their heads with exhaustion.

Slowly, the dust-clouds that had obscured the field drifted aside and dissipated. The field was a terrible sight.

Our squadron was scattered over the entire plain. I counted five chariots whose wheels had shattered during the chase, and the up-ended vehicles looked like the broken toys of a petulant giant. The injured men lay on the sandy earth beside their shattered chariots, with their comrades kneeling over them as they tended their wounds.

Even those chariots that had survived undamaged were halted. The horses were blown and exhausted. Their flanks heaved as they strained for breath, and the white froth dripped from their muzzles. Each one of them was soaked with sweat, as though it had swum across the river.

The game was scattered upon the field in the same disorder and lack of purpose or design. Many of the great beasts were dead, and their carcasses lay stretched out on their sides. Many others were crippled and maimed. Some stood with their heads hanging. Others limped away through the dunes with slow and halting gait. Each arrow-shaft left a dark stain of wet blood upon the pale, roan-coloured hide.

This was the pitiful end to every hunt, when the heat and excitement have cooled and the wounded game has to be gathered up and put out of its misery.

Near us I saw one old bull oryx sitting on his paralysed haunches with his front legs stiff in front of him. The arrow that had crippled him stood out so high from his back that I knew that the point had severed his spine. I took the second bow from the rack on the side-panel of our chariot, and I jumped down from the footplate to the ground. As I walked towards the crippled bull, he swung his head to watch me. Then he made one last courageous effort, and dragged his crippled back legs as he came at me. He slashed those long black horns at me, but his eyes swam with the tears of mortal agony. I was forced to drive two arrows deep into the cavity of his chest before he gave one last groan and rolled over on to his side, kicked once convulsively, and was still.

When I climbed back into the chariot, I glanced at the prince's face. His eyes were wet with tears

191

and his blood-smeared face was crumpled into an expression of pity for the oryx. He turned his face away from me, so that I could not see his tears, but I was proud of them. He who lacks compassion for the game he pursues is no true huntsman.

I took his curly head in my hands and turned his face back to me. Gently, I cleaned the wound on his forehead and bandaged it with a strip of linen.

We camped that night upon the plain of flowers, and their sweet perfume scented the darkness, and overlaid the smell of fresh-spilled blood.

There was no moon, but the stars filled the entire sky. The hills were bathed in their silver luminosity. We sat late at the camp-fires and feasted on the livers and hearts of oryx roasted on the coals. To begin with, the prince sat between Tanus and me at the fireside, but the officers and men vied for his attention. He had stolen all their hearts, and at their invitation he moved easily from one group to the next. They mended their language and banter to fit his ears, and the prince was at ease in their company.

They made a great fuss of his bandaged head. 'Now you are a real soldier,' they told him, 'just like one of us.' And they showed him their own scars.

'You did the right thing by allowing him to come with us,' I told Tanus, as we both watched him proudly. 'This is the best training any young cadet can ever have.'

'The men love him already,' Tanus agreed. 'There are two things that a general needs. One is luck and the other is the devotion of his troops.'

'Memnon must be allowed to go out with every expedition, just as long as it is not too dangerous,'

I decided, and Tanus chuckled.

'I leave you to convince his mother of that. There are some things that are beyond my powers of persuasion.'

On the other side of the camp-fire, Kratas was teaching Memnon the expurgated version of the lyrics of the regimental marching songs. The prince had a sweet, clear voice, and the men clapped the time, and came in on the chorus. They protested loudly and rudely when at last I tried to send Memnon to the bed I had prepared for him under the body of the chariot, and even Tanus supported them.

'Let the boy stay with us a little longer,' he ordered, and it was well after midnight when at last I was able to roll the prince in my sheepskin rug.

'Tata, will I ever be able to shoot the way that Lord Tanus does?' he asked sleepily.

'You will be one of the great generals of our very Egypt, and one day I will carve an account of your victories on obelisks of stone, so that all the world will know of them.'

He thought about that for a while and then sighed. 'When will you make me a real bow, not just a baby's toy?'

'As soon as you can draw it,' I promised.

'Thank you, Tata. I should like that.' And he went to sleep as suddenly as I would blow out the flame of a lamp.

We returned in triumph to the fleet, the wagons loaded with the salted and sun-dried meat of the oryx herd. I had expected my mistress to tax me severely for having abducted the prince. I had prepared my defence and was determined to place the blame squarely on the broader shoulders of Lord Harrab.

However, her censure was milder than I had anticipated. She told Memnon that he was a wicked child for having caused her worry, and then hugged him until he was in danger of suffocation. When she turned to me, I launched into a long explanation of Tanus' role in the affair, and the valuable training and experience that the prince had received, but she seemed to have dismissed the entire episode.

'When did you and I last go fishing together?' she asked. 'Fetch your fishing-spears, Taita. We will take one of the skiffs. Just the two of us on the river, the way we used to be in the old days.'

I knew that we would do little fishing. She wanted me alone on the water where we could not be overheard. Whatever was troubling her was of serious importance.

I paddled downstream on the shrunken and slow green waters until the bend of the river and the high rocky bluff hid us from the fleet. All my attempts at conversation had failed, so I put aside my paddle and took up my lute. I strummed and sang the tunes she loved best, and waited for her to speak.

At last she looked up at me, and her eyes were

filled with a strange mixture of joy and worry.

'Taita, I think I am going to have another baby.'

I can think of no reason why this statement should have surprised me so. After all, every night since we had left Elephantine, she and the commander of her army had been locked in secret conclave, while I kept guard at the door of her cabin. Nevertheless, I was so alarmed that my hand froze on the lute strings and the song died in my throat. It was some moments before I could regain my voice.

'My lady, did you use the infusion of herbs that I prepared for you?' I asked diffidently.

'At times I did, but at others I forgot.' She smiled shyly. 'Lord Tanus can be a very impatient man. Besides which, it is so unromantic to fiddle with pots and jars, when there are better and more urgent things waiting to be done.'

'Things like making babies who have no royal father to claim them.'

'It is rather serious, isn't it, Taita?'

I struck a chord on the lute while I framed a reply. 'Rather serious? Oh, I think that is the wrong word. If you give birth to a bastard, or if you take a husband, then you will be obliged to relinquish the regency. That is the custom and the law. Lord Merkeset would be the next in line as regent, but there will be covert warfare amongst all the nobility for the position. Without your protection as regent, the prince would be in great danger. We would be torn by internecine strife—' I broke off, and shuddered at the prospect of it.

'Tanus could become regent in my stead, and then I could marry him,' she suggested brightly.

'Don't think I have not thought of that before,' I

195

told her sombrely. 'It would be the solution to all our difficulties. But then there is Tanus.'

'If I ask him, he will do it gladly, I am sure of that,' she smiled with relief, 'and I will be his wife. We need no longer play these shams and subterfuges to be alone together.'

'I wish it were that easy. But Tanus will never agree. He cannot—'

'What is this silliness?' The first sparks of anger lit her eyes, and I hurried on.

'That night at Thebes, the night that Pharaoh sent men to arrest Tanus on charges of sedition, we tried to force Tanus to declare for the crown. Kratas and all his officers swore their support, and that of all the army. They wanted to march on the palace and place Tanus on the throne.'

'Why did Tanus not agree to this? He would have been a fine king, and it would have saved all of us so much heartache.'

'Tanus spurned their offer. He declared that he was not a traitor, and that he would never mount the throne of Egypt.'

'That was long ago. Things have all changed,' she cried with exasperation.

'No, they have not changed. Tanus swore an oath that day, and he called on the god Horus to witness it. He swore that he would never take the crown.'

'But it no longer counts. He can go back on that oath.'

'Would you go back on an oath that you had sworn in the sight of the god Horus?' I demanded, and she looked away and hung her head.

'Would you?' I insisted, and she shook her head reluctantly.

'No,' she whispered, 'I could not.'

'The same code of honour binds Tanus. You cannot call upon him to do what you dare not do yourself,' I explained gently. 'Of course, we can put it to him, but you and I both know what his reply must surely be.'

'There must be something that you can do?' She looked at me with that blind trust that angered me. Whenever she had run herself into the deepest danger, she simply turned to me and said, 'There must be something that you can do?'

'There is something, but you will not agree to it, any more than Tanus will agree to wear the crown.'

'If you care anything for me, you will not even suggest it.' She understood me immediately, and recoiled from me as though I had struck her. 'I would rather die myself than kill this miracle of love that Tanus has placed in my womb. The child is him and me and our love. I could never murder all of that.'

'Then, Your Majesty, there is nothing more that I can suggest to you.'

She smiled at me with such sublime trust and confidence that it took my breath away. 'I know you will think of something, my darling Taita. You always do.'

And so I had a dream.

I related my dream before a full session of the council of state called by the regent of this very Egypt.

Queen Lostris and Prince Memnon were seated upon the throne high on the poop-deck of the *Breath of Horus*. The galley was moored to the west bank of the Nile. The members of the council were seated upon the beach below her.

Lord Merkeset and the nobility represented the secular arm of the state. The high priests of Ammon-Ra and Osiris and Hapi represented the sacred arm. Lord Harrab and fifty of his senior officers stood for the military.

I stood upon the open deck below the throne and faced this distinguished gathering. I had taken even greater pains than usual with my appearance. My make-up was subtle and cunning. My hair was dressed with fragrant oils, and coiled in the fashion that I had made popular. I wore the two chains of the Gold of Praise around my neck, and my chest and arms were shaped and hardened by chariot-driving. I must have presented an extraordinary figure of beauty to them, for many of them gaped at me, and I saw the lust in the eyes of those whose inclinations ran in that direction.

'Your Majesties,' I made the low salutation to the pair upon the throne, and Prince Memnon grinned at me cheekily. His head was still bandaged, although it was no longer necessary. He was so proud of his war wound that I had let him keep it on. I frowned at him, and he adjusted his expression to be more in keeping with the

198

occasion.

'Your Majesties, last night I dreamed a strange and wonderful dream which I feel it is my duty to relate. I beg your leave to speak.'

Queen Lostris replied graciously, 'Every person in this company is aware of the sacred gift that you have. The prince and I know that you are able to see into the future, and to divine the will and the wishes of the gods through dreams and visions. I command you now to speak of these mysteries.'

I bowed again and turned to face the council.

'Last night I slept at the door to the royal cabin, as is my duty. Queen Lostris lay alone upon her couch, and the prince slept in his alcove beyond her bed.'

Even Lord Merkeset leaned forward and held his cupped hand behind his good ear, the other being stone-deaf. They all loved a good story and a fruity prophecy.

'In the third watch of the night I awoke, and there was a strange light glowing throughout the ship. I felt a cold wind blowing upon my cheek although every door and porthole was closed.'

My audience stirred with interest. I had struck the right ghostly tone.

'Then I heard footsteps echoing through the hull, slow and majestic footsteps, such as never were made by mortal man.' I paused dramatically. 'These weird and eerie sounds came from the hold of the galley.' I paused again for them to absorb this.

'Yes, my lords, from the hold where the gold coffin of Pharaoh Mamose, the eighth of that name, lies awaiting burial.'

Some of my audience shuddered with awe, while

199

others made the sign against evil.

'These footsteps drew closer to where I lay at the queen's door. The heavenly glow of light grew stronger, and while I trembled, a figure appeared before me. It was the shape of a man, but it was not human, for it glowed like the full moon and its face was a divine reincarnation of the king as I had known him, yet altered and filled with all the terrible divinity of his godhead.'

They were rapt and silent. Not a man stirred. I searched their faces for any sign of incredulity, but I found none.

Then suddenly a child's voice broke the silence, as the prince cried out high and clear, '*Bak-Her!* It was my father. *Bak-Her!* It was Pharaoh!'

They took up the cry, '*Bak-Her!* It was Pharaoh. May he live for ever!'

I waited for the silence, and when it returned I let it draw out to the point where they were almost overwhelmed by the suspense.

'Pharaoh came towards me, and I could not move. He passed me and entered the cabin of Her Gracious Majesty, Queen Lostris. Though I could neither move nor utter a sound, I saw all that came to pass. While the queen still slept, the divine pharaoh mounted upon her in all his splendour, and he took his husbandly pleasure with her. Their bodies were joined as man and woman.'

There was still no sign of disbelief on any face. I waited for the full effect of my words and then I went on, 'Pharaoh rose from the bosom of the sleeping queen, and he looked upon me and he spoke thus.'

I am able to mimic the sound of other men's voices so faithfully that others believe they hear the one I am imitating. I spoke now in the voice of Pharaoh Mamose.

'I have endowed the queen with my godhead. She has become one with me and the gods. I have impregnated her with my divine seed. She who has known no man but me, will bear a child of my royal blood. This will be a sign to all men that she enjoys my protection, and that I will watch over her still.'

I bowed once more to the royal pair upon the throne. 'Then the king passed back through the ship, and entered once more his golden coffin where he now rests. That was all my vision.'

'May Pharaoh live for ever!' shouted Lord Tanus, as I had coached him, and the cry was taken up.

'Hail, Queen Lostris! May she live for ever! Hail, the divine child she bears! May all her children live for ever!'

That night when I prepared to retire, my mistress called me to her, and she whispered, 'Your vision was so vivid and you told it so well that I shall not be able to sleep lest Pharaoh come again. Guard the door well.'

'I dare say there may be one bold and importunate enough to disturb your royal slumber, but I doubt that it will be Pharaoh Mamose. If some rascal does come to take advantage of your kind and loving nature, what should I do?'

'Sleep soundly, dear Taita, and stop your ears.' Her cheeks glowed pink in the lamplight as she blushed.

Once again my premonition of future events was proved accurate. That night there came a secret visitor to my mistress's cabin, and it was not the ghost of Pharaoh. I did what Queen Lostris had ordered. I stopped my ears.

 The Nile flooded once again, reminding us that another year had passed. We had reaped the corn that we had planted upon the islands, and we gathered in our herds. We broke down the chariots and packed them on the open decks of the galleys. We rolled up the tents and stowed them in the holds. Finally, when all was ready for our departure, we laid out the ropes upon the bank and put every able-bodied man and horse into the traces.

It took us almost a month of heart-breaking labour to make the transit of this fearsome cataract. We lost sixteen men drowned, and five galleys broken and chewed to splinters by the fangs of black rock. But at last we were through, and we set sail upon the smooth flow of the river above the rapids.

As the weeks turned to months, the Nile described a slow and majestic bend beneath our keels. Since leaving Elephantine, I had charted the course of the river. I had used the sun and the stars to give me direction, but I had come upon a great difficulty in measuring the distance that we travelled. At first I had ordered one of the slaves to walk along the bank and count every pace he took, but I knew that this method was so inaccurate that it would set all my calculations to nought.

The solution came to me one morning while we were out on chariot manoeuvres. I watched my right-hand wheel turning, and realized that each revolution of the rim made an exact measure of the ground that it had covered. Thereafter a chariot followed the bank of the river. One wheel had a flag on the rim, and a reliable man sat on the footplate and made a mark on a scroll for each time the flag came around.

Each evening I calculated the direction and distance we had travelled during the day, and marked it up on my chart. Slowly, the design and shape of the river made itself clear to me. I saw that we had made a vast loop out into the west, but that now the river had turned back into the south, as the priests of Hapi had predicted.

I showed my findings to Tanus and the queen. Many nights we sat late in the royal cabin, discussing the course of the river and how it would affect our plans to return to Egypt. It seemed that every mile along the river that we travelled, far from dimming my mistress's determination, served but to enhance the force of the vow she had made to return.

'We will build no temple nor palace of stone in the wilderness,' she ordered. 'We will set up no monument or obelisk. Our sojourn here is transitory. We will build no cities, but will live in our ships, or under tents and huts made of grass and reeds. We are a caravan on a journey that in the end will take us back to the city of my birth, beautiful Thebes of a hundred gates.'

In private she counselled me, 'Keep your charts well, Taita. I trust you to find the easy way home for us.'

So our river caravan journeyed onwards, and the desert on either hand changed its face with every mile, and yet in the end was unchanged.

We who sailed upon the river had become a close-knit community, almost an itinerant city without walls or permanent structure. Life burgeoned and faded. Our numbers increased, for most of those who had come with us from Elephantine were in the full bloom of life, and the women were fruitful. Young couples married upon the river-bank, and broke the jar of Nile water between them. Children were born, and we watched them grow.

Some of our old people died, and there were accidents and dangers that took toll of the younger ones. We embalmed them and dug tombs for them in the wild hills and left them to their slumber, and went onwards.

We observed the festivals and prayed to our gods. We feasted and fasted in the correct season, and danced and sang and studied the sciences. I held lessons for the older children upon the deck of the galley, and Memnon was the prize of all my students.

Before the year had run out, and while the course of the river still ran southwards, we came upon the third cataract that bestrode the course of the Nile. Once again we went ashore and cleared the land and planted our crops, while we waited for the Nile to rise and help us through.

It was here at the third great cataract that another joy came to fill my life to overflowing.

In a linen tent upon the bank of the river, I attended my mistress in her labour, and brought forth into this world the Princess Tehuti, the acknowledged daughter of the long-dead Pharaoh Mamose.

In my eyes Tehuti was beautiful as only a miracle might be. Whenever I had the opportunity, I sat beside her cot and examined her tiny feet and hands with wonder and awe. When she was hungry and waited for her mother's nipple, I would sometimes place my little finger in her mouth for the pleasure of feeling her chewing on it with her bald gums.

The river rose at last and allowed us to make the transit of the third cataract. We sailed onwards, and almost imperceptibly the river turned back into the east, describing a vast loop beneath our keels.

Before the year was out it was necessary for me to dream another of my famous dreams, for my mistress had once more suffered a virgin pregnancy that could only be explained by supernatural means. The ghost of the dead pharaoh had been on the prowl again.

My mistress was huge with child when we reached the fourth great cataract of the river. This chute of tumbling waters and rocks like the teeth of crocodiles was even more formidable than those that had come before, and there was much despondency in our company. When they thought

205

that no one could overhear them they complained to each other, 'We are beset by these infernal rock barriers. The gods have placed them across the river to prevent us going onwards.'

I read their lips as they huddled together on the bank of the river. None of them realized that I was able to understand what they said without hearing their words.

'We will be trapped behind these terrible rapids, and we will never be able to return down-river. We should turn back now, before it is too late.'

Even at the councils of state, I saw the words on the lips of some of the great lords of Egypt who sat at the back of the gathering and spoke to each other in muted tones. 'If we go on, we shall all die in this desert, and our souls will wander eternally through it without rest.'

There was an element amongst the young nobility that was both arrogant and headstrong. They were fostering discontent, and hatching insurrection. I knew that we had to act swiftly and with resolution, when I saw the Lord Aqer say to one of his henchmen, 'We are in the hands of this woman, this little harlot of a dead king, when what we really need is a strong man to lead us. There must be some way we can rid ourselves of her.'

Firstly, with the help of my old friend Aton, I ferreted out the names of all the malcontents and potential traitors. It did not surprise me that at the head of this list was this same Lord Aqer, the eldest son of Lord Merkeset, on whose lips I had read those traitorous sentiments. Aqer was an angry young man with inflated ideas of his own worth and importance. I suspected that he had the gall to see a vision of himself seated upon the throne of the two kingdoms with the double crown upon his head.

When I explained to Tanus and my mistress what I thought must be done, they called a full and solemn state council on the river-bank.

Queen Lostris opened the conclave. 'I know very well how you pine for your own land, and how you weary of this long voyage. I share with you every dream of Thebes.'

I saw Aqer exchange meaningful glances with his cronies, and had my suspicions strengthened.

'However, citizens of Egypt, nothing is as bad as it seems. Hapi has watched over our expedition, as he promised. We are much closer to Thebes than any one of you can imagine. When we return to our beloved city, we will not have to retrace our same weary footsteps. We will not have to face once again the dangers and the hardships of those hellish cataracts that block the course of the river.'

There was a stirring through her audience, and whispers of doubt and disbelief. Aqer laughed, not loud enough to cross the borders of respect and propriety, nevertheless my mistress singled him out. 'I see, Lord Aqer, that you question my word?'

'By no means, Your Majesty. I curse such a disloyal thought.' Aqer made a hasty retreat. He was not yet strong enough, nor sure enough of his support, to force a confrontation. I had caught him out before he was prepared.

'My slave, Taita, has plotted the course of the river that we have covered in these last years,' Queen Lostris went on. 'You have all seen the chariot with the flagged wheel that has measured the ground, and Taita has studied the heavenly bodies to find the direction of our journey. I order him now to arise before the council and reveal to us his calculations.'

Prince Memnon had helped me to trace copies of my chart on to twenty new scrolls. At nine years of age, the prince was already a fine pen-man. I passed these out to all the senior nobles, so that they might follow my lecture more clearly. I drew their attention to the almost circular course that we had followed since we had left Elephantine.

Their astonishment was evident. Only the priests had some prior knowledge of what had occurred, they also studied the stars and had some expertise in navigation. But even they were taken aback by the extent of the river's loop. This was not surprising, since the copies of the map that I showed them were not entirely accurate. I had taken certain liberties with the facts for the benefit of Aqer and his faction, and made the distance across the bight seem shorter than my calculations suggested was the case.

'My lords, as you can see by these charts, since we left the second cataract we have travelled very nearly a thousand miles, but we stand now not much more than a few hundred miles from the point of our departure.'

Kratas rose to his feet to ask a question that I had placed in his mouth before the meeting began. 'Does this mean that it should be possible to take this short cut across the desert and reach the second cataract in the same time as it takes to travel from Thebes to the Red Sea and return? I have made that journey several times.'

I turned to him. 'I was your companion on that same journey. Ten days in each direction it took us, and we did not have horses then. The crossing of this narrow strip of desert would be no more onerous. It means that from here one could be back in the city of Elephantine within a few short months, and it would be necessary to transit only the first cataract at Assoun.'

There was a buzz of comment and amazement. The maps were passed from hand to hand and scrutinized avidly. The entire mood of the assembly changed, as I watched. There was a pathetic eagerness amongst all of them to accept my theory. This unexpected proximity to home and the land they knew cheered all of them.

Only Aqer and his friends were out of countenance. He had been deprived of the top dice in the game he was playing. As I had hoped he would do, he rose angrily to his feet now to put the next question to me.

'How accurate are this slave's scribblings?' His tone was offensive and his expression haughty. 'It is a simple matter to make a few pen-strokes on a scroll, but when those are turned into miles of sand and rock, it is another matter entirely. How will this slave prove that these wild theories of his are fact?'

'My lord Aqer has come to the very heart of the matter,' my mistress intervened pleasantly, 'and, in so doing, has proven his astute grasp of the problem that faces us. I intend to send an expedition of good men to cross the neck of the desert and to open up our return route to the north, the road home to beautiful Thebes.'

I saw Aqer's expression change suddenly as he caught the slant of the queen's speech and realized the trap that had been set for him. He sat down

209

again hurriedly, and tried to appear remote and disinterested. However, my mistress continued remorselessly, 'I was undecided as to who was best suited to lead this expedition, but now Lord Aqer has, by his perception and understanding, proposed himself for this vital task. Is that not the case, my lord?' she asked sweetly, and then went on smoothly before he could refuse.

'We are grateful to you, Lord Aqer. You are to have whatever men and equipment you require. I command that you make your departure before the next full moon. The moon will make it easier for you to travel during the night, and so avoid the heat of the day. I will send with you men who are able to navigate by the stars. You could win through to the second cataract and be back here before the end of the month, and, if you succeed, I will place the Gold of Praise upon your shoulders.'

Lord Aqer stared at her with open mouth, and he was still sitting rigid with shock on his stool after all his companions had dispersed. I fully expected him to find some excuse to back out of the task that we had tricked him into, but in the end he surprised me by coming to me to ask for my advice and help in arranging the scouting party. It seemed that I might have misjudged him, and that now he had been given some worthwhile mission, there was a chance that he would change from a trouble-maker to a useful member of the company.

I selected some of our best men and horses for him and gave him five of our most sturdy carts, which could carry water-skins that, if used sparingly, would last them for thirty days. By the time the full moon came around, Aqer was quite cheerful and optimistic, and I felt guilty about having minimized the distance and the hazards of the journey.

When the expedition set out, I went a short way into the desert with them to point them on the right road, and then I stood alone and watched them merge into the silvery moonlit wastes, aimed at that set of stars we call the Lute which marks the northern horizon.

I thought of Aqer every day over the weeks that followed while we lay below the fourth cataract, and I hoped that the map I had given him was not as inaccurate as I feared it was. At least the immediate threat of a rebellion had disappeared with him into the north.

While we waited, we planted our crops on the cleared islands and the river-banks. However, the lie of the land was steeper than at the other sites lower down the river. It was more difficult to raise the water to irrigate our crops, and I could see that the quantity and the quality of the harvest must suffer in consequence.

Naturally, we had set up the traditional shadoofs on their long, counter-balanced arms to lift the water from the river. These were worked by a slave who swung the clay pot at the end of the arm into the water and then lifted and spilled it into the irrigation ditch on the bank. It was a slow and back-breaking task. When the bank was high, as it was here, it was also an extremely wasteful method of collecting water.

Each evening Memnon and I drove our chariot along the river-bank, and I was troubled by the paucity of the harvest that we watched growing there. We had many thousands of mouths to feed, and cornmeal was still the staple of our diet. I foresaw a time of famine, unless we were able to bring more water to the fields.

I do not know what made me think of the wheel for this purpose, except that the science of the wheel had by this time become an obsession and a passion in my life. I was still plagued by the problem of the bursting of the wheels of our chariots. My dreams were filled with turning and spinning and shattering wheels, wheels with bronze knives on the rim or with flags to measure the distance run. Large wheels and small, the images haunted me and troubled my sleep.

I had heard from one of the priests of Hapi that some varieties of timber can be made harder and more resilient by soaking them in water for a long period, so I was driven to experiment with this idea. As we were lowering one of the chariot wheels into the river for this purpose, the current playing on the rim began to turn the wheel on its hub. I watched this idly, but as the wheel sank lower in the water, the movement ceased, and I thought no more about it.

Some days later, one of the small boats crossing between the islands capsized, and the two men in it were swept into the rapids and drowned. Memnon and I watched this tragedy from the bank, and we were both distressed by it. I took the opportunity to warn the prince once more of the danger and the power of the river.

'It is so strong that it will even turn the wheel of a chariot.'

'I don't believe you, Tata. You are saying that to frighten me. You know how I love to swim in the river.'

So I arranged an exhibition for him, and we

212

were both duly impressed by the wheel turning, seemingly of its own accord, when it was dipped into the running water.

'It would go faster, Tata, if it had paddles fixed around the rim,' Memnon gave his opinion at last, and I stared at him in wonder. He was a little over ten years old at the time, and yet he saw all things with a fresh and enquiring eye.

By the time the full moon came around again, we had built a wheel driven by the river which lifted the water in a series of small baked-clay jars and spilled it into a canal lined with clay tiles at the top of the high Nile bank. Even with her big belly, my mistress came ashore to watch this wondrous contraption. She was delighted by it.

'You are so clever with the things you do with water, Taita,' she told me. 'Do you remember the water-stool you built for me at Elephantine?'

'I could make another for you now, if only you would allow us to live in a decent home like civilized people.'

Tanus was similarly impressed with the water-wheel, though of course he would not show it. Instead, he grinned at me.

'Very clever, but when will it burst like one of your famous chariot wheels?' he demanded, and Kratas and those other military oafs thought that was hugely funny. Thereafter, whenever a chariot wheel broke, they said that it had 'gone Tata', the pet name that the prince called me.

Despite this levity, the fields of dhurra soon grew dense and green in the loamy soil on the high banks, and the ears of golden corn drooped heavily in the bright Nile sunlight. This was not the only harvest that we gathered in at the fourth cataract.

213

Queen Lostris gave birth to another little royal princess. If anything, the infant was more exquisite than her elder sister.

It was passing strange that Princess Bekatha was born with a cap of golden-red curls. Her divine and ghostly father, Pharaoh Mamose, had been of swarthy cast, and her mother's hair was dark as the wing of the black eagle. No one could think of any reason for this aberrant coloration, but all agreed how pretty it was.

Princess Bekatha was two months old when the Nile began to rise once more, and we made our preparation for the transit of the fourth cataract. By now we were experienced in what had become an annual labour, and we had learned every trick and artifice to beat the rapacious river.

 We had not yet begun the transit, when there was tremendous excitement in the encampment. I heard the shouting and the cheering from the far bank of the river where Prince Memnon and I were inspecting the horses and making certain that all was ready for the ascent of the cataract.

We hurried back to the boats and crossed to the east bank, to find the camp in an uproar. We pushed our way through the crowds who were all waving palm-fronds and singing the songs of welcome and honour. At the centre of all this we found a small caravan of battered wagons and skeletal horses, and a band of lean, travel-hardened veterans, burned black by the sun and tempered by the desert.

'Seth damn you and that map of yours, Taita,' Lord Aqer shouted at me from the leading wagon. 'I don't know which of you lies worst. It was almost twice as far as you promised us.'

'Did you truly reach the north side of the river loop?' I shouted back at him, hopping with excitement and trying to fight my way through the crowd.

'There and back!' he laughed, mightily pleased with his accomplishment. 'We camped at the second cataract and dined on fresh fish from the Nile. The road back to Thebes is open.'

My mistress ordered a feast to welcome back the travellers, and Lord Aqer was the man of the day. At the height of the celebration, Queen Lostris placed the Gold of Praise around his neck, and promoted him to the rank of Best of Ten Thousand. My gorge rose to see the fellow preen and strut. As if that was not enough, she gave him command of the fourth division of chariots, and issued him a warrant that would entitle him to one hundred feddan of prime land on the river-bank when we returned to Thebes.

I thought all this a little excessive, especially the gift of so much land which must come out of my mistress's own estate. After all, Aqer had been on the brink of mutiny, and though his achievement had been laudable, it was I who had proposed and planned the expedition. In the circumstances, it seemed to me that another gold chain for the poor slave Taita might not have been out of place.

Nevertheless, I had to applaud my mistress's cunning and statesmanship. She had transformed Lord Aqer, who had been potentially one of her most dangerous enemies, into an ardent and loyal

215

adherent who would prove his value to her many times in the years ahead. She had a way with all men, and was gaining in statecraft each day.

The taming of Lord Aqer and the discovery of the route across the bight had secured our rear, and we could go on above the fourth cataract with high spirits and brave heart.

We had not travelled more than a month before we realized how our fortunes had changed and how the goddess had made good her promise.

It was clearer each day that we had come through the worst. The desert was behind us at last, and the broad, smooth flow of the river turned into the south once more and carried us into a land such as none of us had seen before.

It was here that for the first time many of our company witnessed the miracle of rain. Although of course I had seen it in the Lower Kingdom, they had never seen water fall from the sky. The rain beat down into our upturned and astonished faces, while the thunder rolled across the heavens and the lightning blinded us with its white fire.

These copious and regular rains engendered a new and exciting landscape, the like of which we could only wonder at. On either bank of the Nile, as far as we could see from the deck of the leading galley, stretched a broad savannah grassland. This magnificent plain, rich with grazing for our horses, set no boundaries to the range of our chariots. We could drive out at will, with no dunes or rocky hills to block our progress.

216

This was not the only blessing that the goddess had bestowed. There were trees. In the narrow valley that was our home, there might once have been forests, no man could tell. But they had fallen centuries before to the appetite and axes of man. Wood was to us Egyptians a rare and treasured commodity. Each stick of it had to be carried in by ship or on the back of beasts of burden, from far and foreign lands.

Now, wherever we looked, we saw great trees. They grew, not in the same dense forests that we had found on the islands in the cataracts, but in lofty groves with broad grassy spaces between the majestic trunks. There was timber enough upon these plains to rebuild all the fleets of all the nations on all the seas of the worlds. More than that, there was enough to rebuild the cities of all the civilized world, and to roof and furnish every room in them. After that there would still be enough left over to burn as fuel over the centuries to come. We who all our lives had cooked our food on bricks made from the dung of our animals, stared around us in wonder.

This was not the only treasure that we found for our taking in this legendary land of Cush that we had reached at last.

I saw them first in the distance and thought that they were monuments of grey granite. They stood upon the yellow grass plains and in the shade beneath the spreading branches of the acacia groves. Then, as we watched in perplexity, these great rocks began to move.

'Elephants!' I had never seen one before, but they could be nothing else. The cry was taken up by those on the deck around me.

'Elephants! Ivory!' These were riches that Pharaoh Mamose, with all his funerary treasure, could not have dreamed of. Wherever we looked, the vast herds stood.

'There are thousands of them.' Tanus gazed around him, the passion of the huntsman beginning to dawn in his eyes. 'Just look at them, Taita. There is no end to their numbers.'

The plains were thronged with living creatures, not only the herds of elephant. There were antelopes and gazelle, some of which we knew, and others that we had never seen or heard of before. We would come to know all of them well in the future, and find names for their abundant and diverse species.

Oryx mingled with herds of purple waterbuck whose horns curved like the bow that I had built for Tanus. There were spotted giraffe with necks that reached to the top branches of the acacia trees. The horns that grew from the snouts of the rhinoceros were as tall as a man and as sharp as his spear. The buffalo wallowed in the mud at the river's edge. They were huge bovine beasts, black as Seth's beard, and every bit as ugly. We would soon learn the malevolence behind that melancholy stare with which they regarded our passing, and the menace of those drooping black horns.

'Unload the chariots from the holds,' Tanus roared with impatience. 'Put the horses into the traces. The hunt is on!'

If I had known the danger that we were riding into, I would never have allowed Prince Memnon to mount the footplate behind me as we drove out on our first elephant hunt. To us who knew no better, they appeared such docile brutes, slow and clumsy and stupid. Surely they would be easy game.

Tanus was bristling with impatience to go out against this new quarry, and he would not wait for all four divisions of our chariots to be reassembled. As soon as the first division of fifty vehicles was ready, he gave the order to mount up. We shouted challenges to the other drivers, and made our wagers on the outcome of the hunt as the long columns of chariots rolled out through the groves along the river-bank.

'Let me drive, Tata,' the prince demanded. 'You know I drive as well as you do.' Although he was a natural horseman with gentle hands and an instinctive way with his team, and he practised the art almost every day, the prince's boast was unfounded. He certainly was not as good a charioteer as I was, no man in the army could make that claim, certainly not a scamp of eleven years.

'Watch me and learn,' I told him sternly, and when Memnon turned to Tanus, he supported me for once.

'Taita is right. This is something none of us has done before. Keep your mouth closed and your eyes open, boy.'

Ahead of us a small herd of these strange grey beasts were feasting on the seed-pods that had fallen from the top branches of the trees. I studied them with avid curiosity as we approached at a trot. Their ears were enormous, and they fanned them out and turned to face us. They lifted their trunks high, and I guessed that they were taking up our scent. Had they ever smelled a man or a horse

219

before, I wondered.

There were small calves with them, and the mothers gathered them into the centre of the herd and stood guard over them. I was touched to see this maternal concern, and I had the first inkling then that these animals were not as slow and stupid as they appeared to be. 'These are all females,' I called over my shoulder to Tanus on the footplate. 'They have young at heel, and their ivory is small and of little value.'

'You are right.' Tanus pointed over my shoulder. 'But look beyond them. Those two must surely be bulls. See how tall they stand and how massive is their girth. Look how their tusks shine in the sun.'

I gave the signal to the chariots that followed us, and we veered away from the breeding herd of cows and calves. We ran on, still in column, through the acacia grove towards those two great bulls. As we drove forward, we were forced to swerve around the branches that had been torn from the trees, and to dodge the trunks of giant acacia that had been uprooted. As yet we knew nothing of the unbelievable strength of these creatures, and I called back to Tanus, 'There must have been a great storm through this forest to wreak such destruction.' It did not even occur to me then that the elephant herds were responsible; they seemed so mild and defenceless.

The two old bulls we had selected had sensed our approach and turned to face us. It was only then that I realized the true size of them. When they spread their ears they seemed to block out the sky, like a dark grey thunder-cloud.

'Just look at that ivory!' Tanus shouted. He was

unperturbed, and concerned only with the trophy of the chase, but the horses were nervous and skittish. They had picked up the scent of this strange quarry, and they threw their heads up and crabbed in the traces. It was hard to control them and keep them running straight.

'That one on the right is the biggest,' squeaked Memnon. 'We should take him first.' The pup was every bit as keen as his sire.

'You heard the royal command,' Tanus laughed. 'We will take the one on the right. Let Kratas have the other, it's good enough for him.'

So I raised my fist and gave the hand-command that split the column into two files. Kratas wheeled away on our left with twenty-five chariots following him in line astern, while we ran on straight at the huge grey beast that confronted us with the yellow shafts of ivory, thick as the columns of the temple of Horus, standing out from his vast grey head.

'Go hard at him!' Tanus shouted. 'Take him before he turns to run.'

'Hi up!' I called to Patience and Blade, and they opened up into a gallop. We both expected the huge animal to run from us as soon as he realized that we menaced him. No other game we had ever hunted had stood to receive our first charge. Even the lion runs from the hunter until he is wounded or cornered. How could these obese animals behave differently?

'His head is so big, it will make a fine target,' Tanus exulted, as he nocked an arrow. 'I will kill him with a single shaft, before he can escape. Run in close under that long, ridiculous nose of his.'

Behind us the rest of our column was strung out in single file. Our plan was to come in and split on each side of the bull, firing our arrows into him as we passed, then wheeling around and coming back in classic chariot tactics.

We were right on the bull now, but still he stood his ground. Perhaps these animals were every bit as dull-witted as they looked. This would be an easy kill, and I sensed Tanus' disappointment at the prospect of such poor sport.

'Come on you old fool!' he shouted contemptuously. 'Don't just stand there. Defend yourself!'

It was as though the bull heard and understood the challenge. He threw up his trunk and loosed a blast of sound that stunned and deafened us. The horses shied wildly, so that I was thrown against the dashboard with a force that bruised my ribs. For a moment I lost control of the team, and we swerved away.

Then the bull squealed again, and he ran.

'By Horus, look at him come!' Tanus roared with astonishment, for the beast was not running from us, but directly at us, in a furious charge. He was swifter than any horse, and nimble as an angry leopard set upon by the hounds. He kicked up bursts of dust with each long flying stride, and was on us before I could get the horses under control again.

I looked up at him, for he towered directly over us, reaching out with his trunk to pluck us from the cockpit of the chariot, and I could not believe the size of him, nor the fury in those eyes. They were not the eyes of an animal, but those of an intelligent and alert human being. This was no porcine sloth, but a courageous and terrible adversary that we had challenged in our arrogance and ignorance.

Tanus got off a single arrow. It struck the bull in the centre of his forehead, and I expected to see him collapse as the bronze point pierced the brain. We did not know then that the brain of the elephant is not situated where you would expect it to be, but is far back in the mountainous skull and protected by a mass of spongy bone that no arrow can penetrate.

The bull did not even check or swerve. He merely reached up with his trunk and gripped the shaft of the arrow with the tip, as a man might do with his hand. He pulled the shaft from his own flesh and threw it aside and came on after us, reaching out towards us with the blood-smeared trunk.

Hui in the second chariot of our line saved us, for we were defenceless against the old bull's fury. Hui came in from the side, lashing his horses and yelling like a demon. His archer from the footplate behind him fired an arrow into the bull's cheek a hand's-span below the eye, and that pulled his attention from us.

The elephant wheeled to chase after Hui, but he was at full gallop and raced clean away. The next chariot in line was not so fortunate. The driver lacked Hui's skill, and his turn away was inept. The bull lifted his trunk high and then swung it down like an executioner's axe.

He struck the near-side horse across the back, just behind the withers, and broke its spine so cleanly that I heard the vertebrae shatter like a brittle potsherd. The maimed horse went down and dragged its teammate down with it. The chariot rolled over and the men were hurled from it. The elephant placed one forefoot on the body of the fallen charioteer and, with its trunk, plucked off his head and tossed it aloft like a child's ball. It spun in the air spraying a bright feather of pink blood from the severed neck.

Then the next chariot in line tore in, distracting the bull from his victim.

I pulled up my horses at the edge of the grove, and we stared back aghast at the carnage of our shattered squadron. There were broken chariots scattered across the field, for Kratas out on the left had fared no better than we had.

The two great bull elephants bristled with arrow-shafts, and the blood streamed down their bodies, leaving wet streaks on their dusty grey hide. However, the wounds had not weakened them, but seemed only to have aggravated their fury. They rampaged through the grove, smashing up the capsized chariots, stamping the carcasses of the horses under those massive padded feet, throwing the bodies of screaming men high in the air and trampling them as they fell back to earth.

Kratas raced up alongside us, and shouted across at us, 'By the itching crabs in Seth's crotch, this is hot work! We have lost eight chariots in the first charge.'

'Better sport than you expected, Captain Kratas,' Prince Memnon yelled back at him. He would have done better to keep his opinion to himself, for up until that moment we had forgotten about the boy in the confusion. Now, however, both Tanus and I rounded on him together.

'As for you, my lad, you have had enough sport for one day,' I told him firmly.

'It's back to the fleet with you, and that right

224

swiftly,' agreed Tanus, and at that moment an empty chariot cantered by. I do not know what had happened to the crew, they had probably been thrown from the cockpit or been plucked out of it bodily by one of the infuriated beasts.

'Catch those horses!' Tanus ordered, and when the empty chariot was brought back to us, he told the prince, 'Out you get. Take that chariot back to the beach and wait there for our return.'

'My Lord Tanus,' Prince Memnon drew himself to his full height, reaching as high as his father's shoulder, 'I protest—'

'None of your royal airs with me, young man. Go back and protest to your mother, if you must.' He lifted the prince with one hand and dropped him into the vacant cockpit of the other vehicle.

'Lord Tanus, it is my right—' Memnon made one last despairing attempt to remain in the hunt.

'And it is my right to wrap the scabbard of my sword around your royal backside, if you are still here when I look around again,' said Tanus, and turned his back on him. Both of us put the boy out of our minds.

'Gathering ivory is not quite as easy as picking up mushrooms,' I remarked. 'We will have to think up a better plan than this.'

'You cannot kill these creatures by shooting them in the head,' Tanus growled. 'We will go in again and try an arrow through the ribs. If they have no brain in their skull, then surely they have lungs and a heart.'

I gathered up the reins, and lifted the heads of the team, but I could feel that Patience and Blade were as nervous as I was at the prospect of returning to the field. None of us had enjoyed our

225

first taste of elephant hunting.

'I'll go at him head-on,' I told Tanus, 'and then turn out to give you a broadside shot into his ribs.'

I put the horses into a trot, and then gradually pushed up their speed as we entered the acacia grove. Dead ahead of us our bull rampaged over the ground that was littered with the wreckage of overturned chariots and the bodies of dead men and broken horses. He saw us coming and let out another of those terrible squeals that chilled my blood, and the horses flicked their ears and shied again. I gathered them up with the reins and drove them on.

The bull charged to meet us, like a landslide of rock down a steep hillside. He was a terrible sight in his rage and his agony, but I held my team steady, not yet pushing them to the top of their speed. Then, as we came together, I lashed them up and yelled them into a full, mad gallop. At the same moment I swung out hard left, opening the bull's flank.

At a range of less than twenty paces, Tanus fired three arrows in quick succession into his chest. All of them went in behind the shoulder, finding the gaps between the ribs, and burying themselves full-length in the seared grey skin.

The bull squealed again, but this time in mortal agony. Though he reached out for us, we raced clear of the stretch of his trunk. I looked back and saw him standing in our dust, but when he bellowed again, the blood spurted from the end of his trunk, like steam from a kettle.

'The lungs,' I shouted. 'Good work, Tanus. You have hit him through the lungs.'

'We have found the trick of it now,' Tanus

exulted. 'Take us back. I will give him another one through the heart.'

I wheeled about and the horses were still strong and willing.

'Come on, my beauties,' I called to them. 'One more time. Hi up!'

Though he was mortally struck, the old bull was still far from death. I would learn just how tenacious of life these magnificent beasts were, but now he charged to meet us once again with a courage and splendour that filled me with reverence. Even in the heat of the hunt and terror for my own safety, I felt shame at the torture we were inflicting on him.

Perhaps it was because of this that I let the horses go in very close. Out of respect for him, I wanted to match his courage with my own. When it was almost too late, I swung my horses out of the charge, meaning to pass him just out of reach of that wicked trunk.

Just then the off-side wheel of the chariot burst under us. There was that giddy moment as I somersaulted through the air like an acrobat, but this was not the first time I had been thrown, and I had learned to fall like a cat. I rode the shock and let myself roll twice. The earth was soft and the grass as thick as a mattress. I came up on my feet unhurt and with my wits still all about me. I saw at a glance that Tanus had not come through as well as I had. He was sprawled flat out and unmoving.

The horses were up, but anchored by the dead weight of the broken chariot. The bull elephant attacked them. Blade was nearest to him and he broke my darling mare's back with a single blow of the trunk. Blade went down on her knees

227

screaming, and Patience was still linked to her. The bull thrust one thick tusk through Blade's chest and jerked his head up, lifting the kicking and struggling animal high in the air.

I should have run then, while the bull was so distracted, but Patience was still unhurt. I could not leave her. The elephant was turned half-away from me, his own ears, spread like a ship's sail, blanketed me from his view, and he did not see me run in. I snatched Tanus' sword from the scabbard on the rack of the capsized chariot, and darted to Patience's side.

Although the great bull was dragging her along by the leather harness that attached her to Blade, and although the blood from the other horse splashed over her neck and shoulders, she was still unhurt. Of course, she was wild with terror, squealing and kicking out with both back legs, so that she almost cracked my skull as I darted up behind her. I ducked as her hooves flew past my head and grazed my cheek.

I hacked at the rawhide tackle that pinned her to the drive-shaft of the chariot. The sword was sharp enough to shave the hair from my head, and the leather split under that bright edge. Three hard strokes, and Patience was free to run. I snatched at her mane to pull myself up on to her back, but she was so terror-struck that she bounded away before I could find a grip. Her shoulder crashed into me and sent me spinning away. I was thrown heavily to the ground, under the side of the wrecked chariot.

I struggled up to see Patience dashing off through the grove; she ran with a free and light stride, so I knew she was unhurt. I looked for

Tanus next. He lay ten paces away from the chariot, face down against the earth, and I thought he was dead, but at that moment he raised his head and looked around at me with a bewildered and groggy expression. I knew that any sudden movement might draw the bull elephant's attention to him, and I willed him to lie still. I dared not utter a sound, for the enraged animal was still standing over me.

I looked up at the bull. Poor Blade was impaled upon his tusk, and the rawhide traces were entangled with his trunk. The bull started to move off, dragging the battered chariot with him. He was attempting to dislodge the weight of Blade's dangling carcass from his tusk. The point of the tusk had ripped open the horse's belly, and the stink of the stomach contents mingled with the reek of blood and the elephant's peculiar rank and gamey odour. Stronger than all that, the stench of the sweat of my own fear filled my nostrils.

I made sure that the bull's head was still turned away from me, before I pushed myself up and ran doubled-over to where Tanus lay. 'Up! Get up!' I croaked in a hoarse whisper, and I tried to lift him to his feet, but he was a heavy man and still only half-conscious. Desperately I looked back at the bull. He was moving away from us, still dragging the whole tangle of broken equipment and the dead horse with him.

I draped Tanus' arm around my neck and put my shoulder into his armpit. With all my strength I managed to lever him to his feet, and he hung against me unsteadily. I swayed under his weight. 'Brace up!' I whispered urgently. 'The bull will spot us at any moment.'

229

I tried to drag Tanus along with me, but he took only one pace before he gave a groan and fell back against me. 'My leg,' he grunted. 'Can't move. Knee gone. Twisted the cursed thing.'

The full realization of our predicament struck me then, as it had not before. My old sin of cowardice overwhelmed me once more, and the strength went out of my own legs.

'Get out of it, you old fool,' Tanus grated in my ear. 'Leave me. Run for it!'

The elephant lifted his head and shook it in the same way that a dog shakes the water from its ears after it has swum back to the shore. Those vast leathery ears slapped and rattled against his own shoulders, and Blade's crushed carcass slid off the tusk and was hurled aside as if it were no heavier than a dead rabbit. The strength of the elephant bull was past all belief. If he could toss the weight of horse and chariot so easily, what might he do with my own frail body?

'Run, for the love of Horus, run, you fool!' Tanus urged me, and tried to push me away, but some strange obstinacy prevented me from leaving him, and I hung on to his shoulder. Afraid as I was, I could not leave him.

The bull had heard the sound of Tanus' voice and he swung around with those ears flaring wide open like the mainsail of a fighting galley. He stared full at us, and we were less than fifty paces from him.

I did not know then, as I would learn later, that the eyesight of the elephant is so poor that he is almost blind. He relies almost entirely on his hearing and his sense of smell. Only movement attracts him, and if we had stood still he would not

230

have seen us.

'He has seen us,' I gasped, and I dragged Tanus with me, forcing him to hop on his good leg beside me. The bull saw the movement and he squealed. I shall never forget that sound. It deafened and stunned me, sending us both reeling so that we staggered together and almost fell.

Then the bull charged straight at us.

He came with long, driving strides, and his ears flapped about his head. Arrows bristled from the great weathered forehead, and blood streamed down his face like tears. Each time he squealed, the lung blood spurted in a cloud from his trunk. As tall as a cliff, and as black as death, he came at us in full charge. I could see every seam and crease in the folded skin around his eyes. The lashes of his eyes were thick as those of a beautiful girl, but such a glare of rage shone through them that my heart turned to a stone in my chest, and weighed down my legs so I could not move.

The passage of time seemed to slow down, and I was overcome with a sense of dreamlike unreality. I stood and watched death bear down upon us with a slow and stately deliberation, and could make no move to avoid it.

'Tata!' A child's voice rang in my head, and I knew that it was a delusion of my terror. 'Tata, I am coming!'

In total disbelief I swung my head away from the vision of death before me. Across the open ground of the grove a chariot was tearing towards us at full gallop. The horses were stretched out and their heads were going like the hammers on a coppersmith's anvil. Their ears were laid back, and their nostrils flared wide open, pink and wet. I could see no driver at the reins.

'Get ready, Tata!' Only then did I see the neat little head, barely showing above the dashboard. The reins were gripped in two small fists, the knuckles white with tension.

'Mem,' I cried, 'go back! Turn back!'

The wind blew his hair out in a cloud behind his head, and the sunlight struck ruby sparks from the thick dark curls. He came on without a pause or check.

'I'll thrash the little ruffian for disobeying me,' growled Tanus, as he teetered on one leg. We had both of us forgotten our own danger.

'Whoa!' Memnon cried, and brought the team down from a full gallop. He wheeled the carriage into such a sharp turn that the inside wheel stopped dead and swivelled on its rim. He had cut in front of the two of us, shielding us for an instant from the charging bull, and as the chariot spun about there was a moment when it was standing still. It was beautifully done.

I heaved my shoulder up under Tanus' armpit and threw him sprawling on the footplate. The very next instant I hurled myself headlong on top of him. As I landed, Memnon gave the horses their heads, and we bounded forward so sharply that I was almost jerked backwards off the platform, but I grabbed at the side-panel and steadied myself.

'Go, Mem,' I screamed, 'for all you're worth!'

'Hi-up!' Memnon screamed. 'Yah hah!' The chariot careered away with the frightened horses driven to full flight by the enraged squeals of the charging bull close behind.

All three of us stared back over the tail-board. The head of the bull hung over us, seeming to fill all my vision. The trunk reached out for us, so close that each time the bull squealed, the bloody cloud sprayed over us and speckled our upturned faces, so that we looked like the victims of some horrible plague.

We could not draw clear of his rush, and he was unable to overtake us. Matched in speed, we went racing through the glade with the great bloody head hanging over us as we cowered on the floorboards of the bouncing chariot. It needed only one small mistake from our driver to send us into a hole or rip our wheels off against a stump of a fallen tree, and the bull would have been upon us in an instant. But the prince handled the traces like a veteran, picking his route through the grove with a cool hand and practised eye. He sent the chariot careening through the turns on one wheel, within an ace of capsizing, holding off the bull's mad charge. He never faltered once, and then suddenly it was all over.

One of the arrows buried in the bull's chest had worked itself in deeper and sliced open the heart. The elephant opened his mouth wide, and a flood of bright blood shot up his throat and he died in his tracks. His legs went out from under him and he came down with a crash that jarred the earth under us, and lay upon his side with one long curved tusk thrust up in the air as if in a last defiant and regal gesture.

Memnon pulled in the horses, and Tanus and I stumbled down out of the carriage and stood together staring back at that mountainous carcass. Tanus clung to the side of the chariot to favour his damaged leg, and slowly turned back to look at the boy who did not know he was his father.

233

'By Horus, I have known some brave men in my time, but none of them better than you, lad,' he said simply, and then he lifted Memnon in his arms and hugged him to his chest.

I did not see much more of it, for those everlasting and tedious tears of mine blotted out my vision. Even though I knew myself for a sentimental fool, I could not staunch them. I had waited too long to see this happen, to watch the father embrace his son.

I only managed to regain control of my errant emotions when I heard the faint sound of distant cheers. What none of us had realized was that the chase had taken place in full view of the fleet. The *Breath of Horus* lay close in against the bank of the Nile, and I could see the slim figure of the queen upon the high poop. Even at this distance her face looked pale and her expression set.

The Gold of Valour is the warrior's prize, higher in honour and in esteem than the Gold of Praise. It is only ever worn by heroes.

We gathered on the deck of the galley, those closest to the queen and the commanders of all the divisions of her army. Stacked against the mast, the tusks of the elephants were on display like the spoils of war, and the officers wore all their regimental finery. The standard-bearers stood to attention behind the throne, and the trumpeters blew a fanfare as the prince knelt before the queen.

'My beloved subjects!' the queen spoke out

clearly. 'Noble officers of my council, generals and officers of my army, I commend to you the crown prince, Memnon, who has found favour in my sight and in the sight of you all.' She smiled down on the eleven-year-old boy who was being treated like a victorious general.

'For his courageous conduct in the field, I command that he be received into the regiment of the Blue Crocodile Guards, with the rank of subaltern of the second class, and I bestow upon him the Gold of Valour, that he may wear it with pride and distinction.'

The chain had been especially forged by the royal goldsmiths to fit the neck of a boy of Memnon's age, but with my own hands I had sculpted the tiny golden elephant that was suspended from the chain. It was perfect in every detail, a miniature masterpiece with garnet chips for eyes and real ivory tusks. It looked well as it hung against the smooth, unblemished skin of the prince's chest.

I felt my tears coming on again as the men cheered my beautiful prince, but I fought them back with an effort. I was not the only one who was wallowing in sentiment like a wart-hog in a mud bath; even Kratas and Remrem and Astes, for all their hardbitten and cavalier attitudes which they usually cultivated so assiduously, were grinning like idiots, and I swear I saw more than one pair of wet eyes in their ranks. In the same way as his parents, the boy had a way with the affections and loyalties of men. Every officer of the Blues came forward at the end to salute the prince and embrace him gravely as a comrade-in-arms.

That evening, as we drove together along the

bank of the Nile in the sunset, Memnon suddenly reined in the horses and turned to me. 'I have been called to my regiment. I am a soldier at last, so you must make me my own bow now, Tata.'

'I will make you the finest bow that any archer has ever drawn,' I promised.

He considered me gravely for a while, and then he sighed, 'Thank you, Tata. I think this is the happiest day of all my life.' The way he said it made eleven years seem like hoary old age.

The next day after the fleet had moored for the night, I went to look for the prince and found him alone upon the bank in a spot that was hidden from casual observation. He had not seen me, so I could observe him for a while.

He was stark naked. Despite my warnings about currents and crocodiles, it was obvious that he had been swimming in the river, for his hair was sopping wet upon his shoulders. However, I was puzzled by his behaviour, for he had selected two large round stones from the beach and was holding one of these in each hand, raising and lowering them in some strange ritual.

'Tata, you are spying on me,' he said suddenly, without turning his head. 'Do you want something from me?'

'I want to know what you are doing with those stones. Are you worshipping some strange new Cushite god?'

'I am making my arms strong so that I can draw my new bow. I want it to have a full draw-weight. You are not to fob me off with another toy, Tata, do you hear?'

236

There was another cataract across the river, the fifth and what would later prove to be the penultimate that we would encounter upon our voyage. However, this was not the same barrier to our progress that the other four had been. With the change in the surrounding terrain, we were no longer restricted to the course of the river.

While we waited for the Nile to rise again, we planted our crops as usual, but we were able to send out our chariots to range far and wide across the savannah. My mistress despatched expeditions southwards to pursue the elephant herds and bring back the ivory.

Those vast herds of the magnificent grey beasts that had greeted us so trustingly when first we had sailed into Cush, were now flown and scattered. We had hunted them ruthlessly wherever we found them, but these sage creatures learned their lesson well and right swiftly.

When we arrived at the fifth cataract, we found the herds grazing in the groves on either bank. The elephant were in their thousands, and Tanus ordered the chariots into action immediately. We had refined our tactics of hunting them and we had learned how to avoid the losses that those first two bulls had inflicted upon us. At the fifth cataract, on the very first day, we killed one hundred and seven elephant, for the loss of only three chariots.

The following day there was not a single elephant in sight from the decks of the ships. Although the chariots pursued the herds, following the roads they had left through the forest as they fled, it was five days before they caught up with them again.

Very often now the hunting expeditions returned to our encampment below the cataract after being out for many weeks on end without having found a single elephant or gathered a single tusk. What had seemed to us at first to be an endless supply of ivory had proved an illusion. As the prince had remarked on that very first day, elephant-hunting was not as simple as it first seemed.

However, those chariots ranging southwards did not return entirely empty-handed. They had found something even more valuable to us than ivory. They had found men.

I had not left the encampment for several months for I had been involved in the eternal experimentation with my chariot wheels. It was at this period that I at last found the solutions to the problem which had plagued me from the very beginning, and which had been such a source of amusement and ridicule to Tanus and his military cronies—the occasional failure of some of my designs.

In the end, it was not a single answer, but a combination of factors, beginning with the material from which the spokes of the wheels were made. I now had an almost unlimited selection of various types of wood to work with, and the horn of oryx and rhinoceros which we hunted close to our settlement, and which, unlike the elephant herds, did not move away after being harassed.

I found that soaking the red heartwood of the giraffe acacia rendered it so hard that it would turn the edge of the sharpest bronze axe-head. I compounded this wood with layers of horn and bound it all up together with bronze wire, very much in the same fashion as I had done with the bowstock of Lanata. The result was that at last I had a wheel that could be driven to the utmost over any type of terrain without collapsing. When Hui and I had completed the first ten chariots with these new wheels, I challenged Kratas and Remrem, who were the most notoriously heavy-handed and destructive drivers in all the army, to try to smash them up. The wager that we agreed on was ten deben of gold a side.

This was a game much to the liking of those two overgrown children, and they entered into the spirit of it with boyish gusto. For weeks thereafter, their raucous cries and the sound of pounding hooves rang through the groves on the banks of the Nile. By the time their limit was up, Hui came to me complaining bitterly that they had worn out twenty teams of horses. However, it was some consolation to him that we had won the wager. Our new wheels had stood the most stringent test.

'If you had given us a few days more,' Kratas groused as he handed over his gold with a marked lack of sporting grace, 'I know I would have managed another Tata.' And he treated us to a pantomime which he thought amusing and which was supposed to suggest a shattering wheel and a somersaulting driver.

'You are a gifted clown, brave Kratas, but I have your gold.' I jingled it under his nose. 'All you have is a tired old jest that has gone sour on you.'

It was then that the scouting expedition, led by Lord Aqer, that had gone out to find elephant, came back with the news that instead they had found human habitation further to the south.

We had expected to come across the tribes as soon as we passed the first cataract. For centuries the land of Cush had produced slaves. These had been captured by their own people, probably in tribal warfare, and carried down with other commodities of trade—ivory and ostrich feathers and rhinoceros horn and gold dust—to the outposts of our empire. Queen Lostris' saucy black handmaidens were natives of this land and had come to her from the slave-markets in Elephantine.

I still cannot explain why we had not found people before this. Perhaps they had been driven back by wars and slave raids, in the same way as we had scattered the elephant herds. They may have been wiped out by famine or plague, it was impossible to say. Up until now we had found scant evidence of human presence.

However, now that we had finally caught up with them, the excitement was an epidemic in our company. We needed slaves more even than we needed ivory or gold. Our whole civilization and way of life was based upon the system of slave ownership, a system that was condoned by the gods and sanctified by ancient usage. We had been able to bring very few of our own slaves with us from Egypt, and now it was imperative for our survival and growth as a nation that we capture more to replace those we had been forced to abandon.

Tanus ordered a full-scale expeditionary force to be sent out immediately. He would lead it himself, for we were uncertain what we would find up-river. Apart from those taken as prisoners of war, we Egyptians had always purchased our slaves from foreign traders, and this was the first time in centuries, as far as I knew, what we were forced to resort to catching our own. It was sport as new to us as elephant-hunting, but at least this time we did not expect our quarry to be either docile or dull-witted.

Tanus would still not ride with any other driver than me, and even Kratas' and Remrem's unsuccessful efforts to destroy them had not yet convinced him of the virtue of my new chariots. We led the column, but the second chariot in line was driven by the youngest subaltern of the Blues, the crown prince, Memnon.

I had chosen the two very best charioteers to act as crew for Memnon. His own weight was so light that the chariot could carry an extra man, and the prince's strength had not developed sufficiently for him to be able to lift his end of the chariot when it was necessary to dismount and carry it over the obstacles that could not be driven over. He needed that extra man to help him.

The first villages we came across were on the river-bank, three days' travel above the cataract. They were groups of miserable grass shelters too rudimentary to be called huts. Tanus sent scouts forward to reconnoitre, and then in the dawn we surrounded them with a single swift rush.

The people that stumbled out of these crude shelters were too dazed and shocked to offer any resistance, or even attempt to run from us. They clung together and chattered and gaped at the ring of chariots and shields that we had thrown around them.

'A fine catch!' Tanus was delighted as we looked them over. The men were tall and lean, with long, slim limbs. They towered over most of the men in our ranks; even Tanus seemed short in comparison as we walked amongst them, sorting them into groups as a farmer might apportion his herds.

'There are some really good specimens,' he enthused. 'Look at that beauty.' He had picked out a young man of exceptional physique. 'He would fetch ten rings of gold on the slave-market at Elephantine on any day.'

Their women were strong and healthy. Their backs were straight and their teeth were white and even. Every mature female carried an infant on her hip and led another by the hand.

Yet they were the most primitive people I had ever encountered. Neither men nor women wore a shred of clothing, and they left their pudenda shamelessly bared, though the younger girls wore a single string of beads made from the shells of ostrich eggs around their waist. I could see at once that the mature women had all been circumcised in the most brutal fashion. Later I learned that either a flint knife or a sliver of bamboo was used for this operation. Their vaginas were scarred and deformed into open pits, and then infibulated with slivers of bone or ivory. The younger girls had not yet suffered this mutilation, and I determined that this custom would be outlawed in the future. I was certain that I could rely on the support of my mistress in this.

Their skins were so dark that their naked bodies appeared purple in the early sunlight, the colour of an over-ripe black grape. Some of them had smeared themselves with a paste of ashes and white clay, on which they had daubed crude patterns with their fingertips. They had dressed

242

their hair with a mixture of ox-blood and clay into a tall, shiny helmet which exaggerated their already impressive height.

One thing that struck me immediately was that there were no old people among them. I learned later that it was their custom to break the legs of the elderly with their war clubs and leave them on the bank of the river as a sacrifice to the crocodiles. They believed that the crocodiles were reincarnations of their dead ancestors, and that by feeding them, the victim became a part of this process.

They had forged no metal artefacts. Their weapons were wooden clubs and sharpened sticks. The potter's art had eluded them and their vessels were the gourds of wild plants. They planted no crops, but lived on the fish they caught in basket-traps, and on the herds of stunted long-horned cattle which were their most prized possessions. They bled them from a vein in the neck and mixed the blood with milk warm from the udder, and drank the curdled mess with the utmost relish.

When I studied them over the months that followed, I found that they could neither read nor write. Their only musical instrument was a drum hollowed from a tree-trunk, and their songs were the grunting and braying of wild animals. Their dances were flagrant parodies of the sexual act in which ranks of naked men and women approached each other, stamping and grinding their hips until they met. When this happened, the imitation was transformed into reality, and the most licentious debaucheries were enacted.

When Prince Memnon questioned me as to

what right we had to capture these people and take possession of them like cattle, I told him, 'They are savages, and we are civilized people. As a father has a duty to his son, it is our duty to lift them from their brutish state, and to show them the true gods. Their part of the bargain is that they repay us with their labour.' Memnon was a bright lad, and after I had explained it to him he never again questioned the logic or the morality of it.

At my suggestion, my mistress had allowed two of her black handmaidens to accompany the expedition. My personal relationship with these little hussies had not been entirely untroubled, but now they rendered invaluable service. Both these girls had childhood memories of the time before their capture, and they retained a rudimentary knowledge of the language of these tribes of Cush. This was just sufficient for us to begin the process of taming our captives. As a musician, I have an ear tuned to the sounds of the human voice; added to this, I have also a natural linguistic ability. Within a very few weeks I was able to speak the language of the Shilluk, which was what these people were called.

Their language was as primitive as their customs and their way of life. Their entire vocabulary did not exceed five hundred words, which I recorded on my scrolls and taught to the slave-masters and to the army instructors whom Tanus appointed over the fresh-caught slaves. For among these people Tanus had found his infantry regiments to complement the chariot divisions.

This first raid gave us no real warning of the true warlike nature of the Shilluk. It had all gone too easily, and we were unprepared for what followed when we swept down on the next straggle of villages. By this time the Shilluk had been alerted, and they were ready to meet us.

They had driven away their cattle herds and hidden their women and children. Naked and armed only with wooden clubs, they came in their hordes against our chariots and recurved bows and swords, with a courage and tenacity that surpassed belief.

'By the putrid wax in Seth's ear-hole,' Kratas swore with delight after we had driven back another charge, 'every one of these black devils is a soldier born.'

'Trained and armed with bronze, these Shilluk will stand out against any other foot-soldiers in the world,' Tanus agreed. 'Leave the bows on the racks. I want as many of them as we can catch alive.'

In the end, Tanus ran them to exhaustion with the chariots, and only when they fell to their knees with even their extraordinary stamina and reckless courage totally expended, could the slave-masters put the ropes on them.

Tanus selected the best of them for his infantry regiments, and he learned their language as readily as I did. The Shilluk soon looked upon him as a god to replace their crocodiles, and Tanus came to love them almost as much as I loved my horses. In the end it was no longer necessary to catch the Shilluk like animals. These marvellously tall and willowy spearmen came out of their hiding-places in the reeds and bushy gulleys of their own accord, to seek Tanus out and to beg to be allowed to join his regiments.

Tanus armed them with long bronze-tipped

spears and shields made from elephant hide, and he uniformed them in kilts of wild-cat tails and head-dresses of ostrich feathers. His sergeants drilled them in all the classic evolutions of war, and we learned swiftly to integrate these tactics with those of the chariots.

Not all the Shilluk were selected for the army. The others proved to be indefatigable oarsmen on the rowing-benches of the galleys, and dedicated herdsmen and grooms, for they were born to tend their herds.

We very soon learned that their hereditary enemies were the tribes that lived further to the south, the Dinka and the Mandari. These other tribes were even more primitive, and lacked the fighting instincts of our Shilluk. Nothing pleased Tanus' new Shilluk regiments better than to be sent south with their Egyptian officers and supported by the chariots against their ancient foes. They rounded up the Dinka and Mandari in their thousands. We used them for the heavy unskilled work. None of them came in willingly, as some of our Shilluk had done.

Once we had brought the fleet up through the fifth cataract, the entire land of Cush lay open to us. With our Shilluk now to guide us, the fleet sailed on up-river, while our chariot divisions ranged widely along each bank, and returned with more ivory and fresh levies of slaves.

Soon we reached a wide river-course that joined the main flow of the Nile from the east. The flow of this river was restricted to a sullen trickle down its shrunken pools. However, the Shilluk assured us that in its season this river, which we named the Atbara, would become a raging torrent, and its waters would augment the annual flood of the Nile. Queen Lostris despatched an expedition of gold-seekers, with Shilluk guides, to follow the Atbara as far as they were able. The fleet sailed on southwards, hunting and slave-raiding along the way.

I worried to see it, and tried to prevent it, but so often these days Prince Memnon's chariot was at the head of one of these flying columns. Naturally, he was supported by good men, I could at least see to that, but there was constant hazard and danger out there in the African bush, and he was still only a boy.

I felt he should spend more time with me and his scrolls studying on the deck of the *Breath of Horus*, rather than disporting himself with the likes of Kratas and Remrem. Those two hooligans had as little concern for the prince's safety as they had for their own. They egged him on with wagers and challenges and extravagant praise for his more daring feats. He was soon as much of a dare-devil as any of them, and when he returned from these forays, he took great pleasure in horrifying me with accounts of his escapades.

When I protested to Tanus, he merely laughed. 'If he is to wear the double crown one day, he must learn to spurn danger and lead men.' My mistress agreed with Tanus in the training of Memnon. I had to content myself with making the most of what time I still had to be alone with my prince.

At least I had my two little princesses. They

were a wonderful consolation. Tehuti and Bekatha grew more enchanting each day, and I was their slave in more than name alone. Because of our peculiar circumstances I was closer to them than their true father could be. The first word that Bekatha ever said was 'Tata', and Tehuti refused to sleep unless I first told her a story. She pined when I was obliged to leave the fleet on other business. I think that this was the most happy period of my life. I felt that I was at the centre of my family, and solid in the affections of all of them.

The fortunes of our nation were almost as bright as my own. Soon one of our gold-seekers returned from the expedition up the Atbara river. He knelt before Queen Lostris and laid a small leather bag at her feet. Then, at her bidding, he opened the neck of the bag and poured from it a stream of gleaming pebbles. Some of these were as small as grains of sand, and others as large as the end of my thumb. All of them shone with that peculiar radiance that cannot be mistaken.

The goldsmiths were summoned and they worked with their furnaces and clay crucibles, and finally declared these nuggets to be veritable gold of an extraordinary purity. Tanus and I rode back up the Atbara to the site where this gold had been discovered. I helped to plan the methods that were used to mine the gravel-beds in the water-course of the river in which the gold had been trapped.

We used thousands of Mandari and Dinka slaves to scoop out basketloads of gravel and carry these up to the sluices that the masons had carved out of the granite slopes in the hills above the river.

To take back to my mistress I sketched pictures

248

of the long lines of naked black slaves, their wet skins gleaming in the sunlight, toiling up the hillside, each with a heavy basket balanced on his head. When we left the miners hard at work and went back to rejoin the fleet, we carried with us five hundred deben of newly smelted gold rings.

 We encountered yet another cataract on our voyage southwards. This was the sixth and final set of rapids, but this transit proved swifter and easier than any of the others. Our chariots and wagons were able to detour around the rapids, and so at last we reached the mystical confluence of two mighty rivers that between them became the Nile we knew and loved so well.

'This is the place that Taita saw in his vision of the Mazes of Ammon-Ra. Here Hapi lets her waters flow and mingle. This is the sacred site of the goddess,' Queen Lostris declared. 'We have completed our voyage. It is at this place that the goddess will strengthen us for the return to Egypt. I name it Qebui, the Place of the North Wind, for it is that wind which blew us here.'

'It is a propitious place. Already the goddess has shown her favour by providing us with slaves and gold,' the great lords of the state council agreed. 'We should voyage no further.'

'It remains only to find a site for the tomb of my husband, Pharaoh Mamose,' Queen Lostris decreed. 'Once the tomb is built and Pharaoh sealed in it, then my vow will have been fulfilled and it will be time to return in triumph to our very

Egypt. Only once that has been done can we go up against the Hyksos tyrant and drive him from our mother-land.'

I think that I was one of the very few of all our company who was not happy and relieved by this decision. The others were consumed by homesickness and weary of the long years of travel. I, on the other hand, had been stricken by a malady even more pernicious, that of wanderlust. I wanted to see what lay beyond the next bend of the river and over the crest of the next hill. I wanted to go on and on, to the very end of the world. Therefore I was delighted when my mistress chose me as the one to seek out the site of the royal tomb, and ordered Prince Memnon to escort me on this expedition with his squadron of chariots. Not only would I be able to indulge this new appetite of mine for travel, but I would once more have the undiluted pleasure of the prince's company.

At fourteen years of age, Prince Memnon was placed in command of the expedition. This was not exceptional. There have been pharaohs in our history who commanded great armies in battle when they were no older. The prince took his responsibilities on this his first independent command most seriously. The chariots were made ready, and Memnon inspected each horse and vehicle personally. We had two spare teams of horses for each chariot, so that these could be changed and rested regularly.

Then the two of us deliberated at great length and in even greater detail as to which direction we should follow in our search for the ideal site for the king's tomb. This should be in some rugged and uninhabited area not readily accessible to grave-robbers. There must be a cliff into which the tomb with all the subsidiary passages could be cut.

There was no area that we had come upon since we had entered the land of Cush that satisfied these requirements. We reviewed what we knew of the land behind us and tried to divine what lay ahead. Where we stood now at Qebui, the meeting-point of the two rivers, was the loveliest place we had visited on all the long voyage.

It seemed that all the birds of the air had gathered here, from tiny jewelled kingfishers to stately blue cranes, from whistling flocks of duck that darkened the sun in their multitudes to plovers and lapwings that scurried along the water's edge, pausing only to ask the plaintive question, 'Pee-wit? Pee-wit?' In the silvery acacia groves and out on the open savannah, the herds of antelope grazed in their countless millions. It was almost as though this seat of the goddess was sacred to all degrees of life. The waters below the juncture of the rivers roiled with shoals of fish, while in the sky above the white-headed fish eagles turned slow circles against the startling blue of the African sky and uttered their weird, yelping chant.

Each of these twin rivers expressed a different character and mood, just as two infants sprung from the same womb can vary in every detail of body and mind. The right-hand branch was slow and yellow, greater in volume than the other, but not so assertive. The eastern branch was a murky grey-blue, an angry, overbearing flood that shoved its twin aside when they met, refusing to mingle its waters, crowding the other against the bank and retaining its own turbid character for many miles

251

downstream before sullenly allowing itself to be absorbed by the gentler yellow stream.

'Which river must we follow, Tata?' Memnon demanded, and I sent for the Shilluk guides.

'The yellow river comes out of a vast and pestilent swamp that has no end. No man can enter there. It is a place of crocodiles and hippopotamus and stinging insects. It is a place of fever where a man might lose his way and wander for ever,' the Shilluk told us.

'What of the other river?' we asked.

'The dark river comes out of the sky, down cliffs of stone that rise up into the clouds. No man can climb the dreadful gorges.'

'We will follow the dark left-hand fork,' the prince decided. 'In those rocky places we will find a resting-place for my father.'

So we journeyed into the east until we saw the mountains rise on the horizon. They formed a blue rampart so tall and formidable as to surpass anything that we had ever seen or believed possible. Beside these great mountains, the hills we had known in the Nile valley were like the scratching of little birds in the sand-banks of the river. Each day as we journeyed towards them they climbed higher into the heavens and dwarfed all the world below.

'No man can go up there,' Memnon marvelled. 'That must be the abode of the gods.'

We watched the lightning play upon the mountains, flickering and flaring inside the tumbling banks of cloud that blanketed the peaks from our view. We listened to the thunder growling like a hunting lion amongst the gorges and the sheer valleys, and we were awestruck.

We ventured no further than the foothills of this terrible range, and then the cliffs and gorges barred our way and turned our chariots back. In these foothills we found a hidden valley with vertical sides of stone. For twenty days the prince and I explored this wild place, until at last we stood before a black cliff-face and Memnon spoke quietly. 'This is where my father's earthly body will rest for all eternity.' He stared up at the sheer stone with a dreamy and mystical expression. 'It is as though I can hear his voice speaking in my head. He will be happy here.'

So I surveyed this place and marked out the cliff, driving bronze pegs into the cracks in the rock, setting out the direction and the angle of the entrance passage for the masons who would come to begin this work. When this was done, we extricated ourselves from the maze of valleys and snarling gorges, and returned down the Nile to the meeting-place of the rivers, where our fleet lay.

 We were camped on the great plains only a few days' travel from Qebui when I was awakened in the night by the eerie grunting cries and the sound of a moving mass of animals that seemed to come from the darkness all around us.

Memnon ordered the trumpeter to blow the call to arms, and we stood to, within the circle of chariots. We threw wood on the watch-fires and stared out into the night. In the flicker of the flames we saw a dark flood, like the spate of the Nile, streaming past us. The eerie honking cries and the snorting sounds were almost deafening, and the press of animals in this throng was so heavy that they bumped into the outer ring of chariots, and some of the vehicles were thrown over on their sides. It was not possible to rest in this uproar, and we stood to arms all the rest of that night. The flood of living creatures never abated in all that time.

When dawn lit the scene, we were presented with the most extraordinary spectacle. In every direction as far as the eye could see, the plains were covered with a carpet of moving animals. They were all travelling in the same direction, trudging onwards with a strange fatalistic determination, heads hanging, shrouded in the dust of their own passage, uttering those weird, mournful cries. Every so often, some section of this endless herd took fright, for no reason, and tossed up their heels. They cavorted and snorted and chased each other in aimless circles, like whirlpools in the surface of a smoothly flowing river. Then they would settle back into the same plodding gait and follow the swarms ahead of them into the hazy distance.

We stood and stared in amazement. Every animal in this vast concourse was of the same species, and each individual was identical in every respect to the next. They were all of a dark purplish hue, with a shaggy-maned dewlap and horns shaped like the crescent moon. Their heads were misshapen, with ugly bulbous noses, while their bodies sloped back from high shoulders to spindly hindquarters.

When at last we harnessed the chariots and resumed our own journey, we passed through this living sea of animals like a fleet of galleys. They opened to allow us passage, streaming by on either hand so close that we could reach out and touch them. They were completely unafraid, and stared at us with dull, incurious eyes.

When it was time for the midday meal, Memnon strung his bow and killed five of these antelope with as many arrows. We skinned and butchered the carcasses as their fellows streamed by us at arm's-length. Despite the animals' strange appearance, their flesh, when grilled on the coals of an open fire, was as good to eat as any wild game I had tasted.

'This is another gift from the gods,' Memnon declared. 'As soon as we rejoin the main army, we will send out an expedition to follow these herds. We will be able to smoke enough meat to feed all our armies and our slaves from now until these beasts come again next year.'

From our Shilluk guides we learned that this incredible migration was an annual occurrence as the herds moved from one grazing-ground to another, several hundred miles apart. The Shilluk called these beasts gnu, in imitation of their strange honking cry. 'This will be a never-ending supply, one that is replenished each year,' I informed the prince.

None of us was then able to foresee the catastrophic events which would flow from this visitation of the ungainly gnu. I might have been warned by the manner in which they threw up their heads and snorted without reason, or by the discharge of mucus from the nostrils of some of these beasts, that I noticed as they streamed past us. However, I gave little thought to this

255

behaviour, and judged them to be mild and harmless creatures who could bring us nothing but great benefit.

As soon as we reached the twin rivers, we reported the migration of gnu to Queen Lostris, and she agreed with Prince Memnon's suggestion. Assisted by Kratas and Remrem, she put him in command of a column of two hundred chariots, supported by wagons and several thousand Shilluk. She ordered him to slaughter as many gnu as could be cut up and smoked for army rations.

I did not accompany the expedition, for the role of butcher's assistant was not to my fancy. However, we could soon see the smoke from the fires, on which the meat was curing, darkening the horizon, and before many more days had passed, the wagons started to return, each one loaded high with blackened slabs of cured meat.

Exactly twenty days from our first encounter with the gnu herds, I was sitting under a shady tree on the bank of the Nile, playing bao with my old and dear friend Aton. As a small indulgence to myself and out of deference to Aton, I had opened one of the precious jars of three-palm quality wine that remained from the stock which I had brought from Egypt. Aton and I played and haggled as old friends do, and sipped the wine with deep appreciation.

We had no means of knowing that catastrophe was rushing down upon us to overwhelm us all. On the contrary, I had every reason to be pleased with myself. The previous day I had completed the drawings and plans for the building of Pharaoh's tomb, in which I had incorporated several features to deter and frustrate the depredations of any

256

grave-robber. Queen Lostris had approved these plans and appointed one of the master masons as the overseer. She told me that I might requisition all the slaves and equipment that I needed. My mistress was determined that she would not stint in making good her vow to her dead husband. She would build him the finest tomb that my genius could design.

I had just won the third successive board of bao from Aton and was pouring another jar of the truly excellent wine, when I heard the beat of hooves and looked up to see a horseman coming at full gallop from the direction of the chariot lines. When he was still at a distance I recognized Hui. Very few others rode astride, and certainly not at such a headlong pace. As he raced towards where we sat, I saw the expression on his face, and it alarmed me so that I stood up abruptly enough to spill the wine and upset the bao board.

'Taita!' he screamed at me from a hundred yards. 'The horses! Sweet Isis have mercy on us! The horses!'

He reined down his mount, and I swung up behind him and seized him around the waist. 'Don't waste time talking,' I shouted in his ear. 'Ride, fellow, ride!'

I went to Patience first. Half the herd was down, but she was my first love. The mare lay upon her side with her chest heaving. She was old now, with grey hairs frosting her muzzle. I had not used her in the traces since the day that Blade had been killed by the elephant bull. Although she no longer pulled a chariot, she was the finest brood mare in all our herds. Her foals all inherited her great heart and vivid intelligence. She had just weaned a

257

beautiful little colt who stood near her now, watching her anxiously.

I knelt beside her. 'What is it, my brave darling?' I asked softly, and she recognized my voice, and opened her eyes.

The lids were gummed with mucus. I was appalled by her condition. Her neck and throat were swollen to almost twice their normal girth. A vile-smelling stream of yellow pus streamed from her mouth and nostrils. The fever was burning her up, so that I could feel the heat radiate from her, as though from a camp-fire.

She tried to rise when I stroked her neck, but she was too weak. She fell back, and her breath gurgled and wheezed in her throat. The thick, creamy pus bubbled out of her nostrils, and I could hear that she was drowning in it. Her throat was closing, so that she had to battle for each breath.

She was watching me with an almost human expression of trust and appeal. I was overcome with a sense of helplessness. This affliction was beyond my previous experience. I slipped the snowy-white linen shawl from my shoulder and used it to mop the streaming pus from her nostrils. It was a pathetically inadequate attempt, for as fast as I wiped it away, fresh trickles of the stinking stuff poured from her.

'Taita!' Hui called to me. 'Every one of our animals has been stricken by this pestilence.' Grateful for the distraction, I left Patience and went through the rest of the herd. Half of them were down already, and those still upright were mostly staggering or beginning to drool the thick yellow pus from their mouths.

'What must we do?' Hui and all the charioteers appealed to me. I was burdened with their trust. They expected me alone to avert this terrible disaster, and I knew that it was beyond my powers. I knew of no remedy, and could not think of even the most drastic and unlikely treatment.

I stumbled back to where Patience lay, and wiped away the latest flood of stinking discharge from her muzzle. I could see that she was sinking away swiftly. Each breath she drew now was a terrible struggle. My grief weakened me, and I knew that in my helplessness I would soon melt into tears and be of no further use to any of them, neither horses nor men.

Somebody knelt beside me, and I looked up to see that it was one of the Shilluk grooms, a willing and likely fellow whom I had befriended and who now looked upon me as his master. 'It is the sickness of the gnu,' he told me in his simple language. 'Many will die.'

I stared at him, as what he said began to make sense in my muddled mind. I remembered the snorting, drooling herds of slate-coloured animals darkening the plains with their numbers, and how we had thought it a gift of the benevolent gods.

'This sickness kills our cattle when the gnu come. Those that live through it are safe. They are never sick again.'

'What can we do to save them, Habani?' I demanded, but he shook his head.

'There is nothing to be done.'

I was holding Patience's head in my arms when she died. The breath choked away in her throat and she shuddered and her legs stiffened and then relaxed. I let out a low moan of grief and was on

259

the very edge of the abyss of despair, when I looked up and through my tears saw that Patience's colt was down, with the yellow slime bubbling up from his throat.

In that moment my despair was replaced with a burning anger. 'No!' I shouted. 'I will not let you die also.'

I ran to the foal's side and shouted to Habani to bring leather buckets of hot water. With a linen cloth I bathed the colt's throat in an attempt to reduce the swelling, but it had no effect. The pus still poured from his nostrils, and the hot skin of his neck stretched out as the flesh ballooned like a bladder filling with air.

'He is dying.' Habani shook his head. 'Many will die.'

'I will not let it happen,' I swore grimly, and sent Hui to the galley to fetch my medicine chest.

By the time he returned, it was almost too late. The colt was in extremis. His breath was choking out of him and I could feel his strength draining away under my frantic hands. I felt for the ridged rings of his windpipe at the juncture of his throat and his chest. With one shallow cut through the skin I exposed the white sinewy pipe, and then I pressed the point of my scalpel into it and pierced the tough sheath. Immediately air hissed through the aperture and I saw the colt's chest swell as his lungs inflated. He began to breathe again to a steady and even rhythm, but I saw almost immediately that the puncture-wound in his throat was closing again with blood and mucus.

In frantic haste I hacked a length of bamboo from the framework of the nearest chariot, and I cut a hollow tube from the end of it and pushed this into the wound. The bamboo tube held the wound open and the colt relaxed his struggles as the air sucked and blew unimpeded through it.

'Hui!' I yelled for him. 'I will show you how to save them.' Before night fell, I had trained a hundred or more of the charioteers and grooms to perform this crude but effective surgery, and we worked on through the night by the wavering, uncertain light of the oil lamps.

There were over thirteen thousand horses in the royal herds by this time. We could not save them all, although we tried. We worked on, with the blood from the severed throats caking black up to our elbows. When exhaustion overcame us, we fell on a bale of hay and slept for an hour and then staggered up and went back to work.

Some of the horses were not as badly affected by this pestilence, which I had named the Yellow Strangler. They seemed to have an in-born resistance to its ravages. The discharge from their nostrils was no more copious than I had seen in the gnu herds, and many of these remained on their feet and threw off the disease within days.

Many others died before we were able to open the windpipe, and even some of those, on which we had successfully operated, died later from mortification and complication of the wound which we had inflicted. Of course, many of our horses were out on expeditions into the plains and beyond my help. Prince Memnon lost two out of every three of his steeds and had to abandon his chariots and return to the Qebui rivers on foot.

In the end we lost over half our horses, seven thousand dead, and those that survived were so weakened and cast down that it was many months before they were strong and fit enough to pull a chariot. Patience's colt survived and replaced his old dam in my affections. He took the right-hand trace in my chariot, and was so strong and reliable that I called him Rock.

'How has this pestilence affected our hopes of a swift return to Egypt?' my mistress asked me.

'It has set us back many years,' I told her, and saw the pain in her eyes. 'We lost most of our best-trained old horses, those like Patience. We will have to breed up the royal herds all over again, and train young horses to take their places in the traces of the chariots.'

I waited for the annual migration of the gnu the following year with dread, but when it came and their multitudes once more darkened the plains, Habani was proved correct. Only a few of our horses developed the symptoms of the Yellow Strangler, and these in a mild form that set them back for only a few weeks before they were strong enough to work again.

What struck me as strange was that the foals born in the period after the first infection of the Yellow Strangler, those who had never been exposed to the actual disease, were as immune as their dams who had contracted a full dose. It was as though the immunity had been transferred to them in the milk that they sucked from their mother's udder. I was certain that we would never again have to experience the full force of the plague.

My major duty now, laid upon me by my mistress, was the construction of Pharaoh's tomb in the mountains. I was obliged to spend much of my time in that wild and forbidding place, and I became fascinated by those mountains and all their moods.

Like a beautiful woman, the mountains were unpredictable, sometimes remote and hidden in dense moving veils of clouds that were shot through with lightning and riven with thunder. At other times they were lovely and seductive, beckoning to me, challenging me to discover all their secrets and experience all their dangerous delights.

Although I had eight thousand slaves to prosecute the task, and the unstinted assistance of all our finest craftsmen and artists, the work on the tomb went slowly. I knew it would take many years to complete the elaborate mausoleum which my mistress insisted we must build, and to decorate it in a fashion fit for the Lord of the Two Kingdoms. In truth there was no point in hurrying the work, for it would take as long to rebuild the royal horse herds and train the Shilluk infantry regiments until they were a match for the Hyksos squadrons against which they would one day be matched.

When I was not up in the mountains working at the tomb, I spent my time at Qebui, where there were myriad different tasks and pleasures awaiting me. These ranged from the education of my two little princesses to devising new military tactics with Lord Tanus and the prince.

By this time it was clear that, whereas Memnon

would one day command all the chariot divisions, Tanus had never outgrown his first distrust of the horse. He was a sailor and an infantryman to the bone, and as he grew older, he was ever more conservative and traditional in his use of his new Shilluk regiments.

The prince was growing into a dashing and innovative charioteer. Each day he came to me with a dozen new ideas, some of them far-fetched, but others quite brilliant. We tried them all, even the ones that I knew were impossible. He was sixteen years old when Queen Lostris promoted him to the rank of Best of Ten Thousand.

Now that Tanus rode with me so seldom, I slowly took over the role of Memnon's principal driver. We developed a rapport which became almost instinctive, and which extended to our favourite team of horses, Rock and Chain. When we were on the march, Memnon still liked to drive, and I stood on the footplate behind him. However, as soon as we engaged in action, he would toss me the reins and seize his bow or his javelins from the rack. I would take the chariot into the fray and steer it through the evolutions we had dreamed up together.

As Memnon matured and his strength increased, we began to win some of the prizes at the games and the military tattoos that were a feature of our lives at Qebui. First, we triumphed in the flat races where our team of Rock and Chain could display its paces to the full; then we began to win the shooting and javelin contests. Soon we were known as the chariot that had to be beaten before anyone could claim the champion's ribbon from Queen Lostris.

I remember the cheers as our chariot flew through the final gate of the course, myself at the traces and Memnon on the footplate hurling a javelin right and left into the two straw-filled dummies as we passed, then the mad dash down the straight, with the prince howling like a demon and the long wind-blown plait of his hair standing out behind his head, like the tail of a charging lion.

Soon there were other encounters in which the prince began to distinguish himself, and those without any assistance from me. Whenever he strode past the young girls, with the Gold of Valour gleaming on his chest and the champion's ribbon knotted into his plait, they giggled and blushed and slanted their eyes in his direction. Once I entered his tent in haste with some important news for him, only to come up short as I found my prince well mounted and oblivious to all but the tender young body and the pretty face beneath him. I withdrew silently, a little saddened that the age of his innocence was past.

Of all these pleasures, none for me could compare with those precious hours that I was still able to spend with my mistress. In this her thirty-third year she was in the very high summer of her beauty. Her allure was enhanced by her sophistication and her poise. She had become a queen indeed, and a woman without peer.

All her people loved her, but none of them as much as I did. Not even Tanus was able to surpass me in my devotion to her. It was my pride that she still needed me so much, and relied upon me and my judgement and my advice so trustingly. Notwithstanding the other blessings that I had to adorn my existence, she would ever be the one great love of my life.

 I should have been contented and replete, but there is a restlessness in my nature that was exacerbated by this new wanderlust that had come to plague me. Whenever I paused from my labours at Pharaoh's tomb, and looked up at them, the mountains beckoned me. I began to make short excursions into their lonely gorges, often alone but sometimes with Hui or some other companion.

Hui was with me when I first saw the herds of wild ibex high above us in the lofty crags of the mountain. They were of a species we had never seen before. They stood twice as tall as the wild goats that we knew from the Nile valley, and some of the old billy-goats carried such a mass of curling horn that they seemed as monstrous as some fabulous beast.

It was Hui who carried reports of these huge ibex back to the twin rivers where the fleet lay at Qebui, and within the month, Lord Tanus arrived at the valley of the king's tomb, with his bow over his shoulder and Prince Memnon at his side. The prince was fast becoming as ardent a huntsman as his father, and was every bit as eager for the chase. As for myself, I welcomed the chance to explore those fascinating highlands in such company.

We had meant to venture only as far as the first line of peaks, but when we climbed to their crest, we were presented with a vista that was breathtaking. We saw other mountains against the sky that were shaped like flat-topped anvils, and were the tawny colour of lions. They dwarfed the peaks on which we stood and lured us onwards.

The Nile climbed in concert with us up through precipitous valleys and dark gorges that churned its waters to gleaming white. We could not always follow its course, but in places were forced to climb above it and follow giddy goat-tracks across the face of a frowning mountain.

Then, when we had been lured deep into its maw, the mountain loosed its full fury upon us.

We were one hundred men in our company, with ten pack-horses to carry our provisions. We were camped in the depths of one of these fathomless gorges, with the fresh trophies of Tanus' and Memnon's latest hunt laid out upon the rocky floor for our appraisal and admiration. These were two goats' heads, the largest we had seen in all our travels, so heavy in horn that it took two slaves to lift one of them. Suddenly it began to rain.

In our Egyptian valley it may rain once in twenty years. None of us had ever imagined anything even remotely like the rain that fell upon us now.

First, dense black clouds roofed over the narrow strip of sky that showed between the cliffs that walled us in, so that we were plunged from sunny noon into deep twilight. A cold wind raced down the valley and chilled our bodies and our spirits. We huddled together in dismay.

Then lightning lanced from the sombre belly of the clouds and shattered the rocks around us, filling the air with the smell of sulphur and sparks struck from flint. Thunder burst upon us, magnified as it rolled from cliff to cliff, and the earth jumped and trembled beneath our feet.

Then the rain fell. It did not come down upon us in the form of drops. It was as though we stood under one of the cataracts of the Nile when the river was in full flood. There was no longer air to breathe, water filled our mouths and our nostrils so that we felt that we were drowning. The rain was so thick that we could see only the blurred outline of the man who stood an arm's-length away. It battered us so that we were thrown down and cringed beneath the nearest rock for shelter. Still it assaulted all the senses and stung our exposed skin like a swarm of angry hornets.

It was cold. I had never known such cold, and we were covered only with our thin linen shawls. The cold sucked the force out of my limbs, and we shivered until our teeth clattered together in our mouths, and we could not still them even though we bit down with all the strength of our jaws.

Then, above the sound of the falling rain, I heard a new sound. It was the sound of water which had become a ravening monster. Down the narrow valley where we lay swept a wall of grey water. It stretched from cliff to cliff, and carried everything before it.

I was caught up in it and tumbled end over end. I felt life being beaten out of me as I was thrown against the rocks, and icy water filled my throat. Darkness overwhelmed me, and I thought that I was dead.

I have a vague recollection of hands dragging me from the flood, and then I was wafted away to some dark and distant shore. The voice of my prince called me back. Before I could open my eyes I smelled woodsmoke, and felt the warmth of the flames on one side of my body.

'Tata, wake up! Speak to me.' The voice was insistent, and I opened my eyes. Memnon's face floated before me, and he smiled at me. Then he called over his shoulder, 'He is awake, Lord Tanus.'

I found that we were in a rock cave and that outside, the night had fallen. Tanus came across from the smoky fire of damp wood and squatted beside the prince.

'How are you, old friend? I don't think you have broken any bones.'

I struggled into a sitting position, and gingerly tested every part of my body before I replied, 'My head is cracked through, and every limb aches. Apart from that, I am cold and hungry.'

'You will live then,' Tanus chuckled, 'though a while ago I doubted any of us would. We have to get out of these cursed mountains before something worse happens. It was madness ever to venture into a place where the rivers come out of the sky.'

'What about the others?' I asked.

Tanus shook his head. 'They are all drowned. You were the only one that we were able to drag from the flood.'

'What about the horses?'

'Gone,' he grunted. 'All gone.'

'Food?'

'Nothing,' Tanus replied. 'Even my bow is lost in the river. I have only the sword at my side and the clothes on my body.'

At dawn we left our rock shelter and started back down that treacherous valley. At the foot of the gorge we found the bodies of some of our men and the horses strewn upon the rocks where they had been stranded when the flood receded.

We scavenged amongst the rocks and scree, and we managed to recover some of our stores and equipment. To my great joy I found my medicine chest still intact, though flooded with water. I laid out the contents on a rock, and while they dried, I fashioned a sling from a leather harness to carry the chest upon my back.

In the meantime, Memnon had cut strips of meat from the carcass of one of the horses and grilled them over another fire of driftwood. When we had eaten our fill, we saved the rest of the meat, and set out on the return.

The journey slowly descended into nightmare as we scaled steep rocky slopes and dropped into the gorges beyond. There seemed to be no end to this terrible wilderness, and our bruised feet in open sandals protested each step. At night we shivered miserably around a smoky little fire of driftwood.

By the second day we all knew that we had lost the way, and that we were wandering aimlessly. I was certain that we were doomed to die in these terrible mountains. Then we heard the river and, as we topped the next saddle between peaks, we found the infant Nile winding through the depths of the gorge below us. That was not all. On the banks of the river we saw a collection of coloured tents, and amongst them moved the shapes of men.

'Civilized men,' I said immediately, 'for those tents must be of woven cloth.'

'And those are horses,' Memnon agreed eagerly, pointing out the animals tethered on the lines beyond the encampment.

'There!' Tanus pointed. 'That was the flash of sunlight off a sword-blade or a spear-head. They are metal-workers.'

'We must find out who these people are.' I was fascinated by what tribe could live in such an inhospitable land.

'We will get our throats cut,' Tanus growled. 'What makes you believe these mountaineers are not as savage as the land in which they live?' Only later would we come to know these people as Ethiopians.

'Those are magnificent horses,' Memnon whispered. 'Our own are not so tall, or so sturdy. We must go down and study them.' The prince was a horseman above all else.

'Lord Tanus is right.' His warning had aroused my usual prudent nature, and I was ready to counsel caution. 'These might be dangerous savages, with but the trappings of civilized men.'

We sat upon the shoulder of the mountain and debated for a while longer, but in the end curiosity got the better of all three of us and we crept down through one of the ravines to spy upon these strangers.

As we drew closer, we saw that they were tall, well-built people, probably more robust in stature than we Egyptians are. Their hair was thick and dark and curled profusely. The men were bearded, and we are clean-shaven. They wore full-length robes, probably woven of wool, and brightly coloured. We go bare-chested and our kilts are usually pure white in colour. They wore soft leather boots, as opposed to our sandals, and a bright cloth wound around their heads.

The women we saw working amongst the tents were unveiled and cheerful. They sang and called to each other in a language I had never heard before, but their voices were melodious as they drew water, or squatted over the cooking-fires, or ground corn on the millstones.

One group of men was playing a board-game that, from where I hid, looked very much like bao. They were wagering and arguing over the play of the stones. At one stage, two of them leapt to their feet and drew curved daggers from their belts. They confronted each other snarling and hissing, like a pair of angry tom-cats.

At that stage a third man, who had been sitting alone, rose to his feet and stretched, like a lazy leopard. He sauntered across and, with his sword, knocked up the daggers. Immediately the two protagonists subsided and slunk away.

The peace-maker was clearly the chief of the party. He was a tall man, with the wiry frame of a mountain goat. He was goat-like in other ways. His beard was as long and thick as that of an ibex ram, and his features were coarse and goaty; he had a heavy, hooked nose and a wide mouth with a cruel slant to it. I thought that he probably stank like one of the old rams that Tanus had shot from the cliff-face.

Suddenly I felt Tanus grip my arm, and he whispered in my ear, 'Look at that!'

This chieftain wore the richest apparel of any of

272

them. His robe was striped in scarlet and blue and his earrings were stones that glowed like the full moon. But I could not see what had excited Tanus.

'His sword,' Tanus hissed. 'Look at his sword.'

I studied it for the first time. It was longer than one of our weapons and the pommel was obviously of pure gold filigree-work, of a delicacy that I had never seen before. The hand-guard was studded with precious stones. It was a masterpiece that clearly had occupied some master craftsman his lifetime.

This was not what had captured Tanus' attention, however. It was the blade. As long as the chief's own arm, it was made of a metal that was neither yellow bronze nor red copper. In colour it was a strange silvery glittering blue, like the living scales of a Nile perch taken fresh from the river. It was inlaid with gold, as if to highlight its unique value.

'What is it?' Tanus breathed. 'What metal is that?'

'I do not know.'

The chief resumed his seat in front of his tent, but now he laid the sword across his lap, and, with a phallus-shaped piece of volcanic rock, began lovingly to stroke the edge of the blade. The metal emitted a ringing thrill of sound to each touch of the stone. No bronze ever resounded like that. It was the purr of a resting lion.

'I want it,' Tanus whispered. 'I will never rest until I have that sword.'

I gave him a startled glance, for I had never heard such a tone in his voice. I saw that he meant what he said. He was a man struck with a sudden

273

overpowering passion.

'We cannot remain here longer,' I told him softly. 'We will be discovered.' I took his arm, but he resisted. He was staring at the weapon.

'Let us go to look at their horses,' I insisted, and at last he allowed me to draw him away. I led Memnon by the other hand. At a safe distance we circled the camp, and crept back towards the horse-lines.

When I saw the horses close up, I was struck with a passion as fierce as Tanus had conceived for the blue sword. These were a different breed from our Hyksos horses. They were taller and more elegantly proportioned. Their heads were noble and their nostrils wider. I knew those nostrils were the mark of stamina and good wind. Their eyes were situated further forward in the skull and were more prominent than those of our animals. They were great soft eyes, shining with intelligence.

'They are beautiful,' whispered Memnon at my side. 'Look at the way they hold their heads and arch their necks.'

Tanus longed for the sword, we coveted the horses with a passion that equalled his.

'Just one stallion like that to put to our mares,' I pleaded to any god who was listening. 'I would exchange my hope of eternal life for a single one.'

One of the foreign grooms glanced in our direction, then said something to the fellow beside him and began to walk in our direction. This time I had no need to insist, and all three of us ducked down behind the boulder that sheltered us and crawled away. We found a secure hiding-place further down-river, amongst a tumbled heap of boulders, and immediately launched into one of those discussions in which all spoke together and none listened.

'I will go in and offer him a thousand deben of gold,' Tanus swore, 'I must have that sword.'

'He would kill you first. Did you not see him stroke it as though it was his first-born son?'

'Those horses!' marvelled Memnon. 'I never dreamed of such beauty. Horus must have beasts like that to draw his chariot.'

'Did you see those two fly at each other?' I cautioned. 'They are savage men, and bloodthirsty. They would rip out your guts before you opened your mouth to utter a word. Besides, what do you have to offer in return? They will see we are destitute beggars.'

'We could steal three of their stallions tonight and ride them down on to the plain,' Memnon suggested, and though the idea had appeal, I told him sternly, 'You are the crown prince of Egypt, not a common thief.'

He grinned at me. 'For one of those horses, I would cut throats like the worst footpad in Thebes.'

As we debated thus, we were suddenly aware of the sound of voices approaching along the river-bank from the direction of the foreign camp. We looked about for better concealment and hid away.

The voices drew closer. A party of women came into view and they stopped below us at the water's edge. There were three older women, and a girl. The women wore robes of a drab hue, and cloths of black around their hair. I thought that they were servants or nursemaids. It did not occur to me then that they were gaolers, for they treated the girl

275

with unusual deference.

The girl was tall and slim, so that when she walked, she moved like a papyrus stem in the Nile breeze. She wore a short robe of rich wool, striped in yellow and sky blue, which left her knees bared. Though she wore short boots of soft stitched leather, I could see that her legs were lithe and smooth.

The women stopped below our hiding-place, and one of the older women began to disrobe the girl. The other two filled the clay jars that they had carried down on their heads with water from the Nile. The river was still swollen with flood-water. No one could safely enter that icy torrent. It was clear that they intended bathing the girl from the jars.

One of the women lifted the girl's robe over her head and she stood naked at the water's edge. I heard Memnon gasp. I looked at him and saw that he had forgotten entirely about stealing horses.

While two of the women poured the water from the jars over the girl, the third woman wiped her down with a folded cloth. The girl held her hands above her head and circled slowly to allow them to wet every part of her body. She laughed and squealed at the cold, and I saw tiny goosebumps rise around her nipples, which were the rich ruby of polished garnets, mounted like jewels on the peak of each smooth, round breast.

Her hair was a dark bush of tight curls, her skin was the colour of the heartwood of the acacia, when it has been buffed and oiled to a high patina. It was a rich, ruddy brown, that glowed in the high sunlight of the mountains.

Her features were delicate, her nose narrow and

chiselled. Her lips were soft and full, but without any thickness. Her eyes were large and dark, slanted above high cheek-bones. Her lashes were so thick that they tangled together. She was beautiful. I have only known one other woman who was more so.

Suddenly she said something to the women with her. They stood aside, and she left them and climbed on those long naked legs towards us. But before she reached our hiding-place, she stepped behind a boulder that shielded her from her companions, but left her full in our view. She glanced around quickly, but did not see us. The cold water must have affected her, for she squatted quickly and her own water tinkled on the rock beneath her.

Memnon groaned softly. It was instinctive, not intentional, a sound of longing so intense as to have become agony. The girl sprang to her feet and stared directly at him. Memnon was standing a little to one side of Tanus and me. While we were concealed, he was full in her view.

The two of them stared at each other. The girl was trembling, her dark eyes enormous. I expected her to run or scream. Instead, she looked back over her shoulder in a conspiratorial gesture, as if to make certain that the women had not followed her. Then she turned back to Memnon and, in a soft sweet voice, asked a question, at the same time holding out her hand to him in a gesture of appeal.

'I do not understand,' Memnon whispered, and spread his own hands in a gesture of incomprehension.

The girl stepped up to him and repeated the question impatiently, and when Memnon shook his head, she seized his hand and shook it. In her agitation, her voice rose as she demanded something of him.

'Masara!' One of her attendants had heard her. 'Masara!' It was obviously the girl's name, for she made a gesture of silence and caution to Memnon and turned to go back.

However, the three women had all started up the slope after Masara. They were chattering with alarm and agitation, and they came round the side of the boulder in a pack and stopped when they saw Memnon.

For a moment nobody moved, and then all three women screamed in unison. The naked girl seemed poised to run to Memnon's side, but as she started forward, two of the women seized her; all four of them were screaming now, as the girl struggled to be free.

'Time to go home,' Tanus jerked my arm, and I was after him in a bound.

From the direction of the camp came the shouts of many men aroused by the screams of the women. When I paused to look back, I saw them coming over the ridge in a body. I saw also that Memnon had not followed us, but had leaped forward to the girl's assistance.

They were all big women and held the girl hard, redoubling their screams. Although Masara was trying desperately to pull free, Memnon could not get her away from them.

'Tanus!' I yelled. 'Memnon is in trouble.'

We turned back and between us grabbed him and hauled him away. He came reluctantly. 'I will come back for you,' he shouted to the girl, looking back over his shoulder as we ran with him between us. 'Be brave. I will come back for you.'

When somebody tells me nowadays that there is no such thing as love at first sight, I smile quietly to myself and think of the day that Memnon first saw Masara.

We had lost time in the struggle to get Memnon away, and our pursuers were already pressing us hard as we took to one of the goat-tracks and ran for the crest of the slope. An arrow flitted past Memnon's shoulder and clattered against the rocks beside the path. It spurred us to greater speed.

We were in single file along the narrow path. Memnon led us and Tanus followed him. I was last in the file, and, burdened by the heavy medicine chest on my back, I began to fall further behind. Another arrow passed over our heads, and then the third struck the pack on my back with a force that made me stagger. But the chest stopped the arrow that would otherwise have transfixed my body.

'Come on, Taita,' Tanus shouted back at me. 'Throw off that cursed box of yours, or they will have you.'

He and Memnon were fifty paces ahead of me and drawing away, but I could not discard my precious chest. At that moment the next arrow struck, and this time I was not so fortunate. It hit me in the leg, in the fleshy part of the thigh, and I went tumbling across the path and fell hard.

I rolled into a sitting position and looked with horror at the reed shaft of the arrow that protruded from my leg. Then I looked back at our pursuers. The bearded chieftain in the striped robe led them, and he had outdistanced his own men by a hundred paces. He was coming up the track in a

279

series of great elastic bounds, covering the ground as swiftly as one of the ibex rams that he resembled in so many other ways.

'Taita!' Tanus called back at me. 'Are you all right?' He had paused on the brow of the slope, and was looking back anxiously. Memnon had crossed over and was out of sight.

'I am arrowed!' I yelled back. 'Go on and leave me. I cannot follow.'

Without a moment's hesitation, Tanus turned back, and came leaping down towards where I lay. The Ethiopian chieftain saw him coming and bellowed a challenge. He drew the glittering blue sword and brandished it as he came on up the hillside.

Tanus reached the spot where I sat, and tried to lift me to my feet. 'It's no use. I am hard hit. Save yourself,' I told him, but the Ethiopian was almost upon us. Tanus dropped my arm, and drew his own sword.

The two of them came together, going for each other in a murderous rush. I was not in any doubt as to the outcome of this duel, for Tanus was the strongest and most skilled swordsman in all Egypt. When he killed the Ethiopian, we would all be doomed, for we could expect no mercy from his henchmen.

The Ethiopian swung first with a full-blooded overhand cut at Tanus' head. It was an imprudent stroke to aim at a swordsman of his opponent's calibre. I knew that Tanus' response would be a parry in the line of the head and a natural riposte, with all the momentum of his shoulder behind it, that would drive the point through the chieftain's beard and into his throat. It was one of Tanus' favourite strokes.

The two blades met, but there was no ringing clash. The blue blade hacked clean through Tanus' yellow bronze, as though it were a wand of green willow. Tanus was left with the hilt in his hand and a finger's length remaining from that once long and deadly bronze blade.

Tanus was stunned by the ease with which the Ethiopian had disarmed him, and he was slow to defend himself from the next stroke that followed like a thunderbolt. He leaped backwards just in time, but the blue point opened a long, shallow cut across the bulging muscles of his naked chest, and the blood came swiftly.

'Run, Tanus!' I screamed. 'Or he will kill us both.'

The Ethiopian went for him again, but I was lying in the middle of the narrow path. He was forced to leap over me to get at Tanus. I seized him around the knees with both arms, and brought him down on top of me in a snarling, thrashing heap.

The Ethiopian was trying to drive the point of the blue sword into my belly, as I lay under him, and I twisted so violently aside that both of us rolled off the path and began to slide away down the steep slope of loose scree. As we rolled more swiftly, gathering momentum, I had one last glimpse of Tanus peering down over the edge of the path, and I screamed in a despairing wail, 'Run! Take care of Memnon!'

The shale and loose scree were as treacherous as swamp quicksands, and gave no anchor or purchase. The Ethiopian and I were flung apart, but both of us were carried to the edge of the torrent. I was battered and hammered to the edge of consciousness, and lay there groaning until rough hands dragged me to my feet, and blows and harsh curses rained upon my head.

The chieftain stopped them from killing me and throwing my body into the river. He was covered with dust, as I was, and his robe was torn and filthy from the fall, but the blue sword was still gripped in his right fist and he snarled at his men. They began to drag me away towards the encampment, but I looked around me desperately and saw my medicine chest amongst the rocks. The leather harness had snapped, and it had come off my back.

'Bring that,' I ordered my captors with as much force and dignity as I could muster, and pointed to the chest. They laughed at my insolence, but the chieftain sent one of his men to retrieve it.

Two men were obliged to support me, for the shaft in my thigh was beginning to cause me crippling pain. Every pace back to the camp was agony, and when they reached it, they threw me roughly to the ground in the open space in the centre of the ring of tents.

Then they argued long and fiercely. It was obvious that they were puzzling over my origins and my motives, and trying to decide what they should do with me. Every once in a while, one of them would stand over me and kick me in the ribs, while he shouted questions at me. I lay as quietly as I could, so as not to provoke further violence.

There was a distraction when the party that had pursued Tanus and Memnon returned empty-handed. There was more shouting and arm-waving as bitter recriminations and insults were exchanged. I was cheered by the thought that the two of them had got clean away.

After a while my captors remembered me, and they came back to vent their frustration on me with more kicks and blows. In the end their chieftain called them off, and ordered them not to torment me further. After that, most of them lost interest in me and wandered away. I was left lying on the bare ground, covered with dirt and bruises, with the arrow still lodged in my flesh.

The Ethiopian chieftain resumed his seat in front of the largest tent, which was clearly his own, and while he stropped the edge of his sword, he regarded me with a steady but inscrutable expression. Occasionally he exchanged a few low words with one of his men, but it seemed that my immediate danger was past.

I judged my moment carefully, and then addressed him directly. I pointed to my medicine chest, which had been thrown against one of the tents, and I made my voice mild and placatory. 'I need my chest. I must tend this wound.'

Although the chieftain did not understand the words, he understood my gestures. He ordered one of his men to bring the chest across to him. He made them set it down in front of him and opened the lid. He unpacked the chest methodically, examining each separate item. Anything that particularly caught his attention he held up, and asked a question to which I tried to give an answer with signs.

He seemed satisfied that, apart from my scalpels, the chest contained no dangerous weapon. I am not sure if he realized at this stage that these were medical items. However, with signs I showed him what I needed to do, pointing to my leg and making a pantomime of pulling the arrow. He stood over me with the sword in his hand, and made it clear that he would lop off my head at the first sign of treachery, but he allowed me to use my instruments.

The arrow had entered at an angle and position which made it awkward for me to reach. In addition to this, the pain that I inflicted upon myself, as I used the Taita spoons to trap and mask the barbs that were buried deep in my flesh, brought me more than once to the point of fainting away.

I was panting and drenched in sheets of sweat when at last I was ready to draw the arrow-head. By this time I had an audience of half the men in camp. They had returned to crowd around me and watch my surgery with garrulous interest.

I took a firm hold on the handles of the spoons, placed a wooden wedge between my teeth and bit down on it hard, and drew the clamped arrow-head out of the wound. There were shouts of wonder and amazement from my audience. Obviously none of them had ever seen a barb drawn with such ease and with so little damage to the victim. They were impressed even further when they watched the skill and dexterity with which I laid on the linen bandages.

In any nation and in any culture, even the most primitive, the healer and the physician have a special place of honour and esteem. I had demonstrated my credentials in the most convincing manner, and my status in the Ethiopian camp was drastically altered.

At the orders of the chief, I was carried to one of the tents and laid on a straw mattress. My medicine chest was placed at the head of my bed, and one of the women brought me a meal of corn-bread and chicken stew and thick sour milk.

In the morning, when the tents were struck, I was placed in a pole-litter behind one of the horses in the long caravan, and pulled along the rough and precipitous tracks. To my dismay, I saw from the angle of the sun that we were headed back into the fastness of the mountains, and I feared that I was lost to my own people, probably for all time. The fact that I was a physician had probably saved my life, but it had also placed such value on me that I would never be turned free. I knew that I was now a slave in more than name alone.

Despite the jolting of the litter, my leg began to heal cleanly. This further impressed my captors, and soon they were bringing to me any member of the band who was sick or injured.

I cured a ringworm and lanced a whitlow under a thumbnail. I sewed together a man who had won too much gambling with his quick-tempered friends. These Ethiopians had a penchant for settling arguments with the dagger. When one of the horses threw its rider down a gulley, I set his broken arm. It knitted straight, and my reputation was enhanced. The Ethiopian chieftain looked at me with a new respect, and I was offered the food-bowl after he had made his selection of the choice cuts, before any of the other men were allowed to eat.

When my leg had healed sufficiently for me to

walk again, I was given the run of the camp. However, I was not allowed out of sight. An armed man followed me and stood over me, even when I was on the most private and intimate business amongst the rocks.

I was kept away from Masara and only saw her from afar at the start of each day's journey, and again when we camped for the night. During the long day's ride through the mountains we were separated; I rode near the head of the caravan, while she was brought along at the rear. She was always accompanied by her female gaolers, and usually surrounded by armed guards.

Whenever we did catch sight of each other, Masara cast the most desperate and appealing looks at me, as though I would be able to help her in some way. It was obvious that she was a prisoner of rank and of importance. She was such a lovely young woman that I often found myself thinking of her during the day, and trying to fathom the reason for her captivity. I decided she was either an unwilling bride, being taken to meet her future husband, or that she was a pawn in some political intrigue.

Without a knowledge of the language I could not hope to understand what was taking place, or to learn anything about these Ethiopians. I set out to learn the Geez tongue.

I have the ear of a musician, and I played my tricks upon them. I listened attentively to all the chatter around me, and picked up the cadence and the rhythm of their speech. Very early on, I was able to deduce that the chieftain's name was Arkoun. One morning before the caravan set out, Arkoun was giving orders for the day's march to his assembled band. I waited until he had delivered a long and heated harangue, and then I repeated it in precisely the same tone and cadence.

They listened to me in stunned silence, and then burst into uproar. They roared with laughter and beat each other on the back, tears of mirth streamed down their cheeks, for they had a direct and uncomplicated sense of humour. I had not the least idea what I had said, but it was obvious that I had got it exactly right.

They shouted excerpts from my speech at each other, and wagged their heads, mimicking Arkoun's pompous manner. It took a long time for order to be restored, but at last Arkoun strutted up to me and shouted an accusatory question at me. I did not understand a word of it, but I shouted the same question back at him, word for exact word.

This time there was pandemonium. The joke of it was too rich to be borne. Grown men clung to each other for support, they screamed and wiped their streaming eyes. One of them fell into the fire and singed his beard.

Even though the joke was on him, Arkoun laughed along with them and patted me on the back. From then onwards, every man and woman in the camp was my teacher. I had only to point at any object and the Geez word for it was shouted at me. When I began to string those words into sentences, they corrected me eagerly, and were inordinately proud of my progress.

It took me some time to fathom the grammar. The verbs were declined in a manner which had no relationship to Egyptian, and the gender and plurals of the nouns were strange. However, within ten days I was speaking intelligible Geez, and had even built up a good selection of choice curses and invective.

While I learned the language and treated their ailments, I studied their mores and manners. I learned that they were inveterate gamblers, and that the board-game that they played endlessly was a passion. They called it dom, but it was a simplified and rudimentary form of bao. The number of cups in the board and the quantity of stones brought into play varied from bao. However, all the objects and the principles were similar.

Arkoun himself was the dom champion of the band, but as I studied his play, I saw that he had no inkling of the classic rule of seven stones. Nor did he understand the protocol of the four bulls. Without a thorough knowledge of these, no bao player could aspire to even the lowly third grade of masters. I debated with myself the risk that I would run in humiliating such a vain and overbearing tyrant as Arkoun, but in the end I decided that it was the only way to gain ascendancy over him.

The next time he sat in front of his tent and set up the board, smirking and twirling his moustaches as he waited for a challenger to step forward, I elbowed aside the first aspirant and settled myself cross-legged opposite Arkoun.

'I have no silver to wager,' I told him in my still rudimentary Geez. 'I play for love of the stones.'

He nodded gravely. As an addict of the board, he understood that sentiment. The news that I was taking the board against Arkoun ran through the camp, and they all came laughing and jostling to watch.

When I allowed Arkoun to lay three stones in

the east castle they nudged each other and chuckled with disappointment that the game would be so swiftly lost. One more stone in the east, and the board was his. They did not understand the significance of the four bulls that I had banked in the south. When I loosed my bulls, they strode invincibly across the board, splitting his unsupported stones and isolating the east castle. He was powerless to prevent it. Four moves and the board was mine. I had not even been called upon to demonstrate the rule of seven stones.

For some moments they all sat in shocked silence. I do not think that Arkoun realized the extent of his defeat for a while. Then, when it sank in upon him, he stood up and drew the terrible blue sword. I thought that I had miscalculated, and that he was about to lop my head, or at least an arm.

He lifted the sword high and then swung it down with a shout of fury. With a dozen strokes he hacked the board to kindling and scattered the stones about the camp. Then he strode out into the rocks, tearing his beard and shouting my death threats to the towering cliffs, that hurled them onwards down the valleys in a series of diminishing echoes.

It was three days before Arkoun set up the board again, and gestured to me to take my seat opposite him. The poor fellow had no inkling of what lay in store for him.

Each day my command of the Geez language increased, and I was at last able to glean some understanding of my captor and the reason for this long journey through the canyons and gorges.

I had underrated Arkoun. He was not a chieftain but a king. His full name was Arkoun Gannouchi Maryam, Negusa Naghast, King of Kings and ruler of the Ethiopic state of Aksum. It was only later that I learned that in this land any mountain brigand with a hundred horses and fifty wives was likely to set himself up as a king, and that at any one time there might be as many as twenty Kings of Kings on the rampage for land and loot.

Arkoun's nearest neighbour was one Prester Beni-Jon, also claiming to be King of Kings and ruler of the Ethiopic state of Aksum. There appeared to be a certain amount of ill-feeling and rivalry between these two monarchs. They had already fought a number of inconclusive battles.

Masara was the favourite daughter of Prester Beni-Jon. She had been kidnapped by one of the other robber chieftains, one of those who had not yet crowned himself, nor taken the obligatory title of King of Kings. In a straightforward trading arrangement, Masara had been sold to Arkoun for a horse-load of silver bars. Arkoun intended using her to gain political ground from her doting father. It seemed that hostage-taking and ransom were very much a part of Ethiopian statesmanship.

Not trusting any of his own men with such a valuable commodity, Arkoun had gone himself to take possession of Princess Masara. Our caravan was carrying her back to Arkoun's stronghold. I gathered this and other information from the gossipy women slaves who brought me my meals, or in casual conversation over the dom board. By the time we reached Amba Kamara, the mountain fortress of King Arkoun Gannouchi Maryam, I was an expert on the complicated and shifting politics of the various Ethiopic states of Aksum, and the numerous claimants to the throne of the empire.

I was aware of an increasing excitement running through our caravan as we approached our journey's end, and at last we climbed the narrow winding pathway, no more than just another goat-track, to the summit of yet another amba. These ambas were the massifs that made up the mountain ranges of central Ethiopia. Each of them was a flat-topped mountain with sheer sides that plunged like a wall into the valley that divided it from the next mountain.

It was easy to see, when I stood at the top of the precipice, how the land was fragmented into so many tiny kingdoms and principalities. Each amba was a natural and impregnable fortress. The man on top of it was invincible, and might call himself a king without fear of being challenged.

Arkoun rode up beside me and pointed to the mountains on the southern sky-line. 'That is the hiding-place of that horse-thief and scoundrel, Prester Beni-Jon. He is a man of unsurpassed treachery.' He hawked in his throat and spat over the edge of the cliff in the direction of his rival.

I had come to know Arkoun as a man of not inconsiderable cruelty and treachery himself. If he conceded Prester Beni-Jon as his master in these fields, Masara's father must be a formidable man indeed.

We crossed the tableland of the Amba Kamara, passing through a few villages of stone-walled hovels, and fields of sorghum and dhurra corn. The peasants in the fields were all tall, bushy-haired ruffians, armed with swords and round copper shields. They appeared as fierce and warlike as any of the men in our caravan.

At the far end of the amba, the path led us to the most extraordinary natural stronghold that I had ever seen. From the main table of the mountain a buttress had eroded until it stood alone, a sheer pinnacle of rock with precipitous sides, separated from the table by an awe-inspiring abyss.

This gulf was bridged by a narrow causeway, a natural arch of stone, that joined it to the tableland. It was so narrow that two horses could not pass each other on the pathway, so narrow that once a horse started out across the bridge, it could not turn round and return, until it had reached the other side.

The drop under the causeway was a thousand feet, straight into the river gorge below. It was so unnerving to the horses that the riders were forced to dismount, blindfold them, and lead them over. When I was halfway across, I found myself trembling with vertigo, and I dared not peer over the edge of the pathway into the void. It required all my self-control to keep walking, and not to throw myself flat and cling to the rocks beneath my feet.

Perched on top of this pinnacle of rock was an ungainly, lopsided castle of stone blocks and reed thatch. The open windows were covered with curtains of rawhide, and the raw sewage and odious refuse running from the fortress stained and littered the cliff beneath it.

Festooning the walls and battlements like pennants and decorations celebrating some macabre festival, were the corpses of men and women. Some had hung there so long that their bones had been picked white by the flocks of crows that circled above the abyss or roosted squawking upon the roofs. Other victims were still alive, and I watched their feeble last movements with horror as they hung by their heels. However, most of them were already dead and in various stages of decomposition. The smell of rotting human carcasses was so thick that even the wind that whined eternally around the cliffs could not disperse it.

King Arkoun called the crows his chickens. Sometimes he fed them on the walls, and at other times he threw their food from the causeway into the gorge. The dwindling wail of another unfortunate victim falling away into the depths was a feature of our life on the pinnacle of Adbar Seged, the House of the Wind Song.

These executions and the daily floggings and chopping-off of hands or feet, or the pulling-out of tongues with red-hot tongs were King Arkoun's principal diversions when he was not playing dom, or planning a raid on one of the other neighbouring King of Kings. Very often Arkoun wielded the axe or the tongs in person, and his roars of laughter were as loud as the screams of his victims.

As soon as our caravan had crossed the

causeway and pulled into the central courtyard of Adbar Seged, Masara was whisked away by her female gaolers into the labyrinth of stone passageways, and I was led to my new quarters which abutted those of Arkoun.

I was allotted a single stone cell. It was dark and draughty. The open fireplace blackened the walls with soot and gave out little heat. Though I wore the woollen robes of the land, I was never warm in Adbar Seged. How I longed for the sunlight on the Nile and the bright oasis of my very Egypt! I sat on those wind-swept battlements and pined for my family, for Memnon and Tanus, for my little princesses, but most of all for my mistress. Sometimes I woke in the night with the tears chilling my face, and I had to cover my head with my sheepskin blanket, so that Arkoun would not hear my sobs through the thick stone wall.

Often I pleaded with him to release me.

'But why do you want to leave me, Taita?'

'I want to go back to my family.'

'I am your family now,' he laughed. 'I am your father.'

I made a wager with him. If I won a hundred successive boards of dom from him, he agreed that he would let me go and give me an escort back down the Nile to the great plains. When I won the hundredth game, he chuckled and shook his head at my naïvety.

'Did I say a hundred? I think not. Surely it was a thousand?' He turned to his henchmen. 'Was the bargain a thousand?'

'A thousand!' they chanted. 'It was a thousand!'

They all thought it a grand joke. When in a pique I refused to play another board with Arkoun, he hung me naked from the walls of the citadel by my heels until I squealed for him to set up the board.

When Arkoun saw me naked, he laughed and prodded me. 'You may have a way with the dom board, but it seems you have lost your own stones, Egyptian.' This was the first time since my capture that my physical mutilation had been revealed. Once again, men called me 'eunuch', much to my shame and mortification.

However, in the end the consequences were beneficial. If I had been a man entire, they would never have let me go to Masara.

 They came for me in the night and led me shivering through the passages to Masara's cell. The room was lit by a dim oil lamp and smelled of vomit. The girl was curled on a straw mattress in the centre of the floor, with her vomit puddled on the stone floor beside her. She was in terrible pain, groaning and weeping and holding her stomach.

I set to work immediately, and examined her carefully. I was afraid that I would find her stomach as hard as a stone, the symptom of the swelling and bursting of the gut that would drench her insides with the contents of her intestines. There was no remedy for this condition. Not even I, with all my skills, could save her, if this was her affliction.

To my great relief I found her stomach warm and soft. There was no fever in her blood. I continued my examination, and though she groaned and screamed with agony when I touched her, I could not find any cause for her condition. I was puzzled and I sat back to think about it. Then I realized that although her face was contorted with agony, she was watching me with a candid gaze.

'This is worse than I feared.' I turned to her two female attendants and spoke in Geez. 'If I am to save her, I must have my chest. Fetch it immediately.'

They scrambled for the door, and I lowered my head to hers and whispered, 'You are a clever girl and a good actress. Did you tickle your throat with a feather?'

She smiled up at me and whispered back, 'I could think of no other way to meet you. When the women told me that you had learned to speak Geez, I knew that we could help each other.'

'I hope that is possible.'

'I have been so lonely. Even to speak to a friend will be a joy to me.' Her trust was so spontaneous that I was touched. 'Perhaps between us we will find a way to escape from this dreadful place.'

At that moment we heard the women returning, their voices echoing along the outside passage. Masara seized my hand.

'You are my friend, aren't you? You will come to me again?'

'I am and I will.'

'Quickly, tell me before you must go. What was his name?'

'Who?'

'The one who was with you on that first day beside the river. The one who looks like a young god.'

'His name is Memnon.'

'Memnon!' She repeated it with a peculiar reverence. 'It is a beautiful name. It suits him.'

The women burst into the room, and Masara clutched her healthy little belly and groaned as though she were at the point of death. While I clucked and shook my head with worry for the benefit of her women, I mixed a tonic of herbs that would do her some good, and told them that I would return in the morning.

In the morning Masara's condition had improved, and I was able to spend a little longer with her. Only one of the women was present, and she soon became bored and wandered away to the far side of the room. Masara and I exchanged a few quiet words.

'Memnon said something to me. I could not understand. What was it he said?'

'He said, "I will come back for you. Be brave. I will come back for you."'

'He could not mean that. He does not know me. He had met me only fleetingly.' She shook her head, and tears filled her eyes. 'Do you think he meant it, Taita?' There was a haunting plea in her tone that moved me, and I could not allow her to suffer more than she had already.

'He is crown prince of Egypt, and a man of honour. Memnon would not have said it unless he meant every word.'

That was all we could say then, but I came back the next day. The very first thing she asked of me was, 'Tell me again what Memnon said to me,' and I had to repeat his promise.

I told Arkoun that Masara was improving in health, but that she must be allowed out each day

297

to walk on the battlements. 'Otherwise I cannot answer for her health.'

He thought about that for a day. However, Masara was a valuable asset for which he had paid a horse-load of silver bars, and at last he gave his permission.

Our daily exercise periods slowly extended, as the guards became accustomed to seeing us together. In the end Masara and I were able to spend most mornings in each other's company, strolling around the walls of Adbar Seged and talking endlessly.

Masara wanted to know everything that I had to tell about Memnon, and I racked my memory for anecdotes about him to entertain her. She had favourite stories which I was obliged to repeat until she knew them by heart, and she corrected me when I erred in the retelling. She particularly enjoyed the account of how he had rescued Tanus and me from the wounded bull elephant, and how he had received the Gold of Valour for his deed.

'Tell me about his mother the queen,' she demanded, and then, 'Tell me about Egypt. Tell me about your gods. Tell me about when Memnon was a baby.' Always her questions returned to him, and I was glad to appease her demands, for I longed for my family. Speaking about them made them seem closer to me.

One morning she came to me distraught. 'Last night I had a dreadful dream. I dreamed that Memnon came back to me, but I could not understand what he said to me. You must teach me to speak Egyptian, Taita. We will start today, this very minute!'

She was desperate to learn and she was a clever

little thing. It went very quickly. Soon we were talking only Egyptian between ourselves, and it was useful to be able to speak privately in front of her guards.

When we were not talking about Memnon, we were discussing our plans to escape. Of course, I had been thinking of this ever since our arrival at Adbar Seged, but it helped to have her thoughts on the same subject to compare with my own.

'Even if you escape from this fortress, you will never pass through the mountains without help,' she warned me. 'The paths are like a skein of twisted wool. You will never unravel them. Every clan is at war with the next. They trust no strangers, and they will cut your throat as a spy.'

'What must we do, then?' I asked.

'If you are able to get away, you must go to my father. He will protect you and guide you back to your own people. You will tell Memnon where I am, and he will come to save me.' She said this with such shining confidence that I could not meet her eyes.

I realized then that Masara had built up an image of Memnon in her mind that was not based on reality. She was in love with a god, not a stripling as young and untried as she was herself. I was responsible for this, with my clever stories about the prince. I could not wound her now and shatter her hope by telling her how forlorn all these imaginings truly were.

'If I go to Prester Beni-Jon, your father, he will think I am one of Arkoun's spies. He will have my head.' I tried to extricate myself from the responsibilities she had laid upon me.

'I will tell you what to say to him. Things that

299

only he and I know. That will prove to him that you come from me.'

She had blocked me there, so I tried a different escape. 'How would I find my way to your father's fortress? You have told me that the path is a tangled skein.'

'I will explain the way to you. Because you are so clever you will remember everything I tell you.'

By this time, naturally, I loved her almost as much as I loved my own little princesses. I would take any risk to shield her from hurt. She reminded me so strongly of my mistress at the same age that I could deny her nothing.

'Very well. Tell it to me.' And so we began to plan our escape. It was a game for me, which I played mostly to keep her hopes alive and her spirits buoyant. I had no serious expectation of finding a way off this pinnacle of rock.

We discussed ways of making a rope to lower ourselves down the cliff, although every time I looked over the causeway from the terrace outside her cell, I shuddered at that gaping void of space. She began to collect scraps of wool and cloth which she hid under her mattress. From these she planned to plait a rope. I could not tell her that a rope long enough and strong enough to support our weight and take us down to the floor of the valley would fill her cell to the ceiling.

For two long years we languished on the height of Adbar Seged, and we never were able to devise a plan of escape, but Masara never lost faith. Every day she asked me, 'What did Memnon say to me? Tell me again what he promised.'

'He said, "I will come back for you. Be brave."'

'Yes. I am brave, am I not, Taita?'

300

'You are the bravest girl I know.'

'Tell me what you will say to my father when you meet him.'

I repeated her instructions, and then she would reveal to me her latest plan of escape.

'I will catch the little sparrows that I feed on the terrace. You will write a letter to my father to tell him where I am. We will tie it to the sparrow's leg, and it will fly to him.'

'It is more likely to fly to Arkoun, who will have us both thrashed, and we will not be allowed to see each other again.'

In the end I escaped from Adbar Seged by riding out on a fine horse. Arkoun was going out on another raid against King Prester Beni-Jon. I was commanded to accompany him, in the capacity of personal physician and dom player.

As I walked my blindfolded horse across the causeway, I looked back and saw Masara standing on her terrace looking down at me. She was a lovely, lonely figure. She called to me in Egyptian. I could just make out her words above the sough of the wind.

'Tell him I am waiting for him. Tell him I have been brave.' And then softly, so I was not certain that I had heard the words right, 'Tell him I love him.'

The wind turned the tears upon my cheeks as cold as ice, as I rode away across Amba Kamara.

The night before the battle, Arkoun kept me sitting late in his tent. While he gave his last orders to his commanders, he stropped the edge of the blue sword. Once in a while he would shave a few hairs off his wrist with the steely, glittering blade to test the edge, and nod with satisfaction.

At last he rubbed down the blade with clarified mutton fat. This strange, silver-blue metal had to be kept well greased, otherwise a red powder would form upon it, almost as though it was bleeding.

The blue sword had come to exert the same fascination on me as it had on Tanus. Occasionally, when he was in a specially benevolent mood, Arkoun would allow me to handle it. The weight of the metal was surprising, and the sharpness of the edge was incredible. I imagined what havoc it could wreak in the hands of a swordsman like Tanus. I knew that if we ever met again, Tanus would want every detail of it, and so I questioned Arkoun, who never tired of boasting about it.

He told me that the sword had been forged in the heart of a volcano by one of the pagan gods of Ethiopia. Arkoun's great-grandfather had won it from the god in a game of dom that had lasted for twenty days and twenty nights. I found all this quite plausible, except the part of the legend about winning the weapon in a dom game. If Arkoun's great-grandfather had played dom at the same standard as Arkoun, then it must have been a very stupid god who lost the sword to him.

Arkoun asked my opinion of his battle plan for the next day. He had learned that I was a student of military tactics. I told him his plan was brilliant. These Ethiopians had as much grasp of military tactics as they had of the play of the dom stones. Of course, the terrain would not allow full use of the horses, and they had no chariots. Nevertheless, their battles were fought in a haphazard and desultory manner.

Arkoun's grand strategy for the morrow would be to split his forces into four raiding parties. They would hide among the rocks and rush out, seize a few hostages, slit a few throats, and then run for it.

'You are one of the great generals of history,' I told Arkoun, 'I would like to write a scroll to extol your genius.' He liked the idea, and promised to provide me with whatever materials I required for the project, as soon as we returned to Adbar Seged.

It seemed that King Prester Beni-Jon was a commander of equal panache and vision. We met his forces the following day in a wide valley with steep sides. The battlefield had been mutually agreed upon some months in advance, and Prester Beni-Jon had taken up his position at the head of the valley before we arrived. He came forward to shout insults and challenges at Arkoun from a safe distance.

Prester Beni-Jon was a stick of a man, thin as a staff, with a long white beard and silver locks down to his waist. I could not make out his features over that distance, but the women had told me that as a young man he had been the most handsome swain in Ethiopia and that he had two hundred wives. Some women had killed themselves for love of him. It seemed clear to me that his talents might be more gainfully employed in the harem than on the battlefield.

Once Prester Beni-Jon had had his say, Arkoun went forward and replied at length. His insults were flowery and poetic, they rolled off the cliffs and echoed down the gorge. I committed some of his pithier remarks to memory, for they were worth recording.

When Arkoun subsided at last, I expected that battle would be joined, but I was mistaken. There were several other warriors on both sides who wished to speak. I fell asleep against a rock in the warm sun, smiling to myself as I imagined what sport Tanus and a company of his Blues would enjoy against these Ethiopian champions of rhetoric.

It was afternoon when I woke and started up at the clash of arms. Arkoun had loosed his first assault. One of his detachments raced forward against Prester Beni-Jon's positions, beating their swords against their copper shields. Within a remarkably short space of time they returned with great alacrity to their starting-point, without having inflicted or suffered casualties.

Further insults were exchanged, and then it was Prester Beni-Jon's turn to attack. He charged and retired with equal verve and similar results. So the day passed, insult for insult, charge for charge. At nightfall both armies retired. We camped at the foot of the valley and Arkoun sent for me.

'What a battle!' he greeted me triumphantly, as I entered his tent. 'It will be many months before Prester Beni-Jon will dare take the field again.'

'There will be no battle on the morrow?' I asked.

'Tomorrow we will return to Adbar Seged,' he told me, 'and you will write a full account of my victory in your scrolls. I expect that after this salutary defeat Prester Beni-Jon will soon sue for peace.'

Seven of our men had been wounded in this ferocious encounter, all by arrows fired at extreme range. I drew the barbs and dressed and bandaged the wounds. The following day I saw the wounded loaded on to the litters and walked beside them, as we started back.

One of the men had received a stomach wound and was in much pain. I knew he would be dead from gangrene within the week, but I did my best to ease his suffering and to cushion the bouncing of the litter over the rougher sections of the track.

Late that afternoon we came to a ford in the river, one that we had crossed on our way to give battle to Prester Beni-Jon. I had recognized this ford from the description that Masara had given me of the countryside and the route to her father's stronghold. The river was one of the numerous tributaries of the Nile that descended from the mountains. There had been rain over the preceding days, and the level of the ford was high.

I began the crossing, wading beside the litter of my patient with the stomach wound. He was already delirious. Halfway across the ford I realized that we had under-estimated the height and strength of the water. The flood caught the side of the litter and swung it sideways. It twisted the horse around, dragging the poor animal into deeper water where its hooves lost purchase on the gravel bottom.

I was hanging on to the harness, and the next

moment the horse and I were both swimming. We were washed away downstream in the icy green flood. The wounded man was tumbled out of the litter, and when I tried to reach him, I lost my hold on the horse's harness. We were swept apart.

The wounded man's head disappeared below the surface, but by this time I was swimming for my own life. I rolled on to my back and pointed my feet downstream. This way I was able to fend off the rocks with my feet, as the current hurled me against them. For a short while some of Arkoun's men ran along the bank beside me, but soon the river swept me through a bend and they could not find a way around the base of the cliff. The horse and I were alone in the river.

Below the bend, the speed of the current slackened, and I was able to swim back to the horse and throw one arm over its neck. For the moment I was safe. For the first time I thought of escape, and realized that the gods had made an opportunity for me. I muttered a prayer of thanks, and used a handful of the horse's mane to steer it on down the middle of the river.

We had come downstream several miles and it was dark before I steered my horse into the bank. We clambered ashore on a sand-bar. I judged that I was safe from pursuit and recapture until morning. None of Arkoun's men would venture down the gorge in darkness. However, I was so chilled that my whole body shivered in uncontrollable spasms.

I led the horse to a sheltered place out of the wind, and then pressed my body to his flank. His wet hide steamed in the moonlight. Gradually the warmth of the animal permeated me, and my shivering subsided. Once I was half-warmed, I was able to gather up driftwood from the sand-bank. Using the Shilluk method, I managed with much difficulty to start a fire. I spread my robes out to dry, and crouched over the fire for the rest of that night.

As soon as it was light enough to see the path, I dressed myself and mounted the horse. I headed away from the river, for I knew that Arkoun's men would concentrate their search along the banks.

Two days later, following the directions that Masara had given me, I reached one of the fortified hilltop villages in the domain of Prester Beni-Jon. The headman of the village expressed the intention of cutting my throat immediately and taking my horse. I made full use of all my persuasive gifts, and eventually he agreed to keep the horse but lead me to the fortress of Prester Beni-Jon.

 The guides who were escorting me to King Prester Beni-Jon spoke of him in warm and affectionate terms. The villages that we passed along the way were cleaner and more prosperous than those of Arkoun. The herds of kine were fatter, the crops well cultivated and the people better fed. The horses I saw were magnificent. Their beauty brought tears to my eyes.

When at last we came in sight of the castle high on another amba, it was in a better state of repair than that of Arkoun, and no grisly trophies decorated the walls.

From close at hand, King Prester Beni-Jon was

indeed an extremely handsome man. His silver hair and beard endowed him with a singular air of dignity. His complexion was fair and his eyes dark and intelligent. At first he was highly sceptical of my story, but gradually his manner changed towards me, as I recited the intimate knowledge with which Masara had armed me.

He was deeply affected by the messages of love and duty that I brought to him from his daughter, and he questioned me eagerly as to her health and welfare. Then his servants led me to quarters that, by Ethiopian standards, were sumptuous, and I was provided with fresh woollen robes to replace my rags.

After I had eaten and rested, the servants led me back to the dank and smoky cell that was Prester Beni-Jon's audience chamber.

'Your Majesty, Masara has been a prisoner of Arkoun these past two years,' I pointed out to him immediately. 'She is a young and tender girl. She pines away in his stinking dungeons.' I embroidered the facts a trifle, to bring home to him the urgency of her plight.

'I have tried to assemble the ransom that Arkoun demands for my daughter,' Prester Beni-Jon excused himself. 'But I would have to melt down every plate and bowl in Aksum to put together such a hoard of silver as would satisfy his greed. In addition, he demands great tracts of my land and scores of my principal villages. To relinquish these to him would weaken my realm and condemn tens of thousands of my subjects to his tyranny.'

'I could lead your army to his stronghold of Adbar Seged. You could lay siege to the castle and force him to hand over Masara to you.'

Prester Beni-Jon looked startled by this proposal. I do not think such a course of action had occurred to him. It was not the Ethiopian way of waging war.

'I know Adbar Seged very well, but it is impregnable,' he answered me primly. 'Arkoun has a mighty army at his back. We have fought many fierce battles against him. My men are lions, but we have never been able to defeat him.' I had seen the lions of Prester Beni-Jon in battle, and I saw that his estimate of the situation was correct. The army he commanded could never hope to storm Adbar Seged and free Masara by force of arms.

The following day I returned with another proposal. 'Great Emperor of Aksum, King of Kings, as you well know, I am of the Egyptian nation. Queen Lostris, the regent of Egypt, lies with her armies at the confluence of the two rivers, where the Nile meets its twin.'

He nodded. 'This I know. These Egyptians have entered my territory without my leave. They are digging mines in my valleys. Soon I will fall upon them and annihilate them.'

It was my turn to be startled. Prester Beni-Jon was aware of the work on Pharaoh's tomb, and our people there were in danger of attack. Accordingly, I modified the suggestion that I was about to put to him.

'My people are skilled in the art of siege and war,' I explained. 'I have influence with Queen Lostris. If you send me safely back to her side, I will prevail on her to extend you her friendship. Her troops will storm the fortress of Adbar Seged and free your daughter.'

Although Prester Beni-Jon tried to disguise the

309

fact, I saw that my suggestion appealed to him. 'What would your queen require in return for her friendship?' he asked carefully.

We haggled for five days, but in the end the bargain was struck. 'You will allow Queen Lostris to continue the mining work in your valley, and you will declare those valleys a prohibited area. Your own people will be forbidden to enter there on pain of death,' I told him. This was for my mistress. It would secure the tomb of Pharaoh from desecration.

'I agree,' said Prester Beni-Jon.

'You will deliver to Queen Lostris two thousand horses that I will choose from your herds.' This was for me.

'One thousand,' said the king.

'Two thousand.' I was firm.

'I agree,' said Prester Beni-Jon.

'Once she is free, the Princess Masara shall be allowed to marry any man she chooses. You will not forbid it.' That was for Memnon and the girl.

'It is against our custom,' he sighed. 'But I agree.'

'When we capture them, Arkoun and the stronghold of Adbar Seged will be handed over to you.' He looked more cheerful and nodded vigorously.

'Finally, we Egyptians shall be allowed to keep all the spoils of war that we capture from Arkoun, including the legendary blue sword.' That was for Tanus.

'I agree,' said Prester Beni-Jon, and I could see that he thought that he had made a bargain.

He gave me an escort of fifty men, and I set out the following day on the return to Qebui, riding a fine stallion that was the king's parting gift to me.

 We were still five days' ride from Qebui, when I saw the swift dust-cloud ahead of us, racing towards us across the plain. Then I saw the chariots dancing through the heat-mirage. As they approached, the columns deployed into attack formation at the gallop. It was beautiful to watch. The dressing was perfect, and the spacing between each vehicle so exact that they looked like a string of beads. I wondered who commanded them.

I shaded my eyes as they drew closer, and my heart leaped as I recognized the horses of the leading chariot. They were Rock and Chain, my own darlings. However, I did not immediately recognize the charioteer behind them. It was almost three years since last I had laid eyes on Memnon. The difference in age between seventeen and twenty is the difference between the boy and the man.

I had taken to riding with saddle-cloth and stirrups, in the Ethiopian manner, and so now I stood high in the stirrups and waved. I saw the chariot swerve, as Memnon recognized me and whipped up the team to full charge.

'Mem!' I howled. 'Mem!' and his answering shout came back to me on the wind.

'Tata! By the sweet milk of Isis, it's you!'

He pulled up the horses, sprang from the footplate and dragged me from my horse. First he hugged me, then he held me at arm's-length and we studied each other avidly.

311

'You are pale and thin, Tata. The bones are sticking out of you. Are those grey hairs I see here?' He tugged at my temples.

He was taller than I was now, lean in the waist and broad in the shoulder. His skin was tanned and oiled to the colour of burnished amber, and cords of muscle stood out in his throat when he laughed. He wore wrist-guards of gold and the Gold of Valour on his bared chest. Although it seemed impossible, he was more handsome than when I had last seen him. He reminded me of a leopard, supple and sleek.

He lifted me bodily and set me on the footplate of the chariot. 'Take up the traces,' he ordered. 'I want to see if you have lost any of your old skill.'

'Which way?' I asked.

'West, to Qebui, of course,' he ordered. 'My mother will be angry if I do not bring you directly to her.'

That night we sat at a camp-fire together, away from the other officers, so that we could talk in private. We sat in silence for a while, looking up at the silver blaze of stars, and then Memnon said, 'When I thought I had lost you, it was as though I had lost a part of myself. You are woven into my very first memory of life.'

I, who deal in words, could find no words to answer him. We were silent again, and then at last he laid a hand on my shoulder.

'Did you ever see the girl again?' he asked, and though his tone was casual, his grip upon my shoulder was not.

'Which girl?' I asked, to tease him.

'The girl at the river, on the day we were parted.'

'Was there a girl?' I frowned, as I tried to

312

remember. 'What did she look like?'

'Her face was a dark lily, and her skin was the colour of wild honey. They called her Masara, and the memory of her still troubles my sleep.'

'Her name is Masara Beni-Jon,' I told him, 'and I have spent two years imprisoned with her in the fortress of Adbar Seged. There I learned to love her, for her nature is even sweeter than her face.'

He seized me with both hands now and shook me without mercy. 'Tell me about her, Tata! Tell me everything. Leave nothing out.'

So we sat the rest of that night beside the fire and we talked about the girl. I told him how she had learned to speak Egyptian for his sake. I told him how his promise to her had sustained her through the dark, lonely days, and in the end I told him the message that she had sent to him, the message she had called out to me from the battlements of Adbar Seged as I rode away and left her.

'Tell him I was brave. Tell him I love him.'

He was silent for a long while, staring into the flames, and then he said softly, 'How can she love me? She does not know me.'

'Do you know her any better than she knows you?' I asked, and he shook his head.

'Do you love her?'

'Yes,' he answered simply.

'Then she loves you in the same way.'

'I made her a promise. Will you help me make good my promise to her, Tata?'

I have never in my life known such joy as was mine on my return to Qebui when I went aboard the *Breath of Horus*.

Memnon had sent a messenger ahead to warn them of my return, and they were all waiting for me.

'By the stinking crust between Seth's toes!' Kratas shouted. 'I thought we had got rid of you at last, you old rogue.' And he crushed me to his chest until I thought my ribs were all staved in.

Tanus seized my shoulders and stared into my eyes for a moment before he grinned, 'But for you, that hairy Ethiop would have had me. He got the better bargain when he took you instead. Thank you, old friend.' I saw how Tanus had aged. Like me, there was grey in his hair now, and his face was weather-beaten, beginning to erode like a granite cliff.

My little princesses were no longer little, but they were still adorable. They were shy towards me, for their memory of me had faded. They stared at me with big eyes as I made my obeisance. The colour of Bekatha's hair had darkened to copper. I looked forward to rekindling her affection.

Tehuti recognized me at last. 'Tata!' she said. 'Did you bring me a present?'

'Yes, Your Highness,' I replied, 'I have brought you my heart.'

My mistress smiled at me as I walked towards her along the deck. She wore the light *nemes* crown and the golden head of the cobra on her brow. When she smiled, I saw that she had lost her first

314

tooth, and the gap marred her smile. She had thickened around the waist, and the heavy affairs of state had furrowed her brow and etched crow's feet at the corners of her eyes. To me, however, she was still the most lovely woman in the world.

She stood up from the throne as I knelt before her. This was the highest mark of her favour. She laid her hand on my bowed head, and it was a caress.

'You have been away from us too long, Taita,' she said, so softly that only I could hear her. 'Tonight you will sleep at the foot of my bed once more.'

That night, when she had drunk the bowl of herb broth that I had prepared for her, and I had covered her with a fur blanket, she murmured softly as she closed her eyes, 'Can I trust you not to kiss me when I am asleep?'

'No, Your Majesty,' I replied, and stooped over her. She smiled as my lips touched hers.

'Never leave us again for so long, Taita,' she said.

Memnon and I had planned our tactics meticulously, and we executed them with the same precision as one of our chariot manoeuvres.

Tanus was easy to convince. His defeat by Arkoun still rankled. In his presence Memnon and I discussed the ease with which the blue sword had sheered his bronze blade, and how Arkoun would certainly have killed him, if I had not intervened. Tanus bristled with humiliation.

Then Memnon questioned me on the magical origins and properties of the legendary weapon. Tanus forgot his pique and joined in with avid questions of his own.

'This Prester Beni-Jon has declared the blue sword a prize of war. Whoever can seize it, may hold it,' I told them.

'If we went against Arkoun, we would not be able to use chariots in those valleys,' Memnon mused. 'It would have to be the infantry. How do you think your Shilluk would fare against the Ethiops, Lord Tanus?' Memnon still addressed Tanus formally. Obviously he had not learned in my absence that Tanus was his real father.

By the time we had finished with him, Tanus was as hot for the venture as either of us. He was totally in league with us as we started our campaign on Queen Lostris.

From the very beginning my mistress had understood, as Tanus never had, just how vital the horses and chariots would be, if ever we were to fulfil the dream of the return to our very Egypt. I displayed the stallion that Prester Beni-Jon had given me, and pointed out to my mistress his finer points of breed.

'Look at his nostrils, Majesty. See the depth of his chest, and the balance of muscle to bone. The Hyksos have nothing to match these Ethiopian horses.'

Then I reminded her of her promise to the dead pharaoh, and told her, 'Prester Beni-Jon will cede the valley of the tomb to you. His warriors will guard it against the grave-robbers. He will place a taboo upon the valley, and these Ethiops are superstitious people. They will respect the

316

prohibition even long after we have returned to Thebes.'

I warned Memnon not to mention to Queen Lostris his amorous interest in an expedition against Arkoun. It would do our cause no good. Every mother is also a lover; she seldom takes any pleasure in seeing her son led away by another younger woman.

No woman, not even a queen, could resist the combined charm and cunning of the three of us, Tanus and Memnon and myself. Queen Lostris gave her consent to our expeditionary force marching on Adbar Seged.

 We left the wagons and the chariots at the valley of Pharaoh's tomb, and struck out into the mountains. Prester Beni-Jon had sent a company of guides to meet us. They were a hundred of his best and most reliable men.

Tanus had selected a full division of his wild and bloodthirsty Shilluk, and promised them all the cattle they could capture. Each of these black pagans carried a cloak of thick jackal fur rolled upon his back, for we remembered the cold wind of the mountain passes.

For support we had three companies of Egyptian archers, led by Lord Kratas. That old ruffian had joined the company of nobles during my sojourn in Adbar Seged. He was spoiling for a real fight. He and every one of his men were armed with the new compound recurved bows that could outdrive the Ethiopian long-bows by two hundred paces.

317

Memnon had selected a small band of the finest swordsmen and rough fighters that we had. Remrem was one of these, of course, as were Lord Aqer and Astes. I was part of this special detachment, not for my warlike skills, but simply because I was the only one who had ever entered the fortress of Adbar Seged.

Hui wanted to come with us and offered me every bribe at his disposal. In the end I gave in to him, mainly because I needed an expert to help me select the horses that Prester Beni-Jon had promised me.

I impressed on both Tanus and the prince how vital it was to move swiftly, not only for reasons of surprise, but also because the rains must soon break upon the mountains. During my days in Adbar Seged I had studied the patterns of the weather and the seasons. If the rains caught us in the valleys, they would prove a more dangerous enemy than any Ethiop army.

We made the approach march to Amba Kamara in less than a month. Our column wound through the passes like a long, deadly cobra. The bronze spear-heads of the Shilluk glittered in the high sunlight like the scales of the serpent. We met no person to oppose us. The villages we passed through were deserted. The inhabitants had fled and taken their herds and their women with them. Although each day the clouds gathered black and sullen on the mountain peaks, and at night the thunder muttered at us, the rains held off and the fords of the rivers were low.

Twenty-five days after setting out, we stood in the valley below the massif of Amba Kamara, and looked up the winding track to the heights looming over us.

On my previous journeys up and down the mountain I had studied the defences that Arkoun had erected along the pathway. These comprised rockfalls and stone-walled redoubts. I pointed these out to Tanus, and we could make out the bushy, unhelmeted heads of the defenders showing above the walls of the strongpoints.

'The weakness of a rockfall is that you can only let it come down once, and my Shilluk are quick enough on their feet to dodge a charging buffalo,' Tanus said thoughtfully.

He sent them up the path in small parties, and when the defenders knocked out the wedges from under the rockfall and sent it rolling down on the track, those long-legged black spearmen ran out to the side with the agility of mountain goats. Once the slide of boulders had rumbled past them, they turned straight up the almost sheer mountainside. Bounding from rock to rock, and howling in such a horrible fashion that they started the hair on the nape of my neck, they drove the defenders up the mountain and over the crest.

They were held up only by Arkoun's archers hidden behind the walls of the stone redoubts. When this happened, Kratas led his archers up the mountain. With their superior bow-range, the Egyptians were able to stand back and shoot massed volleys, almost straight into the sky.

It was fascinating to watch a swarm of arrows climb into the air like a flock of black birds and then drop down on to the redoubt so steeply that the stone wall afforded the men behind it no protection. We heard their screams and then saw them break and scurry away up the slope.

Immediately the Shilluk were after them, baying like a pack of hunting dogs. Even from the bottom of the valley I could hear their battle cry, '*Kajan! Kajan!* Kill! Kill!'

Though my legs were hard and my wind strong with so much marching, I had difficulty keeping up with Memnon and the rest of our small group. The years were beginning to take their toll.

We were all wearing long woollen Ethiopic robes, and we carried the traditional round shields of our enemies. However, we had not yet placed the horse-hair wigs on our heads. It would have been extremely unwise to resemble the Ethiopian too closely while the Shilluk were in their present mood.

When at last I came out on the flat tableland of the amba, I saw at a glance that Tanus was rallying and regrouping his infantry. The one fault of the Shilluk as fighting men is that once they have wet their spears with blood, they go berserk, and it is almost impossible to control them. Tanus was roaring like a bull elephant and laying about him with his golden whip of rank. Once more in hand, the Shilluk formed ranks and moved forward against the first village where the Ethiopians were waiting behind the stone walls. As the wave of tall black figures, topped by a foam of white ostrich-feather head-dresses, washed towards them, they loosed a shower of arrows from their long bows. But the Shilluk had their tall shields up.

As the Shilluk charge burst upon them, some of the Ethiopians rushed forward, brandishing their swords. They were not lacking in courage, but this type of warfare was new to them. They had never been forced to meet a charge that was carried through to the death.

I stayed long enough to see them heavily engaged, and then I called to Memnon and his band, 'The wigs!' Each of them pulled one of the wigs of black horse-hair over his scalp. I had made these with my own hands, and styled them on the Ethiopian model of beauty, full and floccose. Clad in the long striped robes and with the wigs on our heads, we could pass as a mob of Arkoun's clansmen.

'This way! Follow me!' I cried, and let out an ululating Ethiopic war cry. They yodelled and howled behind me, as we skirted the village where the fight was still raging, and ran in a disorderly bunch through the cornfields.

We had to reach the fortress and be at Masara's side to protect her when Arkoun finally realized that he had lost the day. I knew that he would not hesitate to kill her as soon as she was no longer of value to him. I thought that he would probably take the blue sword to her or throw her from the causeway into the gorge. Those were his favourite means of despatching his victims.

As we made our way across the amba, we found the entire tableland in turmoil. Bands of bushy-headed warriors milled about in confusion. Women dragged their children by the arm, their possessions piled on their heads, wailing with terror as they ran about like frightened chickens who smell the fox. Herds of goats bleated, and cattle lowed and churned the dust. The herd-boys had fled. Nobody paid us the least attention as we trotted through the fields and kept clear of the villages.

We followed the general movement towards

Adbar Seged at the far end of the table, and as we neared the causeway the crowds thickened and congealed until we were obliged to force our way through them. There were guards at the head of the causeway. They were turning the fugitives back with drawn swords and clubs. Women were screaming and pleading for shelter in the fortress, holding up their babies for mercy's sake. Some of them were knocked down in the press and were trampled under the feet of those coming on from behind.

'Form the tortoise.' Memnon gave the order quietly, and our small band closed up and locked the edges of our Ethiopian shields. We cut through the crowd like a shark through a shoal of sardines. Some of the weaker ones at the front were pushed forward and forced over the edge of the precipice. Their screams added to the panic. When we reached the head of the causeway, the guards there tried to stop us, but they were themselves so crowded by the mob that they could not swing their weapons, and were in danger of being overwhelmed and thrown over the cliff.

'We are under King Arkoun's direct orders. Stand aside!' I shouted at them in Geez.

'The password?' the captain of the guard yelled at me, as he struggled to stay on his feet. The crowd surged back and forward in panic. 'You must give the password.' He poked his sword at me, but Memnon struck the blade aside.

During my imprisonment I had heard the password repeated a thousand times, for my cell had been above the main gate. It might have been changed since then, and I was ready to have the captain killed, as I yelled the old password at him:

'The mountain is high!'

'Go across!' He stood aside, and we struggled out of the throng, kicking and shoving back those who tried to follow us. We ran out on to the bridge. So urgent was the need to reach Masara that I barely noticed the drop on either hand, and without a qualm I led them across the gaping void.

'Where is King Arkoun?' I shouted at the guards who blocked the gateway. When they hesitated, I told them, 'The mountain is high! I have urgent despatches for the king. Stand aside! Let us pass!' We barged through the open gate before they could decide to oppose us, and, with twelve good men at my back, I raced for the outer staircase that led to the upper terrace.

There were two armed men at the door to Masara's chamber, and I rejoiced to see them. I had worried that the girl might have been moved to another part of the fort, but the presence of the guards assured me that she had not.

'Who are you?' one of them shouted, and drew his sword. 'By what authority—' He did not finish the challenge. I stepped aside and allowed Memnon and Remrem to brush past me. They flew at the guards and cut them down before they could defend themselves.

The door to Masara's chamber was barred from within, and when we hurled our combined weight against it, there came a chorus of feminine screams and wails from the other side. At the third attempt the door gave way and I was propelled through the opening into the room beyond. It was in deep gloom, and I could barely make out the huddle of women in the far comer.

'Masara!' I called her name, as I plucked the wig

323

from my head, and let my own hair fall around my shoulders. She recognized me by it.

'Taita!' She bit the wrist of the woman who tried to hold her, and ran to me. She flung both arms around my neck, and then she looked over my shoulder and her grip slackened, her dark eyes opened wide and the colour flooded her cheeks.

Memnon had pulled off his wig. Without it, he was strikingly and unmistakably a prince. I stepped aside and left Masara standing alone. The two of them stared at each other. Neither of them moved or spoke for what seemed like an eternity, but was a moment only. Then Masara said softly and shyly in Egyptian, 'You came. You kept your promise. I knew that you would.'

I think that this was the only time that I ever saw Memnon at a loss. He could only nod his head, and then I witnessed an amazing phenomenon. Blood flooded up his neck and suffused his face, so that even in the gloom of the chamber it glowed. The Crown Prince of Egypt, son of Pharaoh, commander of the first division of chariots, Best of Ten Thousand, holder of the Gold of Valour, stood there blushing and as tongue-tied as a peasant clod.

Behind me one of the women squawked like a startled hen, and before I could put out a hand to hold her, she had ducked under my arm and darted down the inner staircase. Her screams reverberated up the stairwell. 'Guards! The enemy has broken into the east wing. Come quickly!' and almost immediately there was a rush of booted feet on the staircase.

On the instant, Memnon was transformed from the blushing young lover to a hard-faced
324

guardsman. 'Take care of her, Tata. Let no harm come to her,' he told me grimly, and stepped past me to the head of the stairs.

He killed the first man coming up with that classic thrust to the throat that Tanus had taught him. Then he placed his foot in the centre of his chest. As he jerked his blade free, he kicked the dead man backwards down the stair-well. The falling corpse tumbled into the other men coming up from below, and swept the stairs clean.

Memnon looked at me. 'Do you think we can reach the gate before they close it?'

'We must,' I answered. 'Our best route is back down the outer staircase.'

'Remrem, lead us. Tata and the princess in the centre. I will bring up the rear-guard,' he said crisply, and stabbed the next man coming up the stairs in the eye.

The Ethiopian dropped his weapon and clutched his face with both hands. Memnon stabbed him again through the chest and pushed him backwards down the stairs, clearing them a second time. 'Follow Remrem,' he shouted at me. 'Don't stand there. After him as fast as you can.'

I grabbed Masara's arm, but there was no need to pull her along. She came with me readily, so quick and agile that she was leading me.

The sunlight struck us as we ran out on to the terrace. After the dark room it dazzled me. I blinked to clear my vision, and then I looked across the causeway to the edge of the tableland on the far side of the gulf. Tanus' Shilluks were there. I saw their feathers dancing and their shields held high.

'*Kajan!* Kill! Kill!' they sang, and their

spear-heads were dulled with fresh blood. The panic-stricken peasants scattered before them, and they reached the head of the causeway.

There were two or three hundred of Arkoun's soldiers there. They had the abyss at their backs, and necessity made heroes of every one of them. Now they had truly become lions. Although a score of them were driven back over the edge, and plunged to their death in the valley far below, the survivors hurled back the first charge of the Shilluk.

I saw Tanus then, exactly where I expected him to be, holding the centre. His helmet shone like a beacon in the dark sea of Shilluk warriors. I saw him throw back his head and begin to sing.

The savage Shilluk words carried over the gulf to where I stood on the terrace of the fortress. The men around him took up the chorus, and they surged forward, still singing. This time nothing could stand before them. They stabbed and hacked their way through the defenders, and Tanus was the first man on to the causeway. He ran lightly for such a big man, and he was still singing. His Shilluk followed him on to the stone arch, but it was so narrow that they were forced into single file.

Tanus was halfway across, when the song died on his lips, and he stopped.

From the gateway of Adbar Seged, below where I stood, another man stepped out on to the causeway to confront Tanus. I was looking down and so could not see his face, but there was no mistaking the weapon in his right hand. The blue sword caught the sunlight and flashed like a sheet of summer lightning.

'Arkoun!' Tanus bellowed. 'I have been looking for you.'

Arkoun could not understand the words, but the sense of them was unmistakable. He laughed into the wind, and his beard blew out like smoke around his goaty face.

'I know you!' He swung the silver-blue blade around his head, and it hissed and whined in the air. 'This time I will kill you.' He started forward, out along the narrow arch of stone, running with long, lithe strides straight at Tanus.

Tanus altered his grip on the handle of his bronze shield, and tucked his head in behind it. He now knew the power in that glittering blade, and I saw that he did not intend meeting it with his own softer bronze. Arkoun had also learned discretion from their last brief encounter. From the way he carried the blue sword, I guessed that he would not attempt another rash overhand stroke.

As they came together, Arkoun gathered himself. I saw his shoulders brace and his weight swing forward. He used the impetus of his charge to send the straight thrust at Tanus' head. Tanus lifted the shield and caught the blue blade in the centre of the heavy bronze target. It would have snapped a sword of inferior metal, but the blue sword sheared through it as if it were goat-skin. Half its silver length was buried in the yellow bronze.

Then I realized Tanus' intention. He twisted the shield at an angle so that the blade was trapped. Arkoun struggled to withdraw his weapon, he wrestled and heaved, throwing his full weight backwards, but Tanus had the blue sword in a vice of bronze.

Arkoun gathered all his strength and pulled back again. This time Tanus did not resist him. He leaped forward in the direction that Arkoun was heaving, and this unexpected move threw Arkoun off-balance.

Arkoun staggered away, tripped and teetered on the brink of the chasm. In order to keep his balance, he was forced to relinquish his grip on the hilt of the blue sword, and to leave it still embedded in the shield.

He windmilled his arms as he swayed out over the drop. Then Tanus shifted his ground, put his shoulder behind the shield and barged forward. The shield crashed into Arkoun's chest, and the pommel of the blue sword caught him in the pit of his belly with all Tanus' weight and strength behind it.

Arkoun was thrown backwards, out into empty space. He turned a slow somersault in the air and then went straight down, with his robe ballooning around him, and his beard streaming like a chariot pennant in the wind of his fall.

From where I stood, I watched him make the same last journey on which he had sent so many other unfortunate souls. From the causeway until he struck the rocks a thousand feet below, he screamed all the way down, on a high, receding note that was cut off abruptly at the end.

Tanus stood alone in the middle of the causeway. He still held the shield on high with the sword buried in the metal.

Slowly the tumult and the fighting died away. The Ethiopians had seen their king vanquished and cast down. The heart went out of them.

They threw down their weapons and grovelled

for mercy. The Egyptian officers were able to save some of them from the blood-crazed Shilluk, and these were dragged away to where the slave-masters waited to bind them.

I had no eyes for any of this, for I was watching Tanus out there on the bridge. He began to walk towards the gateway of the fortress, and the men cheered him and raised their weapons in salute.

'There is plenty of fight in the old bull yet,' Memnon laughed in admiration, but I did not laugh with him. I felt the chill premonition of some awful tragedy, like the air stirred by the beat of vultures' wings as they settle to their gruesome feast.

'Tanus,' I whispered. He walked with a slow and hampered gait. He lowered the shield as he came down the bridge of stone, and only then did I see the stain spreading on his breastplate.

I thrust Masara into Memnon's arms and ran down the outer staircase. The Ethiopian guards at the gate tried to surrender their weapons to me, but I pushed my way past them and ran out on to the causeway.

Tanus saw me running towards him and he smiled at me, but the smile was lop-sided. He stopped walking and slowly his legs buckled beneath him, and he sat down heavily in the middle of the bridge. I dropped on my knees beside him, and saw the rent in the crocodile-skin of his breastplate. Blood oozed from it, and I knew that the blue sword had bitten deeper than I had believed possible. Arkoun had driven the point through the bronze shield, on through the tough leather breastplate, and into Tanus' chest.

Carefully I untied the straps that held his

armour, and lifted away the breastplate. Tanus and I both looked down at the wound. It was a penetrating slit the exact width of the blade, like a tiny mouth with wet red lips. Every breath that Tanus drew frothed through that horrid opening in a rash of pink bubbles. It was a lung wound, but I could not bring myself to say it. No man can survive a sword-cut through one of his lungs.

'You are wounded.' It was an asinine remark, and I could not look at his face as I said it.

'No, old friend, I am not wounded,' he replied softly. 'I am killed.'

Tanus' Shilluk made a litter with their spears, and covered it with a rug of sheepskin. They lifted him and carried him, gently and slowly, into the fortress of Adbar Seged.

We laid him on the bed of King Arkoun, and then I sent them all away. When they were gone, I placed the blue sword upon the bed beside him. He smiled and laid his hand on the gold and jewelled hilt. 'I have paid a high price for this treasure,' he murmured. 'I would have liked to wield it just once upon the battlefield.'

I could offer him no hope or comfort. He was an old soldier, and he had seen too many lung wounds. I could not hope to deceive him as to the final outcome. I bound up the wound with a pad of wool and a linen bandage. While I worked, I recited the incantation to quell the bleeding, 'Retreat from me, creature of Seth—'

But he was sinking away from me. Each breath

330

he drew was an effort, and I could hear the blood stirring in his lungs like a hidden creature in the deep swamps.

I mixed a draught of the sleeping-flower, but he would not drink it. 'I will live every minute of my life,' he told me. 'Even the very last one.'

'What else is there that I can do for you?'

'You have done so much already,' he said. 'But there is no end to the demands that we all make upon you.'

I shook my head, 'There is no end to what I would give.'

'These last things then I ask of you. Firstly, you will never tell Memnon that I am his sire. He must always believe that the blood of the pharaohs runs in his veins. He will need every strength to meet the destiny that awaits him.'

'He would be as proud to share your blood as that of any king.'

'Swear to me you will not tell him.'

'I swear it,' I replied, and he lay a while gathering his strength.

'There is one other boon.'

'I grant it before you name it,' I said.

'Take care of my woman who was never my wife. Shield and succour her as you have done all these years past.'

'You know I will.'

'Yes, I know you will, for you have always loved her as much as I have. Take care of Lostris and of our children. I give them all into your hands.'

He closed his eyes, and I thought that the end was close, but his strength surpassed that of other men. After a while he opened them again.

'I wish to see the prince,' he said.

'He waits for you on the terrace,' I answered, and went to the curtained doorway.

Memnon stood at the far end of the terrace. Masara was with him, and the two of them stood close together but not touching. Their expressions were grave and their voices muted. They both looked up as I called.

Memnon came immediately, leaving the girl standing alone. He went directly to Tanus' bed and stood looking down at him. Tanus smiled up at him, but the smile was unsteady. I knew what effort it had cost him.

'Your Highness, I have taught you all I know of war, but I cannot teach you about life. Each man must learn that for himself. There is nothing else I have to tell you before I start out on this new journey, except to thank you for the gift of knowing and serving you.'

'You were ever more than a tutor to me,' Memnon answered softly. 'You were the father I never knew.'

Tanus closed his eyes, and his expression twisted.

Memnon stooped and took his arm in a firm grip, 'Pain is just another enemy to be met and overcome. You taught me that, Lord Tanus.' The prince thought it was the wound that had affected him, but I knew that it was the pain of the word 'father'.

Tanus opened his eyes. 'Thank you, Your Highness. It is good to have you to help me through this last agony.'

'Call me friend, rather than highness.' Memnon sank on one knee beside the bed, and he did not release the grip on Tanus' arm.

332

'I have a gift for you, friend.' The congealing blood in Tanus' lungs blurred his voice. He groped for the handle of the blue sword that still lay on the mattress beside him, but he did not have the strength to lift it.

He took Memnon's hand from his arm and placed it upon the jewelled hilt. 'This is yours now,' he whispered.

'I will think of you whenever I draw it from its scabbard. I will call your name whenever I wield it on the battlefield.' Memnon took up the weapon. 'You do me great honour.'

Memnon stood up, and with the sword in his right hand took the classic opening stance in the centre of the room. He touched the blade to his lips, saluting the man lying on the bed.

'This is the way you taught me to do it.'

Then he began the exercise of arms, in which Tanus had drilled him when he was still a child. He performed the twelve parries, and then the cuts and the lunges with an unhurried perfection. The silver blade circled and swooped like a glittering eagle. It fluted and whined through the air, and lit the gloom of the chamber with darting beams of light.

Memnon ended it with the straight thrust, aimed at the throat of an imaginary enemy. Then he placed the point between his feet and rested both hands upon the pommel.

'You have learned well,' Tanus nodded. 'There is nothing more that I can teach you. It is not too soon for me to go.'

'I will wait with you,' Memnon said.

'No.' Tanus made a weary gesture. 'Your destiny waits for you beyond the walls of this dreary room. You must go forward to meet it without looking back. Taita will stay with me. Take the girl with you. Go to Queen Lostris and prepare her for the news of my death.'

'Go in peace, Lord Tanus.' Memnon would not degrade that solemn moment with futile argument. He crossed to the bed and kissed his father on the lips. Then he turned and, without a backward glance, he strode from the room with the blue sword in his hand.

'Go on to glory, my son,' Tanus whispered, and turned to face the stone wall. I sat at the foot of his bed and looked at the dirty stone floor. I did not want to watch a man like Tanus weep.

 I woke in the night to the sound of drums, those crude wooden drums of the Shilluk, beating out there in the darkness. The doleful sound of the Shilluk's voices chanting their savage dirge made me shudder with dread.

The lamp had burned low, and was guttering beside the bed. It threw grotesque shadows on the ceiling, like the beating and fluttering of the wings of vultures. I crossed slowly and reluctantly to where Tanus lay. I knew that the Shilluk were not mistaken—they have a way of sensing these things.

Tanus lay as I had last seen him, with his face to the wall, but when I touched his shoulder I felt the chill in his flesh. That indomitable spirit had gone on.

I sat beside him for the remainder of that night and I lamented and mourned for him, as his

Shilluk were doing.

In the dawn I sent for the embalmers.

I would not let those crude butchers eviscerate my friend. I made the incision in his left flank. It was not a long, ugly slash, such as the undertakers are wont to perform, but the work of a surgeon.

Through it I drew his viscera. When I held Tanus' great heart in my hands, I trembled. It was as though I could still feel all his strength and power beat in this casket of flesh. I replaced it with reverence and love in the cage of his ribs, and I closed the gash in his side and the wound in his chest, that the blue sword had made, with all the skill at my command.

I took up the bronze spoon, and pressed it up his nostril until I felt it touch the thin wall of bone at the end of the passage. This flimsy partition I pierced with one hard thrust, and scooped out the soft matter from the cavity of his skull. Only then was I content to deliver him over to the embalmers.

Even though there was no more for me to do, I waited with Tanus through the forty long days of the mummification in the cold and gloomy castle of Adbar Seged. Looking back upon it now, I realize that this was weakness. I could not bear the burden of my mistress's grief when first she heard the news of Tanus' death. I had allowed Memnon to assume the duty that was rightfully mine. I hid with the dead, when I should have been with the living who needed me more. I have ever been a coward.

There was no coffin to hold Tanus' mummified body. I would make him one when at last we reached the fleet at Qebui. I had the Ethiopian women weave a long basket for him. The mesh of the weave was so fine that it resembled linen. It would hold water like a pot of fired clay.

 We carried him down from the mountains. His Shilluk easily bore the weight of his desiccated body. They fought each other for the honour. Sometimes they sang their wild songs of mourning as we wound our way through the gorges and over the windswept passes. At other times they sang the fighting songs that Tanus had taught them.

I walked beside his bier all that weary way. The rains broke on the peaks and drenched us. They flooded the fords so that we had to swim ropes across. In my tent at night, Tanus' reed coffin stood beside my own cot. I spoke aloud to him in the darkness, as if he could hear and answer me, just as we had done in the old days.

At last we descended through the last pass, and the great plains lay before us. As we approached Qebui, my mistress came to meet our sad caravan. She rode on the footplate of the chariot behind Prince Memnon.

As they came towards us through the grassland, I ordered the Shilluk bearers to lay Tanus' reed coffin under the spreading branches of a giant giraffe acacia. My mistress dismounted from the chariot and went to the coffin. She placed one hand upon it, and bowed her head in silence.

I was shocked to see what ravages sorrow had wrought upon her. There were streaks of grey in her hair, and her eyes were dulled. The sparkle and the zest had gone out of them. I realized that the days of her youth and her great beauty were gone for ever. She was a lonely and tragic figure. Her bereavement was so evident, that no person who looked upon her now could doubt that she was a widow.

I went to her side to warn her. 'Mistress, you must not make your grief clear for all to see. They must never know that he was more than just your friend and the general of your armies. For the sake of his memory and the honour that he held so dear, hold back your tears.'

'I have no tears left,' she answered me quietly. 'My grief is all cried out. Only you and I will ever know the truth.'

We placed Tanus' humble reed coffin in the hold of the *Breath of Horus*, beside the magnificent gold coffin of Pharoah. I stayed at the side of my mistress, as I had promised Tanus I would, until the worst agonies of her mourning had subsided into the dull eternal pain that would never leave her again. Then, at her orders, I returned to the valley of the tomb to supervise the completion of Pharaoh's sepulchre.

Obedient to my mistress, I also selected a site further down the valley for the tomb of Tanus. Though I did my very best with the material and craftsmen available to me, Tanus' resting-place would be the hut of a peasant compared to the funerary palace of Pharaoh Mamose.

An army of craftsmen had laboured all these years to complete the magnificent murals that decorated the passages and the subterranean chambers of the king's tomb. The store-rooms of the tomb were crammed with all the treasure that we had carried with us from Thebes.

Tanus' tomb had been built in haste. He had accumulated no treasure in his lifetime of service to the state and the crown. I painted scenes upon the walls that depicted the events of his earthly existence, his hunting of mighty beasts and his battles with the red pretender and the Hyksos, and the last assault on the fortress of Adbar Seged. However, I dared not show his nobler accomplishments, his love for my mistress and his steadfast friendship to me. The love of a queen is treason, the friendship of a slave is degrading.

When at last it was completed, I stood alone in Tanus' modest tomb, where he would spend all eternity, and I was suddenly consumed by anger that this was all I could do for him. In my eyes he was more a man than any pharaoh who had ever worn the double crown. That crown could have been his, it should have been his, but he had spurned it. To me he was more a king than ever Pharaoh had been.

It was then that the thought first dawned upon me. It was so outrageous that I thrust it from me. Even to contemplate it seriously was a terrible treason, and offence in the eyes of men and the gods.

However, over the weeks that followed, the thought kept creeping back into my mind. I owed Tanus so much, and Pharaoh so little. Even if I was damned to perdition, it would be a fair price to pay. Tanus had given me more than that over my lifetime.

I could not accomplish it alone. I needed help, but who was there to turn to? I could not enlist either Queen Lostris or the prince. My mistress was bound by the oath she had sworn to Pharaoh, and Memnon did not know which of the two men was his natural father. I could not tell him without breaking my oath to Tanus.

In the end there was one person only who had loved Tanus almost as much as I had, who feared neither god nor man, and who had the brute physical strength I lacked.

'By Seth's unwiped backside!' Lord Kratas roared with laughter when I revealed my plan to him. 'No one else but you could have dreamed up such a scheme. You are the biggest rogue alive, Taita, but I love you for giving me this last chance to honour Tanus.'

The two of us planned it carefully. I even went to the lengths of sending the guards at the entrance to the hold of the *Breath of Horus* a jug of wine heavily laced with the powder of the sleeping-flower.

When Kratas and I at last entered the hold of the ship where the two coffins lay, my resolve wavered. I sensed that the Ka of Pharaoh Mamose watched me from the shadows and that his baleful spirit would follow me all the days of my life, seeking vengeance for this sacrilege.

Big, bluff Kratas had no such qualms, and he set to work with such a will that several times during the course of the night, I had to caution him against the noise he was making as we opened the golden lids to the royal coffin and lifted out the mummy of the king.

Tanus was a bigger man than Pharaoh, but fortunately the coffin makers had left us some space, and Tanus' body had shrunk during the embalming. Even so, we were obliged to unwind several layers of his wrappings before he fitted snugly into the great golden cask.

I mumbled an apology to Pharaoh Mamose as we lifted him into the humble wooden coffin, painted on the outside with a likeness of the Great Lion of Egypt. There was room to spare, and before we sealed the lid we packed this with the linen bandages that we had unwrapped from Tanus.

After the rains had passed and the cool season of the year returned, my mistress ordered the funeral procession to leave Qebui and set out for the valley of the tomb.

The first division of chariots, headed by Prince Memnon, led us. Behind followed fifty carts loaded with the funerary treasure of Pharaoh Mamose. The royal widow, Queen Lostris, rode on the wagon that carried the golden coffin. I rejoiced to see her take this last journey in the company of the one man she had loved, even though she thought it was another. I saw her glance back more than once towards the end of the long caravan that crept dolefully across the plains, five miles from its head to its tail.

The wagon at the rear of the column that carried the lighter wooden coffin was followed by a regiment of Shilluk. Their magnificent voices carried clearly to us at the head of the column as they sang the last farewell. I knew that Tanus would hear them and know for whom the song was sung.

340

When we at last reached the valley of the tomb, the golden coffin was placed beneath a tabernacle outside the entrance to the royal mausoleum. The linen roof of the tent was illuminated with texts and illustrations from the *Book of the Dead.*

There were to be two separate funerals. The first was the lesser, that of the Great Lion of Egypt. The second would be the grander and more elaborate royal funeral.

So it was that three days after our arrival at the valley, the wooden coffin was placed in the tomb that I had prepared for Tanus, and the tomb was consecrated by the priests of Horus, who was Tanus' patron, and then sealed.

During this ritual, my mistress was able to restrain her grief and to show nothing more than the decent sorrow of a queen towards a faithful servant, although I knew that inside her something was dying that would never be reborn.

All that night the valley resounded to the chant of the Shilluk regiment as they mourned for the man who had now become one of their gods. To this day they still shout his name in battle.

Ten days after the first funeral, the golden coffin was placed on its wooden sledge and dragged into the vast royal tomb. It required the efforts of three hundred slaves to manoeuvre the coffin through the passageways. I had designed the tomb so precisely that there was only the breadth of a hand between the sides and the lid of the coffin and the stone walls and roof.

To thwart all future grave-robbers and any

341

others who would desecrate the royal tomb, I had built a labyrinth of tunnels beneath the mountain. From the entrance in the cliff-face, a wide passage led directly to an impressive burial vault that was decorated with marvellous murals. In the centre of this room stood an empty granite sarcophagus, with the lid removed and cast dramatically aside. The first grave-robber to enter here would believe that he was too late and that some other had plundered the tomb before him.

In fact, there was another tunnel leading off at right-angles from the entrance passage. The mouth of this was disguised as a store-room for the funerary treasure. The coffin had to be turned and eased into this secondary passage. From there it entered a maze of false passages and dummy burial vaults, each more serpentine and devious than the last.

In all there were four burial chambers, but three of these would remain forever empty. There were three hidden doors and two vertical shafts. The coffin had to be lifted up one of these, and lowered down the other.

It took fifteen days for the coffin to be inched through this maze, and installed at last in its final resting-place. The roof and walls of this tomb were painted with all the skill and genius with which the gods have gifted me. There was not a space the size of my thumbnail that was not blazing with colour and movement.

Five store-rooms led off from the chamber. Into these were packed that treasure which Pharaoh Mamose had accumulated over his lifetime, and which had come close to beggaring our very Egypt. I had argued with my mistress that, instead of being buried in the earth, this treasure should be used to pay for the army and the struggle that lay ahead of us in our efforts to expel the Hyksos tyrant and to liberate our people and our land.

'The treasure belongs to Pharaoh,' she had replied. 'We have built up another treasure of gold and slaves and ivory here in Cush. That will suffice. Let the divine Mamose have what is his—I have given him my oath on it.'

Thus on the fifteenth day, the golden coffin was placed within the stone sarcophagus that had been hewn out of the native rock. With a system of ropes and levers, the heavy lid was lifted over it and lowered into place.

The royal family and the priests and the nobles entered the tomb to perform the last rites.

My mistress and the prince stood at the head of the sarcophagus, and the priests droned on with their incantations and their readings from the *Book of the Dead*. The sooty smoke from the lamps and the breathing of the throng of people in the confined space soured the air, so it was soon difficult to breathe.

In the dim yellow light I saw my mistress turn pale and the perspiration bead on her forehead. I worked my way through the tightly packed ranks, and I reached her side just as she swayed and collapsed. I was able to catch her before she struck her head on the granite edge of the sarcophagus.

We carried her out of the tomb on a litter. In the fresh mountain air she recovered swiftly, but still I confined her to her bed in her tent for the rest of that day.

That night as I prepared her tonic of herbs, she lay quietly and thoughtfully, and after she had drunk the infusion she whispered to me, 'I had the most extraordinary sensation. As I stood in Pharaoh's tomb, I felt suddenly that Tanus was very close to me. I felt his hand touch my face and his voice murmur in my ear. That was when I fainted away.'

'He will always be close to you,' I told her.

'I believe that,' she said simply.

I can see now, though I could not see it then, that her decline began on the day that we laid Tanus in his grave. She had lost the joy of living and the will to go on.

 I went back into the royal tomb the next day with the masons and the corps of slave labourers to seal the doorways and the shafts, and to arm the devices that would guard the burial chamber.

As we retreated through the maze of passageways, we blocked the secret doorways with cunningly laid stone and plaster, and painted murals over them. We sealed the mouths of the vertical shafts so that they appeared to be smooth floor and roof.

I set rockfalls that would be triggered by a footstep on a loose paving slab, and I packed the vertical shafts with balks of timber. As these decayed over the centuries and the fungus devoured them, they would emit noxious vapours that would suffocate any intruder who succeeded in finding his way through the secret doorways.

But before we did all this, I went to the actual burial chamber to take leave of Tanus. I carried with me a long bundle wrapped in a linen sheet. When I stood for the last time beside the royal sarcophagus, I sent all the workmen away. I would be the very last to leave the tomb, and after me the entrance would be sealed.

When I was alone I opened the bundle I carried. From it I took the long bow, Lanata. Tanus had named it after my mistress and I had made it for him. It was a last gift from the two of us. I placed it upon the sealed stone lid of his coffin.

There was one other item in my bundle. It was the wooden *ushabti* figure that I had carved. I placed it at the foot of the sarcophagus. While I carved it, I had set up three copper mirrors so that I could study my own features from every angle and reproduce them faithfully. The doll was a miniature Taita.

Upon the base I had inscribed the words: 'My name is Taita. I am a physician and a poet. I am an architect and a philosopher. I am your friend. I will answer for you.'

As I left the tomb, I paused at the entrance and looked back for the last time.

'Farewell, old friend,' I said. 'I am richer for having known you. Wait for us on the other side.'

 It took me many months to complete the work on the royal tomb. As we retreated through the labyrinth, I personally inspected every sealed doorway and every secret device that we left behind us.

I was alone, for my mistress and the prince had gone up into the mountains to the fortress of Prester Beni-Jon. They had gone with all the court to prepare for the wedding of Memnon and Masara. Hui had accompanied them to select the horses from the Ethiopian herds that were part of our payment for the storming of Adbar Seged, and the recovery of Masara.

When at last my work in the tomb was completed and my workmen had sealed the outer entrance in the cliff-face, I also set off into the mountains, over those cold and windy passes. I was anxious not to miss the wedding feast, but I had left it late. The completion of the tomb had taken longer than I had planned. I travelled as hard as the horses could stand.

I reached Prester Beni-Jon's palace five days before the wedding, and I went directly to that part of the fortress where my mistress and her suite were lodged.

'I have not smiled since last I saw you, Taita,' she greeted me. 'Sing for me. Tell me your stories. Make me laugh.'

It was not an easy task she set me, for the melancholy had entered deeply into her soul, and the truth was that I was not myself cheerful or light-hearted. I sensed that more than sorrow alone was affecting her. Soon we abandoned our attempts at merriment, and fell to discussing affairs of state.

It might have been a love match, and a meeting of twin souls blessed by the gods as far as the two lovers were concerned, but for the rest of us, the joining of Memnon and Masara was a royal wedding and a contract between nations. There were agreements and treaties to negotiate, dowries to be decided, trade agreements to draw up

346

between the King of Kings and ruler of Aksum, and the regent of Egypt and the wearer of the double crown of the two kingdoms.

As I had predicted, my mistress had been at first less than enchanted by the prospect of her only son marrying a woman of a different race.

'In all things they are different, Taita. The gods they worship, the language they speak, the colour of their skins—oh! I wish he had chosen a girl of our own people.'

'He will,' I reassured her. 'He will marry fifty, perhaps a hundred Egyptians. He will also marry Libyans and Hurrians and Hyksos. All the races and nations he conquers in the years to come will provide him with wives, Cushites and Hittites and Assyrians—'

'Stop your teasing, Taita.' She stamped her foot with something of her old fire. 'You know full well what I mean. Those others will all be marriages of state. This, his first, is a marriage of two hearts.'

What she said was true. The promise of love that Memnon and Masara had exchanged in those fleeting moments beside the river was now blossoming.

I was especially privileged to be close to them in these heady days. They both acknowledged and were grateful for my part in bringing them together. I was for both of them a friend of long standing, somebody that they trusted without question.

I did not share my mistress's misgivings. Though they were different in every way that she had listed, their hearts were turned from the same mould. They both possessed a sense of dedication, a fierceness of the spirit, a touch of the ruthlessness

347

and the cruelty that a ruler must have. They were a matched pair, he the tiercel and she the falcon. I knew that she would not distract him from his destiny, but rather that she would encourage and incite him to greater endeavour. I was content with my efforts as a matchmaker.

One bright mountain day, watched by twenty thousand men and women of Ethiopia and of Egypt who crowded the slopes of the hills around them, Memnon and Masara stood together on the river-bank and broke the jar of water that the high priest of Osiris had scooped from the infant Nile.

The bride and the groom led our caravan down from the mountains, laden with the dowry of a princess and the treaties and the protocols of kinship sealed between our two nations.

Hui and his grooms drove a herd of five thousand horses behind us. Some of these were in payment for our mercenary services, and the rest made up Masara's dowry. However, before we reached the junction of the two rivers at Qebui, we saw the dark stain on the plains ahead as though a cloud had cast its shadow over the savannah—but the sun shone out of a cloudless sky.

The gnu herds had returned on their annual migration.

Within weeks of this contact with the gnu, the Yellow Strangler disease fell upon our herd of Ethiopian horses, and it swept through them like a flash-flood in one of the valleys of the high mountains.

Naturally, Hui and I had been expecting the plague to strike when the gnu returned, and we had made our preparations. We had trained every groom and charioteer to perform the tracheotomy, and to treat the wound with hot pitch to prevent mortification until the animal had a chance to recover from the Strangler.

For many weeks none of us enjoyed much sleep, but in the end, fewer than two thousand of our new horses died of the disease, and before the next flooding of the Nile, those that survived were strong enough to begin training in the chariot traces.

 When the floods came, the priests sacrificed on the banks of the river, each to his own god, and they consulted the auguries for the year ahead. Some consulted the entrails of the sacrificial sheep, others watched the flight of the wild birds, still others stared into vessels filled with water from the Nile. They divined in their separate ways.

Queen Lostris sacrificed to Hapi. Although I attended the service with her and joined in the liturgy and the responses of the congregation, my heart was elsewhere. I am a Horus man, and so are Lord Kratas and Prince Memnon. We made a sacrifice of gold and ivory to our god and prayed for guidance.

It is not usual for the gods to agree with each other, any more than it is for men to do so. However, this year was different from any other that I had known. With the exception of the gods Anubis and Thoth and the goddess Nut, the heavenly host spoke with one voice. Those three, Anubis and Thoth and Nut, are all lesser deities. Their counsel could be safely discounted. All the great gods, Ammon-Ra and Osiris and Horus and Hapi and Isis and two hundred others, both great and small, gave the same counsel: 'The time has come for the return to the holy black earth of *Kemit*.'

Lord Kratas, who is a pagan at heart and a cynic by nature, suggested that the entire priesthood had conspired to place these words in the mouths of their patron gods. Although I expressed shocked indignation at this blasphemy, I was secretly inclined to agree with Kratas' opinion.

The priests are soft and luxurious men, and for almost two decades we had lived the hard lives of wanderers and warriors in the wild land of Cush. I think they hungered for fair Thebes even more than did my mistress. Perhaps it was not gods, but men who had given this advice to return northwards.

Queen Lostris summoned the high council of state, and when she made the proclamation that endorsed the dictates of the gods, the nobles and the priests stood and cheered her to a man. I cheered as loud and as long as any of them, and that night my dreams were filled with visions of Thebes, and images of those far-off days when Tanus and Lostris and I had been young and happy.

Since the death of Tanus, there had been no supreme commander of our armies, and the war council met in secret conclave. Of course, I was excluded from this assembly, but my mistress repeated to me every word that was spoken.

After long argument and debate, the command was offered to Kratas. He stood before them, grizzled and scarred like an old lion, and he laughed that great laugh of his and he said, 'I am a soldier. I follow. I do not lead. Give me the command of the Shilluk, and I will follow one man to the borders of death and beyond.' He drew his sword then and pointed with it at the prince. 'That is the man I will follow. Hail, Memnon! May he live for ever.'

'May he live for ever!' they shouted, and my mistress smiled. She and I had arranged exactly this outcome.

At the age of twenty-two years Prince Memnon was elevated to the rank of Great Lion of Egypt and commander of all her armies. Immediately he began to plan the Return.

Though my rank was only that of Master of the Royal Horse, I was on Prince Memnon's staff. Often he appealed to me to solve the logistical problems that we encountered. During the day I drove his chariot with the blue pennant fluttering over our heads as he reviewed the regiments, and led them in exercises of war.

Many nights the three of us, the prince and Kratas and I, sat up late over a jar of wine as we discussed the Return. On those nights Princess

Masara waited upon us, filling the cups with her own graceful brown hand. Then she sat on a sheepskin cushion at Memnon's feet and listened to every word. When our eyes met, she smiled at me.

Our main concern was to avoid the hazardous and onerous transit of all the cataracts on the way down-river. These could only be navigated in flood season, and would thus limit the periods in which we could travel.

I proposed that we build another fleet of barges below the fifth cataract; with these we could transport our army down to the departure-point for the desert crossing of the great bight. When we regained the river above the first cataract, we would rebuild another squadron of fast fighting galleys and barges to carry us down to Elephantine.

I was sure that if we timed it correctly, and if we could shoot the rapids and surprise the Hyksos fleet anchored in the roads of Elephantine, we would be able to deal the enemy a painful blow and capture the galleys we needed to augment our force of fighting ships. Once we had secured a foothold, we would then be able to bring down our infantry and our chariots through the gorge of the first cataract, and engage the Hyksos on the flood-plains of Egypt.

We began the first stage of the Return the following flood season. At Qebui, which had been our capital seat for so many years, we left only a garrison force. Qebui would become merely a trading outpost of the empire. The riches of Cush and Ethiopia would flow northwards to Thebes through this entrepôt.

When the main fleet sailed back into the north, Hui and I, with five hundred grooms and a squadron of chariots, remained behind to await the return of the gnu migration. They came as suddenly as they always did, a vast black stain spreading over the golden savannah grasslands. We went out to meet them in the chariots.

It was a simple matter to capture these ungainly brutes. We ran them down with the chariots, and dropped a noose of rope over their ugly heads as we ran alongside them. The gnu lacked the speed and the spirit of our horses. They fought the ropes only briefly and then resigned themselves to capture. Within ten days, we had penned over six thousand of them in the stockades on the bank of the Nile which we had built for this purpose.

It was here in the stockades that their lack of stamina and strength was most apparent. Without cause or reason, they died in their hundreds. We treated them kindly and gently. We fed them and watered them as we would our horses. It was as though their wild wandering spirits would not be fettered, and they pined away.

In the end we lost over half of those that we had captured, and many more died on the long voyage to the north.

 Two full years after Queen Lostris had commanded the Return, our people assembled on the east bank of the Nile above the fourth cataract. Before us lay the desert road across the great bight of the river.

For the whole of the previous year the caravans of wagons had set out from here. Each of them had been laden with clay jars filled to the brim with Nile water, and sealed with wooden plugs and hot pitch. Every ten miles along the dusty road we had set up watering stations. At each of these, thirty thousand water jars had been buried to prevent them cracking and bursting in the rays of that furious sun.

We were nearly fifty thousand souls and as many animals, including my dwindling herd of captured gnu. The water-carts set out from the river each evening. Their task was unending.

We waited on the river-bank for the rise of the new moon to light our way across the wilderness. Although we had planned our departure for this the coolest season of the year, still the heat and the sun would be deadly to both man and beast. We would travel only at night.

Two days before we were due to begin the crossing, my mistress said, 'Taita, when did you and I last spend a day together fishing on the river? Make ready your fish-spears and a skiff.'

I knew that she had something of deep import that she wished to discuss with me. We drifted down on those green waters until I could moor the skiff to a willow tree on the far bank, where we were out of earshot of the inquisitive.

First we spoke of the imminent departure along the desert road, and the prospects of the return to Thebes.

'When will I see her shining walls again, Taita?' my mistress sighed, and I could only tell her that I did not know.

'If the gods are kind, we might be in Elephantine

354

by this time next season when the Nile flood carries our ships down the first cataract. After that, our fortunes will ebb and flow like the river, with the hazards and fortunes of war.'

However, this was not what she had brought me out on to the river to discuss, and now her eyes swam with tears as she asked, 'How long has Tanus been gone from us, Taita?'

My voice choked as I answered, 'He set out on his journey to the fields of paradise over three years ago, mistress.'

'So it is longer than that by many months that I last lay in his arms,' she mused, and I nodded. I was uncertain in which direction her questions were leading us.

'I have dreamed of him almost every night since then, Taita. Is it possible that he might have returned to leave his seed in my womb while I still slept?'

'All things in heaven are possible,' I replied carefully. 'We told the people that was how Tehuti and Bekatha were conceived. However, in all truth and seriousness, I have never heard of it happening before.'

We were both silent for a while, and she trailed her hand in the water and then lifted it to watch the drops fall from her fingertips. Then she spoke again without looking at me. 'I think I am to have another child,' she whispered, 'My red moon has waned and withered away.'

'Mistress,' I answered her quietly, and with tact, 'you are approaching that time of your life when the rivers of your womb will begin to dry up.' Our Egyptian women are like desert flowers that bloom early but fade as swiftly.

She shook her head. 'No, Taita. It is not that. I feel the infant growing within me.'

I stared at her silently. Once again I felt the wings of tragedy brush lightly past me, stirring the air and raising the hair upon my forearms.

'You do not have to ask me if I have known another man.' This time she looked directly into my eyes as she spoke. 'You know that I have not.'

'This I know full well. Yet I cannot believe that you have been impregnated by a ghost, no matter how beloved and welcome that ghost might be. Perhaps your desire for another child has fathered your imagination.'

'Feel my womb, Taita,' she commanded. 'This is a living thing within me. Each day it grows.'

'I will do so tonight, in the privacy of your cabin. Not here upon the river where prying eyes might discover us.'

 My mistress lay naked upon the linen sheets, and I studied first her face and then her body. When I looked upon her with the eyes of a man, she was still lovely to me, but as a physician I could see clearly how the years and the hardships of this life in the wilderness had wrought their cruel change. Her hair was more silver than sable now, and bereavement and the cares of the regency had chiselled their grim message on her brow. She was growing old.

Her body was the vessel which had given life to three other lives. But her breasts were empty now, there was none of the milk of a new pregnancy

356

swelling them. She was thin. I should have noticed that before. It was an unnatural thinness, almost an emaciation. Yet her belly protruded like a pale ivory ball out of proportion to those slim arms and legs.

I laid my hands lightly upon her belly, upon the silvery streaks where the skin had once stretched to accommodate a joyful burden. I felt the thing within her and I knew at once that this was not life beneath my fingers. This was death.

I could not find words. I turned away from her and went out on to the deck and I looked up at the night stars. They were cold and very far away. Like the gods, they did not care. There was no profit in appealing to them, gods or stars.

I knew this thing that was growing within my mistress. I had felt it in the bodies of other women. When they died, I had opened the dead womb and seen the thing that had killed them. It was horrible and deformed, bearing no resemblance to anything human or even animal. It was a shapeless ball of red and angry flesh. It was a thing of Seth.

It was a long time before I could gather the courage to return to the cabin.

My mistress had covered herself with a robe. She sat in the centre of the bed and looked at me with those huge, dark green eyes that had never aged. She looked like the little girl I once had known.

'Mistress, why did you not tell me about the pain?' I asked gently.

'How do you know about the pain?' she whispered back. 'I tried to hide it from you.'

Our caravan set out into the desert, travelling by moonlight across the silver sands. Sometimes my mistress walked at my side, and the two princesses frolicked along with us, laughing and excited by the adventure. At other times, when the pain was bad, my mistress rode in the wagon that I had equipped for her comfort. Then I sat beside her and held her hand until the powder of the sleeping-flower worked its magic and gave her surcease.

Every night we travelled just as far as the next watering-station along the road that was now well beaten by the thousands of vehicles that had preceded us. During the long days we lay beneath the awning of the wagon and drowsed in the sweltering heat.

We had been thirty days and nights upon the road when in the dawn we saw a remarkable sight. A disembodied sail upon the desert, moving gently southwards over the sands. It was not until we had journeyed on for many more miles that we saw how we had been deceived. The hull of the galley had been hidden from us by the bank of the Nile, and below the dunes the river ran on eternally. We had crossed the loop.

Prince Memnon and all his staff were there to greet us. Already the squadron of new galleys had almost completed fitting out. It was the sail of one of these that we had first descried as we approached the river again. Every plank and mast had been cut and sawn on the great plains of Cush, and transported across the loop of the river. All the chariots were assembled. Hui had herded all the horses across the desert, and the wagons had carried their fodder with them. Even my gnu were waiting in their stockades upon the river-bank.

Although the wagon caravans carrying the women and the children still followed, the main body of our nation had been brought across. It had been an undertaking that almost defied belief, a labour of godlike proportions. Only men like Kratas and Remrem and Memnon could have accomplished it in so short a time.

Now only the first cataract still stood between us and the sacred earth of our very Egypt.

We went on northwards again. My mistress sailed in the new barge that had been built for her and the princesses. There was a large and airy cabin for her, and I had equipped it with every luxury that was available to us. The hangings were of embroidered Ethiopian wool, and the furniture was of dark acacia wood inlaid with ivory and the gold of Cush. I decorated the bulkheads with paintings of flowers and birds and other pretty things.

As always, I slept at the foot of my mistress's bed. Three nights after we sailed, I woke in the night. She was weeping silently. Although she had stifled her sobs with a pillow, the shaking of her shoulders had awakened me. I went to her immediately.

'The pain has come again?' I asked.

'I did not mean to wake you, but it is like a sword in my belly.'

I mixed her a draught of the sleeping-flower, stronger than I had ever given to her before. The pain was beginning to triumph over the flower.

She drank it and lay quietly for a while. Then she said, 'Can you not cut this thing out of my body, Taita?'

'No, mistress. I cannot.'

'Then hold me, Taita. Hold me the way you used to do when I was a little girl.'

I went into her bed, and I took her in my arms. I cradled her, and she was as thin and light as a child. I rocked her tenderly, and after a while she slept.

 The fleet reached the head of the first cataract above Elephantine, and we moored against the bank in the quiet flow of the river before the Nile felt the urging of the cascades and plunged into the gorge.

We waited for the rest of the army to be ferried down to us, all the horses and the chariots and Lord Kratas' pagan Shilluk regiments. We waited also for the Nile to rise and open the cataract for us to pass down into Egypt.

While we waited, we sent spies down through the gorge. They were dressed as peasants and priests and merchants with goods to trade. I went down with Kratas into the gorge to map and mark the passage. Now, at low water, every hazard was exposed. We painted channel-markers on the rocks above the high-water line, so that even when the flood covered them, we would still know where those obstacles lurked.

We were many weeks at this labour, and when we returned to where the fleet was moored, the army was assembled there. We sent out scouting parties to find a route for the chariots and the horses through the rock desert down into Egypt. We could not risk such a precious cargo to the wild waters of the cataract.

Our spies began to return from Elephantine. They came in secretly and singly, usually in the night. They brought us the very first news of our mother-land that we had heard in all the years of exile.

King Salitis still reigned, but he was old now, and his beard had turned silver-white. His two sons were the mighty men of the Hyksos legions. Prince Beon commanded the infantry and Prince Apachan commanded the chariots.

The might of the Hyksos exceeded all our estimates. Our spies reported that Apachan disposed of twelve thousand chariots. We had brought down only four thousand from Cush. Beon had forty thousand archers and infantry. Even with Kratas' Shilluk, we could muster only fifteen thousand. We were heavily outnumbered.

There was cheering news also. The great bulk of the Hyksos force was held in the Delta, and Salitis had made his capital at the city of Memphis. It would take months for him to move his forces south to Elephantine and Thebes. He would not be able to bring his chariots up-river until the floods abated and the land dried. There was only a single squadron of chariots guarding the city of Elephantine, one hundred chariots to oppose our entry. They were of the old solid-wheel type. It seemed that the Hyksos had not yet perfected the spoked wheel.

Prince Memnon laid out his battle plan for us. We would pass through the cataract on the flood, and seize Elephantine. Then, while Salitis moved southwards to oppose us, we would march on Thebes, raising the populace in insurrection as we went.

We could expect Salitis to give battle with his full army on the flood-plains before Thebes, once the Nile waters had subsided. By then we could hope that the disparity in the numbers of the two armies would be redressed in part by the Egyptian troops that would rally to our standard.

We learned from our spies that the Hyksos did not suspect the presence of our army of liberation so close to their border, and that we could expect to gain the element of surprise with our first assault. We learned also that Salitis had adopted our Egyptian way of life. These days he lived in our palaces and worshipped our gods. Even his old Sutekh had changed his name to Seth, and was, very appropriately, still his principal god.

Although all his senior officers were Hyksos, many of Salitis' captains and sergeants had been recruited from amongst the Egyptians, and half the common soldiers were of our own nation. Most of these would have been infants or not yet born at the time of our exodus. We wondered where their loyalties would lie, when Prince Memnon led our army down into Egypt.

All was in readiness now. The scouts had marked a road through the desert of the west bank, and the water wagons had laid down stores of fodder and water jars along the length of it, enough to see our chariots through to the fertile plains of our very Egypt. Our galleys were rigged and manned for battle. When the Nile flooded, we would sail, but in the meantime there was one last

362

ritual to complete.

We climbed the bluff above the river to where the obelisk that my mistress had raised over two decades before, still stood, a tall and elegant finger of stone pointing into the cloudless blue of the African sky.

My mistress was too weak to climb the rugged pathway to the summit. Ten slaves carried her up in a sedan-chair, and set her down below the tall monument. She walked painfully slowly to the foot of the pillar on the arm of Prince Memnon, and gazed up at the inscription carved in the granite. Our whole nation watched her, all those souls who had found their way back to this point from which we had set out so long ago.

My mistress read the inscription aloud. Her voice was soft, but still so musical that it carried clearly to where I stood behind the great lords and the generals.

'I, Queen Lostris, Regent of Egypt and widow of Pharaoh Mamose, the eighth of that name, mother of the Crown Prince Memnon, who shall rule the two kingdoms after me, have ordained the raising of this monument...'

When she had finished the reading, she turned to face her people and spread her arms.

'I have done that which was required of me,' she said, and her voice regained some of its old power. 'I have led you back to the border of your land. My task is completed and I relinquish the regency.' She paused, and for a moment her eyes met mine over the heads of the nobles. I nodded slightly to encourage her, and she went on.

'Citizens of Egypt, it is fitting that you have a true Pharaoh to lead you the last steps of the way

363

home. I give to you the divine Pharaoh Tamose, who once was the Crown Prince Memnon. May he live for ever!'

'May he live for ever!' the nation roared in one voice. 'May he live for ever!'

Pharaoh Tamose stepped forward to face his people. 'May he live for ever!' they shouted the third time, and our new pharaoh drew the blue sword from its jewelled scabbard and saluted them with it.

In the silence that followed, his voice rang and echoed from the gaunt red crags of the hills.

'I take up this sacred trust. I swear on my hope of eternal life to serve my people and my land all my days. I shall not flinch from this duty, and I call upon all the gods to witness my oath.'

 The flood came. The waters rose up the rocks that guarded the entrance to the gorge, and the colour changed from green to grey. The cataract began to growl like a beast in its lair and the spray-cloud rose into the sky and stood as high as the hills that flanked the Nile.

I went aboard the leading galley with Lord Kratas and Pharaoh. We dropped our mooring and shoved off into the stream. The rowers on the benches were stripped to their breech-clouts, their faces turned up to watch Kratas as he stood high in the stern, gripping the steering-oar in his bear-like fists.

In the bows two teams of sailors under the king stood ready with heavy oars to fend off. I stood beside Kratas, with the map of the rapids spread on the deck in front of me, ready to call the twists and turns of the channel to him as we came to them. I did not really need the map, for I had memorized every line drawn upon it. In addition to which, I had stationed reliable men on the sides of the gorge and on the islands in the main stream ahead of us. They would use signal flags to show us the way through.

As the current quickened beneath our keel, I cast one last glance backwards and saw the rest of the squadron fall into line astern behind us, ready to follow us down the cataract. Then I looked forward again, and felt the fist of fear tighten on my bowels so that I was forced to squeeze my buttocks together. Ahead of us the gorge smoked like the mouth of a furnace.

Our speed built up with deceptive stealth. The rowers touched the surface lightly with the blades of the oars, just enough to keep our bows pointed downstream. We floated so lightly and so smoothly that we seemed to be drifting. It was only when I looked at the banks, and saw them streaming past us, that I realized how fast we were running. The rock portals of the gorge flew to meet us. None the less, it was only when I noticed the grin on Kratas' craggy face that I realized the true danger of what we were attempting. Kratas only grinned like that when he saw death crook a bony finger at him.

'Come on, you rogues!' he shouted at his crew. 'This day I'll make your mothers proud of you, or I'll find work for the embalmers.'

The river was split by three islands, and the channel narrowed.

'Bear to port, and steer for the blue cross.' I

tried to sound casual, but at that moment I felt the deck tip beneath my feet, and I clutched at the rail.

We flew down a chute of grey water, and our bows swung giddily. I thought that we were already out of control, and waited for the crunch of rock and for the deck to burst open beneath my feet. Then I saw the bows steady, and the blue cross painted on the wall of rock was dead ahead.

'Hard to starboard as we come up to the flag!' my voice squeaked, but I picked out the man on the centre island flagging us into the turn, and Kratas put the steering-oar over and yelled at the benches, 'All back right, pull together left!' The deck canted sharply as we spun into the turn.

The wall of rock flashed past us, and we were going at the speed of a galloping horse. One more turn and the first rapids lay ahead. Black rock stood across our path, and the waters piled upon it. The water took on the shape of the rocks beneath it. It bulged and stood in tall static waves. It opened into smooth green gulleys. It curled upon itself and exploded into veils of white through which the rock snarled at us with black fangs. My stomach clenched as we leaped over the edge and dropped down the slope. At the bottom we wallowed and spun, like a stalk of dry grass in a whirlwind.

'Pull left!' Kratas bellowed. 'Pull till your balls bounce!' We steadied and aimed for the next gap in the rock, and the white water dashed over the deck and into my eyes. It hissed alongside, running in tandem with us, and the waves stood taller than our poop-deck.

'By Seth's tattered and festering foreskin, I've not had so much sport since I tupped my first ewe!' Kratas laughed, and the rock sprang at us like a charging bull elephant.

We touched once, and the rock rasped along our belly. The deck shuddered beneath our feet, and I was too afraid to scream. Then Memnon's team poled us free and we raced on down.

Behind us I heard the shattering crash as one of the other galleys struck hard. I dared not look round as I judged our next turn, but soon there were wreckage and the heads of drowning men bobbing and swirling in the torrent on both sides of us. They screamed to us as they were borne away and dashed upon the spurs of rock, but we could offer them no succour. Death pressed hard upon our heels and we ran on with the stench of it in our nostrils.

In that hour I lived a hundred lives, and died in every one of them. But at last we were hurled from the bottom of the cataract into the main body of the river. Of the twenty-three galleys that had entered the gorge, eighteen followed us out. The others had been smashed to flotsam, and the corpses of their drowned crew washed down beside us in the grey Nile flood.

There was not time for us to celebrate our deliverance. Dead ahead lay the Island of Elephantine, and on both banks of the river stood the well-remembered walls and buildings of the city.

'Archers, string your bows!' King Tamose called from the bows. 'Hoist the blue pennant! Drummer, increase the beat to attack speed!'

Our tiny squadron flew into the mass of shipping that clogged the roads of Elephantine. Most of it was made up of trade barges and transports. We passed these by, and went for the Hyksos galleys. The Hyksos had manned their fighting ships with Egyptian sailors, for nobody knew the river better. Only their officers were Hyksos. Most of them were ashore, carousing in the pleasure-palaces of the docks.

Our spies had told us which was the flag of the southern admiral, a swallowtail of scarlet and gold so long that the end of it dipped in the water. We steered for the ship that flew her, and Memnon boarded her over the side with twenty men at his back.

'Freedom from the Hyksos tyrant!' they roared. 'Stand up for this very Egypt!'

The crew gaped at them. They had been taken completely by surprise, and most of them were unarmed. Their weapons were locked away below decks, for the Hyksos officers trusted them not at all.

The other galleys of our squadron had each picked out one of the enemy fighting-ships and boarded it as swiftly. On all of them the reaction of the crew was the same. After the first surprise they shouted the question, 'Who are you?'

And the reply was, 'Egyptian! The army of the true Pharaoh Tamose. Join with us, countrymen! Cast out the tyrant!'

They turned on their Hyksos officers and cut them down before we could reach them. Then they embraced our men, roaring out a welcome.

'For Egypt!' they cheered. 'For Tamose! For Egypt and Tamose!'

The cheering jumped from ship to ship. Men danced upon the rails and swarmed up the masts to tear down the Hyksos banners. They broke open the arms stores and passed out bows and swords.

Then they poured ashore. They dragged the Hyksos from the taverns and hacked them to bloody shreds, so that the gutters discharged a scarlet flood into the harbour waters. They ran through the streets to the barracks of the garrison, and fell upon the guard.

'For Egypt and Tamose!' they chanted.

Some of the Hyksos officers rallied their men, and held out for a while in pockets surrounded by the rabble. Then Kratas and Memnon came ashore with their veterans, and within two hours the city was ours.

Most of the Hyksos chariots were abandoned in their lines, but half a squadron was escaping through the east gate and galloping away over the causeway that crossed the inundated fields to the dry ground beyond.

I had left the ship and hurried through the back alleys, that I knew so well, to the north tower on the city walls. From there I knew I would have the best view over the city and the surrounding countryside. Bitterly, I watched the escaping detachment of chariots. Every one that got away now would have to be fought later, and I wanted those horses. I was about to turn away and watch what was happening in the city below me, when I saw a little finger of dust rising from the foot of the harsh southern hills.

I shaded my eyes and stared at it. I felt the quickening of excitement. The dust was coming towards us swiftly, I could make out the dark shapes beneath it.

'By Horus, it's Remrem!' I whispered with

delight. The old warrior had brought the first division of chariots through the bad ground of the hills quicker than I would have believed possible. It was only two days since we had parted.

I watched with professional pride as the first division opened from columns of four into line abreast. Hui and I had trained them well. It was perfectly done, and Remrem had the Hyksos in enfilade. Half their vehicles were still on the causeway. It seemed to me that the enemy commander was not even aware of the massed squadrons bearing down upon his exposed flank. I think he must still have been looking back over his shoulder. At the very last moment he tried to swing into line abreast to meet Remrem's charge, but it was far too late. He would have done better to have turned tail and run for it.

Remrem's chariots poured over him in a wave, and he was washed away like debris in the stream of the Nile. I watched until I was certain that Remrem had captured most of the Hyksos horses, and only then did I sigh with relief and turn to look down into the city.

The populace had gone wild with the joy of liberation. They were dancing through the streets, waving any piece of blue cloth that came to hand. Blue was the colour of Pharaoh Tamose. The women tied blue ribbons in their hair, and the men wound blue sashes around their waists and tied on blue arm-bands.

There was still some isolated fighting, but gradually the surviving Hyksos were cut down or dragged from the buildings they were trying to defend. One of the barracks with several hundred men still inside it was put to the torch. I heard the screams of the men as they burned, and soon the aroma of scorched flesh drifted up to me. It smelled like roasting pork.

Of course there was looting, and some of our upstanding citizens broke into the taverns and the wine shops and carried the jars out into the street. When one of the jars broke, they went down on all fours and guzzled the wine out of the gutter like hogs.

I saw three men chase a girl down the alley below where I stood. When they caught her they threw her down and ripped her skirt away. Two of them pinned her limbs and held her spread-eagled while the third man mounted her. I did not watch the rest of it.

As soon as Memnon and Kratas had stamped out the last pockets of Hyksos resistance, they set about restoring order to the city. Squads of disciplined troops trotted through the streets, using the shafts of their war spears as clubs to beat sense into the drunken and delirious mob.

Memnon ordered a handful of those taken in the act of rape and looting to be strangled on the spot, and their corpses were hung by the heels from the city gates. By nightfall the city was quiet, and decent men and women could once more safely walk her streets.

Memnon set up his headquarters in Pharaoh Mamose's palace, which had once been our home on Elephantine Island. The moment I stepped ashore I hurried to our old quarters in the harem.

They were still luxuriously appointed and had escaped the looters. Whoever had occupied them had treated my murals with the respect they warranted. The water-garden was a profusion of

371

lovely plants, and the ponds were filled with fish and lotus. The Egyptian gardener told me that the Hyksos garrison commander who had lived here had admired our Egyptian ways, and had tried to ape them. I was thankful for that.

Within days I had restored the rooms and garden to a state in which they were once more fit to receive my mistress. Then I went to Memnon to ask permission to bring the queen home.

Pharaoh was distracted by the burden of taking firm hold of his kingdom. There were ten thousand matters that demanded his attention, but he put them aside for the moment and embraced me.

'It all goes well, Tata.'

'A happy return, Your Majesty,' I replied, 'but there is still so much to do.'

'It is my royal command that when you and I are alone like this, you continue to call me Mem.' He smiled at me, 'But you are right, there is much to do, and little time left to us before Salitis and all his host march up from the Delta to oppose us. We have won the first little skirmish. The great battles lie ahead of us.'

'There is one duty that will give me great pleasure, Mem. I have prepared quarters for the queen mother. May I go up-river and bring her home to Elephantine? She has waited too long already to set foot on Egyptian soil.'

'Leave at once, Tata,' he commanded, 'and bring Queen Masara down with you.'

The river was too high and the desert road too rough. One hundred slaves carried the litters of the two queens along the banks of the Nile, through the gorge and down into our green valley.

It was not pure coincidence that the first

372

building we came to as we crossed the border was a small temple. I had planned our route to bring us here.

'What shrine is this, Taita?' my mistress drew aside the curtain of her litter to ask.

'It is the temple of the god Akh-Horus, mistress. Do you wish to pray here?'

'Thank you,' she whispered. She knew what I had done. I helped her down from the litter, and she leaned heavily upon me as we entered the cool gloom of the stone building.

We prayed together, and I felt certain that Tanus was listening to the voices of the two people in all the world who had loved him most. Before we went on, my mistress ordered me to hand over all the gold that we had with us to the priests, and promised to send more for the upkeep and the beautification of the temple.

By the time we reached the Palace of Elephantine, she was exhausted. Each day the thing in her womb grew larger as it fed upon her wasting body. I laid her on a couch under the barrazza in the water-garden, and she closed her eyes and rested for a while. Then she opened them again and smiled at me softly. 'We were happy here once, but will I ever see Thebes again before I die?' I could not answer her. It was idle to make promises to her that were not mine to keep.

'If I die before that, will you promise to take me back and build me a tomb in the hills from where I can look across and see my beautiful city?'

'That I promise you with all my heart,' I replied.

In the days that followed, Aton and I resuscitated our old spider's web of spies and informers across the Upper Kingdom. Many of those who had once worked for us were long dead, but there were also many who were not. With the bait of gold and patriotism, they recruited other younger spies in every village and city.

Soon we had spies in the palace of the Hyksos satrap in Thebes, and others as far north as the Delta of the Lower Kingdom. Through them we learned which Hyksos regiments were billeted in each town, and which of them were on the march. We learned their strength, and the names and foibles of their commanders. We had an exact count of the numbers of their ships and their chariots, and as the flood-waters of the Nile receded, we were able to follow the southward movement of this huge mass of men and fighting machines, as King Salitis marched on Thebes.

I smuggled secret messages in the name of Pharaoh Tamose to those Egyptians in the regiments of the enemy, urging them to revolt. They started to trickle in through our lines, bringing more valuable intelligence with them. Soon the trickle of deserters from the Hyksos armies became a flood. Two full regiments of archers came marching in under arms, with the blue banner waving over them, and chanting, 'Egypt and Tamose!'

The crews of a hundred fighting galleys mutinied and slew their Hyksos officers. When they came sailing up-river to join us, they drove before them a fleet of barges that they had captured in the port of Thebes. These were laden with grain and oil and salt and flax and timber, all the sinews of war.

By this time, all our own forces were down through the cataract and deployed around the city, except only the small herd of tame gnu. These I had left until the very last. From my lookout in the north tower, I could see the horse-lines extending for miles along both banks, and the smoke from the cooking-fires of the regimental encampments turned the air blue.

Each day we were growing stronger, and the whole of Egypt was in a ferment of excitement and anticipation. The heady aroma of freedom perfumed each breath we drew. *Kemit* was a nation in the process of rebirth. They sang the patriotic anthems in the streets and the taverns, and the harlots and the wine merchants grew fat.

Aton and I, poring over our maps and secret despatches, saw a different picture emerging. We saw the Hyksos giant shaking itself awake, and stretching out a mailed fist towards us. From Memphis and every city and town in the Delta, King Salitis' regiments were on the march. Every road was crowded with his chariots, and the river ran with his shipping. All of this was moving south upon Thebes.

I waited until I knew that Lord Apachan, the commander of the Hyksos chariots, had reached Thebes and was encamped outside the city walls with all his vehicles and all his horses. Then I went before the war council of Pharaoh Tamose.

'Your Majesty, I have come to report that the enemy now have one hundred and twenty

375

thousand horses and twelve thousand chariots massed at Thebes. Within two months, the Nile will have subsided to the level that will enable Apachan to begin his final advance.'

Even Kratas looked grave. 'We have known worse odds—' he began, but the king cut him short.

'I can tell by his face that the Master of the Royal Horse has more to tell us. Am I right, Taita?'

'Pharaoh is always right,' I agreed. 'I beg your permission to bring down my gnu from above the cataract.'

Kratas laughed. 'By Seth's bald head, Taita, do you intend riding out against the Hyksos on one of those clownish brutes of yours?' I laughed with him politely. His sense of humour has the same subtlety as that of the savage Shilluk he commands.

The next morning Hui and I set off up-river to bring down the gnu. By this time there were only three hundred of these sorry creatures left alive out of the original six thousand, but they were quite tame and could be fed from the hand. We herded them down at a gentle pace, so as not to weaken them further.

The horses that Remrem had captured in that first brief battle with the escaping Hyksos chariots had on my orders been kept separated from our own horses that we had brought down with us from Cush. Hui and I moved the gnu into the same pasture with them, and after the first uneasiness between the two species, they were all feeding peaceably together. That night we penned gnu and Hyksos horses in the same stockade. I left

376

Hui to watch over them and returned to the palace on Elephantine Island.

I will admit now to a great deal of uncertainty and worry over the days that followed. I had invested so much faith in the success of this ruse, which, after all, depended on a natural event that I did not fully understand. If it failed, we would be faced with the full fury of an enemy that outnumbered us by at least four to one.

I had worked late with Aton and had fallen asleep over my scrolls in the palace library, when I was shaken awake by uncouth hands, and Hui was shouting in my ear. 'Come on, you lazy old rascal! Wake up! I have something for you.'

He had horses waiting at the landing. We hurried to them as soon as the ferry put us ashore, and mounted up. We galloped all the way along the river-bank in the moonlight, and rode into the horse-lines with our mounts in a lather. The grooms had lamps lit and were working in the stockade by their feeble yellow light.

Seven of the Hyksos horses were down already with the thick yellow pus pouring from their mouths and nostrils. The grooms were cutting into their windpipes and placing the hollow reeds to save them from choking and suffocating.

'It worked!' Hui shouted, and seized me in a coarse embrace and danced me in a circle. 'The Yellow Strangler! It worked! It worked!'

'I thought of it, didn't I?' I told him with all the dignity that his antics allowed me. 'Of course it worked.'

The barges had been moored against the bank these weeks past, ready for this day. We loaded the horses immediately, all of those who could still stand upright. The gnu we left in the stockade. Their presence would be too difficult to explain where we were going.

With one of the captured Hyksos galleys towing each of the barges, we rowed out into the current and turned northwards. With fifty oars a side and the wind and current behind us, we made good speed as we hurried down to Thebes to deliver our gift to Lord Apachan.

 As soon as we passed Kom-Ombo we lowered the blue flag, and hoisted captured Hyksos banners. Most of the crew of the galleys that were towing the barges had been born under Hyksos rule, some of them were of mixed parentage and spoke the foreign language with colloquial fluency.

Two nights north of Kom-Ombo, we were hailed by a Hyksos galley. They laid alongside and sent a boarding party over to inspect our cargo.

'Horses for the chariots of Lord Apachan,' our captain told them. His father was Hyksos but his mother was an Egyptian noblewoman. His deportment was natural and his credentials convincing. After a cursory inspection they passed us through. We were stopped and boarded twice more before we reached Thebes, but each time our captain was able to deceive the Hyksos officers who came aboard.

My chief concern by this time was the state of the horses. Despite our best efforts, they were beginning to die, and half of those still alive were in a pitiful condition. We threw the carcasses overboard, and ran on northwards at our best speed.

My original plan had been to sell the horses to the Hyksos quartermasters in the port of Thebes, but no man who knew horseflesh would look at this pitiful herd. Hui and I decided upon another course.

We timed the last leg of our voyage to arrive at Thebes as the sun was setting. My heart ached as I recognized all the familiar landmarks. The walls of the citadel glowed pinkly in the last rays of the sun. Those three elegant towers that I had built for Lord Intef still pointed to the sky, they were aptly named the Fingers of Horus.

The Palace of Memnon on the west bank, which I had left uncompleted, had been rebuilt by the Hyksos. Even I had to admit that the Asiatic influence was pleasing. In this light the spires and watch-towers were endowed with a mysterious and exotic quality. I wished that my mistress was there to share this moment of homecoming with me. We had both longed for it over half her lifetime.

In the fading light we were still able to make out the vast concourse of men and horses and chariots and wagons that lay outside the city walls. Although I had received accurate reports, it had not been possible to visualize such multitudes. My spirits quailed as I looked upon them, and remembered the gallant little army I had left at Elephantine.

We would need every favour of the gods, and more than a little good fortune to triumph against such a host. As the last light faded into night, the fires of the Hyksos bloomed and twinkled upon the plain, like a field of stars. There was no end to them—they stretched away to the limit of the eye.

As we sailed closer, we smelled them. There is a peculiar odour that a standing army exudes. It is a blend of many smells, of dung-fires and of cooking food, the sweet smell of new-cut hay and the ammoniacal smell of the horses, and the stench of human sewage in open pits, of leather and pitch and horse-sweat and woodshavings and sour beer. Most of all it is the smell of men, tens of thousands of men, living close to each other in tents and huts and hovels.

We sailed on, and the sounds floated across the star-lit waters to our silent ship; the snort and the whinny of horses, the sound of the coppersmiths' hammers on the anvil beating out spear-heads and blades, the challenges of the sentries, and the voices of men singing and arguing and laughing.

I stood beside the captain on the deck of the leading galley and guided him in towards the east bank. I remembered the wharf of the timber merchants outside the city walls. If it still stood, it would be the best point at which to disembark our herd.

I picked out the entrance to the dock, and we pushed in under oars. The wharf was exactly as I remembered it. As we came alongside, the harbour-master came fussing on board, demanding our papers and our licence to trade.

I fawned upon him, bowing and grinning obsequiously. 'Excellency, there has been a terrible accident. My licences were blown from my hand by the wind, a trick of Seth, no doubt.'

He blew himself up like an angry bullfrog, and then subsided again as I pressed a heavy gold ring into his fat paw. He tested the metal between his teeth, and went away smiling.

I sent one of the grooms ashore to douse the torches that illuminated the wharf. I did not want curious eyes to see the condition of the horses that we brought ashore. Some of our animals were too weak to rise, others staggered and wheezed, they drooled the stinking mucus from mouth and nostrils. We were forced to place head-halters on them and coax them out of the barge on to the wharf. In the end there were only a hundred horses strong enough to walk.

We led them down the wagon-track to the high ground where our spies had told us the main horse-lines were laid out. Our spies had also provided us with the password of the Hyksos first division of chariots, and the linguists among us replied to the challenges of the sentries.

We walked our horses the entire length of the enemy encampment. As we went, we began to turn our stricken animals loose, leaving a few of them to wander through the lines of every one of the Hyksos' twenty chariot divisions. We moved so casually and naturally that no alarm was raised, we even chatted and joked with the enemy grooms and horsehandlers we met along the way.

As the first streaks of dawn showed in the eastern sky, we trudged back to the timber wharf on which we had disembarked. Only one of the galleys had waited to take us off, the rest of the flotilla had cast off and turned back southwards as soon as they had discharged their cargo of diseased horses.

We went aboard the remaining ship, and although Hui and the other grooms threw themselves exhausted upon the deck, I stood at the stern-rail and watched the walls of my beautiful Thebes, washed by the pure early light, sink from view behind us.

Ten days later, we sailed into the port of Elephantine, and after I had reported to Pharaoh Tamose, I hurried to the water-garden in the harem. My mistress lay in the shade of the barrazza. She was pale and so thin that I could not keep my hands from trembling as I stretched out to her in obeisance. She wept when she saw me.

'I missed you, Taita. There is so little time left for us to be together.'

 The Nile began to shrink back into her bed. The fields emerged from under the inundation, glistening black under a thick new coat of rich mud. The roads began to dry out, opening the way northwards. Soon it would be time for the plough, and the time for war.

Aton and I waited anxiously, perusing every report from our spies in the north. It came at last, the intelligence for which we had waited and prayed. The news was carried by a fast felucca, flying to us on the wings of the north wind. It docked in the third watch of the night, but the messenger found Aton and me still working by lamplight in his cell.

I hurried with the dirty scrap of papyrus to the royal apartments. The guards had orders to let me pass at any hour, but Queen Masara met me at the curtained doorway to the king's bedchamber.

'I will not let you wake him now, Taita. The

382

king is exhausted. This is his first night's uninterrupted sleep in a month.'

'Your Majesty, I must see him. I am under his direct orders—'

While we still argued, a deep young voice called to me from beyond the curtain, 'Is that you, Tata?' The curtain was thrown aside and the king stood before us in all his naked splendour. He was a man as few others I have ever known, lean and hard as the blade of the blue sword, majestic in all his manly parts, so that I was all the more conscious of my own disability when I looked upon him.

'What is it, Tata?'

'Despatches from the north. From the camp of the Hyksos. A terrible pestilence is sweeping through the lines of the Hyksos. Half their horses are stricken, and thousands of others fall prey to the disease with each new day.'

'You are a magician, Tata. How could we have ever mocked you and your gnu!' He gripped my shoulders and stared into my eyes. 'Are you ready to ride to glory with me?'

'I am ready, Pharaoh.'

'Then put Rock and Chain into the traces, and fly the blue pennant over my chariot. We are going home to Thebes.'

 So we stood at last before the city of a hundred gates with four divisions of chariots and thirty thousand foot. King Salitis' host lay before us, but beyond his multitudes the Fingers of Horus beckoned to us, and the walls of Thebes shone with a pearly radiance in the dawn light.

The Hyksos army deployed ponderously in front of us, like the uncoiling of some gigantic python, column after column, rank upon rank. Their spear-heads glittered and the golden helmets of the officers blazed in the early sunlight.

'Where is Apachan and his chariots?' the king demanded, and I stared at the Finger of Horus that stood nearest the river. I had to strain my eyesight to make out the tiny coloured scraps that waved from the top of the tower.

'Apachan has five divisions in the centre, and he holds six more in reserve. They are hidden beyond the city wall.'

I read the flag signals of the spy I had posted in the tallest of the three towers. I knew that from there he had a falcon's view across the battlefield.

'That is only eleven divisions, Tata,' the king fumed. 'We know he has twenty. Where are the others?'

'The Yellow Strangler,' I answered him. 'He has fielded every horse that can still stand.'

'By Horus, I hope you are right. I hope that Apachan is not planning a pretty little surprise for us.' He touched my shoulder. 'The dice are in the cup, Tata. It is too late to change them now. We must play this coup with what the gods have given us. Drive out in review.'

I took up the reins and wheeled the chariot out in front of our army. The king was showing himself to his troops. His presence would give them heart, and stiffen their spines. I took the horses down the long ranks at a tight hand-trot. Rock and Chain were brushed until their coats shone like polished copper in the sunlight. The carriage of the royal

384

chariot was dressed in a thin skin of gold-leaf. This was the only concession I had made, in my quest for lightness.

The gold was beaten thinner than a papyrus sheet, and it added less than a hundred deben to the overall weight of our vehicle, yet it made a dazzling display. Friend or enemy who looked upon it could not doubt that this was Pharaoh's chariot, and take heart or be struck by awe in the thick of battle. On its long, whippy bamboo rod the blue pennant nodded and streamed in the breeze high above our heads, and the men cheered us as we drove down their ranks.

On the day we had left Qebui to begin the Return, I had made a vow not to cut my hair until I had made sacrifice in the temple of Horus in the centre of Thebes. Now my hair reached to my waist, and to hide the streaks of grey in it, I had dyed it with henna imported from those lands beyond the Indus river. It was a ruddy gold mane that set off my beauty to perfection. I wore a simple starched kilt of the whitest linen, and the Gold of Praise upon my naked chest. I did not wish in any way to detract from the glory of my young pharaoh, so I wore no make-up and no other ornament.

We passed in front of the massed regiments of the Shilluk spearmen in the centre. Those magnificent bloodthirsty pagans were the rock that anchored our line. They cheered us as we rode by, '*Kajan!* Tanus! *Kajan!* Tamose!' Their ostrich feathers seethed white as the foam of the river in the cataracts as they raised their spears in salute. I saw Lord Kratas there in the midst of them, and he shouted at me. His words were lost in the roar of ten thousand voices, but I read his lips: 'You and I will get puking drunk tonight in Thebes, you old hooligan.'

The Shilluk were stacked in depth, file upon file and regiment upon regiment. Kratas had exercised them ceaselessly in the tactics that I had helped him evolve to deal with chariots. Apart from their long spears, each of them carried a bundle of javelins, and a sling of wood and leather to launch these with added power. They had set the sharpened wooden staves into the earth to form a palisade in front of their line. The Hyksos chariots had to break through that spiny barrier to reach them.

The Egyptian archers were drawn up behind them, ready to move forward through their ranks or retreat again, as the vagaries of the battle called for each differing tactic. They raised their recurved bows on high and cheered Pharaoh. 'Tamose! Egypt and Tamose!'

Pharaoh wore the blue war crown, with the golden circlet of the *uraeus* around his brow, the heads of the vulture and the cobra of the two kingdoms entwined, their jewelled eyes glittering. He returned their salute with the bare blade of the blue sword held high.

We wheeled around our own left flank, and before we started back, Memnon stopped me with a hand on my shoulder. For a short while we looked back over the field. The Hyksos were moving forward already. Their front line was twice the length of our own.

'From your own treatise, Tata,' he quoted, ' "A circumspect defence until the enemy is committed, and then the rapid and audacious attack." '

'You have remembered the lesson well, sire.'

'It is certain we will be outflanked, and Apachan will probably throw in his first five chariot divisions at the start.'

'I agree with you, Mem.'

'But we know what we have to do, don't we, Tata?' He tapped my shoulder and we started back to where our own chariots were holding in the rear.

Remrem headed the first division, Astes had the second, and Lord Aqer the third. Newly promoted to the rank of Best of Ten Thousand, Captain Hui commanded the fourth division. Two regiments of Shilluk guarded our baggage and the spare horses.

'Look at that old hunting dog,' Memnon nodded at Remrem. 'He is chafing to be away. By Horus, I'll teach him a little patience before this day is done.'

We heard the horns sounding in the centre.

'It begins now.' Memnon pointed to the front, and we saw the Hyksos chariots looming through the dust-clouds. 'Yes, Apachan has turned loose his chariots.'

He looked back at our divisions, and Remrem raised his sword high. 'The first is ready, Majesty,' he called eagerly, but Memnon ignored him and signalled to Lord Aqer. The third division came forward in column of fours behind us, and Pharaoh led them out.

The Hyksos chariots lumbered forward, heavy and majestic, aimed at the centre of our line. Memnon cut across in front of them, interposing our thin column between their hordes and the infantry. Then, at his signal, we wheeled into line abreast and we flew straight at them. It seemed suicidal, as futile as charging one of our frail wooden galleys at the rocks of the cataract.

As we came together, our archers fired head-on into the Hyksos, aiming for the horses. Gaps opened in their line as the animals were brought down by our arrows, then at the last possible moment our own line dissolved like wind-driven smoke. Our drivers used their superior speed and manoeuvrability. Instead of coming into collision with the Hyksos line and being crushed beneath the juggernaut, we swerved into the gaps and raced through them. Not all our chariots escaped, and some were broken and overturned, but Lord Aqer led four out of every five of them through.

We emerged in the rear of the Hyksos charge and spun around in a full-locked turn, re-forming the line at the gallop and again using our speed to overhaul the Hyksos, coming into them from the rear, firing our arrows into them at shortening range.

The Hyksos chariots were designed to give protection to the crew from the front, and their archers were stationed on the footplate to fire their arrows forward. Confusion spread down their line as they tried to meet our attack from the rear. Hard-pressed, some of the drivers attempted to turn back to confront us, and they collided with the chariots alongside. Those fearsome wheel-scythes cut into the legs of the neighbouring horses, and brought them down in a screaming, whinnying tangle.

The confusion spread among them just as the first volley of arrows from the Egyptian archers rose up over the massed ranks of Shilluk and dropped among the Hyksos. Immediately this happened, Memnon gave the order, and we

388

wheeled away and let them run down on that palisade of sharpened staves. Half their horses were maimed or killed by those fierce points. Those who broke through were met by the Shilluk and a cloud of javelins. Struck by stake and arrow and javelin, their horses panicked, kicking and rearing in the traces.

Those chariots that were still under control hurled themselves into the Shilluk phalanx. They met no resistance. The black ranks opened before them, allowing the horses to run through, but then they closed up behind them.

Every one of those tall, willowy black devils was an athlete and an acrobat. They leaped up on to the footplate of the racing chariots from behind, and they stabbed and hacked at the crew with dagger and spear. They swallowed that first charge of chariots the same way a jellyfish engulfs a swift silver sardine in its myriad arms and amorphous body.

The Hyksos spearmen were moving forward to follow up and exploit the chariot charge, but now they were exposed. Loose horses and the surviving chariots tore back into their massed ranks, and forced them to open up and let them through. For the moment they were stranded in disorder in the middle of the field, and Memnon skilfully seized the opportunity.

Lord Aqer's horses were blown, and Memnon led them back into reserve. He and I changed teams. It was but a moment's work for the grooms to loosen the tack that coupled Rock and Chain, and to lead in a fresh team from the horses being held in reserve. We had six thousand fresh horses ready in the rear. I wondered how many Hyksos horses had escaped the Strangler, how many fresh teams they were holding.

As we wheeled back into line, Remrem called to us desperately, 'Your Majesty! The first! Let my first division go!'

Pharaoh ignored him and signalled to Astes. The second moved forward behind us and formed up at the trot.

The Hyksos infantry was still tangled in the middle of the field. They had extended to overlap our shorter line, but had lost their dressing. The line was crumpled and twisted. With a general's eye, Memnon picked out the weakest point, a salient in their left flank.

'The second division will advance. Trot-march! Forward! Pods of eight, charge!'

We tore into the salient in the line, eight chariots abreast. Pod after pod, we crashed into them and ripped them open. Their left flank buckled, while their right still pressed forward. We had them canted across the field, their centre was shearing, and Memnon re-formed the third division at the gallop, and set them up to tear open the enemy centre.

At the moment before we were committed to the charge, I glanced across at the city. Dust had almost obscured the range, but I glimpsed the two white flags on the summit of the Finger of Horus. It was the warning signal from my lookout posted there, and I swivelled round and looked back at the eastern fort of the city.

'Sire!' I cried, and pointed back. The king followed my arm, and saw the first squadron of Hyksos chariots trot out from concealment behind the curve of the wall. The others followed, like a

390

column of black warrior ants on the march.

'Apachan is throwing in his reserves to save his infantry,' Memnon shouted, above the din of battle. 'A moment more, and he would have had us in enfilade. Well done, Tata.'

We had to let the infantry escape, as we wheeled into line to face Apachan's chariots. We charged at each other across a field littered with smashed and overturned chariots, loose arrows and javelins, dead and wounded horses and dying men. As we came together, I stood taller on the footplate and peered ahead. There was something unusual about the run of the enemy chariots, and then it dawned upon me.

'Sire,' I cried, 'look at the horses! They are running sick animals.' The chests of the leading teams were painted with a glistening coat of yellow mucus that streamed from their gaping mouths. Even as I watched, one of the horses coming towards us staggered and fell headlong, bringing its team-mate down with it.

'Sweet Isis, you are right. Their horses are finished before they have begun,' Memnon answered. He saw instantly what he had to do. It was the measure of his superb control that he was able to deflect a charge of his chariots once it was fully launched. At this very last moment he declined the head-on engagement.

We opened like a flower before their charge, peeling away on either side of them, turning and running back for our own lines, drawing them on, straining their sick and gasping horses to their utmost.

We ran before them in a tight, compact formation. Their own line began to waver and fall apart as the weaker horses broke down. Some of them fell as though struck in the head by an arrow. Others merely slowed and stopped, standing with their heads hanging, mucus pouring from their mouths in shiny golden ropes.

Lord Aqer's own horses were almost blown by now. They had driven two furious charges without a rest. Still pursued by the remnants of Apachan's division, Memnon led them back to where Hui's fourth division was drawn up alongside Remrem and his first.

'Pharaoh! The first is ready. Let me go! In the name of all the gods, let me go!' Remrem howled with frustration.

Memnon hardly glanced in his direction. I turned my chariot in alongside that of Hui. A team of grooms slipped our sweat-soaked horses from the traces and led in a fresh pair. While Lord Aqer's exhausted division streamed back past us, we faced the oncoming Hyksos.

'Are you ready, Captain Hui?' Memnon called to him, and Hui raised his bow in salute.

'For Egypt and Tamose!' he shouted.

'Then forward march. Charge!' Memnon laughed, and our horses jumped against the traces and we shot forward.

There were six full divisions of Apachan's chariots scattered across the field in front of us. Half of them were broken down, with the horses fallen or drooping in the traces, suffocated and dying from the Yellow Strangler. Most of the others were reduced to a walk, the horses staggering and wheezing. However, the remaining chariots came on in good order.

We went out to meet them face to face. In the

392

centre of their charge rode a tall chariot, its coachwork clad in shining bronze. On the footplate stood a man so tall that he towered above his driver. He wore the high golden helmet of Hyksos royalty, and his dark beard was plaited with coloured ribbons that fluttered in the wind like pretty butterflies hovering over a flowering shrub.

'Apachan!' Memnon challenged him. 'You are a dead man.'

Apachan heard him, and he picked out our golden chariot. He swerved to meet us, and Memnon tapped my shoulder.

'Lay me alongside the bearded hog. It's time for the sword, at last.'

Apachan loosed two arrows at us as we closed. Memnon caught one on his shield. I ducked under the other, but I never lost my concentration. I was watching those terrible spinning scythes on the hubs of Apachan's wheels. They could hack my horses' legs out from under them.

Behind me I heard the gravelly rasp as Memnon drew the blue sword from its scabbard on the side panel, and from the corner of my eye I caught the steely flash of the blade as he went on guard.

I swung my horses' heads over, feinting to the right to confuse the Hyksos driver, but the instant we started to turn away, I changed direction again. I avoided his scythes and passed him close, then I turned in sharply behind him. With my free hand I snatched up the grappling-hook and tossed it over the side-panel of the other chariot. Now we were locked together, but I had achieved the advantage, for we lay across his stern.

Apachan swivelled around, and aimed a sword-cut at me, but I fell to my knees under it, and Memnon gathered up the blow on his shield, then swung the blue sword. A shard of bronze curled from the edge of Apachan's weapon, sliced away by the steel, and he shouted in angry disbelief, and flung up his copper shield at the next blow.

Apachan was a superb swordsman, but no match for my king and the blue sword. Memnon mangled his shield to strips, and then swung hard at his bronze blade, as Apachan tried to defend his head. The blue blade sheared the bronze cleanly, and Apachan was left with only the hilt in his fist.

He opened his mouth wide and bellowed at us. The teeth in the back of his jaw were black and rotten, and his spittle blew into my face in a cloud. Memnon used that classic straight thrust to end it. He drove the point of the blue blade through Apachan's open mouth, deeply into the back of his throat. His angry bellow was drowned out by the torrent of bright blood that burst through his hairy lips.

I cut the rope of the grappling-hook, and let the Hyksos chariot run free. The horses were out of control and they slewed away and ran down the line of locked and battling chariots. Apachan clutched at the dashboard, holding himself erect even though he was dying, and the blood spurted from his mouth and cascaded down his breastplate.

It was a sight that struck dismay into the hearts of his charioteers. They tried to disengage their sick and staggering horses, but we ran hub-to-hub with them and hurled our javelins into them. We followed them all the way back, until we came within range of their archers, and flocks of arrows fell around us and forced us to break off.

'It is not over yet,' I warned Memnon, as we walked our tired horses back. 'You have broken Apachan's chariots, but you still have to deal with Beon's infantry.'

'Take me to Kratas,' Pharaoh ordered.

I stopped our chariot in front of the massed regiments of Shilluk, and Memnon called across to Kratas, 'What heart, my Lord?'

'I fear, sire, that my fellows will fall asleep if you cannot find a little work for us to do.'

'Then let us hear a tune from them as you take them forward to seek employment.'

The Shilluk began their advance. They moved with a curious shuffling gait, and every third pace they stamped in unison with a force that made the ground jump beneath their horny bare feet. They sang in those deep, melodious African voices, a sound like a swarm of angry black bees, and they drummed their spears upon their rawhide shields.

The Hyksos were disciplined and brave, they could not have conquered half the world if they had not been so. We had smashed up their chariots, but they stood to meet Kratas' advance behind a wall of bronze shields.

The two armies came together like fighting temple bulls. The black and the white bulls locked horns and fought it out breast-to-breast and spear-to-spear.

While the two armies of foot-soldiers mauled each other, Pharaoh held back his chariots, using them with skill and daring only when there was an opening or a weakness in the enemy positions. When a pocket of the Hyksos infantry was isolated on the left, he sent in Aqer's division, and annihilated them with two swift charges. When Lord Beon tried to send reinforcements forward to assist his beleaguered front, Pharaoh despatched Astes with five hundred chariots to frustrate him.

The Hyksos rallied every one of their remaining chariots, and every one of their horses that could still stand, and threw them against our right. Memnon sent Hui and Astes out to meet them, and to break up their attack. He left Remrem cursing and pleading and stamping up and down beside his chariot, and ignored his pleas.

Pharaoh and I circled the fighting in the golden chariot, watching each shift and change in the conflict. He pushed in his reserves in exactly those places where they were most needed, and with the timing and anticipation that can never be taught or learned. It was as though the pulse and the tempo of the battle beat in his heart, and he sensed it in his blood.

Always I looked for Kratas in the thick of it. Many times I lost him, and I dreaded that he was down, but then his helmet showed again with the ostrich-feather plume cut away, and the bronze splattered with his own blood and the blood of other men.

It was there in the centre where Kratas fought that the Hyksos ranks began to give. It was like the first trickle through the earth wall of a dam, their line bulged and stretched to the breaking-point. Their rear ranks began to fall in upon themselves under the relentless pressure.

'By the love of Horus and the compassion of all the gods, Tata, this is the moment of our victory.' Memnon saw it even before I did.

We galloped across to where Remrem still

waited, and Pharaoh hailed him, 'Are you ready, my Lord Remrem?'

'I have been ready since dawn, sire, but I am no lord.'

'Would you argue with your king, sir? You are a lord now. The enemy centre is breaking. Take your chariots and chase them back to Memphis!'

'May you live for ever, Pharaoh!' Lord Remrem roared, and he sprang to the footplate. He led out the first. Their horses were fresh and strong, and their fighting spirit was chafed raw and angry with long restraint.

They crashed into the Hyksos right flank. They cut through them with barely a check, and swung round and went into the enemy centre from the rear. It was the perfect moment when the battle teetered, and the Hyksos centre broke. Within the time it takes to draw and hold a long breath, they were in rout.

They streamed back towards the city gates, but even Kratas' Shilluk were too far-gone to follow them. They stood knee-deep in the piles of dead and dying men, they rested on their spears and let the Hyksos go. This was when the genius of Memnon was made apparent. He had kept the first in hand for this moment. They took up the chase, and I saw Remrem's sword rise and fall to a terrible rhythm as he drove them on.

The first of the fleeing enemy reached the city gates, but they found them slammed closed in their faces. My spies and agents had done their work well. The populace of Thebes was in revolt, and the city was ours. They barred the gates to the broken Hyksos legions.

Remrem pursued the Hyksos until night fell and

his horses were exhausted. He drove them back thirty miles, and every yard of the north road was littered with their discarded weapons and the bodies of the slain.

 I drove Pharaoh's golden chariot up to the main gate of the city, and he stood tall on the footplate and shouted to the sentinels on the parapet above us. 'Open the gates! Let me pass through!'

'Who is it that demands entry to Thebes?' they called down.

'I am Tamose, ruler of the two kingdoms.'

'Hail Pharaoh! May you live for ever!'

The gates swung open, and Memnon touched my shoulder. 'Drive through, Tata.'

I turned to face him. 'Forgive me, Majesty. I have taken oath that I will not enter the city, except at the side of my mistress, Queen Lostris. I must pass the reins to you.'

'Dismount,' he ordered me gently. 'Go! Fetch your mistress and make good your oath.'

He took the reins from my hand, and I climbed down into the dusty roadway. I watched him drive the golden chariot through the gateway, and the sound of cheering was like the thunder of waters in the cataracts at high flood. The people of Thebes greeted their king.

I stood at the roadside as our depleted and battered army followed Pharaoh into the city. I realized what a bitter price we had paid for our victory. We would not be fit to pursue the Hyksos until we had rebuilt our army. By this time King

Salitis would be strong again, and his horses recovered from the Yellow Strangler. We had won the first battle, but I knew that many more lay ahead of us before the tyrant could be cast out of this very Egypt.

I looked for Kratas as the Shilluk regiments marched past, but he was not there.

Hui had a chariot and fresh horses for me. 'I will ride with you, Taita,' he offered, but I shook my head.

'I will travel faster alone,' I told him. 'Go into the city and enjoy your triumph. A thousand pretty maids are waiting to welcome you home.'

Before I took the south road, I drove first to the battlefield. The jackals and the hyena were already at the feast that we had set for them, their growls and howls blended with the groans of the dying. The dead were piled like the flotsam on the river-bank when the flood-waters recede.

I drove the chariot through to where I had last seen Kratas, but this was the most gruesome corner of that awful field. The corpses were piled high as my chariot wheels. I saw his helmet lying in the dust that blood had turned to thick mud. I dismounted and took it up. The crest was gone and the helm was all dented and battered in by heavy blows.

I threw the helmet aside and began to search for Kratas' body. I saw his leg protruding like the branch of a giant acacia from beneath a pile of bodies. They were Shilluk and Hyksos lying together in the truce of death. I dragged them aside and found Kratas on his back. He was drenched in clotted black blood, his hair was matted with it and his face was a black, crusted mask.

I knelt beside him, and I whispered softly, 'Must they all die? Every one I truly love, must they all die?' I leaned forward and kissed his bloody lips.

He sat up and stared at me. Then he grinned that wide boyish grin of his. 'By the plug of dried snot in Seth's left nostril, that was a real fight,' he greeted me.

'Kratas!' I stared at him with delight. 'You will truly live for ever.'

'Never doubt it for a moment, my lad. But right now I need a noggin.'

I ran to the chariot and fetched the wine flask. He held it at arm's-length and let the red wine squirt down his throat without swallowing. When the flask was empty he threw it aside and belched.

'That will do well enough for a start,' he winked at me. 'Now point me towards the nearest tavern, you old reprobate.'

Faster than any ship could sail against the current, I carried the news to Elephantine. I was one man in the chariot, and the horses ran lightly. I changed the teams at every relay station along the south road, and galloped on without a check. The grooms handed me a flask or a crust of corn-bread and cheese as they changed the horses, and I never slept or even rested.

During the night, the stars and the moon revealed the path to me, and Horus guided my weary hands upon the traces, for though I ached in every limb and I reeled on the footplate with fatigue, I met with no mishap.

At each relay station and in each village along the way, I shouted the joyous news. 'A victory! A mighty victory! Pharaoh has triumphed at Thebes. The Hyksos is cast down.'

'Praise to all the gods!' they cheered me. 'Egypt and Tamose.'

I galloped on, and they still speak of my ride to this day along the south road. They tell of the gaunt rider with wild bloodshot eyes, his robe thick with dust and the stains of dried blood, his long hair blowing in the wind, the harbinger of victory, bringing the news to Elephantine of the battle that set Egypt on the road to freedom.

I drove from Thebes to Elephantine in two days and two nights, and when I reached the palace, I barely had the strength left to stagger into the water-garden where my mistress lay, and throw myself down beside her couch.

'Mistress,' I croaked through cracked lips and a throat that was parched with dust, 'Pharaoh has won a mighty victory. I have come to take you home.'

We sailed down-river to Thebes. The princesses were with me to keep their mother company and to cheer her. They sat with her on the open deck and sang to her. They rhymed and riddled and laughed, but there were tones of sadness in their laughter and deep concern in their eyes as they watched over my mistress.

Queen Lostris was as frail as a wounded bird.

There was no weight to her bones and her flesh was as translucent as mother-of-pearl. I could lift and carry her as easily as I had done when she was ten years of age. The powder of the sleeping-flower was no longer able to still the pain that gnawed into her belly like some terrible clawed crab.

I carried her to the bows of the galley when at last the walls of Thebes opened to our view around the last bend in the river. With an arm around her thin shoulders I supported her, as we delighted together in all those long-remembered scenes, and lived again a thousand joyous memories of our youth.

But the effort tired her. When we docked below the Palace of Memnon, half the populace of Thebes was waiting to welcome her. Pharaoh Tamose stood at the head of this vast throng.

When the litter-bearers carried her ashore, they cheered her. Although most of them had never laid eyes upon her, the legend of the compassionate queen had persisted during her long exile. Mothers lifted up their infants for her blessing, and they reached out to touch her hand as it trailed from the edge of the litter.

'Pray to Hapi for us,' they pleaded. 'Pray for us, Mother of Egypt.'

Pharaoh Tamose walked beside her litter like the son of a commoner, and Tehuti and Bekatha followed close behind. Both the princesses smiled brightly, though the tears jewelled their eyelids.

Aton had prepared quarters for the queen. At the door I sent them all away, even the king. I laid her on the couch beneath the vine arbour on the terrace. From there she could look across the river to the shining walls of her beloved Thebes.

402

When darkness fell, I carried her to her bedchamber. As she lay upon the linen sheets, she looked up at me. 'Taita,' she murmured, 'one last time, will you work the Mazes of Ammon-Ra for me?'

'Mistress, I can refuse you nothing.' I bowed my head and went to fetch my medicine chest.

I sat beside her bed, cross-legged upon the stone slabs, and she watched me prepare the herbs. I crushed them in the alabaster pestle and mortar, and heated the water in the copper kettle.

I raised the steaming cup and saluted her with it.

'Thank you,' she whispered, and I drained the cup. I closed my eyes and waited for the familiar but dreaded slide over the edge of reality, into the world of dreams and visions.

When I returned, the lamps were guttering and smoking in their brackets, and the palace was silent. There was no sound from the river or from the sleeping city on the far bank, only the sweet trill of a nightingale in the gardens, and the light breath of my mistress as she lay upon her silken pillow.

I thought she was sleeping. But the moment I lifted my trembling hand to wipe the cold and nauseous sweat from my face, she opened her eyes. 'Poor Taita, was it so bad?'

It had been worse than ever before. My head ached and my vision swam. I knew that I would never work the Mazes again. This was the last time, and I had done it for her alone.

'I saw the vulture and the cobra stand on either side of the river, divided by the waters. I saw the waters rise and fall one hundred seasons. I saw one hundred sheaths of corn, and one hundred birds

403

fly over the river. Below them, I saw the dust of battle and the flash of swords. I saw the smoke of burning cities mingle with the dust.

'At last I saw the cobra and the vulture come together in congress. I saw them mating and entwined on a sheet of pure blue silk. There were blue banners on the city walls and banners of blue flew on the temple pylons.

'I saw the blue pennants on the chariots that drove out across the world. I saw monuments so tall and mighty that they would stand for ten thousand years. I saw the peoples of fifty different nations bow down before them.'

I sighed and pressed my fingers into my temples to still the throbbing in my skull, and then I said, 'That was all my vision.'

Neither of us spoke or moved for a long while thereafter, then my mistress said quietly, 'One hundred seasons must pass before the two kingdoms are united, one hundred years of war and striving before the Hyksos are at last driven from the sacred soil of this very Egypt. It will be hard and bitter for my people to bear.'

'But they will be united under the blue banner, and the kings of your line will conquer the world. All the nations of the world will pay homage to them,' I interpreted the rest of my vision for her.

'With this I am content.' She sighed and fell asleep.

I did not sleep, for I knew that she still needed me near her.

She woke again in that hour before dawn which is the darkest of the night. She cried out, 'The pain! Sweet Isis, the pain!'

I mixed the Red Shepenn for her. After a while

404

she said, 'The pain has passed, but I am cold. Hold me, Taita, warm me with your body.'

I took her in my arms and held her while she slept.

She awoke once more as the first timid rays of dawn crept in through the doorway from the terrace.

'I have loved only two men in my life,' she murmured, 'and you were one of those. Perhaps in the next life, the gods will treat our love more kindly.'

There was no reply I could give. She closed her eyes for the last time. She stole away quietly and left me. Her last breath was no louder than the one before, but I felt the chill in her lips when I kissed them.

'Goodbye, my mistress,' I whispered. 'Farewell, my heart.'

 I have written these scrolls during the seventy days and nights of the royal embalming. They are my last tribute to my mistress.

Before the undertakers took her away from me, I made the incision in her left flank, as I had done for Tanus. I opened her womb and took from it that terrible incubus that had killed her. It was a thing of flesh and blood, but it was not human. When I cast it into the fire, I cursed it, and I cursed the foul god Seth who had placed it in her.

I have prepared ten alabaster jars to hold these scrolls. I will leave them with her. I am painting all the murals of her tomb with my own hand. They are the finest I have ever created. Each stroke of my brush is an expression of my love.

I wish that I could rest with her in this tomb, for I am sick and weary with grief. But I still have my two princesses and my king to care for.

They need me.

AUTHOR'S NOTE

On 5 January 1988, Doctor Duraid ibn Al Simma of the Egyptian Department of Antiquities opened and entered a tomb on the west bank of the Nile in the Valley of the Nobles. The reason why this tomb had not been previously excavated was that in the ninth century AD an Islamic mosque had been built over the site. It was only after long and delicate negotiations with the religious authorities that the excavation was permitted.

Immediately upon entering the passage that led to the burial chamber, Dr Al Simma was greeted by a marvellous display of murals which covered all the walls and the ceilings. They were the most elaborate and vivacious that he had ever encountered in a lifetime spent studying the monuments.

He told me that he knew at once that he had made a significant find, for from amongst the hieroglyphics on the walls stood out the royal cartouche of an Egyptian queen who had not been previously recorded.

His excitement and anticipation increased as he approached the burial chamber, only to be dashed as he saw that the seals upon the doorway had been damaged, and the entrance had been forced. In ancient times, the tomb had been robbed and stripped of its sarcophagus and all its treasures.

Nevertheless, Dr Al Simma was able to date the tomb with reasonable accuracy to that dark night of strife and disaster that overwhelmed Egypt in about 1780 BC. For the next century the Two

407

Kingdoms were in a state of flux. We have little record of the events of this period, but from the chaos eventually rose a line of princes and pharaohs that finally expelled the Hyksos invader, and lifted Egypt into its period of greatest glory. It gives me pleasure to think that the blood of Lostris and Tanus and Memnon ran strongly in their veins.

It was almost a year after the tomb was first opened, while Dr Al Simma's assistants were copying and photographing the decorations of the walls, that a section of the plaster fell away to reveal a hidden niche in which stood ten sealed alabaster vases.

When Dr Al Simma asked me to assist in the transcription of the scrolls contained in the vases, I was both honoured and filled with trepidation. I was not, of course, qualified to work on the original scrolls, which were written in the hieratic script. This work was done at Cairo Museum by a team of international Egyptologists.

Dr Al Simma asked me to rewrite this original transcription in a style that would make it more accessible to the modern reader. With this end in view I have included some anachronisms in the text. For instance I have, in places, used such comparatively modern measures of distance and weight as miles and ounces. I have also indulged myself with words such as 'djinn' and 'houri' and 'hooligan' which Taita never employed, but which, I feel certain, he would have used if they had formed part of his vocabulary.

Very soon after beginning work on the texts all my reservations began to evaporate as I became totally involved in the times and character of the ancient author. Despite all his bombast and vainglory, I developed an affinity and affection for the slave Taita that reached back over the millennium.

I am left with a realization of how little the emotions and aspirations of man have changed in all that time, and a lingering excitement that to this day somewhere in the Abyssinian mountains near the source of the Blue Nile the mummy of Tanus still lies in the unviolated tomb of Pharaoh Mamose.

W. S.